The Fatal Diners' Club

Doug Booth

The Fatal Diners' Club

The Fatal Diners' Club

Written for Linda who, like Lorie and Priscilla,
Believes that petite must not become an archaic concept

Part One
1
Late 1890s

Thatcher Riley was a God-fearing young man despite the fact that not once in his life had he seen the inside of a church. Nor had he once thought to seek forgiveness or solace in prayer because neither did he trust in God.

Whorehouses and saloons were more to his liking. He tended to fear God the most when the occasional opportunity to meet his Maker came upon him in the form of a bullet hole threatening to locate somewhere on his person, put there by an adversary not quite as adept at poker as young Thatcher, or a husband whose young and pretty wife Thatcher could not distinguish from a willing and eager whore.

He feared God primarily because he didn't trust God to keep him safe from harm.

He was a charmer who was quite certain neither whiskey nor gambling would be his downfall. This future and inevitable event he attributed in advance to women whose husbands preferred them in aprons and bent over a woodstove to being naked in their marital beds bent over them. In the meantime Thatcher Riley was providing a much needed service for what he believed was the common good and, for that reason, he never remained in one locale very long.

The Fatal Diners' Club

Neither was he very often obliged to pay for his lodging. Why would he sleep in a public bed alone, when for two bits more he could bathe with a whore to ensure a fresher scent and sleep in her bed until dawn?

Thatcher Riley always had two bits more.

He was twenty, 5'10" in his boots, older than his years in his thinking, a ladies' man, and chose to wear a long, black ponytail tied with a black leather thong rather than a hat. He wasn't at all like other men. His chiselled face and torso were tanned from the sun because he saw no purpose in soiling his shirt with dust and sweat while riding between towns in search of gaming tables and pretty women. The rest of him was pasty white.

His eyes were crystal blue, his teeth chalk white and even while other men, those who did possess teeth, could spit through gaps bordered by yellowed chips speckled with brown rot.

He had a black horse he called Horse, and two six-shooters in black holsters he had taken from the foot of his drunken daddy's bed before leaving home early one morning at eighteen with lacerated lips, blackened eyes and swollen balls for having slept with his father's nubile and unspoiled bride on her wedding night.

He possessed one pair of black polished boots, one pair of black cowhide breeches, a black collarless shirt and a single pair of long woolen underpants of various shades which he would wash each time he bathed, hung out any window to dry as he pleasured that particular young whore, wife, or enthusiastic female. He might have been a gunslinger, had such a breed of men ever existed. They did not. Most gunfights took place from behind water troughs, windows, or wherever else a man could squat to shit himself amongst a hail of haphazard bullets.

That was until 1896 when she wasn't a whore at all, or a wife. Not yet.

She was a pastor's daughter, a very appealing and

5

marriageable daughter a year from her majority who was unable to sleep one night thinking of him, her mind troubled, her body coated with his pungent smell melding with her sweat from a hot summer's night, her flesh tingling from his persistent ardour. Though, despite her yearning, her joy at becoming a woman, she feared certain damnation for what she had done.

She confessed her lustful ways to her father the very next day, believing in her heart that he and the good Lord would forgive her because Thatcher Riley had professed his undying love throughout the previous afternoon and into the evening when she had lied about the reason she was late for dinner.

The father went at once to the saloon, calling Thatcher Riley into the street to stand in judgement before his weeping daughter, his distraught wife, the gathering townsfolk and the Lord God Almighty who would smite him onto his knees and cast him into the raging fires of Hell for the wickedness of his ways and the evil he had done.

Yes, Thatcher confessed. He had done wrong. He had indeed sinned, driven to the very fringes of that everlasting inferno by his unbridled lust and unquenchable love for… He looked at her, striving to remember…his daughter.

Before God, he loved her. He did. And he would do right by her.

On his knees the young man pleaded for her hand, tears streaming from the girl's eyes upon hearing her mother and father agree, the townsfolk applauding. The couple would be wedded at week's end.

He stood, dusting his breeches. He kissed his betrothed's quivering hands and her flushed cheeks; he embraced his new mother and met his new father's dark eyes with obvious glee. He had been lost for so long, but now he was found, saved by a young girl's affectionate heart. Hallelujah! Hallelujah! Praise the Lord!

The Fatal Diners' Club

Five days later Thatcher Riley was 300 miles from the girl's not so affectionate heart, fixed in a place familiar to him: Between two freshly scented and nubile thighs. He loved her aroma and her taste. He loved her soft skin, her body and the golden silkiness he would bury his face into between his frequent and urgent forays.

She hadn't been a whore very long, he supposed, at first surprising him with her girlish whimpers and muffled cries. The delicate folds beneath her soft curls hadn't yet lost their pinkish hue and were tightly positioned together.

She was Betty, not that he cared. What need did any whore have of a name? Nor did he care to know her age. She had a woman's shapely body, that's all he needed to know of her. What mattered most was the condition of her skin, the moistness of her clefts and the responsive pink tips of her firm breasts. Though he did have to concede they were not the plumpest he had ever fondled or drawn into his mouth.

She was blonde, her hair the colour of hay on a sunny autumn day. She stood 5'6" in the nude, equipped with breasts for his pleasure that he could completely conceal with his hands. Not a single freckle or natural mark marred her skin that was a colour less harsh than white, as though she were standing naked under a setting sun. What else did he need to know, beyond the tightness of her principal orifice and the heat from her buttocks that all but burnt his fingertips as he clenched her in place?

He had seldom, if ever, kissed a whore. He could not recall, certain he had not. Why would he? Why would any decent man when a whore's mouth was the principal orifice of ne'er-do-wells and indigents in search of more affordable release, or of losers at the table who could no longer afford a woman's natural and intended portals. But Betty's teeth were perfect, her breath was sweet and clean, her tongue so inviting between pouty lips painted red. He touched her lips, pressing gently with his fingertips, penetrating, touching the ridges of her teeth, his finger probing the soft wetness of her mouth.

"I ain't no horse, mister. If you're done with me, pay me my two bits and leave. You ain't the only deprived man in this town and I have to make myself ready for my next."

He left her sitting crossed-legged on her bed. He wasn't much into conversation.

He strode to the window, raising the pane, peering into the street. "Sorry, miss. Truly, I am. Ain't no one nearby fighting for his place in line. Nope. Not so far as my eyes can see. Besides, as it happens, I ain't quite done with you. What I want is to soak with you a while, poke you a few more times. Can't recall when I had a whore as pretty."

"You want to take a bath with me, mister?"

"Yes, ma'am, I do. After I wash my underclothes I'll wash you. Not that I think you're dirty. Want to. That's all. Fact is, you're the cleanest whore I've coupled with to my recollection. You smell real good, fresh, like trout from the river. And don't fret; I'll make my time with you worthwhile. So keep your 'busy' sign on the knob. If anything, me being with you will be good for business. No man wants to bed a whore who ain't busy."

"Show me your money, mister, and it's another two bits for each time. No favours."

He did, settling the account in advance.

Betty's eyes bulged, her mind rapidly doing the arithmetic, not realizing she was grimacing. She hadn't expected to earn as much throughout her first week, let alone her first night.

She'd be raw meat by sunrise unless she could pleasure him to her advantage. Either way, she needed the money. She had run away from home a week earlier, well before dawn, miles away from her stepfather's groping hands and her mother's shrugging shoulders. Men had needs, she was told more than once by her no longer handsome mother. What was the harm with a father's occasional loving attention, the occasional squeeze of her tits or a playful hand between her legs?

They were family like any other. No different.

She was aware men had needs. So let them pay. Just not old men, broken men or cripples, and earlier that very day she had set up shop with rent and bills to pay. Thatcher Riley was her first customer, her first man, and he was getting no part of her for free. No matter how good-looking he was, he was a man with his brain stuck in the tip of his cock and he would pay her what she was worth.

She filled her tub with well water, not thinking to wear a robe, heating what she could in a pan on her woodstove to lessen the chill. She had never bathed with a man, not certain how she felt, though she was surprised by how quickly she did feel comfortable being naked with him and he had already been a few times into her private parts for longer than she thought possible.

So she couldn't see what the harm could be.

Of one thing she was certain. If all men took as long with her each time, they would come to her with more than two bits in their breeches. Or not come at all.

She watched him scrubbing his long underpants, ignoring her, wringing them into a damp log and whipping them straight before hanging a single leg out the window. When he finished he sank into her tub and beckoned her.

She stepped in between his legs the way he told her, facing away from him. She was clumsy, uncertain about what she should do. She slipped, crashing her full weight against him, forcing a grunt from deep in his throat.

She thought he might smack her or laugh at her. He was bigger than her, older and stronger. He didn't. He took her under the arms, easing her forward onto her knees, pressing his parts teasingly against her buttocks.

She squeezed her eyes shut at the thought, dreading the

pain, the humiliation. She had not once thought to imagine a man would want her that way. Still, she was a whore with a whore's body.

"That'll be an extra two bits each time, mister. I don't mind, not really, but that ain't the natural way and you ain't got no right to hurt me."

He ignored her, splashing water onto her back. His hands were gentle, probing, caressing. She wanted to die. Yet she had never felt so good, so warm inside, so right. She wanted to weep. Not once in her life had she dreamed of being a whore. This man, the one behind her, washing her and caressing every part of her with lukewarm suds, he was her dream. She needed to cry. He was the first of so many others to come, and most would not be as handsome or kind.

"What?"

"I ain't never washed a woman's backside before. I think I'll wash all my whores from now on." He inched backwards. "Fact is, I know I will."

She held her breath. She was ready, squeezing the rim of her porcelain tub with tiny hands, his hands caressing more than exploring her buttocks. "I'm ready, mister." She blurted an involuntary moan, feeling the soft pressure. He was kissing her backside. She relaxed. Maybe...

"Lean against me. Let me wash your hair. Can't say I ain't curious to know, though I ain't never hurt a woman and I can't see spending double what I am paying to hurt one as pretty as you."

She eased into him, feeling his arms around her, his hands pressing into her breasts. Part of her wanted him to take his money and go, part of her wanted him never to leave her. She didn't want to feel what she was feeling. In another room, another town and time, he might have been her husband or at least a good friend. But men didn't marry whores and one day, she knew, she would no longer be as pretty because most of her others would not be as gentle with her.

The words burst from her mouth before she could think. "Where's your extra skin, mister. Don't men have hoods on their cocks?"

The question caught him off guard. "You should know better than me, since you've seen more than I ever wish to see. Truth is, my last whore tore it away with her teeth. Ripped it clean off. So you can relax. Because of that I ain't got the slightest inclination to feed another."

She nodded, her head foaming into a white cloud, his fingertips lulling her into a daze. She was lost in time and space, cold water startling her from her reverie. She jerked.

"What?"

"Your tits, you ain't got much to grab. Most whores got a bit more in the front. Given your shyness about your backside and my reluctance to choke you, you don't leave a man much to play with."

"Seems to me your cock doesn't much care, mister. So why should you?" She stood. "Thank you for washing me, and my hair."

She wrapped her hair into a turban and went to lie on the bed, watching as he dried himself with a threadbare towel and peer once again from the window. She wanted to giggle at his half-brown, half-white body yet she didn't. She was a whore and tomorrow or the next day he would be with another. And so would she.

She wanted to tell him that she had only been a whore for a few hours, not that he would believe her.

He checked his watch.

"Got someone waiting for you, mister? A deal's a deal. Taking back what you paid me ain't right."

"What's your name?"

"I told you. I'm Betty, Betty McGilly. What's yours?"

"I'm Thatcher Riley, and I'm very happy at the moment that you're a whore and not a pastor's daughter." He eased the towel from her head, crawled between her legs and patted her back dry as she lay with her head resting on her crossed forearms. "The money's yours and I'm here till morning. You're right. A deal's a deal." He ran his hands lightly across her smooth buttocks. "Can't say I'll likely forget your backside anytime soon, Betty. About the finest I've seen, makes a man forget your small tits."

"I haven't stopped growing, mister."

He chortled. "Neither have I since seeing you."

He raised her up from the waist to meet him, easing into her from behind, which Betty didn't seem to mind as she wiggled onto her elbows, doing her best to ignore her bare backside in the air, doing her best to think of other matters as he rocked her to and fro. Anything other than she was beginning to like him as much as his gentle touch.

Although she could tell he wasn't a real gentleman by his clothes and the manner of his speech, in her mind she made him one. And she was a lady with a gentleman lover.

When he was done she lay flat, watching as he went for the whiskey bottle and two glasses. He was a happy man, happier than he had ever been. Betty could see in his eyes that he was happy. He was a good and sensitive man, with her because he had no woman of his own to share his bed.

He and Betty, in fact, each had cause for celebration: Betty for earning five silver dollars for a single night's work, Thatcher for increasing his wealth at the table earlier in the day to an extent he would not have believed and for listening to the disgruntled rants of men in despair.

That Thatcher Riley had not learned to read or write mattered not at all. He'd learned all that he had to from men in fancy suits with thick wallets. Excited, unable to sleep, he maintained his vigorous rhythm with Betty throughout what remained of the night with promises of another silver dollar in her purse for good measure. She was an excellent whore, her body well-suited to its purpose.

As for Betty, as the night wore on, she became more determined with each word he spoke that Thatcher Riley would never forget her.

*

Dawn the next day seemed reluctant to brighten the dark sky, when finally he slipped from inside her to dress himself and buckle his gun belt.

Betty McGilly lay as she was. Her hair was soaked with sweat, her body glistening, her private parts throbbing and sore from a week's worth of work in one night. She eased onto her side, cupping a warm hand between her legs, too exhausted to clean herself.

"Thatcher, can I tell you something that I swear ain't no lie?"

"Tell me anything you want, whether it's a lie or not. I won't be seeing you again, Betty."

"Until yesterday, with you, I wasn't no whore." She waited. "Do you believe me, Thatcher?"

"For what it matters. Can't say I see a difference between a whore and any other woman. Married women do as much for a place to live and a man to pay their bills, and not many as pretty as you. You'll do well for yourself, Betty." He tossed her a silver dollar. "Another coin well-earned and better spent, Betty. Can't say I've ever been as eager for any woman and I'm sorry for what I said about your small tits. They're a fine match for your other enviable parts."

"You can stay a while longer if that's what you want, Thatcher...for free. I can sleep later. I don't mind."

She wanted badly for him to stay, for him to tell her more of his plans. She hadn't yet figured out how to tell him, to make him want her. All she knew was she wanted to go with him.

He fashioned his hair into a ponytail, smiling. "What I need is a jar of ointment, not more of you. Fact is, Betty, thinking of your sweet parts won't make my day in the saddle any easier. Just as well my whoring days are done for a while, I suppose. Can't say I've heard tell of whores north of the line less they're Indians. Even so, can't properly imagine one of them with a backside as well-formed as yours."

Betty sat straight. "Then take me with you. I can be your whore for as long as you need me."

"Womenfolk have their purpose, Betty. If they're not parting their legs or cooking a meal they're wasting their days having babies. They can't be expected to do a man's work. You'd be a burden on me, slow me down. You've found a good trade, Betty. Be content with what you are."

"I won't ever be a burden, Thatcher. And I'll never refuse you. Not ever. Not as long as you need me to poke. I heard what you said, that a man digging for gold ain't got much need of friends, just more reason to look over his shoulder. And from what I heard, less you were lying to me; he ain't got much reason to find his bed in the night either."

She stood, naked and vulnerable. Her green eyes were clear, sparkling with hope, her mouth dry. Her heart was pounding more than when she first undressed for him. "Please, Thatcher, stay with me a while longer. I've got a plan to tell you. Please, Thatcher. And I swear to you that before you I wasn't no whore."

Giving in to her that early autumn day in 1896, studying her as she nursed her body with a cool, damp cloth between her legs as she spoke to him, captivated not merely by the sight of her daubing scented balm where he had spent the better part of the night, he didn't merely alter his life beyond the imaginable, he altered the world in a far distant future he would not live to witness or comprehend.

2
The Klondike

Thatcher Riley had once heard tell of Canada, though he had no idea of the place or why he would ever think to find himself in a barren wilderness. He'd heard more tales than he wanted to hear about the savages, the untamed Indians and their pagan ways, their hatred for the White man. He'd been told by many about the cold and the colour of snow, nothing about places to drink and places to whore which were of much greater importance. He didn't know, nor did she.

What he did know was that he was going north to make his fortune. What she knew was that she was going with him. The journey would be long and arduous by sail and on horseback, she insisted. Unless he was the worst kind of liar for what he had made her believe when, between their heated bouts, she squatted in her tub to soothe and sweeten her overworked parts.

He would need a whore, she insisted. A man could not live months at a time without a woman's wide-open legs, her firm buttocks and soft tits.

Besides, even if they did have whores, they would be old and used with loose and smelly orifices and, likely as not, with rotting teeth and foul breaths. She kissed him, forcing her sweet tongue into his mouth. She was none of that. She was young and fresh and eager, apart from the temporary damage he'd inflicted upon her. And, she pointed out, well-formed according to his very words.

Her mind was determined. She was going with him. With thousands of men without women in a desolate land she would be in high demand by others if he didn't want her after a time. And with a bit of gold in her purse she could afford a fine establishment to work in and become known.

He would pay her way in exchange for her body and her womanly skills. She would care for him in all ways and leave him once she was settled and independent of him. Not once would she be a burden or a nuisance.

He agreed. He had nothing to lose as he could see, other than a few hundred dollars for her new wardrobe and a horse. She would go with him, if she would agree that any child she might occasion by error or want would not be his. They shook hands and she dressed, departing not long after without the slightest idea of what lay ahead, thinking they would arrive simply to dig gold from the earth and to whore in their respective ways in any of a dozen newly and poorly constructed boomtowns once their agreement was concluded.

They arrived in the early spring of 1897 amongst fewer than half the 100,000 souls that set out before them, anxious to be the first, or trailed behind with hopes of filling tattered pockets with whatever remained in the ground.

There was plenty to go around. That's what the papers said… what they promised.

Their bodies and minds were toughened and depleted by a savage winter of wind and cold that would freeze snot on a man's lip and hot tears on a woman's cheek; snow so deep that neither man nor beast could take a single step without sinking or stumbling. Yet they persisted, while others perished with broken legs and broken hearts, undaunted, their hearts strong with the heated desire of new love, hauling and dragging what would not fit on the backs of their horses.

They were amongst the fortunate few, the obsessed, the driven. They came with food for a year and the best equipment paid for by those less gifted at cards, though Betty Riley never did leave him. Nor did she know any other man from then on.

Indeed, she loved him to such a great extent that she kept her promise not to bear him a child.

The couple remained in the Klondike twenty-four months and not by the grace of God.

While others went to Him each Sunday morning to raise their voices in joyful song and pray for divine intervention of the mineral kind, Thatcher swung his pickaxe and Betty swirled her pan.

They were amongst the last to leave in the spring of '99 watching month after month as thousands of their neighbours returned home too soon, defeated; surrendering to a cruel and harsh land as increasing numbers of new and desperate dreamers arrived. Thatcher, listening to his bride, bought and sold those deserted claims and many more belonging to those who died unenviable deaths while doing all they could to survive and become rich.

That money, as he promised too many times alongside soaked and fetid deathbeds, he sent home to unknown widows and orphans.

They were exhausted; their faces weathered, tanned deep-amber by the cold glare of winter's blinding white as much as summer's scorching sun. Their hands and fingers were sore and raw from permafrost and freezing temperatures they never thought to believe existed as much as from the cutting edges of newfound deposits of ore they believed would glitter, but did not. That she stayed with him, he believed, was a wonder. He did not believe in miracles intended for lesser men. Yet the time had come to take her away. They'd struck gold, and plenty of it, the richest of the four thousand men who did.

They sold their pack-horses at a fair price, offering their

equipment to men whose gear was much poorer in quality, beginning their trek one bright spring morning after winter's unceasing threat had passed. The tedious journey lasted three months, some evenings spent at humble inns, others on hard ground cushioned by lush grass and the softest blankets they could buy that were seldom soft enough by morning.

The farther south they travelled, the warmer the days became and the evenings more pleasant.

They no longer needed their blankets. Betty would enjoy a clean and down-filled-bed for the first time in her then entire life and for several days she would luxuriate by the edge of what the hotel manager told them was a bathing pool while his staff pampered her and catered to Mr. Riley's gentlemanly needs.

By week's end her skin was fragrant and soft, her hands and fingers delicate and smooth, her fingertips were painted pale prune to match her lips and her hair was fashioned into a French braid she had never once heard tell of. For his part, Thatcher eyed the steamer trunk in their room wondering how on earth he would strap the thing to Horse.

The answer was very simple, supplied to him matter-of-factly by Betty. She would not spend another day on a horse until settled into her new home. He could do what he wanted; she was travelling to Houston by coach and train and wearing fine dresses, like a lady. Her days of plaid shirts, rolled-up jeans and laced boots thick with mud were behind her.

For the difficult years she'd lived, though mostly because he loved her so deeply, he was anxious to give her a comfortable and easy life in a magnificent and stately home. He'd spent the week planning and drawing as best he could when he wasn't being fitted with new clothes, refusing to wear starched shirts and breeches with braces or shoes that went no higher than his ankles.

That's what he wanted. That's what his woman

deserved.

Regarding his future, he had no expectations of what he would do with the rest of his life. Betty was anxious to wear fashionable clothes and voyage together with her husband to Europe where she would learn to become a gracious lady. She was no longer a whore, not since weeks before her wedding day. Most of all she wanted to replace her ring Thatcher had carved from a splinter of wood with a diamond set in gold melted from the first nugget they'd mined. She wanted to be his bride once again in a church. She wanted to wear a beautiful and flowing gown; not standing by his side in a borrowed dress trimmed with mud and dung.

That's what she wanted the most.

*

Betty Riley would do all that and more because, like Thatcher Riley, she had never once heard tell of oil.

3
Houston, Texas

Thatcher and Betty Riley arrived home in the autumn of 1899, not far from three years to the day that he sat watching her squatting in the tub.

What remained of their homeward journey, as one might expect, was much less demanding and a great deal more exhilarating for Betty. In the previous two years of hard labour with his wife by his side, Thatcher had mined 56,000 dollars in gold: Sixty million in 2024 terms. What he made from his real-estate transactions amounted to five-thousand more.

He was twenty-three. His bride, dressed in white and veiled, was recently twenty, married as she had longed for on the outer steps of a real church by a pastor who had reluctantly agreed to make certain concessions for the groom who was willing to pay for the pastor's new horse and carriage.

She would at last have her diamond ring, crafted for her from her past hardship and sweat during their honeymoon in Chicago, though her wedding gift came first in Houston: Thirty-one of the 61,000 dollars. He didn't want her staying for the money. He wanted her to want him. When she stopped crying they walked a short distance together to meet with the architects who had set up a tent in the middle of their far-reaching land. The plans were set. Construction would last a full year, neither one able to realize for a moment what they had begun.

They departed the next day by coach and train for Chicago where they remained in stylish comfort for a week before travelling on to New York, onward to London and Paris by steamer before travelling to Rome and Brussels by train. They returned home a year later, much wealthier than when they left, to a real home that days before had been completed as a centre-piece on 1000 acres that were one-half marsh, one-half grassland: An elegant yet unpretentious mansion Betty would never have thought to dream about.

She cried for the better part of a day. He laughed, though not at her. No. He laughed at his father whose young bride years earlier had come to his bed of her own volition and need to escape her future for at least a few hours of youthful delight.

The next day a man knocked at their door, eager to speak with Mr. Riley, surprised to see a man dressed in polished riding boots and kid leather pants with the sleeves of his open shirt rolled to the elbows of sinewy arms and sporting a ponytail. More surprised was he to see Mrs. Riley in jodhpurs, riding boots and a sweater requiring little imagination to fully appreciate the handsome configuration of her chest for, as she had once retorted to a forward and persistent young customer at the outset of a previous and short-lived life, she hadn't then stopped growing.

She was buoyant, smiling, taking his hand firmly in hers to welcome him. She was about to become a proper equestrian with her very own black Arab, silver tack and an English saddle. That was her anniversary gift.

The gentleman was very happy for her and told her so, thankful when she offered him a libation of chilled wine so that he might turn his attention to her husband, thinking for a brief moment as she strode away that her posterior proportions were no less admirable than those of her front.

Thatcher was no less attentive. He was not a man given

to jealousy. He was proud.

The gentleman was an investor, a speculator, part of a consortium willing to stake their combined resources in the name of greater prosperity for themselves and the land and Thatcher's name had spread quickly during his extended tour of Europe. Nor did Thatcher harbour any doubt that his wife's proclivity for being Betty Riley would spread quickly. Yet he was a patient man, unhurried, and, for that reason, not that day, but one week later, subsequent to several meetings with several other men in the company of his lawyers, Mr. Thatcher Riley became an oil baron.

What made him most proud was Betty's signature beside his. They would never be apart, nor one better than the other, and Mrs. Elizabeth Riley would soon become the talk of Houston, Texas.

Once again Betty spent the better part of her day weeping happy tears. And once again Thatcher laughed, this time at himself. He no longer feared God. Those dark days were over. And, despite being married twice to the same lovely bride, he hadn't once stepped into a church.

God would have to do His work in minds other than his, minds more needful and trusting. His was clear and free of guilt. He had no need of eternal salvation or the promise of a better world. Thatcher Riley would make the world a better place by not making it worse.

*

The Lucas gusher erupted at Spindletop near Beaumont, Texas one year later, not more than a two-day ride in the saddle from their homestead. He left immediately without her, returning within the week with the news. He was downtrodden, his face sunken with shame, most of their fortune poured into mere speculation and the little they could hope to extract.

Betty shrugged. They'd been through worse together, mister, she said. How little, though, might they expect to salvage, she asked?

He filled a goblet with wine, his expression grave, searching for the right words before he answered without the slightest glimmer of hope in his eyes or fluctuation in his voice: "Several hundred-thousand, Betty, and millions more very soon."

She believed him, kissing him, patting his cheek all the same as though he'd been telling tales, leaving him to help the newly hired cook prepare his dinner. She would never accept that she was better than anyone brought in to help her manage her expansive home. Who was she to put on airs? He watched her go. She was playacting. She was as ecstatic as he. He knew damned well she was. She was being Betty, playacting to get the better of him. She always did.

After dinner she had a surprise for him, pulling him from his leather chair as he thought to relax with a cognac, though he still did prefer a good shot of whiskey.

She thought differently. They each had homework to do. In his absence she had hired a tutor to teach them reading, writing and numbers and he was already behind in his lessons. The tutor for their table manners and social graces would be by the house the next day. She wanted her gentleman, as long as the real Thatcher Riley promised never to leave her completely.

*

God was not the only entity Thatcher Riley did not believe in. He didn't much care for money, paper money. He preferred gold and silver. In addition to which, and most decidedly, he did not like or condone the way the world was turning. To which end, with each successive year, more of that gold and silver was finding its way into the vault beneath the floors of the mansion.

Horse had died years earlier, though now they had stables with a dozen horses of Horse's calibre and better. He was a horseman, always would be. Still, in 1910 he gave in to Betty and bought his first combustion engine vehicle which he didn't much like. The thing was noisy, smelled of oil, was slow and uncomfortable. Horses were faster and more responsive. They fouled the air only once in a while and required less maintenance.

By 1914 he was thirty-eight, a multimillionaire, an avid reader, traveller, and president of the fifth largest oil producing company in the state, still partnered with the original group of four. He was considered too old to go to war, by the government and by Betty. Though she did declare unashamedly on January 01st, 1915, that he was not too old to become a father and that Casey Riley would be delivered to his father on the first of July.

He was furious, enraged, upset with her beyond description, sipping his cognac and fuming behind a beaming grin he could not hope to contain as he waved a scolding finger at her for becoming such a disrespectful wife and scandalously errant woman. She spent the night crying warm tears into his chest, she was complete. She was no longer merely the finest and most sought after hostess in Texas, the best horsewoman at any event, the best-read of any of her neighbours and friends. She was a mother and her Thatcher loved her so deeply.

By 1929 the boy was fourteen, well-read and well-bred mostly by his mother's concerted efforts. Together father and son were incorrigible. He could ride a horse as well as his father; he could hit a silver coin with his father's well-preserved twin Smith & Wessons and his schoolmaster knew not to discourage him from being his own man. Men made mistakes, and from those mistakes true and honest men learned.

Although young Casey was more than once called upon to immediately atone for his inherited single-mindedness with reddened palms without his father's intervention: The result of his inborn honesty. However, on those occasions when he did, in fact, claim innocence, the case was closed forthwith in his favour. Men lied for two reasons, neither one good: The fear of something or the fear of someone. Neither deficiency applied to a Riley and, like his father, Casey Riley was a man before his time.

He'd been blessed with the good-looks and charm of his parents, the patience of his mother and the forthrightness of his father and Casey Riley was already etched into the hearts and minds of most young and privileged ladies.

4
Casey Riley

In October of 1929 Thatcher Riley sat alone one evening in his study relishing a newly acquired cognac sent to him directly from his favoured estate in France as part of his annual shipment. He was one of the lucky few. He had survived that century's Black Tuesday while others of his associates and neighbours did not.

While most others had believed in and trusted the banks to guard their wealth and brokers in Dallas, New York and Chicago to multiply that wealth, he did not. His one trusted portfolio was gold and silver. His diversification was his fortune spread across a dozen or more respectable banks around the country as well as the Swiss banking system which he became aware of when he first went with Betty to Europe, although his largest reserves remained beneath his feet. The question was: Would he survive the long term?

He would indeed.

A year later he entered into real-estate, buying houses at fair market value which the less fortunate could no longer afford, renting those same houses to those same people for next to nothing so that they might not lose their homes, promising as well to return the deed of each home once the cataclysmic depression was over and at whatever the market deemed fair. He honoured his promise many years later to all but a few who had chosen an easier and more permanent solution to their woes, substantially increasing his wealth in the process.

Of greater concern was what to do with Casey. The boy was sixteen, nearing the end of his secondary education and becoming increasingly restless. He wanted to work with his father one day, the next he thought to work in the oilfields to make his way independently in life when he wasn't talking about running the family ranch. To which his father replied: "You've got your boots, your pants, your shirts, a bed for a short while, and whatever food your mother sees fit to feed you. That's what you've got, boy. The rest belongs to your mother and me until the two of us are dead. What you mistakenly believe is a family ranch won't be yours to run for a very long time, so make plans for yourself and your future that make sense and your mother proud. We didn't bring you into the world to become a costly house decoration."

Despite the jovial mood, the message was intended to be heard and understood and Casey spent the next twelve months pondering his future, asking questions of his parents and his father's many partners. He wrote letters and spent hours each week learning about trades, professions, requisite skills, the business world and the law with which he was most intrigued.

One evening midway through 1932, Betty turned into her pillow distraught.

"You are a despicable man, Thatcher Riley. The boy is barely seventeen. You have no right to send him away." She paused, jerking from his touch, burying herself deeper under her quilted bedcover. "And don't you dare think to laugh at me."

"The boy is seventeen, my love. That's true. The same age as a forward young vixen who once forced me to drag her along to the Yukon against my will and better judgement. So do you believe your son's weaker than a seventeen-year-old girl? If so he's your progeny, no son of mine."

"That was a different time. The world was a less violent place." She stifled a sob. "I'm afraid I won't ever see him again."

"He's going to school, my love, not into a war. He'll be fine. We will be fine. And when he's home again you can help him find a good woman. We both know he won't come across one without help. He's more than a little awkward around the females in the herd, which is a little surprising given the paternal side of his parentage." He patted her still firm cheeks from under her silk nightgown, squeezing gently, enjoying her heat, not letting go. "We both know he'll be fine. Don't we? And now that we're finished with him, perhaps you might see to the more urgent needs of a man who is deeply in love."

She nudged herself closer into his warmth, inhaling a deep breath, breathing out a whisper of sweet air.

"I know you love me, that you want me. But, darling, I'm too sad to please such a selfish and pitiful man with my beautiful body. Honestly, I don't know whether I will ever be happy again because of you. Goodnight, darling. We'll talk again when I'm feeling more myself…perhaps in five years. We both know you'll be fine. Don't we?"

He moved his hand from the youthful curves of her buttocks to her breasts, pulling her in even closer with the other, quietly watching her surrender to sleep. What seemed not more than a few brief hours of restless slumber later, Betty woke to the bright light of morning to gather their nightclothes from the floor.

Thatcher was awake, watching her, grinning mutely, Betty ignoring him. He had discovered at some point between darkness and dawn, though not unexpectedly, that Betty had quite freely begun to regain her happiness. In fact she had very quickly become unquestionably delirious in her enthusiastic pursuit of her temporarily misplaced bliss.

The Fatal Diners' Club

One week later Casey Riley kissed his mother's cheek, hugging her tightly with one arm, his other hand firmly grasping his father's. He would not see his parents for five years. The times were too difficult, the country too unstable, and the pending demands on father and son would prove too burdensome for either man to ignore their respective responsibilities. Casey Riley would find his way, or he would not. What better time or age to discover his self-worth?

The one promise levied upon his son by Thatcher in private was that the boy was not to return home with either a woman or a child. He was not being sent away to frolic under loosely belted skirts or to test his preferences in the tastes, colours and textures of the available and willing female populations of Cambridge or Boston. He was traversing the country alone, as his father had once done, to become a man, to become educated in law and return home to protect his family's interests, not to squander his monthly allowance and masculine seed on deliberately wanton girls in search of an easy future.

If the need arose, when the need arose, he was to pay for the prettiest and the youngest of whores plying their trade in respectable houses. He was never to fill the purse or anything else of a common street whore, no matter what her physical bearing or the intrigue of whatever speciality she might propose.

Casey agreed, red-faced. That his father had any interest at all in what he might choose to undertake with his private parts was somewhat disconcerting to the young man. He left them not long after at the train station. He was stoic, pretending, not believing his good fortune, knowing full well that in his heart he was fearful of his newfound freedom, refusing to worry his mother and disappoint his father, watching as the two people he loved most in the world grew smaller before disappearing into a haze of blue-grey smoke.

The Fatal Diners' Club

That evening, propped on an elbow in their bed, Betty punched Thatcher in the ribs, curious to hear from him what might have become of them had a certain young vagabond of dubious reputation and despicable manners not squandered his masculine seed into a vulnerable and beautiful young woman at a time when she was hoping and dreaming of a better life. Or, better said, had she not seen fit to mould him into a proper gentleman and make him tolerable to most, though certainly not to all acquainted with him. Furthermore, as she clearly recalled, he hadn't once, not then or now, bewailed or shied away from her particular specialities.

He chortled, lamenting the unfortunate lack of privacy in his own home. He kissed her, she pushed him away. He kissed her again and for the next hour Betty Riley didn't once think of her son. Thatcher had never changed from the trim man in black cowhide, polished boots and a ponytail.
*

Five birthdays and five Christmases without him came and went, five years without the reprieve of vacations; long years sprinkled with weekly phone calls plagued with static and party-line interruptions to make the years seemingly pass quickly when they did not.

Thatcher Riley would not summer in the Europe or winter on the Gulf Coast when others were standing long hours in food lines to stave off hunger, or labouring through eighteen-hour days to earn much less than their worth. For her part Betty understood. She saw the sunken faces of malnourished men each day as she filled their tin cups and plates at the mission she operated as Thatcher did his part, hiring men whose service he did not require in the hopes of a better and brighter not too distant future.

They all knew what was coming, many anxious for the prosperity of war, none thinking of death or disfigurement. The men at least were anxious, not so the mothers of young men or boys filled with bravado who believed themselves invincible and ready to fight.

Casey had been gone four months longer than five years and hadn't spoken with his mother in close to three; promising then he would be home with her soon.

Late autumn's cooler air had quelled the oppressive heat of a Southwestern summer. Betty was enjoying her one diversion. She was riding. In an era when other women her age were wearing the current trend of frumpy dresses over girdles, thick shoes and the fur of dead animals around the collars of heavy coats, Betty wore riding boots and knee-length skirts with bolero jackets and capes. She never wore girdles. When stockings were required she wore garters, favouring camisoles over the discomfort of housing her breasts in wire-lined fabric cups that would lend them the unnatural appearance of two unyielding cones.

This day she was atop a knoll in jodhpurs, a leather waistcoat and boots. She was gazing out over the several thousand acres she and Thatcher now owned, as comfortable in her saddle as other women might be in cushioned rocking chairs. She hadn't once thought of leaving her home of almost forty years for another. Nor could she remember the day he left her as a boy the way she once thought she would forever, until the day he would return to her unharmed.

She knew how he looked in sepia, how he had matured each year, each precious photograph scarred by the jagged creases he had made to accommodate the prints in envelopes bursting with pages of heartfelt letters, each moment in time annotated on the back in dark blue ink. In the last photograph he was standing at the podium, graduating, waving at her. He wrote that he was. He was proud and smiling at her, for her. He understood why they hadn't come to witness his most glorious day. He admired them for doing what they must, he told her in his most recent letter. He was coming home soon, he wrote to her, not telling her when.

That was four months earlier and she was beginning quietly to worry.

A single tear splashed into her gloved hand, another followed, blurring her vision, blurring the sudden plume of brown dust in the far distance streaking noiselessly towards her.

She was right not to have gone to him when so many others needed her and Thatcher. That he was now a lawyer wasn't important to anyone other than her. What would matter to others one day was that he would become the best of his profession.

She glanced towards the ranch house, mildly curious. Thatcher was home unusually early. She would wait a few moments longer, giving him time to change. He would know where to find her. He was so handsome in the saddle. How could it be that he was sixty-one? Worse: How could she be fifty-eight with so little advance notice, when in her mind she was a seventeen-year-old girl smitten with a brash young gambler and gadabout, so afraid he would refuse to take her on his journey?

She wiped her eyes. She hadn't wept in five years, four months and eight days. Besides, she was Elizabeth Riley, the wealthiest woman in the state and, together, they were the tenth wealthiest family in the country.

Something was terribly wrong. Thatcher never hurried. He was always measured and calm. He was racing towards her, waving his arms frantically, his suit jacket and tie whipping hectically in the wind, his hat flying from his head. He would never do such a thing. What was he thinking? What was so wrong? What horrible news had he heard of Casey? What was he yelling? What voice was she hearing?

She screamed, clutching at her wide-open mouth. Her son had come home to her. Casey was home. To hell with what Thatcher would think. She burst into tears, lunging her beast forward to meet him, her curvaceous jodhpurs barely touching the saddle, her tears streaming into her hairline with the wind in her face, the stallion and palomino jolting to a stop a mere few inches apart, son pulling mother from her saddle no less deftly than a practiced rogue, not letting her slip from his arms until the flood of tears subsided and he was able to ease her gently to the ground.

Sliding from his saddle he joined her. He might have been facing an older sister; she was seeing a younger Thatcher Riley. All he was missing were the ponytail, black leather and six-shooters.

They walked quietly hand in hand, their mounts trailing behind, mother and son lost in time, neither knowing what to ask or what to say, silence usurping emotion.

That evening at the dinner table Thatcher's mind struggled for the right words to speak at seeing the three settings and his wife dressed in a long, form-fitting silk gown: Her most recent and most favourite. The front was décolleté, her neck sparkling with a chain of sapphires and rubies, her hair coiffed into a simple updo to enhance her one earring that was deep red, the other that was deep blue. She had also insisted that he dress for dinner as befit the occasion.

What occasion? However Thatcher Riley always did know when to fold, when to walk away, albeit facing the foe. He sat facing her in black tie, swirling his drink.

"Betty, my love, this is foolishness. The boy will be home when he gets here. It's that simple. That he isn't yet tells me he's got something in his mind. He wouldn't disappoint you without the best of intentions."

"Stop fussing, darling. I'm very content to wait until he arrives in his good time."

He sipped his whiskey. "You're beautiful, Betty, as beautiful and young as the first day we met...and a very bad liar. I know you. You're strung tighter than fence wire." He downed the drink. "Tomorrow I'll hire a man or two to search for him. He'll be here in a week. I promise."

"Thank you, darling, however there's no need. He'll be here when he's here. Didn't you say so yourself?"

He loosened his necktie. He never did like the damned things. Nor did he like shit on his shoes and he had a bad feeling he was sinking straight into a deep and dirty shit pond.

"All the same, you want him home. He won't be hard to find, though I have to believe he won't appreciate being chased by his mother, not at his age. He isn't a boy any longer, Betty. What I mean to say is, don't expect him to stay with you very long once he walks through the door. He has a life to build, as did we."

"You're right about that, father, which is the reason I didn't wait any longer. Tell me, do I look very much like a future and successful attorney at law?"

Thatcher Riley had learned very early in life never to let a man read his eyes and to keep his holsters well-oiled. Living men never tugged at their handguns. No. Hand and pistol grip would always join easily together for a common purpose of survival. That was the difference between walking away and being carried. He remained as he was.

He filled his glass two-fingers deep, then another sitting empty at the third setting, ignoring Betty's single stamp of her foot. She was flustered, annoyed with him. Good. Let her be for deceiving him since he arrived home. Casey stood relaxed behind his father.

"You're late for dinner, Casey, as usual. I see your manners haven't improved much. Sit down and tell me about your day. I assume you've discovered the taste of whiskey...amongst certain other equally intoxicating aromas."

Their wife and mother gasped.

Casey Riley sat, keeping his hands to himself, raising his glass to his father.

"Thank you, father. I do appreciate a good whiskey, particularly after a long and exhausting day." He inhaled the aroma. "A decent whiskey is very much appreciated. Truly, I would have preferred a good sleep, but mother...Well, you know how she is."

Thatcher nodded. "I do. And make damned sure you don't fall into the same trap. Sweet and tender meat doesn't last well if not properly cured. To my deepest regret, I waited too long to hang her by her feet and smoke her."

Betty's mouth dropped open.

"From what I see, father, your sweet and tender meat is turning sour before our very eyes. At this particular moment I'm truly grateful that she's yours and not mine."

Betty stepped in between them, first slapping her husband, then slapping her incorrigible son before walking away to don an apron. No one but she would cook her son's first meal at home, facing away to hide quiet tears as father and son stood wordlessly to embrace and thump each other's back as though urging a stubborn mule forward. Men were such fools.

Casey had returned home without gifts. He was currently without employment and saw no purpose in buying gifts for his parents with their money. What he did have, however, was a loan pending with the Houston Bank. All that was missing was his father's co-signature as the banks did not believe, nor would they ever, in a person's potential.

He had actually been in Houston for the better part of a week, a piece of news that turned his mother's face pale. His father displayed no reaction, patiently waiting.

He couldn't think of coming home without a plan for his future. He had located an available property in Houston which would perfectly suit his Law Office. All he required was a short-term loan in order to establish himself and hire a capable assistant.

Thatcher enquired as to the amount of the loan and the

amount of interest imposed by the bank. His son replied: One thousand, sir, at three percent annually and perhaps a thousand more in a few months' time at four percent to cover unforeseen expenses. He would, of course, endeavour to repay the loan in the shortest possible time. The property would also provide him with a temporary domicile while he proved himself and became known in the community. News that did not sit well with the only woman seated at the table. In fact, if not apparent to Casey, Thatcher was steadily aware of a cold front permeating his home. The chill was undeniable.

Thatcher reached into his formal jacket for his chequebook. He wrote a cheque for five-thousand, telling his son to do things properly from the start. The interest would be two percent annually, repayment to begin in a year's time and the loan would be called in ten years. Father and son shook hands. Enough said. Nothing in life was free.

With dinner finished Betty joined them for a single digestive before going to bed depleted, her mind a whirlwind of unasked questions, of words unspoken. Tomorrow was another day when she would have her son to herself.

More than weary, she was tired of their silly playacting. Her men needed time without her witnessing their emotions. She kissed them both and retired.

*

Casey Riley had no girlfriend, no lover, save a few favorites he'd paid for twice monthly in Cambridge or his occasional weekends in Boston.

He asked his father, prompted by Thatcher's snicker, whether he'd ever bedded a whore. He was also curious about another personal matter.

"Father, you were born in the West in a different time. Did you ever see a man killed?"

"Killed? No. However, men mixed in a gunfight, yes. I did very often, with their breeches filled with fetid matter as they searched for places to hide. As for whores, I remember having enjoyed a few until I met your mother, though not a day or any part of a day since."

"I was always too young before leaving home to care how you met mother. Might I know now?"

"Your mother ran from a difficult home as a very young girl. I ran from mine for quite a different reason. We met by chance with a common urgency to make our lives better and we fell in love. On our way north I could wait no longer for her and married her. If not for your mother, neither of us would be here today. You would be your mother's dream and I would likely be one with the soil beneath our feet. So, Casey, we have a great deal to be thankful for, you and I. And I remind myself each day, as should you. Lest you punish yourself with good reason one day."

5
2023, New Year's Eve

The choice of wines was excellent, Melvin Horn believed.

For the entrées of consommé aux xérès sprinkled with fresh herbs and a salad of grilled chicken breasts and roasted vegetables laced with a creamy parsley sauce, the host for the evening had proposed a delicate Chablis Premier Cru Vaillons 1984.

His name was Hilary Basil, his name synonymous with The Diners' Club.

For the main courses, a temptation of tender beef ribs prepared in teriyaki sauce and ginger, followed by a platter of roast beef on a bed of caramelized onion sauce, steamed légumes and pommes de terre purées coated with thick and spicy pepper sauce, he proposed his finest red: An almost extinct Château Malescot St. Exupéry Margaux 1986. Dessert was a selection of delicate wafers and imported cheeses complemented by his richest, aubergine-coloured Spanish port.

Then, too soon, and much to the dismay of the Gourmands, the succulent feast was at an end. The specially designed long and narrow white-linen tabletop was not littered with empty, hand-crafted fine china now criss-crossed with silver flatware that no longer gleamed. Not there. Instead the dishware and cutlery were plain, stained with the dullness of moist and eager hands.

The Fatal Diners' Club

Finely cut stemware did not stand neatly expectant, their ridges smudged by coloured lips, their torsos smudged by indulgence and those same moist hands. Not there. Instead plain tumblers lay scattered and empty.

For such a special occasion one might have expected fine linen napkins to lay neatly folded, a sign of respect. Not there. Instead crumpled paper napkins lay as they might, tossed carelessly here and there, no longer useful, no longer clean and crisp.

Melvin Horn was one of the guests. He never refused an invitation.

The members' sole interest was food. There was no spacious drawing room richly decorated with abstract art and sculptures of nude and exotic women to excite the heart, nor were there large and plush lounge chairs luring the men to continue their celebration in comfort while the women chatted well away from thin wispy clouds of blue smoke soon permeating the room.

There was none of that in the hall. The purpose was satiation. Gourmands had no interest in the refinement of art or the art of discussion.

The Gourmands were jovial, well-fed, laughing and light-hearted more so than usual. The evening was one of merriment and fellowship more so than usual, the privileged guests raising their plastic champagne flutes three-quarters full with exotic effervescences awakening in what Melvin Horn believed was his host's prized and decades-old De Venoge.

In unison they counted backwards from ten with 2023 at death's door, Melvin Horn the most jubilant with good reason. He was alive, living to mock The Agency that wanted him dead. Three months earlier he had declined their indifferent invitation to voluntarily end his life. What did they know of his pain and his suffering?

The arrival of midnight was cause for the greatest celebration, greeted with bursts of raucous cheers and the high-pitched squeals of garish party favours. The Diners' Club was welcoming in its eighth year and the membership was not in decline, maintaining its strength and right to exist in a despotic new world by the hard work of Hilary Basil, his people, and the commitment of his members.

Hilary Basil with his glass held high promising many more years to come.

Melvin Horn drained his glass, holding out his hand for more as the din diminished to murmurs, no one in the hall thinking to miss the easy listening of romantic music. None there cared about dancing because no one could dance. None had danced for years, if ever. No one cared about auld lang syne and fond memories. No one cared about warm embraces, heated bodies and the paralyzing apogee of lovemaking.

All that mattered at such times was the gratification of one's palate, the melodies of tantalizing aromas, the lingering complexities of distinct flavours striving for recognition and honourable mention inside their sensory-deprived brains: Their sole escape from physical pain and the torment of ridicule.

They were Gourmands. They were clandestine, and illegal, each one at the precipice of their discovery and death.

6

Beautiful, Alone…and Pissed-off

Lorie Wilson lay in her soaker, heated and fragrant suds cloaking her 5'8" slender frame.

She was alone, mildly drunk and not so mildly pissed-off. At the moment she hated and despised Dwayne Michaels with a passion, whereas normally she simply thought of him as arrogant, self-centred and constantly annoying. 2024 had minutes earlier burst into her life to remind her she was single at thirty-eight. Screw him.

The bottle of Dom Pérignon staring at her from the trolley and the old-fashioned clutched in her hand were half empty, like her life. Her life was shit. All she had was her job. She moved to twist the satin nickel drain plug, reaching for the matching handle dotted with crimson red, like the hole she wanted to put into the centre of his empty forehead. He was shit. She wasn't ready to get out. She was miserable and wanted to drown in misery. Screw him. She grunted a caustic laugh, wondering who might be, or who was screwing him. Whoever she was, she was a whore and a complete bitch. Yes, definitely a bitch. They deserved each other.

Lorie Wilson knew she was beautiful and sexy. So did everyone around her who caught a glimpse of her on the street or was fortunate enough to watch her sauntering along the shoreline of her favourite beach dressed in a tiny Rio she wished was a thong smaller than an eye patch, the one

41

she wore or didn't wear at times on her private patio. None of them possibly able to imagine what she might do for a living, none of them caring when more fanciful and appealing images and thoughts came so readily to mind.

Her life sucked big time. Just once she wanted to run naked along the shore and into the waters of Long Beach, to roll naked in the sand and make angels, to do something absolutely crazy and wild the way she had those fun times with Priscilla. So what if someone saw her. Good for them.

Her straight hair was lustrous, dark mahogany streaked with black, and not from a bottle, which most days she pulled into a tight bun. The reason why was her business, no one else's. Though when she was alone, which accounted for most of her nights, the long fine strands draped past her shoulders or floated in hot, sweetly scented water across her untouched breasts enshrouding them in a soft, silky mantle.

Yes, untouched, she accused him out loud, hating that no one could hear her, smashing a delicate palm into the water, a delicate palm that could easily smash his larynx or turn him into a eunuch. No. Too easy, she mused, when she could as easily drive his nuts into his simple brain with a simple flick of her foot.

"I hope you're happy with your one-night whore because you will never know what you missed. No frigging way."

God, she was talking to herself. She was so pitiful. She wanted him out of her head, too angry to expel him. She needed him in her head to loathe him.

She squirmed deeper into the white cloud. She caressed the contours of her body from her breasts that hadn't been touched or kissed for as long as she could remember, to her hips that were slim and smooth and eager to hold a real man in place. She swirled concentric circles in the water, parting her knees, raising and lowering her hips from the acrylic floor, shallow swells she couldn't see sweeping across her, the gentle rush beneath the snow-white blanket titillating and inciting.

She closed her eyes, drifting, her fingers of one hand strumming lightly against delicate folds devoid of mahogany or any other colour, her glass-filled hand reaching blindly for the Dom Pérignon.

She was content, humming. Time lost its meaning, silent lyrics becoming low moans usurped by spasmodic grunts. Her eyes flashed open, her body twisting, hectic water cresting over the acrylic rim, splashing to the floor, suds flying.

Flushed by heated water and delirium she inhaled deep breaths, composing her mind and her heartbeats. Sex was her single pleasure. She hadn't once in her life since discovering the incumbent pleasures of puberty thought of her proclivity for herself as a vice. As much as she had once enjoyed non-motorized male participation in her lovemaking, men she might consider as deserving were few and far between and the rare recipients of her attention who had so long ago met her stringent criteria hadn't endured more than a short while, preferring less demanding, less autonomous and autocratic females.

She knew what she wanted.

Untouched by a man for as long as she could remember Lorie Wilson didn't like anyone, without exception, invading her life with questions, particularly when she was mandated, instructed to lie about who and what she was. Not even her parents were remotely aware of her true career. She needed no one in her life. What she wanted was another matter, someone who wouldn't run from her high-rise penthouse condo and wealth, her Corvette or her penchant for diamonds. She wanted him. She wanted the jerk, a man more eager for a young and different vagina each weekend than a beggar dying of thirst in the desert would be for water.

She gulped a mouthful, cupping a hand over her alluring

and responsive folds. She loved that part of being a woman. "But this one…in your dreams, jerk."

He was a jerk. Because of him she had become her own best lover, which wouldn't change any time soon. What's worse, he'd bought her a cardigan for Christmas. How original. Why even bother? A frigging cotton sweater she wouldn't think to buy her ailing grandmother, if she had a grandmother, which he gave her at the office as she was about to invite him to her condo two days later for a Christmas dinner, alone, the two of them alone.

At least then she would have known beyond the slightest doubt, irrespective of the clear possibility that he might be gay.

She'd been more thoughtful, or more stupid. She'd bought him a masculine stainless steel bracelet, engraved, which she didn't give him. Instead she sauntered into her private office, measuring her steps, measuring her intake of air, calming her pulse rate to put a ribbon on a bottle of JW Black, wanting to tell him where he could shove the neck if not the entire frigging bottle.

Merry Christmas, jerk.

She had thought of returning the rag to the store, but then she would have known how little he spent. Instead she dropped the thing into a mission box on her way home.

He should have known better. She wore short skirts, short enough, because she could, and sheer pantyhose without panties. When she wore slacks designer thongs accentuated a perfect ass he never once glanced at or complimented the way any normal man would. Perfect? No way. Her ass was fantastic. He probably didn't know she had one, which she thought was strange since he was such a total asshole himself. And, hello, women love guys ogling their asses. Jerk.

She wore expensive push-up bras under sheer blouses when she wore blazers that, once in a while at dinner with him during business trips, she would remove for no other reason than a simple reaction.

Nothing. Nada. The man was definitely a eunuch, stupid, blind or gay. No. She drained her glass. No. He certainly wasn't gay. She'd seen him too often after their dinners charming his way into slutty one-night panties: Bimbos whose idea of going Dutch on a date was opening their legs or playing doggie on-demand between last call and dawn in the hopes of staying for breakfast.

She chortled. For Michaels that would be a long-term commitment. He might even remember their names, if he thought to ask in the first place. He'd taken long enough to understand that Sweetie Pie or Girl or Cupcake were not synonyms for Lorie.

She dropped her glass onto the trolley, changing her mind mostly because the bottle was empty, standing, facing the mirror, her wet skin glistening and pink.

Yeah, she was beautiful. In fact she was perfect. Not a single flaw: An exceptional example of the human female specie. And she was pure female. She scrunched her face. No. She wasn't. She was a frigging nun.

The Agency demanded fitness. Two hours each workday in the gym were requisite to keeping her job, which prompted another spontaneous thought: Spandex. What was she doing wasting her time working out with him in form-fitting Spandex that put her on display virtually naked? He should have had some clue about what to buy her for Christmas. He saw every day how she dressed. It's not as though she was expecting diamonds, which he couldn't afford, which was no excuse.

Perhaps Dwayne Michaels was gay after all. Or blind, definitely blind. Perhaps she would buy him a white cane and beat him with it. She gurgled a curt laugh, the colour of the cardigan piercing her thoughts: Greyish pink. The colour of Kaopectate, as though she needed any reminder at all that he was a complete asshole, a total shithead.

No way! He simply didn't like older women and thirty-eight was closer to fifty than twenty. He wanted bimbos young enough to be his daughter with tight pussies, perky tits and smooth asses. When, for the record, as if he cared, she was tight, she was perky and she was smooth absolutely everywhere. Not only that, she was a fantastic lover, incredibly insatiable in bed. With a real man to love she would never need to work out in a gym.

"So there, jerk," she blurted into the mirror.

She climbed over the high rim of the tub, first one leg then the other, glancing over her shoulder into the mirror, pausing, delighting. Why not? No one else was with her to delight in what she was seeing. She did have a great butt and legs, to-die-for legs, and her pussy was as tight as anything luring him into a blonde twenty-year-old wearing a pleated skirt, stay-ups and a halter top for daddy.

He was the idiot. She wanted to cry. Not because of him, because of her turkey and her ham, because she had spent Christmas Day with her mother and father instead of sharing a romantic candlelight dinner with a jerk.

Lorie Wilson wasn't one of those women who stayed at home until thirty-five. No. She left home at eighteen, fully independent, fully prepared, paying for her advanced education in criminal law without anyone's help, which made her mother's frequently stated and sympathetic view of her current social dilemma all the more annoying.

How often would she have to hear that one day she would find a good man, a man like her father? Yeah, right. That's what she needed, wanted; a man like her father who continued to believe his little girl was still a frigging virgin midway between her cradle and her coffin. Get a life, old man.

She chortled: Men, where did they get off being the valiant Guardians of the Vagina? Well, she didn't need her vagina guarded. She wanted the damned thing invaded, mercilessly ravaged before her hymen began to grow back.

Far worse than Christmas, or the jerk and his

thoughtless gift, her mother and father expected her for New Year's Day dinner because they knew she had no one in her life. The ham she had bought thinking he might have enjoyed his bracelet, her Christmas dinner, and perhaps her, she wanted to stuff down Dwayne Michaels' throat because she would willingly let herself be taken and gang-banged by Gourmands before ever again thinking to invite him to her private and exclusive sanctuary for dinner.

Besides, why would she call him to hear girlish giggles in the background? Instead she took her empty glass and bottle to the kitchen, plucked a bottle of Ultimat vodka from the freezer, a shot glass from her dining room hutch, and zigzagged her way to bed to discuss him with her matted and long-abused teddy bear that had no opinion either way.

7
Jerk

Dwayne Michaels valued his private time and his space. He cherished his time alone. Still he was human and not gifted with the restraint of a monk.

He was a man blessed with above average good looks, though with basic needs for which he was admirably equipped to satisfy, according to many, albeit not as frequently since knowing her.

He loved gorgeous, well-maintained women. He loved their hair, the euphoria of their plural scents. He loved the intimate ballet of undressing them and watching them undress. In spite of which what he wanted most in his empty life was to be with one woman, *a* woman, a stunning, erudite woman who would know when to stop talking about herself, who could be a predatory female as well as a lady, not merely confusing femininity and sensuality with a one-night dip-and-soak as suitable payback for a freebie meal or a few drinks.

He'd been there. He'd done that too many times. Meeting her had forced him to reconsider, to regroup. Inviting suitably attractive and mutually-driven females to spend a memorable evening in a five-star venue which also served the requisite purpose of avoiding the inevitable issue of a farewell breakfast was now far less compelling.

He had waged and won so many battles; never quite

conquering the right heart until the day she made him realize he was tired of the war that never varied beyond the colour of their hair and scent of their perfume. In spite of which they kept coming; all but the one he wanted, or thought he might have a chance with.

They were the physical entities of his dream, her stand-ins.

Women, particularly younger women searching for love, suffered from short-term memory loss. They forgot the come-ons, the demure smiles and gentle pressure on his arms or hands, the longing in their eyes if for no other reason than a meal that was better than what they could afford, or the equality thing their foremothers had once fought for, strived for and won.

What's good for a man is good for a woman, the goose and the gander theory. That was the ancient concept of the 70s and 80s, forgotten in the nineties and reborn in the new millennia by a more promiscuous generation, an equality intended to dissolve rapidly upon penetration, a few groans, pinching and kissing.

Women were not equal to the male of the specie and never would be, not in matters of the heart, which in the second decade of the 21st century meant the gratification of one's genitalia and getting off would forevermore trump whatever romance grandma and grandpa were the last to truly enjoy.

He had always managed to leave before they woke. In those younger years stealth was his profession, his survival. Better that way. He never once hesitated or delayed his departure to gloat, to rub defeat in faces twisted with loathing. The possibility of reprisal was far too great. He knew by each sunrise he would no longer be the conquering hero, simply a manipulative, smooth-talking prick and a son-of-a-bitch.

Nor did he ever glance over his shoulder at them or stand in the doorway lamenting their disappearance from his life. What was done was done: Mutual needs evolving into mutual satisfaction. He didn't need or want the emotion of teary eyes or empty promises.

Nor did he desire in any way the scarred memories of blurred eyes, slurred speech, streaked mascara and matted hair. No matter how pretty or desirable they might be as a prelude to the evening, no matter how intense or willing as an appendage to the evening, they were never as pretty or as vital in the morning. Not the way she would be.

Sunrise, he had determined years earlier, was not a girl's best friend.

He preferred memories preceding night before: The hunt, the game, the innuendos and deceit, the anticipation. In fact, he remembered none of them once he was gone. What was the point?

But now he was enjoying occasional time-out. He needed more in his life. He had for some time; convincing himself he was searching when in fact he was procrastinating, deferring the inevitable, delaying by weekly increments the inescapable consequence of his inaction. He had to man up. He had already found her three years earlier for the second time and she was slipping away once again. History was repeating itself.

He wanted a woman who could be a shameless slut one moment and an elegant lady the next, more than an acquiescent receptacle with a pretty face on a head without a brain, which was the primary reason he did not like most women. Wishful thinking, he knew, placing him somewhere between a lonely and desperate existence and male hypocrisy, a rock and a hard place.

The fact was he did not like most people.

He joined The Agency as a favour to his uncle Ned who saw promise in him, who saw in him one of very few men who could get the job done for the president.

Ned Michaels was his family since the day his parents were killed with his grandparents in a plane crash when he was a boy. His father was a developer, his mother the daughter of wealthy parents whose brokerage firm had for decades made Michaels a familiar name in high-finance circles. Their combined estates worth tens of millions and bequeathed to Ned Michaels were equally divided between uncle and nephew and wisely invested throughout his school years and his years with SEAL Team Two. An unselfish generosity Dwayne never forgot.

Then and now he didn't have to work for anyone. He was wealthy, although at first Dwayne Michaels wasn't entirely convinced. Working for President Pricilla Vendôme would dictate his immediate discharge from the US Navy. He would no longer be a SEAL, no longer follow his dream of doing something very few others could do. He was elite, his unit was elite, and then he met Priscilla Vendôme and understood.

Now the only person Michaels could depend upon to cover his back was Lorie Wilson: The untouchable Ice Queen.

She was an anomaly, a constant pain in the butt, a complete mystery to him. She had nice tits. No, that wasn't true. She had great tits, a fabulous ass, a flat stomach, full and pouty lips and a voice that was at once soft and sensually hoarse. She had hypnotic black eyes splashed with green, a slender aquiline nose and, man, did she smell good. In spite of which she was prissy, standoffish, and more than a little bitchy most days, way beyond the tampon-induced bitchiness most guys learn to deal with about the time menopause sets in to carry on the male curse.

She wasn't warm and fuzzy. She was contradictory. More than once at dinner while on the job, either late-night or out of town she had, yeah, flashed her wares. Look, yes, but don't touch. Please look. Oh yeah, big time, crossing her legs this way and that, doing the bra thing as though he hadn't noticed the extra undone button or two, which was sort of pointless given that her blouses many times were sheer. He wasn't dead. Not to mention her beautiful dark hair.

He could imagine, and did imagine the finer details of what she kept hidden under her designer silk and satin.

Shit. If anything, she was killing him. Why not shoot him? Get it over with. She had a gun. Why not? She was a tease, pure and simple. Those dinners, expensed dinners, were fine. Yet each time he would ask her to join him at the sports bar, where he hung out after hours most evenings before going to an empty home that wasn't a home, for some beers and a few dogs…No way! That's all she ever said: No way! That's all he ever heard: No way! After making certain, of course, as she climbed into her shiny Corvette, that he would see a little more of what he would never touch, kiss or smell. Give him a break. Please.

She was a relentless tease. Probably for the best, he thought. She was the type to have serrated teeth or a designer bear trap surgically implanted into her vagina as a means of reducing the male population.

He poured two more fingers of the Johnnie Walker Black she'd given him into the engraved old-fashioned she'd given him the previous Christmas. At least she had good taste. He sipped, smiling contentedly. He'd done well with his gift also. As well as he could when what he had really wanted to buy her was something sexy and small.

He inhaled deeply, sipping again. She seemed to like her sweater, scurrying into her office to get his gift. She wasn't easy to read.

Dwayne Michaels was thirty-six, 5"11", athletic and slim. He could kill swiftly and accurately without remorse with a gun, a knife, a credit card, a garrotte, or a dozen other ways. Of course he preferred not killing. Proactive killing was no longer his job, more of a skillset to call upon when the need might arise. He derived no joy in taking a life despite the necessity, whether by abject submission of the person or his or her eventual non-compliant termination for the sake of their deliverance from misery.

What mattered was the greater good, the end result etched into his mind and hers for the sole purpose of equilibrium while remaining human as much as humane. It's what they did, what they believed in. What they did in life, for life, mattered. If not for them and six elite covert men and women like them, for what they did, what then, what would happen then?

The destruction of the human race was an unlikely probability, at least for several more decades if not centuries. That theatrical threat came and went with the propaganda and paranoia of the ancient Mayan calendar in 2012 when he was twenty-four. He snorted. Worse than a sucker born every minute, idiots populated the world every second. The world was inundated with them. Too bad fetal brain scans were never made compulsory the way ultrasounds were used to calm anxious soon-to-be parents. Mommies and daddies all worried about junior missing something or other, a leg or a finger, whatever. So why did no one ever give a shit about half, three-quarters or no brain at all?

More likely, however, when first meeting with President Vendôme, was the eventual and not very distant catastrophic collapse of society, chaos, and the inability of the entire continent to defend itself. That was his mission, his raison d'être and hers.

His grandfather, long since dead, had believed the Chinese would one day rule the world. The Great Yellow Scourge conquering Europe and the Americas by systematic immigration. That was not allowed to happen. Whereas his father once believed China would, in his lifetime, conquer the world by incrementally and insidiously controlling the production, fabrication and assembly of the world's limitless needs, which didn't happen either. The world woke up in time, taking back ownership of their respective countries, deciding to care more about their families, their unemployed men and women than an uncontrollable Chinese population.

The real danger was much worse, more insidious: A continent of 400 million seven years earlier dying by the thousands each day, a society that was once a new world borne of hope and determination teetering on the verge of calamitous ruin from within, forging a path of self-destruction amidst an indifferent world anxiously awaiting the day.

The platform of Priscilla Vendôme's first term seven years earlier was healthcare. Her unspoken mandate, her covert intent, was to reverse the country's decaying mindset and infused malaise.

That was his mandate. That was Lorie Wilson's mandate: To make certain Vendôme's mandate was carried out. They were, in fact, America's first and invisible line of defence.

Dwayne Michaels' charm was disarming to women, intimidating to men. His eyes were chocolate brown, liquid, penetrating and searching; his brown hair was thick and flowing. Women wanted him close, men did not. Men could sense danger when women, most women, sensed one elusive chance at rapture or perhaps something longer lasting. That was until they would awaken alone in a hotel suite which was never as luxurious as what they remembered from the night before.

He eased deeper into his steaming spa. Christmas didn't mean much to him, nothing at all really. His uncle lived in Washington, D.C. They called each other a few times each year and went for beers the times Dwayne was in town on Agency business, both men agreeing years earlier that buying each other Christmas gifts and singing laments at New Year's was pretty much the bottom of the barrel.

Sympathy wasn't one of Michaels' strong suits. He was impervious to grief, to death. How could he not be? He was equally impervious to being alone. Casual sex with blondes and redheads in their twenties or the occasional thirty-year-old wasn't living. It was getting by. They were a release, a means to an end, vehicles loaned to him for short and pleasant journeys. He couldn't pretend what he didn't feel.

He was happier now, more complete and not into glossy magazines and tissues.

He didn't mind the New Year thing, the passage of time. People grew old and died. He was good with being alone, without the need to escape before their eyes fluttered open, before he had to remember their names.

He was content to know Lorie had a loving mother and father to celebrate Christmas with and in a few hours she would again be with family who cherished her. He hadn't seen her in eight days. Neither he nor Lorie worked between the two festive days and he missed her.

He often thought of her naked with his hands on her spectacular ass, his mouth on hers, her fabulous breasts, kissing them. Thing was she was into older guys, more mature men. She'd once told him so, which put him SOL. She wasn't interested. And the way she'd sneered at him from out of the blue the last time he'd suggested a meal together, grabbing a fast bite. If that wasn't a message, what was?

He half-wondered why she'd even thought to buy him a gift.

He pushed himself upright, put aside the glass and towelled. Five past twelve, ooh-ha, Happy New Year. Yeah, really: Another year of what, working with the beauty to vanquish the beast or at least diminish the herd? He blew a deep breath.

There was light at the end of the once long and dark tunnel according to Vendôme. Yet the job seemed as endless as it was thankless. The country and the world didn't know. No one did, not even Ned Michaels who had recruited him for a fictitious purpose.

They didn't need to know. The problem wasn't theirs to

feign concern about. Neither was the solution. In that regard nations were no different from nosey neighbours, always wanting to hear shit that wasn't their business. The Agency was doing things right, getting the job done.

He poured two-fingers, flipping the light switch, feeling his way through the dark to his bed. He wanted to sleep, alone on the premier party night of the year. Not that he cared. He didn't.

Not having close friends spared him the constant lies. He didn't need the bullshit: Too much effort and too much trouble for the sake of a few barbeques and social evenings. No one would understand, not to mention he would be relieved from duty and punished forthwith, probably by Lorie with a smile on her face. The Agency wasn't tolerant. What the public might think or suspect, and what they must never know, were mutually exclusive situations.

He knew the rules and had signed on for better or worse, as did Lorie when their primary contact, their first-level link to the president first brought them together three years earlier. In fact the penalty for even the most innocent disclosure was sufficient motivation for secrecy. He was too young for either consequence, Lorie was too beautiful and the president was not a woman to carelessly disregard.

He drained his glass, eased under the covers and closed his eyes. His first image was of Lorie, certain he had her nude body perfected in his mind after their years together: Three short and long years working with a dark-haired angel in purgatory.

He inhaled deeply, smiling in the darkness. She was hot, very hot. He should have invited her to his home for Christmas dinner. At least he should have tried. Then he would have known. But he didn't, and he was much too late to celebrate New Year's.

8
January 01st, 2024

Lorie Wilson lay in bed wide awake wondering when and if she would ever get laid by a man she could love.

She refused to settle for second best or a long line of penis-driven and disappointing hopefuls. She thought she could love him, maybe, perhaps, possibly, which wasn't to say she would wait much longer. Time was running out. That was the last thought she remembered.

She woke in the dark, the half-filled glass clasped in her hands. She'd fallen asleep alone in a king size bed on New Year's Eve. How pathetic was that? She hadn't stirred. She ached. Her neck was stiff and her bum was cold with prickly numbness. She hated winter. The mere thought of winter made her shiver. She hated winter clothes. She hated the thought of wearing a silk skirt and blouse to sit eating a ham and baked potatoes with her commiserating mother and myopic father. What was the point of having a killer body and fabulous clothes if no one could see her? What was the point of buying exclusive lingerie to wear sitting in bed talking to herself at 8:30 AM on a cold winter morning?

She wondered whether his bitch had gone home. Probably not, she decided, too early. The slut was lying in his bed hung-over and naked, too stupid to fry an egg. Not like the morning delicacies she would have served him in bed wearing her panties and bra, or a sheer teddy, or an unbelted robe, or nothing at all.

Instead he was stuck with a semi-conscious bimbo he would ditch before evening unless he was thinking of keeping her another night for seconds because she was already there, broken in. Besides, nothing young or good is out there on New Year's Day. But Michaels wasn't into long-term relationships and two nights running for him was tantamount to a proposal. He was more the hourly kind of guy so her money was on a lonely second day of January before seeing her on the third. The man was a self-infatuated pig.

She was expected for dinner at two: Almost six hours remaining, every minute counting, minus a one-hour drive toward her personal hell. That was her New Year's: Six hours of evasive conversation, helping mom with the dishes, her father sleeping, her father snoring and missing the Rose Bowl half-time blonde bimbo show. Then she would do another sixty-minute drive before getting home at nine to select her wardrobe for the next day and go to bed.

Lorie had never visited Dwayne Michaels' home. She was never invited, nor did she want to experience that part of him. She needed to believe the man was a conceited jerk, albeit well-dressed, educated and infuriatingly quiet. She never understood what he was thinking. Nor did she ever ask because she wouldn't then know what to believe. She was content with their status quo.

He was good-looking, she conceded. She had to admit that much. And he was a consummate lover despite his questionable taste in women. That she did believe. Each day at the gym left her with too many undeniable images for the subsequent and desperate evening that would predictably follow.

The man was perfection wasted on young sluts, a man who walked quietly and did not need a big stick.

She kicked away her duvet, half snorting, half coughing a laugh into her dresser mirror. So was she terrific in bed, with herself, thinking of him. So what if she was thirty-eight. She looked late twenties which, she reminded the young woman leering at her, was years younger than him.

She put her glass on the dresser considering her dress code du jour.

A short silk skirt, sheer stockings, garters and a satin thong with a matching three-quarter bra, for her mother and father, wasted. No way. Her new three-inch patent leather pumps, her new silk blouse, wasted as well. She was depressed, despondent, most of all because drinking before noon was never a good sign and she wanted a drink. She wanted to get drunk and bury herself under her covers.

Every woman she knew was less attractive, less successful, less affluent and married. Some of them had kids, while others, the happier ones, did not. Not that she ever for a moment wanted kids. She didn't. No way. Her life was disappointing enough. She stared into the mirror, into her eyes, chortling, imagining a bizarre future, whispering, "Mommy, what do you and daddy do at work? Can you come to school with daddy and tell my friends?"

No way, not a chance. She shook her head vigorously, tousling her hair hands-free. She didn't need shitty diapers and colic as highly regarded rewards for blotchy stretch marks on a flawless body and baggy eyes from sleepless nights. She already had sleepless nights because of 'daddy', the jerk.

She didn't love him. No way did she love him. How ridiculous would that be? Love grew from tender moments, gentle touches, the unmasking of one's inhibition. Most times she didn't even like him, let alone whispering endearments.

She worked with him, knew him too well. That's why people hated each other after divorce, because they knew each other too well: Their secrets and faults, their misdemeanours and multiple shortcomings. That's what would happen: Divorce. She would bring him home one night, serve him a candlelight dinner, get laid, sweat, scream and moan, and in the morning he'd be gone and she would feel like a slut. Worse, he would know more than he should about her. He would know her breath, her lips, her intimate scents and the feel of her intimate flesh.

That was the problem. He never gave her the time of day, never said how pretty she was or how nice she looked. So what would he think or say when seeing her naked? Or when he was doing her, the thirty-eight-year-old? She knew. He'd leave feeling good, believing he'd done the old hag a favour. No way, frigging asshole.

She reached for her phone. Dinner was off. Something had come up, an emergency requiring her immediate response. She was sorry, mom. She was sorry, dad. She felt terrible. She would see them soon. She loved them.

She pressed END. She wasn't sorry and she didn't feel terrible. Well, she did, but not for the white lie, although she was relieved when her mother's message centre took her call. She was fed up. No way would she wear those clothes for her parents without a man escorting her through their door. No way.

She often remembered her times with Priscilla Vendôme, protecting her, spending privileged time with her. Now she was doing important work for The Agency searching for the elusive Hilary Basil. That was her life. She was so pathetic.

She needed to debug her mind and her body. She needed to sweat, to kick something, to hurt something. After which she was going to dinner, dressed to kill. Not to the most exclusive restaurants where she was known. Most single men, or men wanting to be single, put a value on getting laid which never included haute cuisine or imported wines.

Instead she would visit a more affordable eatery and bar. What she would not do was come home to an empty penthouse to lie in bed pretending her deft and attentive fingers were his.

She put her wardrobe du jour into a suitcase with her

cosmetic bag, checking her gym bag for all things skimpy and clean, her water and her phone. She brushed out her hair, dressed in jeans, a halter top, a leather jacket and boots and walked out ignoring the chimes of her personal number.

Mother was calling. Mother always called in a dither when plans went awry. No way. No way! Not this time. Mother would just have to learn to once in a while…stay out of her frigging life!

9
Withdrawal Pangs

Dwayne Michaels woke at nine, instinctively reaching out to the left, tentatively more than gently, blindly exploring with his hearing on high alert for the slightest breath or murmur. He was a right-handed sleeper, a question of habit. Properly managing a female body was easier from that side of a bed and his women didn't seem to care either way. What mattered was the assault, the completion of the campaign, their decisive and breathless defeat from all quarters under his expert touch. No less critical, however, than the escape, his retreat to higher ground when the battle was won so that he might regroup and strategize to conquer the feeble race once again.

He'd been dreaming, or thought he was. Or was she real? He wasn't certain. He'd waited so long, dreamed so many nights of that night, of that dream. Her body so warm and real in his arms, the pressure of her moist legs clamped to his hips so real.

She wasn't there. He hadn't screwed up and slept in late to "can we spend the day together?" Or "I think I want to be exclusive with you," which was impossible. They weren't like other people.

Anyway, one-nighters weren't her style. She was too classy, too special.

His heart rate began to slow, which seldom happened until the door was closed behind him.

The first day of January, no different from any first day of any month except for the cold, and the entire day was his. Saturday, when he would usually commit a portion of his day to thinking about the one he'd met on Wednesday or Thursday while getting ready for his date with her that evening. This Saturday was different, however, as would Sunday's sunrise be.

He was a new man, resolved. 2024 would be his year. He wasn't going to screw up. Not with Lorie, not with Hilary Basil.

He made his bed and dressed. His home was immaculate, his wardrobe, a collection of who's who, was arranged by workday suits, evening attire, casual, casual sport and training.

In the kitchen he filled his favourite coffee mug with black, steaming Columbian richness. He seldom ate a breakfast of more than a piece or two of dry toast. Food too early in the day slowed him down, dulled his senses, affecting his training, his mood.

Training, though, wasn't uppermost on his mind. She was, and the nagging thought that he should invite her to dinner despite the last-minute invitation. He was a talented cook, something about him she didn't know. She would forgive him for that reason alone. He excelled in matters culinary with a cellar of exceptional wines to complement any creation. He was also a good dancer. The rest he would necessarily take incrementally, giving her the lead.

They had worked together for three years without a single evening together that wasn't work-related. Why was that? Bizarre, he thought, for two unattached and healthy people. What was her problem? She didn't have to sleep with him to lose her attitude. But if she were to let her guard down, what would the harm be? The Agency had no specific ruling against co-ed teams having dinner together, or sex for that matter. Inter-marriage was verboten, which he understood, which was a non-issue. She wasn't the marrying kind. She'd made her feelings pretty clear several times, often out of the blue as though the couples in her line of vision could hear or care about her opinion. Besides, who could ever get close enough without risking severe frostbite?

She was complex, and annoying, beautiful and exotic. He reached for his phone. What the hell. Perhaps she was warmer on weekends. The worst case scenario would be ridicule or a cold shoulder until she found something else to bitch about.

Her message centre took over on the third chime. They, meaning she, weren't available. He was to leave her a detailed message, which he did by pressing END. She had Caller Display. She already knew he was calling at 9:30 on a Saturday morning. She wasn't picking up. She was in the shower getting ready for her parents, or she wasn't interested in talking with her partner, giving him the finger. Talking wasn't her strong point unless she was bitching.

A Saturday and everything was closed. His new resolve quickly creating unexpected issues. He hadn't planned for a day of nothing. His reader was jammed with books he hadn't yet read; his sixty-inch screen mounted in the wall was on stand-by mode waiting to come alive with Brenda and Bambi or Luscious Lucinda and Debbie Divine, his preferred late-night instructional entertainment. He could think of no better way for any man to perfect what women enjoyed, wished for, than to observe two women eagerly sharing the heat of what each one desired from the other: The finest in ongoing home study. He was very much the avid learner.

The thought, however pleasant, without a woman to anticipate, somehow seemed desperate. And any woman he might find later in the day sitting on a stool in a near-empty bar would be no less desperate.

He wasn't into consoling despairing or beleaguered women drinking their failed pasts and bleak futures into tolerable realties. Nor would he ever do a woman simply to make her feel wanted, pretty or young. His women were pretty and young. Case closed.

Nor could he spend a few hours with one of his recent favourites, another pretty yet younger woman whose life was uncertain, who was eager to learn from him. She was having dinner with her parents the way she'd promised him.

He grabbed his training bag and left. He had top clearance and he had a key. He needed to workout, sweat, grunt and groan away his wasted day.

10
Miss Florence Whitten

Casey had been home, meaning Houston, one year and a bit. One earlier evening, a month or so following his return from Cambridge, while sharing a cognac with his father, Thatcher had graciously evicted him from the family hearth without the slightest apology either to his son or to his wife.

If the young man was of an age and maturity to represent the law, he was old enough to make his way. And he did.

From the moment he pulled the brown paper from his storefront window, proudly displaying C. Riley's Law Office in bold script, Casey kept long hours protecting his clients.

At the beginning most were associates or friends of the Riley family with minor and mundane matters to address, however soon Casey Riley was searching for a partner, finding one where he least expected. Her name was Florence Whitten. She was twenty-two and seated in front of him waiting for him to finish reading the history of her life and education that she saw fit to present to him.

His legal training, notwithstanding his father's early influences, had taught him restraint.

He thanked her for her interest and bid her good day. She left with elegant reserve, showing neither disappointment nor disdain for his cavalier treatment of her. In fact she was seething. She was at the top of her graduating class and might have joined any number of firms in New York or Boston. She was hardly about to beg a man of his shallow character for work or charity.

Instead she crossed the street to the Houston Hotel where she enquired as to the cost of their least expensive room.

That night Casey Riley found himself obsessed with immoral thoughts. He loathed himself, not for what he was thinking of her, lewd images of her flooding his mind. He was afraid he might have dismissed her too quickly, that she might feel bitter towards him and that he might now lose her entirely.

He dressed quickly in a clean shirt and freshly laundered suit and made his way to the hotel where he left a note with the nighttime clerk who assured him several times that Miss Whitten would receive his letter without fail in the morning.

He spent a sleepless night, the morning no less worrisome, waiting and wondering, peering through his window at the hotel between each impatient breath, too proud to call, too uncertain to cross the street.

Miss Whitten did, in fact, receive and read his note on her way to the dining hall for her breakfast the following morning. She sat staring at the page-long missive wondering how much she truly disliked him, or how little she might eventually like him, how well she could work with such a rude and forthright young man.

He certainly lacked feelings, possibly for having been born without a heart. The previous day after reviewing her history and letters of reference from the highest offices of her university, he had simply thanked her for coming in as though she had gone to the grocery store for a pound of potatoes.

He stood, reached over his desk to shake her hand and remained standing, waiting for her to stand and leave. She was horrified, hating him instantly. She had never once met such a discourteous man. His parents, she believed, must either be completely ashamed of him or completely vulgar themselves.

On the other hand, he did come to her late at night to apologize for his poor conduct, offering her employment, and she did need to work. She did need the money. She'd spent most of her savings on her journey to meet with him. She had heard so much about Casey Riley during her last year of school that she simply had to work with him. And her professors agreed.

Besides, she believed that one day he might work for her. One day the Whitten name would mean something and she would treat him badly.

She made her way across the street, sauntering, not hurrying. She was certain he was following her every footstep. She opened and closed his door nonchalantly, scanning the outer office as she turned to face him, her face impassive. After all, she was a lawyer as much as he was, and quite likely a much better one.

"I will accept your offer, Mr. Riley, on the conditions that I earn no less than twenty percent less than you, that I do not act as your office girl, that I maintain a separate office with a door, and that eventually and contractually you will see to the installation of a separate and private facility for me and our women clients."

"Is that all?" He stood, disguising his excitement. "Miss Whitten, I have no indication of your competencies other than a few letters written to help you on your way. I find your demands somewhat excessive. Perhaps..."

"Nor do I have the slightest indication of how good an associate you will be, or how I will advance my career in accordance with my goals by accepting your offer."

"I believe twenty-five percent less and a PRIVATE sign for the shared men's facility would be a reasonable beginning, Miss Whitten."

"Twenty percent and a separate powder room appropriately appointed for ladies."

She stood her ground, waiting. She was adamant.

He stood facing her, his thumbs tucked into his waistband, waiting. They were at an impasse. Not really. She needed the job. She would most certainly soon give in.

She crossed her arms, arching an eyebrow, glancing towards a stack of files on his credenza.

She drew her lips inward, pursing them, the way he used to watch his mother applying her lip colours before a going to social evenings with his father. She was lovely and unmoved. She was lovely and he could imagine her in a courtroom, in his arms.

She was exasperating and would be difficult to work with.

"Fifteen percent, a powder room appointed any way you see fit and dinner with me this evening. That's my final offer, Miss Whitten. Take it or leave me to my work."

He took his seat, trying not to blink.

Her arms remained crossed. "Agreed, and my office with a door should be suitable in colour and décor for a lady as well."

"Done."

He noticed her shoulders dropping imperceptibly, her eyes suddenly sparkling, her arms not uncrossing. Rather she appeared to hug herself indiscernibly. She was pleased. She had won her first case.

"Then if we have nothing further to discuss, Mr. Riley, I will prepare the contract for our signatures."

He nodded, watching her saunter into her office which, as yet, had no door.
*

Within a few weeks Miss Florence Whitten had her private office with a door and a powder room which was the envy of any fine hotel. Then she wanted a library. A law office should appear as one, she insisted, and not as a stationary room. Their best clients would expect an air of wisdom and authority.

Not many weeks later they had one to share.

She had a small apartment within walking distance and worked six-day weeks to grow her client list. She had no gentleman friend, no gentlemen callers, and didn't want any. She had no time, though she never refused dinner with Casey Riley, not after she came to like him by degree.

Eventually several of those dinners were at the invitation of Betty Riley directly to her. They became good friends and Florence loved Thatcher like a father who taught her to ride and shoot much to the envy of his son. She had never in her life thought to shoot a gun or gallop over and down endless green hills and shallow valleys.

Betty, however, viewed matters quite differently.

Within a year the law office had doubled its clientele, while revenues had more than doubled. They were taking on more important clients, more critical cases, and winning. He didn't want to lose her, yet he could see a difference in her. She was vexed without probable cause. She was preparing to leave, yet she had become irreplaceable to him.

He could not bear the thought of missing her terribly each day. He made her a partner, inviting his mother and father to join their celebration that weekend. Betty graciously accepted, while Thatcher, hearing of the invitation and the reason thereof, reiterated his pride in the young people and believed himself prudent to say nothing else.

On their way home from a jubilant evening Betty declared in the car to her husband's surprise that his son was, in fact, a clueless idiot. That beautiful young girl, she admonished, would not wait much longer. She needed more than shooting guns and riding horses on her day off. What she needed was to mount something with two fewer legs and, if not the idiot, someone more deserving would one day soon come along to take her hand at the altar.

Thatcher had little to add. He knew when to keep his thoughts private in times when his concurrence was as inciting as any discordant thinking he might propose. She was right, of course. A mother would certainly recognize whether or not her son was a mindless buffoon.

That evening Florence Whitten wrote a letter to her mother and father explaining her promotion, telling them how much she loved him and that the partnership had come as a complete surprise. What she had expected was to see Casey Riley, her boss, on his knees, begging for her heart with a gold ring cupped in his hands. That did not happen and never would. She was certain of that now, after all this time.

She tore the carefully worded note into little pieces. Her parents were dead, though she often wrote them letters from her heart.

She had put herself through law school on what little money they left her, a small insurance policy and working at whatever menial employment she could find throughout her school years.

She deserved the partnership. They were equals, thanks in part to Betty's influence and endless encouragement. In fact she was beginning to believe she was remaining with the law office more for Betty and Thatcher than for her future.

She knew Betty was silently aware, frustrated. Florence saw her own disappointment and disillusionment in her older friend's eyes as clearly as she saw the truth in Casey's eyes each day. She had no idea what to do; determined she would never humiliate herself by asking any man to marry her.

She wouldn't cry. She was too forlorn to lie in bed weeping. She would not give him the satisfaction. Instead she went to her phone and called Betty who sat listening through static and long wordless moments.

That night Thatcher found no peace in quiet slumber,

determined to seek revenge on his son who, the next morning, was summarily ordered to dinner without explanation.

When he arrived at the office for work, Florence was not there. When he called her apartment later that morning thinking she might be ill, she was either not there or chose not to answer. He went to her home during his lunch hour and knocked on her door. Still she did not answer and he left confused, returning once more after closing early for the day, after several frantic calls which she chose not to answer.

*

Florence sat in her own saddle, a birthday gift from Betty, mounted on her own horse, a gift from Thatcher. Over the year she had become a confident and capable horsewoman.

She wore a deep-pleated skirt, a high-neck sweater and bolero jacket. The boots in her silver stirrups came to her knees and gleamed in the sunlight.

They could see for miles from their vantage on Betty's favourite hillside. He was coming, clearly with a purpose. He'd called his father and mother separately earlier in the day. He was worried. Something had happened to Florence.

Betty patted Florence's knee, kissing her cheek before riding alone to meet her son whose day was about to worsen. He was a good man, a smart man, and she had taken all the foolishness from him that she could tolerate.

She dismounted from her horse in a single fluid motion, stopping him in his tracks with an open palm, leaning against his vehicle, giving him no chance to speak.

"You never met your father's father, Casey, because he was a horrible and heartless man, beating his wife until she died to escape him. My mother's second husband, if he's still alive, mistreated me badly until one day I ran away. Both men were unfit for this world and deserve to never rest in peace."

"Father once told me how you met, mother. I know the story."

"Your father lied to you. Now shut up and listen. I ran until I felt safe. I was ignorant and uneducated, though I had a young woman's body. So I set up shop not far from a saloon and made known to the men of the town that I would soon be available for two bits a visit, twenty-five cents for as long as they lasted. Your mother, Casey, was beginning her life as a whore." She thrust a silencing finger. "My first man was so handsome and seemed so dangerous to me. He was dressed completely in black. He had a long ponytail and wore guns on his hips that frightened me. Still, I let him have his way with me for as long as he wanted. He was gentle and kind with me, though I supposed most other men would be hurtful and thoughtless. He remained all night with me, paying me with six silver dollars which was more money than I hoped to earn in a busy week. We didn't sleep, not for a moment. He was so anxious to tell me of his plans, of his future, and I believed him. I was so frightened when he prepared to leave in the morning, so frightened that I refused to let him leave me behind. I made him take me. I would be his private whore until I was settled, which never happened. We married. We were meant to share a future and to have you."

Casey's face was struggling with mixed emotions, his expressions almost comical to her.

"Yes, I know. Your mother was a whore…for a night and, from the moment I mounted my new horse and set out with him, I knew I would always be with him. I still have those six silver coins and your father, I can tell you, still has vivid memories of me soaking my sore parts in my tub. Sorry to shock you, my boy. I don't recall when exactly, though at some point he stopped calling me his favourite whore, albeit kindly, and began using my name. Then one night that I do remember he told me he loved me, and not once, all through the night, and that he wanted and needed to marry me as quickly as possible."

"Mother, I'm stunned. What you're telling me…it's unbelievable."

"No, you're not stunned. You're intrigued, the same way you were taken aback the first time you paid for a whore to experience a naked woman with your father's hard-earned money. The truth is, Casey, if your mother hadn't thought to begin her life as a whore, you wouldn't be here making her so very ashamed of you."

His shock was real, his mouth agape, futile words choking in his throat. "I don't understand. I've only worked to make you proud of me, mother. What could I have…?"

"Shut up, Casey. I married your father in a mud field, with horse dung on my work boots and a hand-me-down dress splashed with wet mud and more dung. Even so, I was the happiest girl and never once thought to discard the ring my husband placed on my finger."

"Mother, your ring is gorgeous. Why would you think to ever…?"

She wanted to smack him, her only son. She absolutely did. Instead, she dug a slender hand into her jodhpurs.

"You're such an unforgivable idiot, Casey. Truly, you are. This is my wedding ring, carved by your father the night before he asked me to marry him. He worked through the entire night from the moment I fell asleep until I woke, whittling and making the wood smooth for my finger. We had a difficult few years, the two of us, with not much to eat or do other than scrape our hands raw and strain our backs. We saw our friends and neighbours die or lose all they possessed in search of a dream and often at night I would weep in your father's strong arms, wanting to believe his comforting whispers. And, because of those words, we endured: Your father, a young and brave man ready to use his guns to protect his woman and his claim from ill-intentioned interlopers, and me, a whore not long after her seventeenth birthday and married to her heart's deepest love at eighteen."

Tears began welling in his eyes. "I never knew. This is not the tale father told me."

"You be careful what you say, boy. Neither my life, nor his, is a tale. And you dry those tears. Your father hasn't cried once in his life. He didn't want you to know I was a whore, albeit his whore who loved him. He wanted you proud of me. And you believe you know the rest, which you do not. You know about our money and your good life, not ours. We came here to make our home and our new lives. What you do not know is that neither one of us could read or write a single word, that we could not hold a knife or a fork properly to eat our meals, that we hired people who knew more than we did to teach us, to make us proper…and after all that I have to stand here and deal with the poor likes of you. Yes, Casey. I am very ashamed of you."

"What have I done, mother? Tell me, please. And where is father?"

"Your father knows better than to show his face, enough said. And if you think you can go to him for some sort of male bonding, you cannot. Not unless he wants to start whoring again after all these years."

"Mother, I apologize for whatever wrong you feel I have committed to disappoint you."

"Your life has been too easy, Casey. You have taken too much for granted. You believe a few years at school and a fancy name on your window makes you a man. You're wrong. That young woman you haven't yet noticed on the hill behind me is what will make you a man. As of today she no longer works with you. I have loaned her the money to become your adversary. She can't work with you any longer because she loves you and you're too simple of mind to understand or appreciate those deep feelings. Are you so much of an idiot that you see her so easily with another man?"

Casey blocked the sun from his eyes, searching, a

sudden gasp stealing his breath, his pulse skipping a beat. She was a vision mounted on a golden steed, sitting there staring down at him. She was motionless, a hypnotic sculpture.

"Mother, I made her my partner in law because I could not stand the thought of losing her. I felt and I do feel myself unworthy of her. I was never able to prove myself as father did, or appear as gallant to any woman as father did to you. Those times are remembered in history books. In that father had and has the upper hand, even when he rides with her most Sundays, when I cannot take my eyes from her. He has a presence I could never for a moment hope to emulate. We are men separated by past and present eras. Still, I do have his blood, and I have yours." He paused. He hadn't once seen his mother this way. "Clearly I have not matured to the point where the mother I love cannot scold me with good reason." He glanced toward the hill, standing straighter. "Mother, might I borrow your horse for a short while, and might I also hope to borrow your wedding ring. It's obvious to me now that I haven't sufficient time to carve my own. I promise to return both, if not together. I do sincerely hope not together."
*

Betty placed the ring into his palm, walking quietly away. She'd said her piece. She wasn't ready to forgive him, though she did admit to Thatcher moments later a certain pleasure in shocking the dim-witted boy to his senses.

Casey threw off his coat and his tie. He rolled his sleeves, undoing his starched collar and top few buttons, springing into the saddle as best he could. He was a good horseman, if not a cowboy. He hesitated, taking her in, absorbing her, imagining himself dressed in black leather, a gun belt and a ponytail. His mouth was dry, his heart keeping rhythm with his deep breathing.

He lunged forward. Betty's horse was strong, sure-footed and fast, carrying an uncertain man at a full gallop to the precipice of an uncertain near future, his heart pounding in concert with the animal's hooves. He reined in the horse several feet from her, stopping, collecting himself, his thoughts, his wished-for cavalier façade failing him. He went to her at a trot, studying her face, her cold, expressionless face.

"Miss Florence Whitten, it has come to my attention that we are no longer partners in law. I require no confirmation of this unfortunate news as my informant is quite reliable. I am also informed that I am, in point of fact, an idiot and a buffoon for having been blind for quite some time regarding a personal matter of considerable interest to both of us. In my defence to the breathtaking court I stand before, may I say that I am neither a buffoon nor blind. I am, however, an idiot for not having the courage to tell the court what I believe to be the entire truth: That I do indeed love this most beautiful court and I would be eternally grateful if Her Honor would deem to impose a penalty in keeping with my inattention of my natural life with her and without any possibility of parole. Miss Florence Whitten, will you marry me on whatever day is convenient to you?"

"Your mother is right, Casey. You are an idiot. It would serve you right to have me as an opponent in court."

"Is that a yes? Will you forgive me and marry me as soon as possible?"

Florence filled her lungs with air, expelling a long breath through lips she intentionally made pouty. That she knew the answer, that she and Betty had discussed the probable outcome earlier, did not mean he had any right to her full disclosure until she saw fit to set his mind at ease.

She gazed at the grass as though studying each blade, the sky as though counting each cloud and measuring their speed. She patted her horse with long, loving strokes. She appeared completely indifferent, ignoring him for interminable minutes, a lifetime of anxious heartbeats until at last she sighed, releasing the pent-up exasperation she'd been practicing all the while in her mind.

"Oh, I suppose with help from your mother I could manage to tolerate you at least as well as she does. And, quite frankly, Casey, I don't see any purpose in letting my hard work and your mother's go to waste. You really are a difficult work in progress."

"I have loved you since I first saw you."

"You mean since you almost lost me the first time."

He smirked. He could tell she was weakening, softening towards him. "Yes, since I ran to your hotel because I couldn't bear to lose you, would never think of losing you." He reached for her hand, bringing her fingertips to his lips, kissing her, slipping his mother's ring onto her finger. "I have moments ago come to know the importance of this ring, Florence, on loan from the one other woman to ever occupy my heart. Love is captured in this ring, Florence, forever a prisoner, theirs and now mine."

"She's my best friend, Casey. I'm glad you didn't make her cry. I would have hated you for a very long time."

"I would never do such a terrible thing, not knowingly. I believe my father has never taken the bullets from the revolvers hanging in his study. I also believe I have made his life sufficiently miserable of late. I would not want to encourage him more than I have."

"You do that very well, Casey, making people miserable. Now, if you're quite finished ingratiating yourself to me, I want to tell Betty and Thatcher that I'm getting married." She reared her horse. "Oh, and by the way, I love you too. However, please remember that your mother loves me more than she loves you. So does your father because I'm nicer than you in so many ways. So do not think to ever look to him for help."

Miss Florence Whitten giggled and bolted away. He let her go, unable to imagine a time when he'd been happier.

That evening Florence received all the attentive

affection due her, and more. She was the bride-to-be, toasted with the finest champagne from Thatcher's cellar.

For his part Casey wisely maintained a low profile, eventually forgiven by degree and with provision.

Six months later Mrs. Casey Riley was throwing a bouquet into the air, not thinking for a moment she would soon lose her adoring husband to a frightful war.

11
December 07th, 1941

Betty and Thatcher Riley were the first to hear that the Pacific Fleet headquartered in the pearl of Hawaii was practically obliterated by the Japanese Imperial Navy.

Florence and Casey had earlier decided they would ignore the world most Sundays. They understood the war in Europe would not end soon, that one day America would be called upon to take part. Everyone knew, and what they didn't hear on any Sunday they would hear on the Monday.

When Betty asked her husband what the attack on Pearl Harbor would mean in real terms, he understood she was afraid of what he might say. He answered the way she would expect of him. "Betty, I believe we may soon have to console our Florence. The best we can hope for is that we console her once and not twice."

Florence and Casey weren't married two years before the letter they were anticipating came to his door, delivered by a postman as though handing out Christmas cards and not the impersonal facsimile of an unsigned death warrant.

Casey was wrong that sunny day on the hill to believe he would never knowingly make his mother cry. The son she loved was going to war without his father's intuitive sense of survival, without a mind and body hardened by arduous times. She was angry and she was afraid. Thatcher had high-level connections and she wanted her son posted at home, beside herself when Thatcher reminded her that his son had not been raised to hide behind his mother's skirt. Nor would he want or expect to.

She at least wanted him sent overseas as an officer, she pleaded, fully aware her husband could make that happen.

Again Thatcher refused, telling her warmly that his son simply was not officer material. Not all men were meant to command others simply because they lived a more fortunate life. Casey was a defender of men, he told her, not one who could for a moment arbitrarily order men to their deaths or disfigurement while he remained safe and sound sending impersonal letters home to comfort mother and wives.

Their son was twenty-six, smarter than most and young enough to learn survival. He would return home, or he would not. This was his life's challenge. What Thatcher would do, however, was to offer his son a choice, which was no choice at all in Betty's maternal mind.

The military arbitrarily wanted Casey in the army. Thatcher gave his son two other options within the sphere of his influence which were refused by his son. Casey could see no advantage in joining the navy. He had no desire to drown in a dark sea or to drift there until eaten. Neither was he enamoured of the idea of hurtling towards Earth in a fire bomb or having his mortal parts exploded into charred tidbits.

He thanked his father sincerely, having considered the matter somewhat theatrically for the benefit of the ladies who were not amused. He would do his time with the army, he decided. He was an excellent shot, taught well. Not many Germans, he supposed, could boast of having a gunslinger for a father and he promised to kill only those Germans who might think to prevent his safe return.

At that remark the men chuckled alone. The women stood and retired to the parlour.

*

Christmas that year was sombre. No attempt was made to

lighten the mood or to disregard reality. Casey did, honouring his father's request, make one easy concession. He and Florence remained that last night and the night before in the guest house of his mother's home.

She and Florence prepared elegant dinners both days, pampering him to where he sought refuge in his father's study. Neither Florence nor Betty was ever told of the men's private conversation. Nor did they ask.

That night Florence wept into Casey's arms, Betty into Thatcher's. They ate an early and quiet breakfast together and at 6:30 AM father and son drove without their wives to the train station. Casey did not want tearful goodbyes amongst thousands of others. That was his second wish. His first was that Florence would remain with his parents until his safe return.

*

Casey's first letters arrived quickly from England, addressed to all of them with an extra page folded in four and marked 'Florence'. All his future letters would arrive that way, although those subsequent letters came slowly, sometimes taking months, sometimes several letters wrapped in a bundle arriving at once, letters he had written and saved. None described the horror of war. None gave Florence or Betty cause to fear for his well-being more than they did.

He had been gone from them one year by Christmas of '42, and by all accounts and unspoken prayers he continued not breaking their hearts. Thatcher did his best to make Christmas Day special for the women. He bought them fine yet simple gifts and took them for a carriage ride and a sumptuous picnic atop Betty's favourite hill. What else could he do but wait for yet another encouraging letter that would give them all hope?

Christmas of '43 was even more special, spent skiing in Vermont. Betty first thought the idea was unconscionable when any day they might be given the worst possible news by strangers at their door. Thatcher thought otherwise. Casey would not want to think they or his young wife were inconsolable to the point where they could no longer live their lives or function. He would want to read in Florence's next letter where they went and what they did. He would want to share times happier than his.

Florence agreed and they departed Houston a few days later arriving in Stowe a week before Christmas. They spent two weeks at an inn where they skied most days wrapped snuggly in fur coats and hats and looking like the Eskimos who dwelled in the frozen North. Something Betty enjoyed much more than trying to skate on a frozen lake, succeeding for the most part when she did in bruising her ankles and knees for which she blamed Thatcher.

Three months later Casey shared photos of his mother bundled in fur and on all fours imploring her uncaring husband for help. Other photos showed his father on his backside with his legs strangely spread apart imploring his unsympathetic wife for help. Many more showed the most beautiful woman in the world smiling and waving at the camera, at him, her cheeks flushed with cold.

She would not cry to make him feel sad.

He would be home soon, he promised in his letter, excusing himself once again for not sending photos of himself or of the men in his troop. On the other hand, he did make humble mention of the fact he was now a sergeant. Florence and Betty, though, would not read his most recent news until midway through June.

In return the women sent his Christmas gifts in July, hoping he might receive his warm underwear, socks and gloves in time for the bitter winter. Thatcher added well-wrapped bottles of scotch and cognac sufficient in quantity for the entire troop to enjoy a merry Christmas, requesting of a certain general that his son receive them on time and in good condition.

However, not a man accustomed to leaving matters to chance, he made certain the general's Christmas would also be quite merry as a matter of self-serving pragmatism.

Casey Riley had been gone thirty months. Thatcher Riley continued working sixty-hour weeks, Betty by his side many of those hours when she wasn't maintaining a ranch, and Florence was by then a well-known and sought after attorney in the law offices of Riley & Riley. She had decided before marrying him that if she could live with an idiot she might just as well continue working with one.

His letters became fewer as the months went on, the family spending their evenings by the radio for whatever news they might hear. Thatcher would not, he told them often, use his connections to ascertain his son's well-being when so many other mothers and wives could not.

The Christmas packages arrived three months early, Casey finding himself somewhat hard-pressed to care for the precious cargo until year's end. The troop was in complete agreement. They could get as drunk at Thanksgiving as easily as at Christmas and saw no particular reason not to be as thankful in September as in November.

Just as well, Casey thought on December 25th, bent at the knees in a rain-filled ditch no deeper than his chest mixed with the piss, vomit and liquefied shit of his troop.

He hadn't washed in a week. Nor had he seen his feet in as many days. He was, by his conservative estimation, twenty pounds, possibly twenty-five slimmer than when he left her. His trousers no longer fit properly, his already loose shirt was looser still, difficult to keep tucked into his belt, and he harboured no doubt whatsoever that he could easily, once at home, leap into the saddle with a single bound as well as any young cowboy bedecked in black.

He hadn't seen her in three years. He'd forgotten her smell and the softness of her skin, her breath and the moistness of her lips. The sound of her voice was a fabrication he struggled each night not to lose and the sight of her naked, he began to believe, was generic.

What he despised most were the lies he wrote to her when he would tell her how he remembered each of those things so vividly.

He wanted to remember. He just couldn't. How could he when all he saw in his mind, in the dark, were the faces of dead Germans who would never again see their girlfriends and wives because of him?

He leaned backward into the damp wall of the trench. His father was right to believe there was no God. Not that Thatcher ever once imposed his beliefs. He had always expected his son to think for himself and to believe what was right for him. He looked to his left, smiling thinly at the man not an arm's length away. The man was pissing over his belt while bent on his knees.

He looked to his right. That man was still dead and would remain so until morning. The bullet had gone through his head not far from midnight on New Year's Eve when he had stood to yank his trousers from his knees. Sure as hell not a way to die, Casey mused.

He and the others had lived in the ditch for a week and the letters he had written over the past several weeks were soaked beyond his memory to rewrite them. He drowned them in the ditch rather than knowing a German might see them and ridicule the dead soldier who'd penned them.

He didn't pray. If it were true that God loved all his children, then why would He give a bugger's damn which side won? Such being the case, Casey wondered what his final words might be, whether he would scream them or not have sufficient time to think of something appropriate to say. He'd seen so many men die, many instantly, many with quizzical expressions, clutching their wounds and wondering what the fuck just happened to them while others cried and others were man enough to shrug, smile one last time and die.

The Fatal Diners' Club

Not one of them had ever thanked God for taking sides. Not one of them had spoken His name with their hands pressed together in prayer. The man beside him had simply expelled a burst of air from his mouth and, seconds later, face down in his own filth, a secondary eruption of gases exploded from between his bare buttocks.

By noon he thought differently. The corpse was gone, dragged from the ditch indelicately, the men of his platoon showing respect by lowering their eyes.

Casey sat on the edge of the ditch, his bare feet dangling not far from the fetid water, staring into the distance. Not more than three hundred yards in front of him lay a field of dead Germans, which to his current train of thought was the best kind of German, his ears ringing from the cacophony of mortar and canon bombardments that had come to save his men hours earlier and days late.

He sat waiting to write his first word. He had a lot to tell her once his eyes dried.

That letter was the last Florence would read from her husband. He was too preoccupied staying alive, which he believed she would understand. Until the day he woke in Amsterdam as drunk as when he went to bed. May 08th, 1945 had come and gone. The war was over. Europe was liberated, which, in truth, was not the reason for his pounding temples. He was alive.

He survived the Battle of the Schelde, the war's worst conflict, marching soon after into Germany to put things right. He was going home.
*

Of course there was no sense in writing. Mail was at a standstill. He would arrive in Boston days, if not weeks, before his letters. Of course his father would feel the full weight of feminine wrath, which is why he waited until arriving in Boston one month later to call Thatcher at his Houston offices. He was home, almost.

That evening Thatcher once again had nothing to tell Florence or Betty. All he knew was that things took time and that no bad news had arrived. He felt no need to tell them that he had chartered several aircrafts to accommodate all the brave men of Houston waiting at the coast.

The next morning was a Saturday. Thatcher slept in, claiming meekly that he needed more rest for an early afternoon meeting in the city, Betty responding with a smirk, accusing him of excessive companionship the evening before with his bottle of whiskey. Strange, she thought, for a man who never drank to excess. Still, he'd been a tower of strength for her and a fretful young wife. He had even, the first Sunday of each month, driven Florence to church despite his lifelong beliefs or lack thereof.

He was quite the spectacle, sitting with his Sunday paper on the front steps of the church, the minister long since having given up any chance of redeeming a lost soul. For all that and more who could begrudge the man an innocent lapse.

Thatcher left at noon, taking the women with him, treating them to lunch before leaving them to attend his meeting, inviting them to join him later in the day for cocktails. He loved them, though at times he simply wished he could, once in a while, get the upper hand. He had, in his bed, thought of the very way.

With the meeting concluded he met them for an early dinner and drove them home, explaining his flushed and contented expression by way of a successfully completed transaction which he would later expound upon for their benefit.

That was very nice. They were happy for him. However the women's preoccupation throughout the afternoon was a husband and son they loved and longed to reunite with. Why could he not understand that?

Once at home Thatcher changed into black leather and riding boots. He was light-hearted, almost elated, garnering a stern and silent glare from his wife who had to concede that some things never change. He could still pull it off at sixty-nine, although the ponytail was destined to live on in photographs.

He asked Florence to ride with him. She declined, too fraught with worry, not knowing whether he was dead or alive, killed on the last day of the war or lost and not able to find his way home.

Thatcher assured her that his son was not a man to lose his way and that he would most assuredly find his way home to a lovely and young wife. In the meantime, however, he, Thatcher, required the company of that young and lovely woman.

She didn't want to go. She wanted to stay with Betty and sit by the phone to wait for his voice she hadn't heard for three years and six months.

"Young lady, you get your finely crafted behind into your jodhpurs and your jodhpurs into your saddle right now. I am not asking. Nor do I expect to be ignored. This is my repayment for tolerating forty-two Sundays on the doorsteps of a yet-to-be-proven heaven and I expect my recompense forthwith. I would also appreciate seeing you in your finest boots and riding jacket with your hair flowing in the wind…if you would be so kind."

"Thatcher, darling, you really do exceed all reasonable limits at times. Please leave the poor girl alone."

"She's been alone long enough, Betty, my love. She needs distraction, not lament." He turned to Florence. "Get changed, young lady, unless you want a real man to dress you."

"Florence, you might want to do as he says and change your clothes." Betty offered. "I know that look and he's right. I believe a good ride would clear your mind, do you the world of good." When Florence left the room Betty wasn't finished. "You, Mr. Riley, have somehow regressed to an earlier time in your life when you were quite unpleasant and demanding."

"Demanding? I was never demanding with you in those early days, Betty. It was all I could do to maintain my enthusiasm with yours. And I can't, truth be told, see that anything has changed in all these years. I love you as much now as when I watched you soaking your sore parts in a tub. And, as I recall, you believed in me then, Betty. Believe in me now. Allow me a few moments with the girl. In the meantime, you might want to set four places for dinner. I've invited an associate to dine with us."

Betty's mouth fell open. She was unprepared.

Thatcher put up his hand. "He's a simple man with simple tastes, brought up by simple parents who taught him humility. He expects nothing more than our cordial company."

Florence walked into the living room, pirouetting. She was delightful: A perfect vision for a long-deprived soldier.

Betty left the room in a huff to see about dinner, wondering what had gotten into him. She had never seen him so out of character, so inconsiderate.

*

Outside, mounted, Thatcher suggested a gentle, unhurried ride, making certain they faced into the sun. After a while they stopped, letting the horses graze. He had difficult thoughts, words best spoken forthrightly.

"Florence, you've been with us a while. We'll miss you, Betty and me, in our home each night."

"Thatcher, I don't understand. You're making me leave?"

"No. You're leaving because you want to, though not until your new home is built. I suppose you and Casey will want to get started on the design as quickly as possible. And, as it happens, I know an excellent architect."

"Do you think he'll come home soon?"

"I do, very soon. And you'll be quite surprised to see

him. He's somewhat of a different man, a good bit slimmer than we remember him. He looks more as though he's worked in the oilfields than fought in a war." Thatcher stood in his stirrups, stretching his legs. When he sat he hunched over the horn seeming despondent. "The man is in desperate need of a tailored suit, Florence. He'll have to spend the entire week with a tailor or go naked."

"Thatcher, he'll be home soon. You've been very strong for me and Betty. Thank you."

"We'll move you into the guest house this evening; otherwise I won't get any rest at all. And I don't suppose he'll spend much time at the dinner table, not after all these years living the life of a monk. And you'll be pleased to know he's much less of an idiot than when he left."

"Thatcher, we should go back. You're tired and you miss him. You'll feel better after a good meal. We all will."

He sat straight. "You're right, Florence. I should go back. We are after all expecting a special guest for dinner."

"I think Betty is a little annoyed with you. What is the name of this secret guest?"

"She won't be angry once she sees him. His name is Casey Riley and he's been watching you for the last ten minutes." Thatcher raised an arm, pointing to Betty's favourite spot. "He's on the hilltop, so what are you waiting for? Get up there. Or must I drag you?"

At first Florence didn't understand, shading her eyes from the late day sun. Then she saw him, his name piercing Thatcher's ears, her horse virtually flying up the hillside, her hair tousled by the wind the way Casey had asked to see her.

Thatcher gave his horse free rein to the stables.

At home Betty was in the kitchen mumbling.

"Thatcher, you really are unforgiveable at times, treating the poor girl the way you did. And who is this associate you expect me to entertain on such short notice when we are all so worried about our son?"

"Your son is fine, Betty, very fine. He is, in fact, our guest for dinner. Or he will be once he's finished with her on the hill." He reached for her arm. "No, Betty. Some things are more important than a mother. Give them the time they need." He chortled. "You'll have him to yourself all day tomorrow while she spends the day soaking in her tub."

12
Melvin Horn: Deceased

Melvin Horn arrived home from The Diners' Club not in a gleaming limousine complete with champagne, music, and a courteous chauffeur to open his door. He arrived home in the dark, in the back of a fifteen-foot truck and strapped to the bulkhead with canvas belts.

He was vertical, harnessed as well into his articulated and motorized lift chair. The driver and his helper worked for The Diners' Club, not Horn.

When the truck stopped, the engine cut, he knew what would come next. He would hear the whir of the hydraulic platform that would lower him to the entrance of his building's garage. The corrugated door would rumble its way into the roof of the cargo area and a light would illuminate his grotesque configuration. Next, the two strongly built men would unstrap him. They would attach a winch cable to the transversal bar above his wheels which would stop him in the event he lost control, in which case Melvin Horn would impact the ground with sufficient force to stop his heart and stifle the scream trapped between his beefy jowls. They would watch as he guided his chair to the platform where they would secure him with chocks, lower him and watch him manoeuvre his way onto the asphalt. Then they would close up the truck and leave him in the dark of night without uttering a word.

That's what they did three nights each month and quite

often four or five nights for the last seven years.

Melvin Horn was a Gourmand, a member of The Diners' Club by selection, chosen in part by Hilary Basil for his money as much as for his obsession with food and his deep sense of secrecy and anonymity to protect and preserve that obsession. He was not by any means a gastronome, he was a Gourmand. He had no highly-trained sense of gastronomy of epicurean delights, he was a glutton.

He lived in a spacious condo on the main floor of his building which several years earlier had required amendments to the covenants so that Horn could renovate two apartments into one.

He kept both kitchens for his convenience, each with two fridges, a redesigned pantry and a washer and dryer. There were no rooms, no artwork on the walls that remained. What he required was functional space. The four washroom areas were open space, more space; the amenities were special-ordered for him and open to view. His two showers were space, encased on three sides by clear acrylic panels with double rainheads centred over a tiled floor formed from four sides into shallow troughs.

For his most personal hygiene, each stall was fitted with a flexible upright nozzle that cleansed him with an adjustable spray where he could not reach, had not reached in years. In a circle around the clinical fountain were smaller jets for the purpose of cleaning under the weighty flaps hanging from his legs and under the fleshy canopy hanging from his gut to his concealed genitals he hadn't had personal contact with in years. When he urinated he did so in the shower as a matter of convenience, activating the smaller jets when he was done to cleanse his inner thighs, ankles and feet.

Neither did he own a towel. What was the point? He was unable to bend or reach behind him. He could barely touch the tips of his fingers together. Instead, stepping out from the panels through an arch, a dozen or more jets of warm air dried him from head to toe.

His two beds were equally spaced midway between the kitchens: One for daytime sleep, the other for nighttime. Until required they stood vertically, reclining no more than 67.5° when his feet would leave the floor.

Sleep required time and preparation. During the spring and summer months he would wear light cotton dresses, through fall and winter a heavier, warmer fabric. Beyond that he had no way to cover himself. Positioning his back against the mattress, stepping onto the steel-reinforced footboard, he would secure himself with a canvas belt intended for hauling boats from the water and press the DOWN button on the remote. The precise angle of 67.5° allowed him to sleep comfortably without choking to death under his weight.

He could easily afford a live-in maid, though she would have nowhere to live, nowhere for a woman's privacy. Nor would anyone needing to work at such menial tasks be of any benefit to him intellectually. For those reasons he hired various women for specific tasks.

One woman came twice each week to gather the clothes he'd worn on the days between her visits from the floor and to launder them. She also cleaned his shower and toilet spaces, washed the few dishes that weren't disposable plastic and retrieved his mail. She was young, foreign, and wore for him what he doubted she would ever tell her boyfriend or husband. He enjoyed watching her work in her panties and bras, thongs in particular. Those were his terms. In return he paid her more than her worth in cash, never touched her, and seldom spoke to her.

Another woman shopped twice each week for his food, taking the better part of each day to complete the specific task without the slightest idea that what she was doing was illegal. One of his two PMCs was counterfeit, deactivated. Melvin Horn did not eat hamburger meat or hotdogs. His palate was refined, as was his preference for superior wines.

He didn't care about The Agency. He cared about Priscilla Vendôme, getting rid of her. He cared about food

Her schedule never coincided with her unknown co-worker. But like the other one she was young and pretty. When she was done placing countless bags of food inside the steel-reinforced front door she would undress where she stood, matter-of-factly, before filling the pantry and, on those two days, she would stay to prepare his meals.

He supposed she worked another job, though, with what he paid her, she certainly didn't need to other than to appease the IRS with weekly contribution slips.

On Saturdays, unless the Gourmands were gathering together, two other women would come to his apartment. They always came together, never missing a scheduled night, Sundays replacing Saturdays once in a while. They were also young, introduced to him by one of his drivers for a fee.

On those nights his bed reclined to 95° so that his head was lower than his feet, allowing the girls to more easily displace his gut for access to his penis which he was never able to reach himself. It's all they could do other than taking turns at smothering him with their wet thighs as they hungrily kissed and fondled each other to forget what they were straddling.

Melvin Horn weighed as much as a small horse and that he might resemble a human being from the neck up was never a matter of divergent opinion for anyone who might see him.

The girls didn't care. He paid them more than any twenty johns combined and got them out of crowded bars where the competition was stiff most Saturdays with garden variety co-ed sluts looking for free shooters they would eventually pay for with open legs once they had one too many. The girls preferred working weeknights, favouring four and five-star hotel bars, often with repeat clients, more often than not waking entwined to enjoy the intimate luxury until check-out and taking Sundays off unless reserved in advance by Melvin Horn.

With him they drank wine they could still not afford and spent most of the evening in his daytime bed intent on loving each other after frolicking in his shower while he gorged himself in the nude because they'd stripped away his formal pants to service him.

On those nights, and nights he was expected to dine with his fellow Gourmands, a retired nurse in the building was paid to trim his finger and toenails, smooth his otherwise neglected body with cream and help him dress. He didn't want the girls seeing him that way, lying on his back, squirming from side to side to assist the woman, unable to pull up his pants on his own. Nor did he want them to see him in a dress.

January 01st was a Monday. 2024 was twenty hours old, the same age as the girls in years. In the strictest sense they were not street whores, visiting with him because most businessmen or interested businesswomen were at home with families they loved.

They were quite a step above, perfecting their trade, selective with all men but Melvin Horn because they could be. They didn't do fifty-dollar BJs with their bare asses hanging from car windows on cold winter nights because they didn't have to. Where they went they went together or not at all, cash up front, no exceptions, and very few johns or bi-curious female clients ever refused the 500-dollar minimum to fulfill a nightlong dream.

They saw nothing wrong with what they did, despite loving each other. Men always paid for sex and women always profited from their natural capability to provide the service. Other women, housewives for the most part, were paid in diamonds, cars, houses and vacations; whereas they were paid in cash for being the surrogate lovers of men whose wives had become less loveable over time; women often approaching them, eager to pay 250 apiece for youthful attention, a more tender touch; but only those women who met the same criteria of not being unsuitably old, feeble or ill. Again, Melvin Horn was an exception.

In two years they had netted 260,000 tax-free dollars with few expenses, 360K with Melvin Horn's contribution to their future, working days in a coffee shop for appearances.

Their primary banking was by way of a Safety Deposit Box until they could find a suitable lawyer familiar with offshore banking. Though they did agree that because of Melvin Horn they could easily retire at thirty and live somewhere nice, perhaps in Europe where they believed people like Melvin Horn did not exist. Such was their dream: to live with beautiful people.

He answered the door dressed in velvet jogging pants and a velvet sweatshirt. The girls were dressed in winter coats, gloves, boots, hats and panties.

They lived modestly for obvious reasons. Pouring double-doubles didn't allow for a penthouse and a fine car without provoking unwanted questions. Their wardrobes were another matter when they weren't in pink and white uniforms wiping tables, though, even then, their shorter and snugger outfits brought better tips. When they wore dresses and skirts, short and décolleté were the order of the day. When they wore slacks, their sweaters and sheer blouses garnered the desired and requisite attention. Not so for Horn. He wasn't interested in their wardrobes. He wanted their nude and nubile bodies, their melding scents and memories of them to last a week.

They never kissed their clients. That their mouths were sewers was understood, conduits for men who insisted on getting the biggest bang for their buck, for some reason preferring a distorted face to one that was pretty with disarming eyes and decidedly more desirable and intriguing ports of entry.

Anyway, they preferred kissing each other. They were

lovers doing a job and they never once kissed Melvin Horn's mouth or anything else for much different reasons despite his frequent requests.

They didn't because they thought his head must weigh 100 pounds, his face was always red because of his angle and his lips were always purple, making him appear ghoulish and even more bloated than he was. His penis, due to constant lack of light and air, they supposed, was far from proportionate to his size. The thing, once coaxed from its hood, was incredibly diminutive and difficult enough to stroke to manageable dimensions let alone draw into their mouths at the side of a mountain.

No. The best Melvin Horn could hope for was a smeared face enhanced by a warm and erotic handshake from one girl while the other laboured at pushing away the landslide.

He greeted them warmly, inviting them in, not waiting very long before lumbering to his night bed where they strapped him in. They had from the very beginning established a routine. They'd been getting him off for two years.

They liked pizza. That was part of the deal: Pizza and red wine. And he didn't mind at all sharing them with the pizza guy for very selfish reasons. The entire building knew about Melvin Horn, though very few had ever seen him. But the pizza guy had seen him many times, Horn driven by the need to wipe the revulsion from the kid's face by pushing his head through a wall.

The kid was a punk, a smartass, working for nickels and dimes on a Saturday night. So Horn had no problem letting the kid see his two young and naked or near-naked girlfriends at the door. The best part was that Horn never tipped the kid. He could go fuck himself.

But business came first. The girls were professionals providing a service and they always preferred working him before eating.

First they would do their job, later playing for a while in the shower, enjoying the jets with gleeful yelps before supporting each other while they danced in tight circles under the dryers until the doorbell chimed.

They enjoyed taunting the boy, sometimes in towels, sometimes one girl whipping away the other's towel, sometimes in panties, sometimes not, sometimes kissing or touching each other while talking to him, not with him.

With the stain of Horn's body odour washed away they jumped onto his daybed to drink his good wine, eat pizza and smudge each other's lips with tomato sauces and cheese where he could see them. Though they never watched him eat. He was disgusting. Securing him and getting him off was one thing. That was business, their version of pro bono work despite his generosity. Such was their purpose in life: Catering to men and women whose once free love was either no longer desirable or attainable for whatever reason.

But watching him wolf down more during one meal while standing at a kitchen counter than they ate together over a few days turned their stomachs. So they didn't look. They ignored him, letting him believe they were acting for him. Changing careers at thirty was too important to them, their life's plan.

He was always gracious and kind to them. He never hurt them, probably very aware of the risk. He was, after all, vulnerable. And when the job was done he never requested further attention, satisfied to watch them enjoy each other.

Strapping him into bed was, of course, requisite prior to their attention to his needs and much less clumsy than when he strapped himself in. If he were to topple onto the floor he would stay there, possibly taking a girl with him. Yet they never tucked him into bed before leaving. He was what he was, as were they, which didn't mean they had to see him in a loose-fitting dress.

The girls were laughing and kissing, one moment watching television, another moment distracted by each other's probes and caresses.

Normally they would leave near midnight, paid in cash. This night, however, they did not. They remained much longer after hearing a melody of curious sounds and turned to see Melvin Horn lying face down on the floor, an assortment of plastic plates and food under and around him as though he were the centrepiece of a ghastly buffet.

He'd taken the entire counter of food with him. He looked comical, unreal, as though learning to swim on the floor. His arms were spread out, sloping oddly downward from his shoulders like the fins of a manatee. His feet, pointing downward at the ends of his layered legs, were suspended several inches over the floor.

The girls remained on the bed. They called his name. He didn't answer. They called out once more, this time louder. Melvin wasn't answering. They stared at each other for long moments, waiting for him to move, make a sound or do something. He did both. He twitched and whistled a long fart.

Holding hands, sliding from the bed, they went to him, their faces twisting into grimaces the closer they went.

At one end Melvin Horn's wide-open mouth was stuffed with food, blocking his gases they heard percolating from somewhere within, his glazed eyes bulging from the mounting pressure or the sudden shock of never again eating. At the other end he was lying in a puddle of urine, the splatter of gases mixed with loose fecal matter sputtering from between massive buttocks to coat his legs and the floor.

Melvin Horn was dead.

The girls stepped back, retching, clutching their stomachs. Their future was ruined.

They at once felt strangely conspicuous being naked and privy to his death. They lost all appetite for their pizza, tossing what was left in their hands onto the countertop. They went to his daybed, dressed into their panties and boots and leaned back to stare at the corpulent corpse.

One girl started crying, her friend and lover embracing her, comforting her with soothing whispers and warm caresses while her thoughts were focused on Horn who had always paid them in cash. So who else did he pay in cash? Maybe they weren't his only release. And who cleaned the place? He didn't. She was certain of that. She kissed her friend and took her by the hand, scanning Horn's space.

The few drawers they could see were in the kitchens at either end of his condo and centred between his beds was a single armoire.

They hurried to the other kitchen first, away from him, pulling out and searching each drawer, each cabinet specially designed for a short-armed hulk to reach into without straining his heart. They found nothing beyond a few plates and cutlery. Nor did they find anything in the first pantry lined with shoulder-high shelves filled with his week's food requirement and cases of expensive wine on the floor that he could never reach. No. Melvin Horn had others to help him live out one week at a time.

They went to the second kitchen bypassing Horn whose condition hadn't worsened or improved, though he had made the air sufficiently foul. They found nothing in the drawers or cabinets, or anything in the pantry but more food and more wine whose names they couldn't pronounce. What they did find was their thousand dollars in hundreds on the counter by a fridge. Then the girl who'd stopped crying had a thought and they each chose a fridge to search, hurrying back to the first kitchen to check those fridges and freezers.

All that remained was the armoire.

Each girl opened a door, not believing the dozens of loose-fitting dresses and his tuxedo jogging suits. They didn't laugh. They were too shocked, possibly or finally realizing how gargantuan the man was.

They pushed the clothes to one side, then to the other

before parting them in the middle. And there they were: Five two-inch stacks of crisp 100-dollar bills. They glanced at Horn, at each other, took the stacks and scurried to the bed where they pushed aside the pizza box. They counted each stack twice, one girl auditing the other, kissing and hugging each other, squeezing out squeals of delight. Horn had left them a quarter of a million dollars in very spendable denominations, more than enough to buy a nice car and a nicer place to live.

They finished the pizza and wine, formulating, a perfect strategy emerging, albeit one that would require attention to detail and a lawyer whose idealism was less than perfect.

They were now worth over 600K. They could have the money sent overseas with sufficient funds returned by a non-existent friend or relative as a non-taxable gift to allow for the purchase of a downtown condo. Of course they would continue working two jobs until thirty. Or quit their day jobs and return to school where professors' wives were never as pretty as their students.

They weren't certain.

The problem was the steel door, once closed they would never get back in. They had no idea what the code was, nor did they want to leave the twenty or so cases of wine. At the price of each bottle he'd once mentioned, how could they leave behind another thirty or forty K?

One girl stayed behind while the stronger of the two spent the better part of an hour loading their car. They didn't care about fingerprints or cameras as neither girl had a record and they were wearing hats. They were unknown. They didn't do street corners, dark alleys or uniformed cops to avoid arrest. No one knew them, no one would.

What they did, however, was to clean up after themselves. They took their wine bottle, the pizza slices from the counter and the pizza box with the date, time of delivery and restaurant name stapled to the lid. They returned the armoire to its original state, called 9-1-1 on his phone, waited for a voice, dropped the phone near his head and left, paid in advance for the next five plus years and anxious to learn about wines.

13
Lorie's Happy New Year

Dwayne Michaels stopped the door from clanging shut, somewhat mystified. What was she doing there?

He thought to retreat, to get out before she noticed him, before he felt forced to say something he would later regret, yet he couldn't. He was fixated. The Ice Queen was too alluring. He often saw her at the gym, almost every day, never like this. He had the greatest urge to sneak up behind her and, he didn't know what, grab her spectacular butt that was, for his current purpose, bare. Or would he cup her breasts, swing her around and kiss her to shock the hell out of her, or all three at once?

Right, then get kicked in the balls. The woman was a fifth Dan with serious attitude.

Instead he stole in behind her and sat watching her. She was slowing, ending her 20K run. She'd been on the treadmill for an hour. That's how she ended each workout, this time without her usual silk scarf at her hips meant to deprive any healthy male, him, who might happen by. She was selfish that way, prissy.

Not imagining her in his bed was impossible. Nothing was moving in a way that it shouldn't. Everything was perfectly in place.

What the hell. He hadn't expected her not to answer phone. He would have spoken to her then. How else would he know?

The Fatal Diners' Club

*

But for her blue second skin and her high-end runners, Lorie Wilson was naked and wet with one empty and one full water bottle strapped to her waist. He wasn't at all curious why she wasn't wearing her usual red thong with the blue to accentuate her incredible ass; he was too damned busy being grateful that she wasn't.

*

She was listening to 60s rock. That's what she did when she was alone. That's what she always did. No way would she listen to his 50s and Latino crap she had to tolerate in the car.

Her parents would be disappointed. Her father would get over it by his bedtime and her mother would remind her until her next New Year's alone. Her life was shit. He would have to be good-looking, not too many drinks ahead of her and preferably single. She would pay for the meal somewhere not too intimidating to him, though he would get the room, a five-star, and take care of practical matters.

She was ready, willing and able. She stopped, her heart rate slowing, her mind racing. She spread her feet, leaned forward, touched her toes, opened her eyes and shrieked.

He was there, smirking, gawking at her, his elbows on his knees, his head resting on two fists, staring at her…Oh, shit!. She wanted to kill him. Or, better yet, she wanted to die. She did want to die. Then she wouldn't have to look at him dead or alive.

She bolted upright, a curtain of silky hair rising and falling across her shoulders.

*

"What do you want, Dwayne?" she snarled.

"Dwayne, not Michaels, that's good. Is that your New Year's resolution, being nice?" He remained as he was. "At the moment I'm thinking I want what any normal guy would want."

"In your dreams."

"That's right. How did you guess?" He grinned, raising his eyebrows, doing his best to annoy her. He had to. That's what Wilson and Michaels did. They annoyed each other. "Very nice without the thong and the ballet thingy you wear to hide those to-die-for cheeks and especially without the granny clumpy thing you do with your hair."

"You're such a total ass." She stepped from the machine, reaching for a fleecy towel, patting her face. "Let's leave the childish banter for Monday, Dwayne. I'm not in the mood."

"Getting in shape for mommy's home-cooking?"

"No, I'm not. I've got a date, if you think it's your business." She paused. "What? Now you think I can't get date? Think again. I can get a date."

He shrugged. "Must be over fifty to have the bucks to pay for what I'm seeing. Personally I'm saving up, biding my time until I'm more mature."

Like that would ever happen. Good luck. She really wasn't in the mood, not unless he was going rip away her clothes and do her right there and then. God! What did a woman have to do to get a good fuck from a guy who knew what buttons to press? And what was with the tank top and shorts when he always wore sweats to the gym?

"Enjoy your workout, Dwayne." She strode to the door he'd come through, turning. "What?"

He hadn't moved. "I said you're very beautiful, Lorie. Whoever he is, he's a very lucky guy. See you Monday."

She scrunched her face, letting the door close behind her.

Very beautiful, her tanned ass. Of course she was beautiful. Jerk. Asshole. She would kick him in the balls. She would shower and dress, come back and kick him in the balls. It would serve him right not to have the thing prodding away for at least one night.

*

Dwayne Michaels never warmed up. Their private gym had twelve pieces of high tech equipment. Five days a week when he wasn't out of town he used each one for nine minutes, taking a minute between to relax his muscles, completing a full-body workout in the requisite two hours. The treadmill she'd been punishing was the closest.

An hour later he was on the universal, dripping, thankful he hadn't asked her, thankful he'd escaped her refusal of dinner at his place. As gorgeous as she was, she was a bit of a hard-ass.

By Monday he would think of a reason for having called her. In the meantime he wouldn't think of her naked in the shower, glistening with body oils, her hair hanging in thick strands across her shoulders and breasts, rivulets of steaming water cascading down her arched back, her chiselled stomach and down her taut legs, one slightly bent, the other straight.

He didn't need the agony.

He winced at the pain, twisting away from the unexpected assault, banging his head into the free-hanging lateral bar.

"You're such a total jerk, Dwayne. You don't ever tell a woman she's beautiful when she stinks with sweat and her mascara's running down her face. That's the reason you need a different bimbo each week. Maybe if you were more of a gentleman you could keep them a day or two longer."

He didn't know what to rub first, his shoulder or his head. "Jesus, Lorie, you got cramps or something? What the hell."

"Cramps. Yeah, well at least I'm old enough to have a period."

"What's your problem?"

"You are, and get your eyes off me."

He was taking her in. He was taking in her midnight

blue sheer blouse and dark blue three-quarter bra pushing her breasts into soft and inviting swells. Her skirt was short, dark blue, pleated and slightly flared, and her legs, the legs his mind saw wet and glistening in the shower, glistening now with the sheen of expensive nylon, her feet planted firmly on the gym floor in patent leather pumps. He couldn't imagine what else. He didn't dare.

"Get my eyes off you. Are you kidding?" He chortled. "First off, you're absolutely stunning, as though you don't already know that. And if you don't want me looking at your breasts, Lorie, why are you showing them to me? And by the way, this isn't the way to your car. You missed the elevator by, oh, a few hundred feet. So I'm thinking, yeah, you want me to see how beautiful you are."

She was becoming angrier by the second, fuming. She couldn't help herself. Because of him some jerkoff she didn't know would be doing his best to screw her brains out in just a few hours. Then what? She knew exactly. Then she would go home to an empty bed after showering and douching to rinse away a memory she didn't want or need. She stared at his crotch, slightly altering her stance, her expression cold.

Dwayne Michaels retreated, instinctively defensive. He knew. "Whoa, Lorie."

She could have. She wanted to. She really did want to.

"You're delusional." She twirled away from him. "Happy New Year, Dwayne. I'm going home. Enjoy your fantasies and your bimbo."

"What about your date?"

"I don't have one. I lied. The spinster's going home alone, if you must know."

She kept walking. She had to get away from him. She hated him.

"I phoned you."

She didn't hear him or didn't want to. She was too near the door.

He yelled, "I said, I phoned you. This morning, I phoned you, Lorie."

He phoned her. What? He never phoned her, not even when they worked out of town. Most mornings he was finished his breakfast before she arrived at the table. Most evenings he was too anxious to get to the bar to finish his meal with her. Asshole. And, yes, she did know she was beautiful. She told herself every day. Someone had to.

Then she was facing him against her will.

"Your hair, you should always wear your hair that way. French braids are very elegant, very sophisticated, very much you."

"I'm surprised you know the term. I would have thought you're more accustomed to blonde ponytails in frilly French maid costumes."

He was taking the higher road.

"I phoned you, but I didn't leave a message. I wanted to invite you for dinner. You know, for New Year's at my place. We never spend time together unless we're working and even then you always head to your room way too early'." He stood his ground. "I'm a great cook, Lorie, and I happen to have a bottle of Ultimat in the freezer."

What was he saying? Jesus H.

She retorted. "Bambi lost in the forest? Can't find her way out and little Dwayne has no one to play with?"

He shrugged. "I was disappointed when you didn't answer, although happy at the same time. I was sort of pushing the last-minute thing and thought you might be a little miffed with me."

"I'm always miffed with you, Dwayne, and you drink scotch."

"I know. I have the vodka for emergencies, in case you ever get locked out of your penthouse and have to go slumming. I've had it for a while."

"You're inviting me for dinner, me, the Ice Queen?"

She enjoyed seeing him cringe.

"Don't take a simple comment out of context. I was making reference to the way you chill your vodka, you know, with a single cube of ice."

"You're a liar."

"Okay, I meant ice is a preservative, like a glacier. You are an ice queen because you're incredibly lovely and eternally young. You always will be. That's what I meant." He waited. "Lorie, help me out. I'm dying here."

She coughed a laugh. "That's hysterical, you and me. No way. What would we even talk about, dead bodies, Gourmands? Goodbye, Dwayne. I'm going home. Have a Happy New Year with whatshername, whomever."

"Maybe we could talk about our next dinner together, at your place. I'm taking a big step here, Lorie. Help me out. I haven't stopped thinking of you since I can't remember when. Let's see now. There's Lorie in the morning. She's incredibly gorgeous and smells so good, her hair's a little ruffled and she's a little difficult until her first coffee. But I don't mind. Then there's Lorie at night. That Lorie's super-hot in silk and satin with her skin so soft and smooth. The bathtub Lorie I'll keep to myself. That's too personal. And the beach Lorie, the oily and sultry Lorie, that Lorie I want to share with everyone."

What the hell was happening, oily, sexy and sultry? Her best dream, her only dream. She had to get out, barely able to breathe let alone move.

"You're hitting on me, me, Lorie Wilson? You must be kidding. No way. Do I look that pathetic? Better yet. Are you that pathetic?"

"I'm telling you that I want to spend time with you off the clock without our weapons. You and me." He grinned widely. "How horrible can one afternoon be? Leave anytime you want. And, Lorie, the Bambis were a defence against you telling me to," he paused, "you know, whatever. Besides, how often have you told me about your thing for much older men?"

"I didn't say much older. I said more mature, which excludes you."

He ignored the barb. "So we can stop by your place for some good wine or we can drink my cheap fifty-dollar stuff, especially since you don't have other plans?"

"Thanks for reminding me."

He went to her, determined. He had nothing else to say. He was done. He simply cupped her face in his hands, tilted her head, stared into her eyes, kissed her for as long as he dared, and retreated to a safe distance.

"You're even more lovely with your cheeks a little pinkish."

He might just as well have sucked the air from her lungs. She wanted to scream. She wanted to smack him, to smear his lips and face with kisses. His lips, she'd felt his warm lips at last. She was in a dream and wanted to wake, to run. But where would she run to, to more sad and lonely nights, more impossible dreams and more lonely mornings?

She could feel the deep heat searing her flushed cheeks. Her mouth was dry and she couldn't swallow.

"Okay. I suppose a glass of your wine wouldn't hurt." She checked the time on her watch for something to do. "But I'm leaving by six, you're taking your shower here, and I hope you understand that was your first and last kiss. Savour the memory and don't ever think to kiss me again."

"I do understand, and I won't. Give me thirty minutes and, as a show of good faith, we'll take both cars."
*

Lorie Wilson sat on the universal watching him leave. When he was gone she walked to a mirror, pausing, not hesitating, inching her skirt to her waist. To-die-for was right. She would die if he was to see that much of her and not give her the time of day the next morning. She would die, after she killed him.

She swirled, pulling the back of her skirt to her waist,

leaning slightly forward, running a hand over her firm curves. He seemed to like that part of her. Really, what wasn't to like? Her gym ensemble had left zero to the imagination without her thong, she knew that, and he did seem to like her breasts. Shit. What was she doing? Dwayne Michaels, self-appointed Mr. Heartthrob coming on to her, thinking what? That he might get laid? Good luck with that.

She let her skirt fall. No way. No frigging way was he getting into her pants or anything else.

Then too soon, what? No way. He wasn't a second longer than thirty minutes.

How bizarre was walking quietly by his side without a weapon on her hip, without holding his hand or without her arms in his after he'd kissed her that way, kissed her as though he might actually love her? Love her? No way. He didn't love anyone or anything he couldn't see in his mirror.

They did take the two cars, though. She was happy for that, insisted on that, the primary reason being Riley Corp. security cameras in the underground parking lot.

She had no idea where he lived or how he lived. She knew he had a long-term lease on a Jag he otherwise couldn't afford despite his quarter-mil income. Nothing else.Why hadn't she ever asked? Because she didn't care, hadn't cared how he entertained his young sluts. She just assumed the place would be well-maintained because he was always impeccably dressed and well-groomed.

She followed him for a brief fifteen minutes in a daze through empty streets, not daring to wonder, afraid to anticipate. She was daydreaming, her reality anything but real. What was she doing? She followed him into his underground parking, driving into the space he signalled, letting him open her door, stepping out.

Dwayne Michaels was opening her door. No way.

At the elevator she stepped in before him. There were eighteen floors, nineteen buttons. She expected perhaps the third or fourth. She didn't know why. She just did, something to think, to occupy her mind, her eyes flickering when he inserted his key and pressed PH.

No way was this happening. No way!

The elevator doors opened onto the expansive living room of his penthouse and beyond to a clear blue sky overlooking the Hudson. So what? Big deal, she thought. Hers overlooked the Atlantic and was four floors higher with a private rooftop patio.

He took her coat, her hat and her gloves. He guided her to a plush sofa, held her hand as she sat, went to his freezer for the Ultimat without speaking a word, poured two ounces of vodka neat with a single large cube, poured a scotch, went to her, excused himself, and went to change into more appropriate attire. Not long after he returned in cords, a V-neck sweater and thick woolen socks. He wasn't into slippers.

Shit! And double shit. What was she seeing? What was she doing there, with him?

"You're still here. That's a good thing, like Dwayne instead of Michaels. I hope your drink isn't too chilled."

"The drink's fine. But do you steal on the side, Dwayne, do drugs, or what? Riley pays well, but not enough for you to keep this place and a Jaguar."

"I don't need Riley's money. Most of that goes to a few pet causes. I'm sort of independent."

"I'm sure it does. Let me guess. I'm thinking blonde, twenty-two and big breasts. Oh, excuse me, I meant to say tits."

"You're partly right. Some are blonde, though not many are in their twenties. A few are." Dwayne Michaels beamed, extending a hand. "Come. Let me show you my girls. I believe you'll be surprised. I hope so."

He took her hand. She grimaced. She didn't want this. He knew she was having a hard time liking him, when the pretence of abhorring him was so much easier. He knew. He led her into his office where the only wall that wasn't glass was lined with photographs of him together with girls and boys in wheelchairs hugging him, children in hospital beds kissing his cheeks, and older folk, women who now had a better life reaching up to pat his cheeks with quivering hands, and frail men grasping his hands between their veined and feeble clutches.

Other photos depicted teenage girls in a dojo, their fists crashing through pine boards.

His office was immaculate. He was immaculate. She had no words. She wanted her vodka.

He wasn't letting go of her hand. She didn't want him to. He led her into the kitchen, the dining room off the living room, his immaculate bedroom and pristine guestroom, completing the tour in his gym room lined with all manner of ancient Japanese and Chinese weapons, weapons familiar to her, weapons she somehow suspected he was adept with. So what was he doing with her, the thirty-eight-year-old Ice Queen?

Why hadn't he ever told her?

"Dwayne, thanks for the tour. I'm stunned to say the least. But I should really go home. This is not a good idea."

"This is a very good idea. You've just learned a little more about me, meaning this place, my life outside of work," his smile was sincere, "and that I'm not such a bad kisser. Please stay, at least until six. Give me at least until six."

"Why?"

"To discover what a great cook I am. What else?"

"Where is this coming from, me and you, here, from nowhere?"

"Not from nowhere, from seven years ago when I first saw you at the White House when I wanted to ask you out. But you didn't like me very much. Then again when I discovered you'd be my partner, when I thought you wouldn't look twice at me because we're a team and all the wrong things you thought of me from day one."

"Shit, Dwayne." In for a penny, that's what her mother always said. "Okay, until six. Not a moment longer and what is for dinner? Don't tell me ham and, just so we're on the same track, I'm not dessert. There is no way I'm sleeping with you. I'm gone by six. Understood? And Monday we don't talk about this. We do not ever talk about this."

"Yes, understood."

*

They sat facing each other spaced safely apart, talking, Lorie on one sofa Dwayne on the other, Lorie gradually softening in part due to her second Ultimat. Or partly because she was realizing she was even more attracted to him because he wasn't a total prick or a jerk. He was possibly a nice guy, possibly.

Though time wasn't standing still and dinner wasn't preparing itself.

She didn't lift a finger. He didn't want her to; her feathers somewhat ruffled when he swept her from the sofa as though she were a feather to plant her on his ceramic countertop with a glass of perfectly chilled Chablis Grand Cru '97 so they wouldn't lose a heartbeat or a word while he prepared a gourmet feast. Much like the Gourmands, working at The Agency came with certain privileges.

The first course was a spring vegetable stir-fry served in wooden bowls with chopsticks which she ate sitting on the counter while he ate his standing, preparing hot and ready to eat spring rolls with sweet dipping sauce.

She let him ease her from the counter, half annoyed that he didn't seem the least bit interested in even attempting to grope her ass. The man was dead, or could be very soon.

The Chablis was finished, Dwayne Michaels searching his extensive wine cooler for the best accompaniment to the main course. Crêpes filled with duck, Chinese cabbage, honey and scallions with a warm salad side dish prepared with thin chicken slices and snow peas, red pepper and baby corn flavoured with chili sauce required a light Pouilly-Fuissé made from grapes harvested the year he was born.

He served her confidently with flair, a panache he no doubt acquired while entertaining his French maid sluts who wouldn't know good wine from stale swill.

Okay, she was impressed. Big deal, she thought, when throughout the entire dinner they sat at right angles to each other, right angles like fucking engineers, not touching each other like tentative and uncertain lovers, not like a man touching a woman who had been in love with him since the first day she'd seen him, since that day she let him walk away from her at the White House. Jerk.

A second bottle of Pouilly-Fuissé wasn't required, neither suggested nor wanted. She was going home. What would she prove by staying once the meal was finished, that she was desperate?

Dessert was not a beautiful woman the way she had anticipated, expected, adamant she would deny her heart's deepest desire. He didn't have to know she was two-faced. That she knew was painful enough. Instead he served home-made mango ice cream served with baked mango clouds, his own creation, individual portions of stewed mandarins in orange flower syrup and fresh pear spears soaked in Anisette which he complemented with a glass of sweet ice wine.

She offered to clear the table and do the dishes, wanting to kill time. He declined, suggesting more soft music in the living room while they enjoyed their wine. She agreed, smiling pleasantly. The meal was beyond excellent; each morsel succulent and mouth-watering. For that and for no other reason she would stay. Leaving before six would be rude. Besides, what was another hour?

The soothing sounds were Latino, meant for lovers and when he stopped talking her reverie was broken. She was in wonderland, heaven, if her version of heaven even existed.

She didn't know where she was. Yet her turn had come at, yeah, right, 05:55. Prick!

He was testing her, looking straight at her. He hadn't once before looked at her that way, silently waiting, his expression calm, turning fleeting seconds into unbearable hours.

No way was she staying. No way would she give him the satisfaction of staying another hour, or maybe two.

She didn't glare at him, as much as she wanted to. She didn't sigh the way people do when it's time to go home after the best time she'd had in years. The most she could hope for now was a handshake or a condescending peck on her cheek considering that since dinner she'd sat facing him like an aunt, a sister or, worse, a partner.

He might at least have patted the cushion beside him, made some sort of weak effort. Screw him. She wiped her face gently with her warm palms for no reason.

"Thank you for dinner, Dwayne. You are a magnificent chef, I must admit, and not quite the completely self-infatuated asshole I thought you were. Thank you for showing me a better side of you."

"You did say six o'clock. So I guess this is goodnight and see you Monday, Miss Wilson."

He didn't say that. He could not have said such a horrible thing.

"Shit, Dwayne… Miss Wilson. Why not just call me an old hag? You really do know how to spoil a good time. Shit."

"I'm sorry. I am. I didn't mean…. Okay, listen, here's the thing, and stop me if I'm getting too personal or making a fool of myself. My mind's been racing here. I thought before this morning that I might, could, or did love you. That's right. Now, after a day with you, I know I love you, Lorie. The worst part was discovering that I've known for three years, if not longer." He was composed, unruffled. "This has not been an easy day for me, having you this close, knowing what I know. And believe me; you are not easy to love. You're not. You are one difficult woman. I don't even know what you're doing here today, but you have saved me a lot of sleepless nights by being at the gym this morning. And I'm sort of thinking you like me enough to stay a while longer and to sit a bit closer to me. I won't bite. I promise" He stood. "Besides, you've had too much to drink, at least if you're driving, which you are. So here's what I'm thinking. Stop me anytime. You stay the night, we dance, we talk, we enjoy a few more vodkas and scotch, not too many, and I put you to bed in the guestroom. Or you put yourself to bed in the guestroom. Either way, in the morning, after your first coffee, which, by the way, is incredible, you leave or you don't. I can't think of anything more romantic with a beautiful woman, with you, than a picnic at the ocean: A man and a woman sitting together, talking, not talking, the waves, the roar, holding hands, maybe kissing, maybe being honest." He paused. "Did I mention sitting together, you know, man, woman…together…you, me?"

Her brain was set to explode. She waited. No. She wouldn't. She had to. She couldn't stop her lips from quivering. Oh, God! No! Her mouth was erupting into a cacophony of hoarse laughter, her eyes flooding with tears.

Dwayne Michaels sat patiently waiting for the tsunami to ebb. She took a while. Who wouldn't laugh at Wilson and Michaels? That didn't matter. What mattered was the sensual sound of her voice, her laughter. How often had he heard her laugh? Not often.

"That was the cruelest thing I could ever imagine you saying to me, Dwayne. We're partners, strictly partners. And despite the fact that I'm about ready to pee my panties, what you just said is not remotely amusing."

"I agree, if I hadn't meant every word of what I said. However, Miss Wilson, Lorie, I do love you. I want to dance with you and I want you with me all day tomorrow.

But I've never forced or tricked any woman to stay with me. And I won't now, despite how much I want her to stay."

She wanted to cry, to scream. She was at the precipice of her worst nightmare, her most wonderful dream. She glanced at her watch.

"Okay, okay. Let's put this love thing behind us, far behind. You're a little drunk, and maybe I am...at least too much to drive. And the evening is early. So I don't see how a dance would kill either one of us while our brains are sufficiently pickled. It couldn't be worse than an office party, really, if we had one. But I'm shutting you down at ten, sleeping alone in your guestroom and leaving here as soon as I wake up. I can make my own coffee at home and you can forget about packing a picnic basket. That won't happen."

"Can I at least offer you a chilled Ultimat and sit beside you? Or would you rather play backgammon over the intercom?"

"Don't be snide. You can top us off, sit beside me and keep your hands to yourself until we dance. Then you can keep them off my ass."

"I'm good with that, in part, though I can't make any promises about your ass, not after what I saw through the door at the gym this morning when I left you to shower. I am a man after all and a cold shower wasn't my first thought or my second as I stood watching you."

Her mouth dropped open from shock, gulping for moisture.

He went to the kitchen for drinks, changed the sound track to Marco Antonio Solis and sat beside her. He kissed her and she let him. She was too stunned. He took her hand and led her to the centre of the room.

They danced for hours without talking, held hands for hours without talking, each one escaping into the music. At midnight he led her to her room, kissed her goodnight, closed the door and went to his room pleased with the evening, as pleased as he could be. Now that she knew, he wasn't giving up.

In her room Lorie undressed, slipping into the silk shirt he laid out on her bed that, for her, was over-sized. She wanted to phone her mother. To say what, that she was in a lover's paradise, a short-lived paradise because she'd spent the evening treating him like shit, laughing at him until she was too exhausted to do anything but curl into his arms and purr? She did purr, counting his heartbeats.

No way! She'd spent the last hour purring in his arms. Shit!

*

The room was pitch-black. She was naked. Not really. She felt naked inside his bed, inside his silk shirt. She was mellow, calm. Dwayne loved her. He told her so. He said he loved her. No way! How could he love her? Unreal words emerging from scotch, words meant to lure. That wasn't love. He was too accustomed to swaying the hearts of bimbos, young blonde co-eds and divorcées, whatever.

She sat, hugging her knees. She hadn't had sex in years since joining the Secret Service. The president had taken all her time and now The Agency was, hoping and dreaming many of those years that she could be with him. And before then, rarely, with no one she could remember. Those few times she had sex because she had a vagina, something they wanted, and at the time she was feeling…whatever. She'd forgotten how she felt then, which was a good thing. Wasn't that a good thing? She believed so. She was happy, content not to remember them.

She wriggled from under the covers, feeling her way to the door, pausing, hesitating.

When he told her he loved her she thought she would die. Instead she laughed like a fool. She'd laughed at the very words she'd waited so many years to hear.

She opened her door, his door, palming her way down a hall she remembered not very well until, in the distance, she saw the moon through the floor-to-ceiling windows of the living room where she'd danced in his arms.

She leaned against the wall outside his room, facing his door, though not facing his door. She was facing her future, her career. She also knew she was good, the best. So what did a career in any one company or agency matter? Truth be told, she didn't have to work.

She pushed herself forward, reaching out, clutching the doorknob. She was so close to him, a door away, closer than she ever thought she would be. She wasn't drunk now and she wasn't drunk at 5:55 when she should have left. But she didn't leave. The time was now or never. The choice was hers, not his. What the hell. At worst he would forget his stupid words, his ridiculous notion of a picnic and mock her, deride her with good reason. Then she would know. Then she would leave him with memories he would relive each morning of her skirt hiked to her waist in the gym. That wouldn't happen. She would quit The Agency Monday morning.

She filled her lungs with a loud intake of air. At least she would know.

Lorie eased the door open, gripping the knob with both hands, stepping in, at first afraid, then thankful for the reddish glow emanating from 1:45 AM illuminating him, outlining his bed and the slim lines of his body. He was sleeping so peacefully.

She closed the door with equal care, her heart pounding in her ears. She inhaled another deep and silent breath, gently easing onto the edge of his bed, reaching out to lightly touch his leg.

She whispered, "Please don't wake up, Dwayne. Please, because I do love you. I always have. That's why I've always hated you without hating you, because I love you so much and couldn't do anything about how I feel. This morning I thought I would die when you saw me running and this evening I stopped breathing when you told me what you saw me doing later in the gym because I was afraid you were laughing at me." She sighed. "I needed to tell you." She touched his leg once more. "Goodnight, Dwayne."

As gently as she could she stood, taking a moment to absorb him, the stillness of the room broken by Dwayne sitting, reaching out to touch her perfect silhouette, a miserable groan escaping her throat. She wanted to die.

"Officially it's morning. Good morning, Lorie, and thank you."

"Thank you, for what? I was a total bitch all day. You should hate me."

"For letting me get at least a little sleep before waking me. You've come this far, Lorie. We both have. We've been foolish long enough and you'll see that my coffee is the richest you'll ever taste, though we may have to fill our picnic basket with your wine which I'm certain is better than mine. And another thing, I would never laugh at the woman I love."

"Dwayne, I thought you were sleeping."

"I wasn't, not really. How would you expect me to sleep? How can either of us sleep, especially now?"

"I never once imagined myself in your bedroom wearing your silk shirt. I think this is where I should be saying No Way!"

"That's one possibility. Or you can wait a while longer to see how great we are together." He reached for her hand. "Would you care to join me, you know, since you're already here and, by the way, drop-dead gorgeous in silk?" He chuckled. "We don't have to talk if you'd rather not."

Lorie hugged herself in the dark. She was crying softly, warm and happy tears staining her face. "Will you be here in the morning? Isn't this about the hour you usually leave town?"

His laugh was warm, inviting. "I promise, unless I'm

brewing coffee. And I won't leave town unless you're with me."

"You're certain about this, Dwayne?"

"Aren't we both?"

"Then I suppose I could stay a while longer, since I'm already here. And, yes, I do have the perfect wine for a picnic."

Her eyes were adapting despite the blur of tears. She moved closer, taking his hand, letting him guide her onto his lap.

The heat of his body was instantly arousing. He wiped her eyes with kisses, kissing her lips.

"Just so you know. I'm more nervous than you right now."

"I love you." She kissed him. "God, I'm in bed kissing Dwayne Michaels and saying I love him." She squeezed him, leaning back, smacking him. "And don't you dare call me anything but Lorie if you want to live. We'll work on something else later unless you disappoint me. I've waited a very long time for this Dwayne Michaels. I'm expecting you to do something very good to me."

14
A Third Generation

Casey and Florence Riley stayed with his parents until one month into 1946.

Not long into his wartime absence Florence had put their home up for rent and Casey Riley no longer saw the house as his dream home. They built something new, something bigger and grander on a parcel of land given to them by his father. Florence had her own stables, her own car and Casey was again being thought of by the who's who of Houston society as a notable attorney in his own right and very close to the brilliance of his wife.

Life was treating them well in return for long hours and six-day weeks. Florence continued riding with her best friend once each week and increasingly they were entertaining men of commerce, industry and politics, many of them the sons of Thatcher's closest associates who were branching out, quitting the fold, many of them with the most vertical of political ambitions.

They were successful lawyers, constantly busy, and the matter of children never came up. One certain reason was that Florence never accepted that she or any other woman should be dismissed to the parlour to discuss female concerns while their menfolk debated matters of social and economic importance in the study with full-bodied brandies in one hand and aromatic blue smoke wafting from eight-inch Cubans held in the other.

She enjoyed a good brandy as much as any man.

Of course, women being women, left to create a truth they were not privy to, gossip began flourishing. Florence was barren. What other possible explanation could one imagine or expect since Florence herself was unwilling to broach the subject? What decent woman would not give herself to motherhood before such a difficult and improbable an age?

Goodness, they agreed, Florence was already thirty-one and a wife of some seven years. She might very well have had her first child before the war and her second directly upon his return, had she a mind to or were she complete as a woman.

How must her husband feel?

Betty never mentioned grandchildren, firmly believing that was not the domain of first generation housemothers now past their usefulness and requiring someone else's new family to fill their empty days. Her days were not empty. Nor did she believe she should interfere in such a personal matter. That aside, at sixty-seven, she didn't need or want to lend advice on good parenting.

Thatcher concurred. He did, and knew that he should.

Prior to the war Betty and Thatcher had pleaded with their friends in Europe to stay with them in Texas until the conflict was resolved. Neither group accepted the generous offer, each of the families politely refused, though by 1952 Betty and Thatcher had resumed their summers in France and Spain.

Betty had achieved fluency in both idioms years earlier with friends in each country, while Thatcher continued to suffer through the simplest menus and road signs when required to spend time alone on those occasions Betty was booked into day spas, hair salons or seamstresses.

Beyond that Thatcher and Betty continued working full days, save for the weeks their European friends came to visit with them in Texas and the Gulf Coast in more peaceful times.

As this vacation drew to an end Betty was eager to arrive home, Thatcher somewhat more pragmatic. He foresaw no great change in his life becoming a grandfather, suffering Betty's anxiousness throughout his flights from Paris to New York to Houston.

At the airport the women kissed and cried and hugged. That's what women did. Thatcher and his son shook hands. What was all the fuss? Women had babies every day. And truth be told, if not for the new mothers imposing the burden of joy on everyone, no one would give a bugger's damn.

Betty and Florence thought a girl would be nice for a change, whereas Casey wanted a son and Thatcher removed himself from any such discussion. A shower was planned, though not a baptism. Casey had not seen the inside of a church until his wedding day, nor would his son who would one day make his private decision as a young man as to what did and what did not exist in the universe. As would he discover what did and what did not exist in the hearts of men.

Of course a gala party was held to include their neighbours and friends in their celebration, followed months later by a shower for the coterie of females Florence and Betty either wanted to invite or felt compelled to invite for their own shared purpose, which Thatcher did not understand at all.

If a person's presence was not wanted in one's house, then just bugger off. That was his stand. Get the hell away.

Betty hushed him and sent him to his study where she knew he was most at home apart from his horses. She expected that tongues would wag and, once again, loose tongues did wag over phone lines and luncheon tables. How brave Florence was to bear a child at such a doubtful age. She was well beyond her most fertile years and might well be ruined as a result. Indeed, the child itself might be born imperfect in body, or in mind, or both.

Very early in '53 Florence Riley screamed her son Edward into the world. He was no less loud, as though shrieking his delight at being set free at last.

Thatcher and Betty continued being the wealthiest couple in the country, thus far having shared none of their wealth with their son and Florence, excepting the subdivision of several thousand acres of their acquired land. Thatcher's sound reasoning being that the kids were not in debt, they lived a privileged life due to hard work and they had sufficient monies in the bank not to worry. So what good would more money do them?

That said, however, Thatcher was seventy-seven. His son was entering reluctantly into his fourth decade of life all too quickly and, with that in mind, Betty agreed. She invited her son and daughter-in-law to dinner.

"Casey, I've been with your mother for fifty-seven years, since the first day she put her enviable charms to work on me."

Casey looked to his mother with a smirk. "I clearly remember the somewhat dissimilar accounts of your first and earliest times together. Although, and without question, I do prefer mother's version, what one would expect from a deliciously exciting novel."

Florence didn't understand Casey's response or Betty's comment that he should mind his manners and be a gentleman.

"Your mother worked hard to shape me as well as you, to make you a good man. I suppose the army did the rest to some lesser extent. She raised you well, never spoiled you with our wealth, never took what we had for granted when uncertain times were the undoing of so many of our friends and our neighbours. Nor do we expect you to spoil your son Edward. I must now have your word that you will raise the boy to be level-headed and that he will one day work for what he gains, not gain from what you will one day leave

127

him, not the indolent beneficiary of our hard work or yours. Give me your solemn word, the two of you. Swear to me now."

"I do most certainly swear. I do not intend for my son to be a slacker. He will make his way on his own merit, not on mine, not on yours or my mother's."

Florence added, "I promise also, Thatcher and Betty. My son will be as fine a man as his grandfather in every way. Or I will not recognize him."

"Then we are agreed." Thatcher sipped his cognac. "To say that Betty and I have been fortunate in life would be an unforgiveable understatement and unquestionably absurd despite our years of hard work. What we do this evening we do for two reasons. Understand that, the both of you. And give me your word that you do. The government would like nothing more than for me to die forthwith. I dare say this very moment would suit their needs propitiously. They see me not as a man successful in business. They see me instead as a source of funds with which to build new streets and repair the old roads, build and paint or repair bridges in disrepair. Need I go on? The second and more important reason is you, Casey, and you, Florence."

"Father, the ambiance in this room has changed somewhat disagreeably. Are you preparing us for horrible news?" He turned to Betty, showing real concern. "Mother, is he?"

"No, he is not. Nor will he appreciate your interrupting him once more. Continue, darling."

Casey had been reminded of his place many times by the hard clack of a gavel when standing before a judge, yet somehow his mother was this time more intimidating even at his mature age. He thought to glance at Florence, choosing for the better not to, giving his father his fullest attention.

"You each have a successful career and you have no obvious need of my and your mother's resources. The reality, however, is that we now must think of the near and distant future. I have recently promoted the president of Riley Corporation to CEO, an ego promotion for the most part to quell his suspicions. I, of course, remain as chairman with full control and voting shares until such time as the corporation becomes yours in full, at which time you may continue as chairman or dispose of the corporation's holdings entirely or in part as you see fit. What he does not know at this juncture, and will soon discover, is that you are now, once you sign the appropriate documents, co-chairman without voting privileges for the time being. There is, you understand, a learning curve and we, your mother and I, expect you to assume your responsibilities at Riley Corporation without much delay should you agree. However, should not agree, should you prefer to continue serving the law, the corporation and all its holdings will be sold by year's end."

"Father, you cannot arbitrarily…"

Thatcher waved his son to silence. "I can do whatever I damn well please. I need time with your mother while she is still young and vital. I've done my time. So has she. We deserve more time together alone. You'll discover one day how quickly the passage of time mocks us and I trust you will remember this moment when you're faced with a future much shorter than your past." Thatcher sipped his cognac. "Now, tell me, do you accept? Or do you need time to mull things over?"

"What your father is saying, Casey, was trying to say, is that you have no real concept of money…not this kind of money, despite the privileged beginning to your life. We took decades to become who and what we are for better or worse, whereas you chose the law to make us proud. However the timing is right for you and Florence to learn on your own, and not simply by what you see here. It is not in any way a responsibility you are accustomed to, despite what you may believe. There is, indeed, a learning curve.

129

To that end, irrespective of your decision to join Riley, we shall be transferring equally to you and Florence twenty million dollars each year until our deaths, with an additional five million each year to Edward until such time as we cannot, to be held in trust until his thirty-fifth birthday. The transfers will, for the most part, be offshore for which we feel not the slightest guilt. We have done our share for our state and our country."

"We also expect, Casey," Thatcher cut in, patting Betty's hand, "that you and Florence will choose an appropriate moment to make your son comfortable with his future and incredible wealth. Our wish is that he set his dreams on a worthwhile course and career of his choosing, not the hedonism of self-serving whims. It is on your shoulders to teach him right from wrong; we'll be long-dead, your mother and I, with whatever we teach him in the years we have left long-forgotten by him."

"We understand. Such was decidedly our intention before this revelation, father."

"So, tell your mother and me. Do you agree to any or all of this?"

"I agree to everything, father. I look forward to our first day working together."

"Florence, speak up, young lady. This is also your burden as well as your gift."

Florence appeared suddenly weak, vulnerable. She shivered, her body trembling for an instant, her face drained of colour, a cold chill surging through her veins.

Betty hurried to sit by her side, embracing her, rubbing warmth into her arms.

Casey reached to touch her hand. "Florence, tell me what's wrong."

Florence shook her head, smiling, downplaying their concern. "This is an incredible turn of events, Thatcher...and Betty, my dearest and closet friends. However Casey has agreed too quickly without comprehending the depth and the extent of what you have too generously proposed. Yes, we need time. We do, of course. No one, not any three people, deserves such a magnanimous gift. Please give us the time we need to consider your faith in us."

*

That evening in their bed Casey put down his book, sliding his reading glasses to the tip of his nose, an older man's habit he'd adopted to enhance his courtroom persona. He hadn't spoken very many words to Florence since returning home from his parents' ranch and certainly not about their incremental inheritance. Neither mind was remotely prepared to discuss what they secretly knew would one day come to pass.

"Florence, my dear, please talk to me. You've had hours to yourself to ruminate and sort through your thoughts and your worries. Tell me, please, what made you blanch with such cold by our parents' raging fireplace."

"I simply can't bear to think that I might one day not ride with Betty. She is my dearest and closest friend. To think of not having her near me is painful in the most extreme way."

"Your friend and my father ride together each evening before dinner. My father can still hit a can of peas from a thousand yards without a scope and hold his side in any debate as much as, I dare say, he can still manage in matters of the heart that are none of our concern. You can see for yourself how they carry on together. Your worry is premature, my dear, years ahead of its appropriate time."

"I saw our son, Casey, years from now in the dark. I saw our son emerging from total blackness. He was handsome and tall with the confidence that accompanies a man who enjoys power over all others, a gentleman as we know he will be. He was older than we are now."

"You created a mother's rendition of the future. What

mother does not imagine or consider her son's future? He will become a fine young man, a credit to his Riley heritage."

"No. He will not. Casey, our son's eyes were cold. His face had no colour. He was staring at me. He saw me as clearly as I saw him and showed me no emotion. He was not a figment of my mother's mind. He was real, Casey. He was real, not in my mind but in my heart. Casey, he had no soul. I shivered from his cold, not my own." She clasped her husband's hands. "Casey, I fear that with what Thatcher proposes our son's heart will choose a darker path, one beyond our ability to contemplate in these innocent times."

"My dear, you're scaring yourself into a frantic state without reason. You are an excellent attorney, the best, not a clairvoyant. Your vivid imagination has gotten the better of you. Leave such premonitions to the theatrics of circus palm readers and would-be fortune tellers. Our son will be fine. He will have the finest education and, as we promised my father and my mother together, he will make his way in life before enjoying his family's good fortune."

"Casey, we must refuse Thatcher's offer."

"I cannot, Florence. I will not. For father's sake and mother's I must continue their work at least until I am no longer able in mind and body. I intend to call father tomorrow and begin my work with him at month's end. The law firm is now entirely yours, Florence. We will see to that as well. My decision is made. Please, stand by me as always."

Her chest swelled with sorrow from the gloom infusing her. She slid under her down-filled covers, burying her face into the warmth of her pillow, trying as hard as she could to recall her son from his place in a future she did not and could not comprehend. She wanted to see him once more as he was, as she was afraid he might be then.

She failed, drifting into a more peaceful world with her husband's hand upon her shoulder.

The Fatal Diners' Club

*

Florence awoke to a bright morning, her heart much lighter than the night before. Casey was right, of course: A mother's fanciful vision. How ridiculous was she to believe otherwise? She had clearly experienced light-headedness due to the weight of Thatcher's unforeseen announcement and the horrible thought of Betty's inevitable passing.

She adored the woman, her friend, and loved her unconditionally.

That evening the papers were signed without much ceremony, Betty riding with Florence before dinner and not her husband. From then on no further mention was made of future events. The subject was closed.

The Riley Corporation had progressed to a second generation.

*

By age five the boy was good on a pony. He could read beyond his level and could not merely write his name but sign his signature, although he was not anxious to leave the vast expanse of his family's land and his pony for the confines and strict structure of private schooling.

By his twelfth year he was well-travelled, familiar with social graces and never forgiven the slightest corporal lapses, be they deliberate or innocent in nature. He was a Riley and with the name came the responsibility of social decorum.

Edward was never invited to travel with his grandparents. That was Thatcher's unyielding rule. As much as he loved Edward he never once mollycoddled the boy. He and Betty bought Christmas gifts and birthday gifts. Such was the extent of their generosity towards him beyond the five million annually of which Edward was not yet informed.

Nor would he be for several years.

At age thirteen his private education continued, working

his summers at Riley Corp. in the basement sorting the mail and at his grandfather's formal retirement celebration he received no special affection or treatment by way of his father's previous instruction to the management.

He was a part-time employee with no special privileges.

At fourteen he advanced to the Courier Room, running messages for middle management, seldom seeing his father before five PM. At fifteen he worked his summer months in the Copy Room, managing the mimeograph and Photostat machines, vacationing with Florence and Casey in the winter months in Miami and the Caribbean while maintaining his studies.

At sixteen he worked his last summer in the Telex and Telephone Room learning the intricacies of the switchboard and increasingly anxious to see more of a woman's body than a mere few inches above her bare knees.

When the oppressive heat of summer was done, replaced by the more pleasant warm days of early September, Edward spent two weeks with his parents at their ranch before leaving with them for the airport. Betty and Thatcher did not go with them.

At their home he shook Thatcher's hand the way he should as a man, stepping back, agreeing that, yes, he would always, in every way, do his family name and his grandmother proud. He hugged Betty warmly, gently, kissing her cheeks, once again stepping back, pausing a moment before walking out the door.

When he was gone Thatcher asked, "What is it, Betty. You're suddenly pale, my love."

She patted his cheek and went to see about his midday meal with the cook. She was his wife and no one else would take his lunch to him in her home.

That evening Florence and Casey ate dinner with their son in England. The next day they left him on the hallowed and ancient steps of Oxford. He would be alone for the first time in his life and not return home for four years and the successful completion of his final year of study before the real world would forever test and challenge him.

Riley Corporation paid the highest salaries, the highest bonuses, for which they expected the best from the best. If you were not in the top five percentile you need not apply for even the most menial position. In addition to which, as per Thatcher Riley's long-established mindset, family was no exception.

Florence and Casey would spend part of those four subsequent summers travelling Europe with their son. That was the plan, though days before the commencement of his first summer vacation, with his grades the highest in his class, he was called home. Thatcher Riley was dead at age ninety-four; the private plane already en route to London, dispatched immediately by Casey Riley upon hearing the devastating news.

The simple funeral was held three days later, Betty orchestrating every detail with Florence to assist her. She wanted her man buried proper like, the way he would want.

He was dressed in black leather breeches, a black cotton shirt without a collar, black leather boots and his gleaming six-shooters. That had always been his unspoken wish, she knew. She knew him so well, more than he had ever been aware, a destiny that had always kept him balanced: To live and be buried the way his shy and young whore had first seen him. Thatcher Riley was not a man of pomp and circumstance. He was simply Thatcher to some and Mr. Riley to others.

None, and not the one man living, had ever heard the true story of young Thatcher Riley and Miss Betty McGilly. For that reason Betty instructed that the lid should be closed, once she put her warm palm to his cool cheek for the last time. Thatcher would go to his final reward hidden from the eyes of those who would see him as an outrageous old man, a cartoon character, not as a man who had more than once used those very guns as a deterrent to less honourable men who would steal his wife or steal his gold. Those days no one had ever heard tell of. Not Casey, not Florence, not anyone. Those times were theirs to remember alone.

She remembered vividly, as though he had stood the day before with unblinking eyes, the hammers pulled back, his cold fingers on the triggers, the unclean faces of men twisted with cowardice trumped by his unyielding bravado. He'd been ready to die for her. He was her man and now he was dead.

Of course governors and senators attended, congressmen and congresswomen, reporters and close friends. Thatcher Riley's funeral was a must do and important occasion.

But what young Betty McGilly needed was her young gunslinger, the young man all dressed in black who promised never to leave her once they were wed. She didn't give a bloody hoot about anyone else.

The internment at the cemetery was a private affair while hundreds of others went to the house by invitation or to the many bars and restaurants in town presumably to chatter about Casey Riley and his son Edward.

Thatcher was dead, no longer a target of curious minds and fuel for wagging tongues.

With her husband laid to rest, the rough mound covered with so many hundreds of flowers, Betty took Florence by the arm, shooing away her son and grandson after kissing and hugging them. She wanted more time alone with Thatcher and sent her best friend away as well a few moments later with a kiss and loving embrace, asking Florence to remain nearby for she had no real idea how long she might be.

Florence hugged her friend gently once more and remained nearby beyond the perimeter of privacy.

Betty eased herself onto the ground, not for a moment feeling her ninety-one years.

She patted the marble stone and the bed of fragrant

blossoms. She was weary after her arduous three days.

"You scared me, mister, waking up to see you looking so peaceful like, like you didn't have a care in the world. You ain't got no right to have gone and hurt me this way, mister. Not after you promised me the way that you did all them long years ago, after I kept my promise not to whore with any other but you. I was yours from the first time you poked me, Thatcher Riley. I didn't once soak myself for any other man. I was yours alone all them long months with wet snow in our faces, with our noses filled with the stink of horse dung stuck to our boots and our hands burnt raw with cold. Do you remember, mister? Wasn't I the best whore whose bed you ever did sleep in?"

She closed her eyes, not to shield them from the bright sunlight, so that she might feel the soothing warmth of the sun's rays upon her face. He wouldn't mind that she was weeping. He would understand she wasn't afraid. She was never afraid when he was with her. She had to feel in her heart once and for all that he knew the truth and that he believed her.

"You were my very first, mister. Ain't never had a man touch me before you did and none after, not a single one before or after."

She needed so much after all these years for him to believe her.

He chuckled, his voice loving. "Never did doubt that you were, Betty McGilly. And I never did have a better whore, despite your small tits. I suppose I knew the first night that we'd pair up, you and me. Suppose I knew deep down I could never think of another man tasting your sweet juices and squeezing them small tits. Must say, though, you did grow into a fine woman. Always did love you so much. Still do, my love."

He was so close. She let her mind wander, her heart skipping a beat.

"You should have gone to church once in a blue moon, mister, wouldn't have hurt you too much. Now you see. You're gone for good and got stuck somewhere that ain't so good."

"I'm fine, Betty. I done my thing for a better world. Religion don't make a man good; don't make a good man better. Just makes him feel that way. Ain't nothing worthwhile in that sort of thinking as I can see. Never did see the need to pinch my nose and pretend."

"It ain't natural, mister, me sitting here alone without you after all them nights watching me in my tub. You ain't got no right at all to go and do what you did without me. We had a pact you and me. We spit into each other's hands that day and shook them tight together the day you bought my first horse. What made you up and leave me, mister? It wasn't right for you not to take me with you, the way that you promised. Ain't no hot water going to remedy that pain."

"Sometimes a man ain't got a choice, Betty, my love."

"I'm tired, Thatcher. Can't imagine my days and my nights without you."

"What you're thinking to do ain't right, Betty. You got work that ain't done yet."

"You were my work, my darling. Now take my hand, the way you did yesterday on our way north."

Thatcher hummed his strong disapproval from deep in his throat. He was not at all certain. In fact he disapproved entirely, but Betty McGilly was possessed of a determined mind.

*

The sun was warm on Betty's face. Florence would understand the tears glistening on her cheeks. She would understand that their close friendship had come to an end. Her lips curved into a pleasant smile. There was no sound. She scarcely heard the birds stop chirping.

"You always were a strong-minded woman, Elizabeth McGilly, since the first morning in your tub when you made me take you with me to buy your first horse."

"Yesterday, darling, when I was seventeen."

"You are seventeen, my love."

"Take my hand, darling. Our work with them is finished. Mine was finished when you were taken from me. I will not go back to them without you."

"Our son, my love, and your grandson… so much grief in such a short time for them to bear. How can we in good conscience…?"

"Casey has Florence to love and I fear that Edward's destiny is set. We did our best for him, my darling, though our Florence those many years ago did clearly see his future. The boy has no soul. I suppose I knew the day he left for his schooling abroad. Yes, I did know. And I watched him again all this week, closely, seeing him quite differently from how others perceived him. You were an inconvenience to him, as I will be now. I never once believed that I might one day despise our grandson, Thatcher, my darling. Yet I do, thoroughly and without regret, for how he mistreated his memory of you."

"Then he will one day be made to atone for whatever wrong he might do, my love. We are what we are, for better or worse. Destinies are not ours to choose or manipulate. We are what we are intended to be. We simply discover who we are, who we have become one day at a time." Thatcher reached out, taking her hand. "Come, my love. We have our own path to walk. That is our destiny."

15
Scent of his Woman

Lorie Wilson lay flat on her front, half her face buried into her pillow, his pillow.

She was naked. She wanted to call his name, afraid he wouldn't answer. She wanted to move, to close her wide-open legs; afraid he might pull back the covers and scoff at her. What was much worse, she needed desperately to pee.

The smell of freshly brewed coffee, rich and thick, permeated the penthouse. Penthouse! No way! The man lived in a frigging penthouse, not the top floor of a whorehouse the way she once wanted to believe. She wanted to scream. The night before had seemed like such a good idea at the time. No one ever had sex with someone new in the morning. Nighttime masked flaws, the same way expensive wine dulled the senses as effectively as cheap booze.

She must have been drunk or insane to sleep with her partner. Sleep: Good word. That wasn't sleeping, especially with Dwayne Michaels. Yet she wasn't hung over. She felt fine. She felt wonderful. She inspected her body in her mind. Her lips were sore and her tongue ached. God, she wanted to die right there in his bed. Her breasts, she couldn't feel them. She wanted to. She wanted to cup them, thinking she would wince from the welcome aftermath of his fondling and kissing. Her vagina was pulsating; throbbing as though she were hanging from a meat hook.

What was the time? When had he finally stopped loving her...or was that loving her? When had she finally collapsed into his arms depleted?

What didn't he know about her, his hands all but glued to her ass when they weren't on her breasts or clasping her face close to his or caressing her legs from her feet to her...Oh, God, he knew that too. She'd never in her life been so totally laid. Shit, no, she thought. She wasn't laid. No way! She was ravaged, plundered, her dream come true.

One time, the fifth or maybe the sixth, she couldn't recall, she couldn't help glancing occasionally at the hands of his crystal cube clock sitting on the bedside table, her body and mind separated, her wet body twisting, grinding, meeting each thrust with heated passion equal to his, her mind crying out after an hour, pleading silently for him not to stop.

Not once did he slow unless he intended to, teasing her, adoring her silhouette with his eyes, savouring her body with his lips, his tongue and his fingertips.

She was going home, with him or without him. She was going home. She would open her panty drawer and throw her motorized boys in the garbage. They were suddenly inadequate, obsolete. She was reborn, reawakened. The past three years and the years before did not exist. She existed. And if he was full of shit she would lick her wounds and get on with her life. No more toys, just men, real men and young men with crystal clocks.

She looked late twenties so she would be late twenties, and next year twenty-nine not thirty-nine, not one year from forty. No one would care. Men lied all the time about their jobs, their wives, their girlfriends and their money. So why couldn't she, the goose and the gander?

He must have told her a thousand times that he loved her. Of course he loved her. For five or six hours before she collapsed into a deep sleep she was naked, wet and slippery, doing everything to him and with him that she could think to do and doing it well. What wasn't to love?

How could she face him? She couldn't, not after everything they'd done, seen, what he'd seen. Shit.

She smelled. The room smelled, smelled of them together. She wanted to raise her head, scan the room, too afraid he might be standing nearby watching her, thinking of something smart to say like 'I've had second thoughts, Miss Wilson. You're too important to me as a partner. We should forget this ever happened. You should go home, but thanks anyway for letting me fuck you so totally', which he did…finally.

A phone chimed, not hers. She listened for footsteps near the bed, and heard nothing. She listened for his voice, and heard nothing. She counted five chimes, listening for a message, and heard nothing.

He wasn't in bed. She was spread like a wishbone and naked. Not him. He would be dressed and clean, his hair combed, his face shaven. The coffee would have taken at least twenty minutes to brew: one of those fancy European machines. He really was so easy to despise, to thoroughly hate.

She felt like a whore. She smelled like a whore. No. She stank like one and she was naked. The way he made her ooze with sweat, dripping from every pore, her face would look like shit and her hair like a rat's nest. He did that to her. She wanted to die. Better dead than him seeing her in the daylight, watching her walk past him in the nude, judging her, vulnerable, gathering her clothes, dressing. Yeah, she definitely needed to die.

How much longer could she stay there, inert, afraid?

"Good morning, something or other."

She jerked, grabbing the edge of his satin sheet, twisting and propping herself onto an elbow in a single movement. He was dressed in a silk robe. His face was, she didn't know, content, his beautiful brown eyes piercing hers. She hated him instantly for how he looked, as though he'd stepped from a glossy magazine.

She could scarcely swallow.

"What do you mean, something or other?"

"Well, you don't want cutie names for a while and I call you Wilson at work. Or I did. It's all I could come up with on such short notice."

"Shit, Dwayne, we're Wilson and Michaels talking about cutie names and I'm sitting naked in your bed. What the hell have we done?"

"I'd say pretty much everything, and then some. That's what you get for sneaking into a man's bedroom late at night."

She cringed. "I did do that. Didn't I?"

He nodded unsympathetically. "Yes, to tell me you love me."

"Yeah, and you told me at least 101 times that you love me. What's up with that, Michaels?"

"Sorry, I'll do better next time."

"I hurt everywhere because of you. Thanks a lot. Are you always this gentle with your women?" She put up a hand. "Don't answer that."

"You're welcome. And there is no other woman, just you, something or other."

"I don't think I like that very much and I stink like a compost heap because of you."

"You smell wonderful." He reached out. "Come. I'll pour a hot bath."

"I need to pee."

"I brought you a robe. Sorry, again, it's a bit big." He waited. "You're not moving.

"That's right. I'm not moving." She glanced at the clock. Her shock was real. "No way! It's noon?"

"He beamed. "I let you sleep. I thought you needed your rest...in a big way."

"Would you please turn?"

"No."

"I'll pee in your bed."

He shrugged. "Lunch is waiting. We'll do the beach another day. I'm thinking fresh sheets and a few glasses of wine. We have a few things to discuss unless we're otherwise occupied. So you might as well get out from under those sheets, something or other. I've already seen your bum in the daylight and we won't always make love in the dark."

"Gee, the same girl twice in a row. Sure you're not too bored."

"The only girl from now on twice in a row, so be nice."

He laid the robe on the bed.

"Shit, Dwayne. You and I are lovers. You're really serious about this? You really do love me? You're not telling the prissy bitch what she wants to hear so you can lay her again? I was so horrible to you yesterday." She didn't give him time to answer. "I've been lying here forever thinking you were going to say something to make me kill you."

"I didn't say I would never piss you off. I said I love you. Not the same thing at all…or maybe it is."

Lorie slipped from under the covers, Dwayne leaning into the doorframe, enthralled. She was perfection. What was her problem?

"This is the daytime me."

"Hmm, I see that. Would you please turn?"

She did, waiting. "Okay, Dwayne. I have a gun. Be careful what comes out of that mouth."

"I'm thinking dream-girl."

"What?"

"You're definitely a dream-girl, my dream-girl."

She faced him. "You're not disappointed."

"Don't search for compliments. You're gorgeous. Go pee. I'll run a bath down the hall."

He swept up the robe and left, ignoring her "No way!

Dwayne, you get back here with that."
*

Lorie sat on his toilet pinching herself, cupping her face in her hands. What happened to her, what was happening to her, was not real, could not possibly be real. She'd spent years dreaming of him, every detail of those unimaginable fantasies now a vivid memory to last forever with so many more to come.

She patted herself, flushed and stood, walking to the mirror to confront the scars of her post-incredibly romantic evening and the shameless lovemaking that she'd dreamed of for so long.

She recoiled, coughing an "ugh," grimacing. What she saw was gruesome. Her hair was pasted to her forehead and face. Her green eyes were red, centred in streaked aureoles of blackish-green. Her lipstick was smudged around her lips and across her chin. She cupped her breasts. Her nipples were tender from his constant attention, which she didn't mind at all. She stood on her tiptoes, peering downward into her reflection, groaning. She looked as though a convoy of armoured vehicles had rammed into her, parked, and stayed the night to party. She felt wonderful, ecstatic, but no way would he see her that way.

She scrubbed her face as hard as she could with soapy hands, smearing what was frightening from her face onto a hand towel, leaving behind a warm glow. Her hair was another matter: A tangled and matted mess. She did what she could with her fingers, running them through until she had no choice but to be satisfied.

She stepped away. One hand towel was left hanging from the stainless steel ring. How stupid would that be? She hugged herself, patting her sculpted stomach, sucking in, thinking she saw a difference, inhaling a deep breath.

Stepping into the hallway soft music filled the condo, the sound of running water guiding her. She was walking through Dwayne Michaels' home in the nude, feeling strange that suddenly she didn't feel strange at all. She felt good. She felt loved. She felt in love and she loved romantic Latin music.

She couldn't imagine what to expect. She was exhausted by how wrong she had been about everything, about him, about them. She took a final deep breath, stepping into his bathroom that resembled a private spa.

He was sitting on a counter, waiting, taking her in. He went to her, embraced her and kissed her, sweeping her into his arms, easing her into the Jacuzzi filled with heated and swirling water scented with apples, peaches and pears.

She invited him in. He refused. She was secretly thankful. She needed time to heal. Instead he went to his gym room. He needed to reenergize, leaving her submerged to her neck and to her thoughts until he walked in on her sometime later. She'd lost track of time.

"Dream-girl, we have fresh sheets and lunch is served. You're staying the night. Going to your place would be like starting over. I don't want that. Tomorrow morning will come soon enough." He sat on the edge of the whirlpool. "How's your...you know, everything?"

"My everything is feeling much better. Thank you for asking. I don't think I'll need stitches. Not yet, anyway."

"Let's get you out and dry."

"This is so weird, Dwayne. What a difference a day makes."

"That's true. Can you believe that only yesterday you were coming on to me at the gym the way you did?"

She splashed him, clambering out with her back to him. Her inhibitions weren't entirely gone, which she believed was a good thing. She wanted to relish every sensation, the pressure of his exploring fingertips, her shyness, the newness of being with him, the heat of their bodies pressed together, each moan, each tender word that now she would believe. She wanted to live forever in the evening past and the one she was soon to share with him.

She let him pat her dry, slipping into the robe he held open for her.

Lunch was a spicy beef and barley soup with a beef dip and a glass of ten-year Bordeaux. For some reason she wasn't surprised he had created the soup from scratch.

They spent the afternoon spooned into a sofa, sipping wine, letting the music speak for them, his hands lazily drifting from one part of her to another without the expectation of more, Lorie often craning her neck to kiss him.

Dinner was light: Consommé aux xérès followed by saumon fumé sprinkled with fresh herbs and spices accompanied by an assortment of brightly coloured steamed legumes. He suggested a Chardonnay, she agreed, wondering who and what she'd fallen in love with. Dessert was frozen lemon sorbet, shaved. Not scooped, she thought, of course not, and with a selection of Belgian chocolate-coated wafers.

Lorie wanted to do the dishes. She insisted.

They spoke about everything and nothing, learning a little more, each one aware of the inevitable conversation facing them, the questions, the impossible reality of what they did together as a team for a living and to make the world a better place.

Lorie didn't want to go to bed early to make love; she wanted him to take her to bed, to do her ten ways from Sunday. Tender and sweet was good, would be good one day. But she hadn't waited eight long years for tender or sweet. She wanted sex, unadulterated, get down and dirty, no holds barred, unrepressed sex. She wanted to get laid every which way until she required medical attention.

Somehow Dwayne understood, whether because of her purring, or possibly how she turned to face him, kissing his mouth, his face, his lips, her soft purrs intensifying to disgruntled groans. Or perhaps what he heard whispered into his ear and the way she was working hard at pulling away his tee-shirt with her lips pressing hard into his.

She got her wish, this time disregarding the clock, waiting as long as she dared before pulling back on his reins. Or was she convulsing, shuddering before crumpling in defeat. She didn't care.

She remained as she was, her arms framing his shoulders, her legs straddling his hips, her straight, wet hair against his cheek.

*

He loved her filet mignons, the firm, meaty bottom curves of her spectacular ass. Seeing her dressed all day would be difficult. Thinking of her as Lorie and not Wilson would be difficult. The Ice Queen had melted into a hot and sultry dream-girl.

Lorie refused to wake, savouring the persistent pats, the warmth of his hands and the pressure of each gentle squeeze. She loved where she was in her dreamy state.

"Good morning, dream-girl."

"No. Don't say that."

"I have to, sorry. The real world awaits us."

She hadn't moved an inch through the night.

She kept her eyes closed. "This really happened? You're Dwayne Michaels, I'm Lorie Wilson and we did all those things all those times?"

"And now we have to shower, have a coffee, something to eat and get to your place. Somehow I don't think garters and short skirts are quite Agency approved, not to mention half covered breasts and sheer blouses. By the way, I do love you. You know, in case you're wondering."

"Thank you, sweetheart." She wriggled to kiss him. "Although I do believe ass-man would be more apropos."

"I can live with sweetheart."

She crossed her arms on his chest. "Who was on the phone yesterday? You didn't answer."

"I have no idea. I don't answer calls on the weekend. The Agency knows that. I can't imagine who else might have called. I never give out my number."

"I'm sorry."

"For what, keeping me up all night?"

"You don't have family, your parents and grandparents."

"My uncle would disagree. He's pretty much a loner, though very much alive." He toppled her onto her side, kissing her. "We get used to being alone. We humans are adaptable that way."

"Now you have me."

"Yeah, I do. Everything comes in good time. We weren't ready before, dream-girl."

"That's easy for you to say. Ever have to get yourself off with eight inches of glow-in-the-dark purple rubber and a motor like you're beating a bowl of whipped cream?"

"Not that I can remember."

She pushed away. "Maybe you should try it tonight at my place." She scrunched her face. "In fact, perhaps I can help you with that."

"Thank you. I believe I'm happy with my status quo."

"You're welcome, sweetheart. And that would be your new status quo, which is a good thing. Besides, you're staying over, so bring a change of clothes."

She went to kneel, grimacing. "Do you hurt? Please tell me you hurt."

"No, I don't. I feel great."

"Then I don't want to hear it."

She moved away, making her way from the bed into the hall. She disappeared, Dwayne waiting for the sound of a door closing before padding into the kitchen to brew his coffee, wondering at the weekend.

When next he saw her she was dressed in her Saturday wardrobe surprised and equally delighted that, when he asked her to turn and lift her skirt, she did with a coquettish smirk.

He had a little vixen on his hands. Now the question was: What would they do with each other? The Agency had rules.

With a breakfast of waffles and Columbian coffee over, the dishes washed, they left hand in hand. He was leaving home with Lorie Wilson, his hot and sultry dream-girl.
*

They took both cars.

Lorie Wilson lived on the twenty-third rooftop floor with a view of the Atlantic. Somehow he wasn't surprised.

He was expecting pinks and lavender, flowers and frills. Not so. What he got was low-profile, simple and cushy European in vibrant blues, greens, yellows, stainless steel and glass. She gave him a full tour, leaving him to think two million, three very likely. Vendôme was recruiting millionaires. Her Corvette was one thing. Anyone could lease a luxury car. This was way over the top, yet she was as nonchalant as though showing him a modest home in the burbs.

He saw her bedroom last, sitting on her king-size watching her exchange a blue thong and bra for red, her stockings and garter for stay-ups, her skirt for form-fitting slacks, one sheer blouse for another and a blazer to match her slacks.

Despite the number of times he'd made love with her, tasted her, inhaled her, he could not believe he was watching the gun-toting and frigid Miss Lorie Wilson stripping and dressing for him. She was performing, teasing, loving every tug, push, pull and snap.

She was exotic, erotic, completely and unexpectedly his from out of the blue. What more could he ask or want? Certainly not millions of dollars; he had millions. Not that he had worked very hard for his wealth. He hadn't. Nor did he have delusions.

The Fatal Diners' Club

His family was filthy rich before they died in his pre-teen years and judging from what he was seeing little Lorie Wilson was doing alright for herself as well and not on the 250K The Agency was paying her. No way, to coin a phrase. What he was seeing of her winter wardrobe was at least twenty K, if not thirty: Tailored suits and dresses, everything else Italian or French.

The girl had some serious coin going on.

He loved her. He would always love her, unable to deny the self-reproach he felt for waiting as long as he did. He could certainly imagine spending forever with her. The problem was that for seven years The Agency had come first in his life. Now he harboured no doubt at all that she would come first. She already was first. He didn't need The Agency, quite the inverse. In fact over the past year he'd become increasingly disenchanted with them, with her, the resolute yet distant president.

Somebody somewhere was making Hilary Basil impossible to find and eliminate and The Agency wasn't doing shit to advance the cause. Twelve people supposedly dedicated for seven years to find one man was bullshit. So what was the point? And Vendôme wasn't much better.

Why wasn't he living in Florida with the pretty people? Why wasn't he drinking margaritas at a beachfront terrace watching, or appreciating bikini-clad women, a bikini-clad woman in something tiny now that he had Lorie to lie on the heated sand with? How phenomenal would she look in a thong, topless, coated with glistening cream?

He didn't have to imagine. He knew. She would fit perfectly well into his dream. So would he. So why wasn't he doing more than dreaming? Here, doing what they did, she stuck out like an angelic nymph on the outskirts of Jurassic Park hunting troglodytes with the notable exception of Riley people who were expected to do gym time each day in the main-floor company fitness centre. That was corporate policy, he was told by the building's watchman, behind a windowed wall that he had on occasion walked by somewhat slower than his usual pace to the silent accusations of the then Ice Queen. Though now he understood the jealousy thing, the female thing.

Pricilla Vendôme's strategy supported by both houses of the Senate, then returned to her and signed into law in January 2017, was inadequate camouflage, borderline at best. The Agency's mandate, their mandate was the real law. To that end not even the Gourmands knew their real purpose, too busy gorging themselves at the trough. No one knew apart from Vendôme and three other Wilson and Michaels teams scattered around the country. They were covert, hidden from a country and a world not yet ready for them.

They were elite: The Special Functions Group on the eighteenth floor of Riley Corp.'s New York offices that no one at Riley cared to associate with.

No one knew who they were. They knew to stay away. They were US Government and wore guns. That was enough to know. They were the supposed crème de la crème, too good for everyone else. That's what everyone thought. But at what, no one knew. They had luxurious office space, came and went at odd hours and never spoke to anyone which created a barrier.

They were never invited to parties or after-hours drinks, despite the men he'd often seen checking out Lorie's everything, and his own close inspections performed by various Riley women of varying potential.

He supposed they seemed too superior with tailored clothes, cars the others couldn't afford and preferential parking for her Corvette, his Jaguar and a corporate SUV.

According to Pricilla Vendôme in a one-time private meeting at the White House he and the members of the other teams were humanitarians. That much he believed. Lorie's meeting came three years later, a few days before he met her for the second time. They were humanitarians, acting outside the law and protected by presidential authority, searching for a man who seemed not to exist.

"What are you thinking, sweetheart?"

He rubbed his face hard, clearing his mind. "I'm thinking of you naked and oily on a Miami or Key West beach, or perhaps somewhere in France this spring."

Her cell phone pinged. She raised a finger. "You keep that thought." She answered on the third tone.

He waited, listening, not that he had to. He knew. If not her, they would have phoned him. She pressed END.

"Sweetheart, Dwayne, looks like we'll do our gym time this afternoon. We've got a dead Gourmand, confirmed."

"Anyone we know?"

"Yes. One of your all-time favourites," she reached for her purse, "the memorable Melvin Horn."

"No kidding. Good old Melvin." Dwayne took a moment, studying his partner, imagining Horn, thinking ne'er the twain, not in this lifetime. "I have to say he took a while. I hope he had at least the good manners to void himself first. Any idea when?"

"We don't know."

"At least he's close by. The last thing I want this week is to fly anywhere."

"What's the first thing?"

"You know very well. So don't get me started. Let's go, Wilson."

She punched him.

*

They knew where he lived. They had been to his home before without any legal right. They knew where most of the Gourmands lived, tracking them wasn't difficult. They knew about everyone except Hilary Basil, founder of The Diners' Club, who was quite possibly a Gourmand, or quite possibly not. They didn't know anything about him except that he was the man Priscilla Vendôme wanted put down along with his chain of supply.

The day was bleak, monochromatic grey skies filling in where grey snow and grey buildings could not. The air was damp and penetrating. Winter was bad enough, he thought; winter without much snow was November all over again. He definitely wanted her on some beach somewhere.

Lorie Wilson and Dwayne Michaels exchanged glances, furtive and private 'I love you' glances before stepping into the building. Michaels surprised when Wilson tugged at his elbow.

"I love you. I want you to know."

He'd sort of figured that out on his own.

The main doors were open. Horn's door was open, two uniformed cops standing around with their hands in their pockets waiting. He dismissed them. Their sole interest was a possible homicide and such wasn't the case. Goodbye. Horn was a No Assist. That was the law: Hands off. Let The Agency take over. Gourmands were not the concern of the law.

Michaels didn't ask whether anything had been touched. He didn't care. He wasn't a cop and dead Gourmands were not a forensic issue. They were a disposal issue pure and simple.

Though the door had been left open and a voiceless call had been placed to 9-1-1 early Sunday morning. So somebody knew Melvin Horn was dead. Again, who knew was not an issue.

He strapped his respirator to his face and gloved his hands in blue latex. Wilson did the same, staring at the greying mass on the floor. Michaels hadn't exhibited disgust in years, though Wilson continued having her moments and Melvin Horn did unquestionably leave the world without much sense of pride.

Seeing Gourmands dead wherever they chose to fall, in a sense gave them meaningful purpose. Yet in Horn's case, as in many cases, they had a choice. They didn't have to die alone, their mouths stuffed with food.

Three months earlier Horn had called for medical assistance when he should have known better. Like hating your loving mother for a lifetime, then screaming out for mommy when faced with fear. Of course he was refused and now his club had one less member. Or so they assumed.

None was very different from this one. Most died naked with their mouths either overflowing with food or leaking with bile or vomit. All died with their eyes wide-open with the shock of disbelief, always the same eyes while lying in puddles of fetid matter until discovered by curious neighbours or anonymous Gourmand friends perhaps missing their company at one of their secret feed fests.

Women or men, so-called, there was no difference. For the most part male and female Gourmands were entirely indistinguishable from each other.

Michaels knelt, thankful for his purified air. He didn't know much about police work. However coming from Black Ops he knew a bit. He knew most people were less than what they pretended. Everyone had secrets. He did. Wilson did, most or some of which would come later.

The wine label held a patchwork of glass together. 2002 from Burgundy and not bought from the corner store.

He jerked his head at Wilson for her to follow. Huge mistake, though her eyes were beautiful despite the punishing scowl. He grimaced, for affect, and she seemed to forgive him.

They checked the kitchens, the pantries, the cupboards and found nothing except shelves of food that would nourish an average family of four over five or six weeks. They checked his armoire and found nothing. Not a single dollar or bottle of wine anywhere.

"Someone had a good time after the party ended."

"Better than any time you'll have tonight, Mr. Michaels."

Ouch. He wasn't forgiven.

"I'm sorry. I am. That was the old me, the work me. That guy's not accustomed to being with an absolutely stunning, intelligent woman."

"So what was I the three years before you got a piece, ugly and stupid?"

"Too lovely to imagine, and I was the stupid one for waiting so long."

"That's right. You were." She smirked. "Good answer."

He was reprieved, change the subject fast.

"Horn has a few bucks in the bank and pays cash for everything. We know that. We should get the blue-shirts to check the videos. Would you please see to that, Miss Wilson? Give me five minutes."

She left, shaking her head, though she knew. That's one part of him she always did like. Even when she hated him he never let her stay very long around the more unpleasant corpses.

Melvin Horn was face down on a tiled floor. He was fortunate. The unlucky ones died outside in any weather not unlike a circus act with oohs and aahs from the crowd who, to a person, would and did think themselves superior.

Take any ten people and you'll find a gay or a lesbian, or both, or a bi-curious, especially females, a thief, probably male, a pedophile, probably male, a cheating husband or wife, or both, a wife beater, an alcoholic or a druggie, or all of the above once the crowd grows to 100 when you can add embezzlers, crooked cops, a pimp or two, a whore or two, insurance frauds, errant fathers and runaway kids who, more likely than not, think that being a whore is okay.

And maybe it is if your life is shit and you're pretty enough to sustain the lucrative hotel trade for a few years before the inevitable car-window BJs are all that's left. Who's to say?

Everyone thought at one time that baby fat was fine: Cuddly little babies. That was total bullshit. Fat was fat.

Nothing fat was fine or beautiful, artistic or acceptable, not in the seventeenth century, not in the twenty-first. Then things changed in January 2017, gradually. Worthwhile change takes time, especially when confronted with negative mind-sets.

President Pricilla Vendôme generally got what she wanted. She had important friends like Edward Riley who somehow figured into the scheme of things. Otherwise his office and Wilson's wouldn't be on the eighteenth floor of Riley's building with Special Functions Group posted on the front entrance directory for suite 1800.

Everyone knew Edward Riley snapped his fingers and things got done. So who was doing what for whom? Who was snapping fingers, Vendôme or possibly Riley? Or were they both? That's what had kept him awake at night when he wasn't making love to Wilson in his dreams or putting her face on a temporary and voluntary stand-in.

The law wasn't cruel. People were cruel to each other, to themselves. Parents were cruel to their fat kids, spouses to each other; doctors who ignored 200 pound ten-year-olds to spare an obese mother's feelings were the worst offenders. And fat begets fat. What tank-top healthy male wants to stud a slothful Clydesdale? So he gets fat too and the corral gets smaller.

He chortled through his mask. Welcome to Jurassic Park. Step aside or risk getting crushed by a starving troglodyte Gourmand.

She tapped his shoulder, stepping into him. They were alone.

"Sweetheart," she paused, "I'm sorry. Michaels, I'm too excited about having a lover, about you. Anyway, two young girls, mid-twenties by appearances, too well-dressed for street girls, between midnight and 2:30 AM Sunday had a bit of post-mortem work going on. Several cases of wine, and I do mean several cases, were taken out to somewhere, presumably to a vehicle parked beyond camera range. They weren't in a hurry and the last sortie fits in with the phone call. They left with a few garbage bags. I would imagine with a good supply of food. And I found this."

She handed Michaels a PMC. The Personal Measurement Card showed Horn's name, not a number, nor was any other information imprinted. The card was bogus, illegal, and free from monitoring. Very few had such cards, exceptions like the Special Functions Group. What the hell was going on? They hadn't once; he hadn't once thought to ask a Gourmand to see his or her card. The Agency had no legal right, nor did a Gourmand to possess a decoded card. So what? Why hadn't he? Covert had very little to do with legal.

"Old Melvin had paid company, probably a little penile resuscitation. Who knows? You're right, though, certainly not street whores? The guy had money enough to pay for higher end. Even so, I can't imagine what kind of girl would want to service something like that any which way?"

She giggled. "Sweetheart, the thought occurs to me. Perhaps if you were to see the video you might recognize them. I don't know, maybe. I'm thinking out loud."

She often stared him down. It's what she did, with eyes blacker than green on demand, unnerving, though he had always attributed the annoying habit to a female's inability to express herself intelligibly when lost for words at the outer reaches of her emotional boundaries. That was then. Now he couldn't stop peering into her eyes: One for his side. Go team.

"You are one spiteful woman, Wilson. Tell me the truth. You ever crush a man's nuts with those tiny feet of yours and laugh?"

"In my dreams, yes…yours, sweetheart, almost every night."

He winced, remembering Saturday at their gym.

She seemed quite satisfied with herself.

"Not funny."

"No. I can imagine not really."

"Is the retrieval team en route?"

"Yes. ETA," she checked her Lady Rolex, "any minute now."

"So, what do you think?'

She answered, "six-fifty. And you?"

"Seven, seven-fifty. Not the biggest we've seen."

The retrieval truck was a flatbed modified for the transport of deceased Gourmands. The steel deck was removable, raised and lowered by an overhead hoist rated for 1200 pounds of cargo. The deck was also articulated, able to slide back past its entire length with extension rails and winches for hauling bodies from inside doorways or low-level windows.

The gurneys were mandatory for window evacuation, each unit fitted with a weigh-scale. In cases such as Melvin Horn the body was rolled by a trained retrieval team of four onto a steel plate, a trolley equipped with locked rollers and a weigh-scale, strapped on and dragged by winch to the flatbed rails. Whatever might be in the way was demolished.

Melvin Horn's family would be notified by their Primary at The Agency, not by them, if he had a family. If not, The Agency would then cremate him, scatter the ashes and close his file. The Agency didn't care about people who didn't care about themselves, nor did most families.

That's what most people didn't know about death: What happened after?

Michaels was certain that Horn hadn't once considered his post-mortem chain of events. Gourmands lived for the day. Once dead, no longer one of them to practice the art of gluttony, they were forgotten, possible fond memories usurped by the next mouthful.

Wilson knew what he was thinking. She hadn't believed him at first, convinced he was trying to shock her.

In her previous life her primary function was to take a

bullet, to put the importance of another's life before her own. She didn't scare easily and went with him to prove him wrong, though he wasn't wrong. The simple fact was that a Gourmand was too enormous a mass to fit into any crematory furnace...in one piece. And then the cost was astronomical, well beyond the norm. For that reason alone Gourmands were never interred, other than rare instances by family. The cost and the entire process were prohibitive.

The retrieval team had arrived. They would be Melvin Horn's final earthly connection unless some relative accepted the burden of his weight. Either way, the carcass would be delivered to the crematory, hoisted onto a steel-reinforced table and dissected by the same team before day's end.

First they would tilt him head downward to increase blood flow to the neck. They would scan him for implants or a pacemaker: A preventive measure to protect themselves and the furnace. Each part of him would then be suctioned to remove the greater part of his fatty bulk with equipment somewhat less delicate than what a surgeon would use to sculpt the breasts, bellies and buttocks of unhappy women.

Boiling fat seeping into refractory more than any other factor was destructive to crematory furnaces. Concurrently his blood would be drained through a tube inserted into his jugular, the one vein they could usually find without further surgical exploration, both steps essential for the maximum reduction of his weight.

Despite dissection the torso would be difficult to manage should the team need to reposition it midway through the burning.

In consideration of such a likely possibility his arms would be removed and placed in a cardboard box fitted with a plywood floor. He would lose his legs, placed in their cardboard box. His head...she remembered the head; she remembered grasping Michaels' hand. How she hated him that first time, believing the contents of her stomach would at any moment hurl from her mouth. How she hated herself for her moment of weakness, for touching him. He was such a self-satisfied prick. Everyone who passed him thought so. Everyone thought he was a self-important, stoic, been there done that Black Ops asshole jerk. What did they know?

They didn't know anything about him. He was romantic, loving and utterly fantastic.

She squeezed his hand quickly, letting go. The team was coming through the door.

Once sectionalized, Horn would be cremated box by box. His head would accompany his arms. If she was accurate about the 650, possibly a bit more, the entire process would take eight hours: Two hours of prepping followed by a minimum six-hour burn time at a full 2200° F. His ashes would weigh twelve, perhaps fifteen pounds and the remaining bones would later be pulverized into disposable bits and pieces.

Melvin Horn would no longer exist. Though of greater importance was getting him off the floor and under a poly sheet as soon as possible. His stench was becoming public. His urine hadn't evaporated and the splatter coating his buttocks and thighs had caked into a thin crust.

The team worked quickly, expertly with less effort than expected. The steel doorframe was sufficiently wide, as was the hallway in order for the trolley to turn freely.

The four men were dressed in rubber boots and tear-resistant disposable overalls, their hands and arms were covered in shoulder-length rubber gloves, their faces with acrylic masks and respirators.

Michaels took Wilson's arm, though he never had before. She obeyed automatically.

On its side, at the brink of self-propulsion, the corpse hesitated, two of the four men hurrying to the other side to prevent the mass from avalanching onto and off the steel deck of the trolley.

Horn lay flat on his back, though Wilson wasn't doing

well at concealing her revulsion. She felt sorry for the girls in the video despite their apparent windfall. The digital readout flashed 802. They were equally wrong. Not that it mattered. Their job was done. So was Horn.

For whatever reason, Horn had decided three months earlier not to opt for a less painful assisted suicide the night he called for assistance. He preferred the prolonged misery of life and a slow death to a simple injection and two minutes of euphoria before blackness and peace.

They never insisted.

*

Dwayne and Lorie drove to The Agency together. They filed and delivered a joint report to an unknown IP address and forgot Melvin Horn.

They did the requisite two hours of gym time in their private setting, more Lorie and Dwayne than Wilson and Michaels.

In her locker room she showered alone, letting the steaming water wash over her from twin oversized heads, happy that she was alone, though she had thought on occasion that working out with the girls on the main floor could be fun. But she would have to lie about her life, about what she did. And, really, they didn't like her very much.

Now that was ironic if anything was. The one woman she had ever thought of as a friend, her only friend, did know what she was. She realized Dwayne had secrets buried deep in his past that he would never reveal. Neither would she reveal hers. They came together from secret pasts. He came from the US Navy SEALs, she came from the US Secret Service and certain services more secret than others.

She giggled, towelling herself. She missed those times; she missed Priscilla more than she believed she could.

In his car on the way to her home they were quiet, holding hands, gently caressing fingertips, comfortable with not talking. At home she poured him two-fingers of JWB, measuring herself the same measure of Ultimat chilled with a single cube. She poured a bath, filling her soaker inches from the brushed-nickel overflow.

She was squeaky clean; she just wanted him with her in the tub. That's how she ended most days. Now she would end her days with him. Above all, she needed for her first workday of the year not to spoil her weekend with him, her dream.

His legs framed her legs and her hips, his arms dangling over the rim. Her feet were planted against his flat abdomen, her breasts submerged, Dwayne doing his utmost to create small waves.

"Sweetheart, I need to tell you something."

"I'm here, dream-girl. Admittedly and understandably a little distracted, but I'm here."

"Okay. You are not a self-satisfied prick or a Black Ops asshole jerk." She sipped from her sweating crystal old-fashioned. "I'm sorry for ever thinking you were. I was being selfish." She sipped again. "I thought you should know before we get serious."

"You're too late. You should have told me Saturday sometime between wanting to crush my boys with your pretty feet," he kissed her toes, first one foot, then the other, "and flashing your perfect ass for me. You're way too late, dream-girl. Besides, we have larger issues than a shy female who can't tell a man how adorable he is, or how much she loves him... and that she can't live without him."

She splashed a wall of hectic water at him, sacrificing her vodka for the greater good of women everywhere.

"Like what issues, sweetheart?"

He saw the curtain of water coming. His scotch held well above the crest.

"For starters, we've got two condos, two beds, two of everything. Not to mention the two of us. I'm thinking it's too late to take things slowly. I'm in, for better and more of better, especially since I'm no longer an asshole jerk."

She grimaced unconvincingly, easing forward. "I suppose you still could be, you know, once in a while. But I am four floors higher with a better view and a private deck." She kissed him. "Also, the rent is reasonable. And another thing, I can live without you. I have lived without you. I just don't want to, not for a moment. So let's temper the male ego thing a little."

"You don't want time to discover my dark side, my secrets? I have them, dream-girl, a real whack of them."

"You were in Black Ops. No kidding. I was Secret Service. Think I'm pure?"

"Yes. I do." Dwayne sipped his scotch, not thinking, simply adoring her. "This one time I was in a corner store, a month or two before meeting with my uncle about Vendôme. There was this guy with a gun. He was irrational, erratic, screaming, threatening everyone, mostly women and kids." He sipped again savouring the sensation, not for affect. "Put a 10mm in his forehead, scared the crap out of everyone and blew his ass into a candy rack. I could have blown his hand off as easily, or a kneecap, but I knew he'd be out within a few months with nothing to lose."

Lorie showed no surprise. "I was assigned to Priscilla Vendôme when she was campaigning in '20. She was way ahead in the polls. Somebody, a crazy, didn't want her in for another term. I shot the messenger."

"I saw the news report, Lorie. I know… eight rounds in three seconds."

Her amazement was real.

"No, you don't, not everything. I know something no one else does, just me and Priscilla."

He chortled. "Priscilla, not Vendôme, not the…"

"That's right… Priscilla. I'm a markswoman. One shot to the chest would have sufficed. I put eight into him, turned his chest into a pudding. Like your guy, I somehow knew he would come back and…"

"And what, dream-girl?"

"I was voting for Vendôme. She's good people. She's also my close friend. She's my best friend, sweetheart. I wasn't protecting the president; I was stopping him from killing my friend."

"Your friend…"

"She's my very close friend, sweetheart. I love her very much. The feeling's mutual. The thing is, once you shoot righteously, you're gone. Friendships take second place. Like a construction guy saved by his belt. He gets rid of it. The thing served its purpose. It's obsolete. And I miss her."

"You did a good thing. And if what I'm seeing is obsolescence, bring it on."

"I'm not finished, sweetheart, and I'm breaking Priscilla's confidence. The shooting wasn't a random act by some madman. He was a Gourmand working for Hilary Basil. His name was Alvin Jasper. No one else knows. He was never identified. You know how that works. How would she explain The Diners' Club?" She scrunched her face, regretting the lost vodka. "Now the only other secrets I have are you, The Agency, and my times with Priscilla on her private island. I taught her archery, sort of a girl's day, just her and me. My parents believe I work for the Speaker of the House reviewing the validity of legal questions and arguments, wasting my life. It's the best I could come up with, you know, like something or other. They're disappointed in me, but I'm good with lying to them. They don't know about the shooting. They couldn't deal with me killing someone and The Agency, no way. My father wants to believe or does believe that I'm saving myself for Mister Right."

"Now you can tell him the wait is over." Dwayne inverted his empty glass. "That's enough revelation for one night, dream-girl. When you come back we'll talk about us."

Her brow furrowed. "Why am I going?"

"It's your place, you're a woman and you're naked, beautiful and all soapy."

Lorie moved slowly, exaggerating each movement, slapping away his hand once, twice, three times. She wrapped herself in a fleecy towel, padding across heated tiles, ignoring his pleas, telling him to deal with it.

She was gone longer than he thought necessary. He called out to her, relaxing into the water when he saw her.

He took his drink from her, wondering, curious.

She put her drink on the bath-side trolley with the narrow gift-wrapped box, slipping under the suds to her shoulders.

"Sweetheart, I love you." She passed him the box. "This is for you and I do have another secret to confess, something awful."

He tore at the wrapping. The box was blue velvet. The bracelet inside read: Dwayne. He took his time. He saw the eagerness in her eyes. He had more to read, an inscription, he guessed. No one ever gave a signet bracelet as a gift without an inscription. He took his time, frustrating her.

How long did he need to read: From me, Lorie, in '23?

She saw his face lose all expression. Her heart was ready to explode.

"The date's wrong," was all he said.

"No it's not. This was your Christmas gift when I wanted to invite you here for Christmas dinner, you and me, alone. The scotch was a second thought. I'm sorry."

She seemed heartbroken.

"This is a lot more than a sweater, Lorie...and for Christmas." His mind was racing to turn back the clock. "You know I would have come."

"No, I didn't. Not at the time and I was angry with you for no reason. I felt so...I don't know."

"But that was a few days before..."

"Yeah, I know."

He pulled their bodies closer with no effort. Her eyes

were wet. She wanted to cry.

"Lorie, I'm the one who's sorry. You have no reason."

"Yes, I do, sort of."

"Help me with the clasp, please. This is my best gift ever. In fact this is my first real Christmas gift since my parents were killed, not that I don't like scotch. Wow. And all I got you was a sweater. Don't think, though, that I wasn't thinking about silk and satin, imagining your expression Christmas morning and maybe planting a thought in that devious head of yours. I was. Thing is I was too afraid." A bright thought flashed in his eyes. "You didn't like the sweater."

Her eyes welled. She kissed, him wrapping her arms tightly around his neck, her soft, hoarse voice an intoxicating whisper in his ear. "Dwayne, sweetheart, about the sweater…"

16
Edward Riley

Edward remained with his parents long enough to lay young Betty McGilly to rest and ever lasting peace alongside roguish Thatcher Riley. He couldn't return soon enough to England.

His timidity and distress of the previous year when abruptly dropped into a life of self-reliance had dissipated into brash confidence. His parents did notice the difference, though not to the extent Betty had, Florence and Casey each assuming a girl was the root cause of his behavior. Although in part they were right, erring only by the number. Edward Riley was not interested in a girl, discovering soon after his arrival at Oxford that one girl was problematic, whereas several girls in his bed were at once instructional and considerably less of a concern.

Nor did the girls particularly care.

The era of free love, hippies, toking and the rampant swapping of partners had arrived for the long-term that would endure for decades. The best part was twofold: The girls were always as eager for new partners and variation as he was and no one, no girl, could ever be certain who the father of her bastard was.

Edward had scoffed at more than one such hopeful girl throughout his four years, arriving home months before his twenty-first birthday with an insatiable appetite for what in his mind were disposable partners.

The Fatal Diners' Club

During his absence his parents had moved into Betty's and Thatcher's home, maintaining theirs as a second residence for visitors and as a pied à terre for out-of-town business associates until their son's return.

Edward's destiny was Riley Corporation. He understood that obligation despite his reluctance to begin his career on the ground floor, his remuneration no better or worse than any of his co-workers, completely unaware his father was pondering the very dilemma Thatcher had debated with himself and Betty: When? The difference was that he and Florence had successful careers before he joined Riley. They didn't need the corporation. He joined as a matter of family pride, not responsibility, whereas Edward had no marketable skills, no future mapped out. Nor did any school, not even Oxford, teach survival in the real world. He still had much to learn.

Edward had no true concept of his parents' wealth. He was aware of their country-wide status to the extent that he knew what Thatcher had wanted the nation to know, which wasn't much. Not even Casey had known until he went into the lower level of his new home, into his father's once off-limits sanctuary, obeying his mother's final instruction to him, to lower the automated floor, open the vault door and raise the floor to its proper level before walking into a few hundred million in gold and silver bars as well as a desk containing information on foreign bank accounts.

Betty's final request of her son and her best friend was that they never reveal the cached fortune to their son, not until the reasonable expectation of their second death. Therein lay the solution to the dilemma: His thirty-fifth birthday. Edward would have that long to prove himself. Until then he would remain as an employee, climbing the corporate ladder in accordance with his measurable and substantive performance.

Time would quickly tell.

Through the years Casey continued diversifying the

family's holdings, the Riley name increasingly recognized in real-estate, urban development, mining and offshore oil exploration, gradually introducing Edward to each facet of the corporation until the day he decided with Florence that their son was unquestionably ill-prepared to assume further responsibility.

By age thirty-five Edward was vice-president and CFO of the Oil & Resource division with a six-figure income, which is where he would remain. His father was seventy-three and not prepared to surrender his chairmanship to a man with no vision beyond the expectation of what he wrongfully considered was rightfully his.

Not once since his return from Oxford had Florence or Casey broached the subject, believing or hoping that one day Edward would recognize the nature of his future with the corporation.

Edward hadn't yet married, nor did he intend to limit his life or his lifestyle to a single woman whose sincere feelings would be impossible to quantify. He preferred the company of women in their twenties with a particular penchant for the younger wives of other men who were less inclined to attach themselves. A practice his mother quietly believed was entirely despicable when his first and foremost responsibility to the family and Riley Corporation was in fact to ensure future generations.

Her premonition had come true, becoming more apparent each day. He was undeserving.

The investment Betty and Thatcher had begun for their then infant grandson had grown impossibly large and Casey was unwilling to transfer over 300 million to his son for no other reason than their symbiotic father-son relationship. Casey harboured little doubt that his son was at Riley solely for the eventual and inevitable outcome of incredible wealth.

The father needed the corporation to remain in the family; the son needed the corporation for his personal gain.

His list of associates and followers in the guise of friends was growing each month.

The birthday celebration was simple. Casey and Florence seldom dined out, the intimacy of fine dining diluted by bodyguards, curious side glances and whispers, and the predictable intrusion of handshakes and promises to meet soon. They were beginning to appreciate Betty's and Thatcher's wisdom.

When the dinner was done and cognacs were served, Casey was very clear in his mind. He would not reward his son for half-merit and overt self-centredness, despite his performance.

"Your grandfather and grandmother, whom we suspect are quite far removed from your thoughts made arrangements for your future well-being, Edward. Their wish was that you receive their gift today. Their further wish was that your mother and I do so at our discretion."

"This is a pleasant surprise. I assume we're talking about a good sum of money."

"We are."

Edward swirled his digestive. "What particular reason did they have to make me wait this long?"

"You have not waited. We wait for what we know exists or anticipate, neither of which apply to this circumstance. Your grandfather wanted you to prove yourself, which you have in part. In part due to your privileged education, in part due to the silver spoon that has fed you these past years. However, and most importantly, as a result of your family name which you seem intent on ignoring. So here's what will happen, Edward."

Casey nodded to Florence, passing his son an envelope.

"Your father's and my wish is that you marry before the year is out. In the envelope is a bank transfer in the amount of one million dollars. An additional fifty million will be transferred once you are married. We also require that our family name continues, which you will honour twice within your first eighteen months together. Once the second is born we will give you a further fifty million, and when the boy or girl is ten yet another 100 million plus interest will be transferred with instructions to our attorney that, upon our deaths, you will receive your grandparents final 100 million...by which time the value should accrue to twice that number."

"You're telling me I've got 300 million."

Mother and father nodded.

"I would say more than 400 once all is said and done. Or one million," Casey added. "The choice is yours."

"That's coercion, and unbecoming of a mother and father."

"That's family responsibility. The family fortune you know nothing about is not a birthright. Should you disagree, which we will understand, you will have a million dollars and a good job. That is until I sell each and every Riley division this year, which you should not interpret as a threat...merely a lifestyle change. Although I cannot envision that your privileged position with the corporation would be welcomed in any way by a potential buyer. Most often the old regime is considered collateral damage by the new people, that sort of thing. Unpleasant, yes, though quite understandable. Conversely, as a wedding gift your income will double, your portfolio will increase significantly and one day Riley Corporation and all that entails will be yours inclusive of our personal wealth."

"You're faulting me for being an only child, for not imposing on your lives what you're now imposing on mine."

Florence retorted. "Some might argue that remark as an only child in the country's wealthiest family. What is your point, Edward? All we ask is that you find a suitable girl of reasonable intelligence and marry her. We do not expect, nor do we require that you remain faithful to her. However we do require two grandchildren. We cannot risk that a single child might share your disinclination towards family or that he or she might lack the intellectual requirement to one day head such a vast corporation."

"I don't even have a lady friend and you expect two kids in two years."

Florence answered. "I believe I said eighteen months, please listen, in order to achieve what is best for you. You're quite free to stay on at Riley until buyers are found. At which time with your savings, the million which you did not expect, and your experience, you can easily build your own business the way your grandparents did."

"When do you expect a reply?"

Casey stood to refill his snifter. "Do not play the village idiot in front of your mother. What is there about 400 million you don't understand? Simply tell the girl, whoever she is, that she'll be married in September and pregnant by October. We assume you're well-practiced in the ways of amorous and self-serving subterfuge. Whatever lies you wish to tell her is your business, which your mother and I will not be a party to. So beware."

*

Faced with pending disaster, Edward Riley left his parents' home in a daze. Not feeling ecstatic over the news of his fortune was impossible, delirious once he was alone, planning to end his evening on the verge of a hangover.

He would marry, soon. He would find a way, his mind processing a rush of possibilities from the irrational to the plausible as he drove along his family's private roads to his home. At the very least he would take the week off. He had some thinking to do.

His favourite girl was Karina. He had others he could call, though he seldom did unless hard pressed. She was twenty-three, everything the most discerning man would wish for in a woman, particularly her husband who travelled frequently on business. Whatever he might do, Edward had no plans to make Karina a casualty of his future. She was too unique, too special.

He took a week's vacation. He needed time away from the office to weigh the pros and cons of each female he knew, Karina lingering in the recesses of his mind.

He could buy her, in a sense. Women had been bought, sold, given as gifts or traded for favours and farm animals for centuries. Everything and everyone had a price. He could make a deal with her husband. She didn't love him, not enough anyway to remain faithful. And what man couldn't be swayed by ten, fifteen million? But she was adamant about not spoiling her incredible body with the irreparable disfigurement inherent to childbirth. Even so, how long before familiarity would fester into contempt? That's what he enjoyed most about her besides the obvious. They met, had dinner or spent the odd weekend together at a coastal resort, enjoyed memorable sex, kissed and went to their respective homes.

He'd known her since she was twenty and single. He'd fucked her, and not for the first time, to celebrate her engagement, again on the eve of her wedding that he attended, standing in the receiving line to kiss the bride, and throughout the first night her husband left town on business following her honeymoon. Expressing undying love was never an issue.

Riley didn't want marriage and Karina's husband had a good job. The trade-off was sex. He wasn't any good in bed or anywhere else, and Riley was, regardless of the venue.

Dealing with her husband was out of the question. If not time, kids would destroy what they now shared.

No. What he needed was twenty-one, thereabouts, and not simply pretty, someone at least as appealing as Karina as a minimum requirement. He wanted someone university educated; clean, with the least possible number of sexual partners, someone willing to trade a privileged life for a family.

He knew no such woman. Most women he took to bed had been with someone else the night or the week before. He wasn't demanding that way. Exclusivity was no less a ridiculous notion than deciding early in life who one would spend his or her entire life with. Yet he had to. He had no choice. He would also have to tell Karina. He needed to assure her that nothing would change between them. He would also tell her that, effective the day of his wedding, she would no longer have to remain married if she chose not to. However he would then require her exclusive devotion and her body whenever and wherever he wished.

His search began in New York midway through his week off on the campus of the Columbia Law School where he spent two days studying bodies. He didn't want a Houston girl. He wanted someone erudite, a long-term stand-in for Karina or any other likely woman those times when he could foresee himself somewhat restrained by family or corporate obligation. What better place than New York?

Her brain didn't matter. That she was in the law school was sufficient proof. What he needed was to see and sample her body, test her body. Karina never said no, often taking the lead. He needed that. Getting laid was easy. He didn't want or need that. He wanted Karina's insatiable drive, her fantasies, her need to reach the ultimate high each time.

The first two didn't work out, each girl benefitting from the luxury of waking in a luxurious hotel setting after an evening of dinner and dancing and a thousand dollars to help with her next year's tuition. The third girl was Vera Batten.

She was twenty-two. He could easily imagine her in bed with Karina, thinking he might make that happen, and she knew of the Riley Corporation. What truly surprised him was that she had applied to Riley Corp. in Chicago for an interview as a prelude to her graduation.

He explained that her interview was not the purpose of

his visit, though quite possibly her future was in a way she had not expected.

He saw no value in pretending. He wanted to invite her to dinner. He wanted to dance with her, talk with her and, if all went as well as he expected, he would need to see her naked. If that went well, though he could not imagine what the source of his disappointment might be, he wanted to spend the night having sex with her for which he would pay her a thousand dollars up front. He needed a wife in the very near future who would be a lady in public and a vital whore in their bed. He would also require two children very soon thereafter.

In return she would have her prestigious career at Riley Corp., any home of her choice in Houston, servants, a nanny, luxury vacations without the children and twenty million dollars the day of the wedding. That commitment would naturally be contractual, prepared by the Riley legal department who would also draw up a prenup excluding her from all his wealth, current or future, with her own windfall contingent on her staying with him as his wife until the death of both his parents who were now in their mid-seventies. He wasn't finished.

At which juncture he would expect her to divorce him and settle for 100 million agreed to in a separate document prepared by his personal attorney prior to the wedding.

Although the marriage would by and large be sexual in nature, a farce, he would expect her to have his children by another man, someone with physical characteristics and traits matching his. She would furthermore sign a document stating that the children were hers as a result of sexual misconduct, affairs with men unknown to her, his children solely by virtue of his kind and forgiving disposition. He did not want children; he needed them and would tolerate her adultery until such time as she became pregnant by someone chosen jointly. He believed the honeymoon might be appropriate timing, something to discuss later. She would not, however, question his adultery at any time. Did she have any questions?

She was stunned, her mouth agape. Certainly she had questions. Like when did he escape? She was ready to leave, back away and run.

He was dead serious.

She wanted to see his driver's permit.

Sure. No problem: Edward Riley, Houston, Texas.

Okay. Why her?

He liked her body and her character. If he had to marry for reasons of family obligations he might as well do so with someone disarming and sexy, which he had yet to determine.

She needed more proof and he was dreaming if he thought for a moment she was going to strip for him. She had a boyfriend.

He believed differently. Her boyfriend was history and he told her so, reciting the public phone number of Riley Corp. in Houston and pointing to a nearby phone booth.

She hesitated, scanning the grounds. She wasn't alone. People were milling around. She had nothing to lose. Why not?

He first called his father's private number with the heads-up, disconnecting, squeezing past her.

She dialled, searching his face before each digit, expecting a hoax. The operator answered her, Vera asking for Casey Riley's private secretary who knew to put the call through to her boss. In those few seconds of silence Edward cautioned her to be discreet.

When she hung up the receiver she was pale.

"What did he say?"

"He said welcome to the family. He and your mother Florence look forward to meeting me.
He'll be calling his legal department to set up an interview for me."

"So, now you believe."

"No, I do not believe this. I'm getting married, but I'm not getting married. I'm having your children with a man I've never met. I'm divorcing you and I've only known you a few minutes. This is too freaky. Freaky, this is too fucking weird."

"That's next. I do have to see you naked and determine if we're compatible in bed. I must also tell you that I do expect a certain energy level."

"Show me the thousand."

He did, counting ten American bills, holding them out to her.

She took them, looking around, students and staff coming and going, sitting or standing, discussing whatever was important to them, though at the moment nothing was more important than giving the son of Mr. Casey Riley the best fuck of his life. She wasn't waiting. She wasn't giving him the chance to find and fuck some other girl. They could eat dinner later.

She eased her arm through his, guiding him to a nearby cluster of trees at the corner of the school where she casually undressed, stooped to neatly arrange her clothes by her legal tomes before standing straight, twirling in slow concentric circles with her arms raised high and laying on the grassy ground under a bright sky with her legs parted and her knees in the air as though in the privacy of her dorm room.

When they were finished he tucked another ten bills into her panties as she was dressing, gave her his Houston address and told her to arrive at his home by Saturday at noon. She had passed her final exam and her adjudicator had to get home to Karina.

17
The 21st Millennia

Vera Batten spent her first thousand dollars on new clothes. She didn't have much. Her parents were average, fortunate to have an above average daughter who hadn't yet told them she was getting married or into what family or that after September they wouldn't have to work another day.

She had travelled to Paris, London and Chicago, not much more. They did what they could to provide her with more than a schoolbook education. She lost her virginity at fourteen with a classmate in an unfinished basement with her blouse undone, her bra pushed to her neck, her skirt pushed to her waist and the guy pushing his way into her while holding her underwear to one side with one hand and groping the closest bare breast with the other. All told, she'd endured ninety seconds of male grunts and bouncing on a stained and dank couch that she had no desire to remember.

Her next experience was three years later en route to her prom in a limousine, sitting on some guy she'd loved for a month, perhaps longer, with her dress hiked to her waist. She remembered him faintly; he wasn't memorable. What she recalled most was the girl beside her, straddling her date. They were best friends, though never close enough or daring enough to confess their curiosity of one another. In fact they never saw each other after that evening. Too embarrassed after the champagne left their bloodstreams, she supposed.

She was in her third year of studies at Columbia with a different guy to mark each year: September to May conveniences to balance the stress of university life, forgetting each other over the summer when she would waitress to help her parents. That was her official count and the third guy wasn't at all pleased with the sudden prospect of searching for a replacement girl to end his year with when all the best were taken.

For his part Edward Riley was quite content with being her sixth, which he considered a reasonable history given modern times.

She arrived at his home Saturday at eleven. When she asked the Riley chauffeur who'd met her at the airport to advise her when they were nearing the property, he answered that they'd been driving through Riley territory for the past ten minutes. What she was seeing as far as the eye could see, and then some, was all Riley.

She had nothing to say.

Several minutes later he opened her door, escorting her to Edward Riley's front entrance where the housekeeper greeted them. The chauffeur bid her farewell, returning to the car to retrieve her single piece of luggage from the trunk.

Edward did not come to the door. He was enjoying a midday cocktail by the pool where they spent the afternoon sunning, swimming and talking about what and what not to say to his parents, Edward explaining how things would play out in his view before and after the wedding.

They were expected for cocktails and dinner at seven and she wasn't to worry. The dress code most times for family was casual.

Florence and Casey greeted them warmly without the slightest pretention, Florence accepting her hostess gift with sincere appreciation. Vera had thought to buy her an Italian silk kerchief, explaining with a smile that she wasn't certain how complete Florence's wardrobe might be.

The ice was broken. Her years at law school had taught her well to confront the unknown with forthrightness and composure.

The initial banter over drinks gave way to more pragmatic conversation over dinner, Casey asking easy questions, nothing intrusive. He already knew every detail of her life, possibly with the exception of her first two ephemeral experiences with the teenage male interpretation of eternal love. Of the other three he knew as much as he cared to.

Florence and Casey agreed with everything Vera had managed to plan in such a short time, very little of which was Edward's doing. Though, as usual, Casey had the last say.

Vera would maintain her studies through to June, indeed, flying to Houston each weekend in First-Class to lessen the strain of frequent travel. She would summer with them at their home and learn to ride. They would introduce her to friends and associates over time, nothing daunting; acquaint her with the intricacies of entertaining as well as the monotony of it and plan a wedding. She had a good deal to learn and many adjustments to make that would enhance, not alter, who she was.

Once her third-year grades were posted she would have her interview before a panel of Riley's most senior attorneys, legal hard-asses which, he warned, most applicants did not survive. Riley hired the best, exclusively.

Once married, once the honeymoon was over, she would return to New York to complete her fourth year. However, given her foreseeable condition, they would not expect her to return after Christmas until her successful fourth and final year. Instead her husband would undertake the responsibility of spending his weekends with her in New York. She would enjoy the finest accommodation with a live-in housekeeper and lack for nothing. She need only ask Edward until such time as she received an appropriate allowance to carry her through to her employment. All he expected of her was that she would maintain her grades and join Riley as soon as possible after her first child.

Not fainting was difficult. She liked them. They were real people, as real as they could be. She was about to become Cinderella with a Prince Charming who, from what she knew of him, was an absolute prick.

Somehow she felt Florence and Casey weren't blind to that character flaw and Vera didn't require much imagination to understand why Edward had insisted on a divorce upon the second of their deaths.

They understood the practicality of the marriage, Florence wanted her to know. Hopefully she did as well. In spite of which, she would discover, they were good people, asking of her quite simply that she not judge them too harshly until she came to know them.

Vera promised with a warm smile that she would.

There was one order of business remaining: The ring.

The stone was a perfect diamond set in a circle of smaller diamonds and mounted on a titanium band.

*

Florence had never flown in First-Class and spent the entire flight recreating the past week in her mind while failing miserably at trying to imagine her future.

Sunday evening she called her parents who thought she must be joking or that she'd been to the campus bar earlier in the day. She didn't argue. She spoke with them once a month. Long distance calls were prohibitive and they had decided together that schoolbooks were a wiser expense.

Their conversations were often brief, to the point. Was she doing well? Was she taking care of herself? Was she being, you know, careful? Yes, yes, yes. Even when she wanted to she never said no. Was she doing well? She snorted. No shit, mom.

What she did say before disconnecting was that they should expect a call from Mrs. Florence Riley who wanted them for a weekend sometime in April at the Riley ranch in Houston, Texas.

She could tell her mother was patronizing her, telling her to get a good night's sleep.

She had no one else to tell. Casey had warned her about security. No one would care about her ring beyond the eager need for fresh gossip. As far as anyone was concerned the thing was a glass bauble. He did, though, understand a young woman's need to tell the world about her upcoming wedding day. The trade-off would be a 24/7 security detail. The so-called good life had a definite downside.

She decided she could live with her secret, content with telling her parents.

She returned to class Monday morning wearing her new clothes and her bauble.

18
Mrs. Vera Riley

Vera Batten lived with her future in-laws each weekend until the end of June when she returned for the summer with a letter addressed to Casey Riley from the Dean of the Faculty of Law confirming that her grades were in fact the highest of the academic year and worthy of a future position at Riley Corporation.

Her successful meeting with the Riley panel took place that week.

Her second sexual encounter with Edward, which was also her pre-marital last, was the first day at his home months earlier. Casey did not want his son's proclivity turning the wedding into any more of a necessity than currently required. The child would come as planned, not a day earlier.

Vera's parents finally did believe her when flying from Chicago to Houston with pampered in-flight service, then certainly when touring the two luxury homes, the stables and Vera's future workplace.

True to their word Florence and Casey took her under their wings, introducing her to their society and making her comfortable with her new life. Furthermore, by late summer she was a passable riding companion for Florence.

Saturday, September 03rd, 1988 was her wedding day. The day before Edward, true to his word, deposited twenty million dollars into her account. Five million more was

184

deposited into Karina's account and that afternoon her lawyer petitioned the court for divorce.

She advised her husband matter-of-factly Friday evening when he returned beleaguered from a week-long trip, astounding him with the news that she was leaving him immediately. She was being fair. What few possessions she wanted had previously been removed. All else was his including the house. She was leaving the country for a two-week vacation to re-evaluate her future and she stood to walk out.

When he asked why, she explained in such taunting detail with dates and particulars that he could scarcely comprehend what she was saying. When he heard the man's name and saw Karina's smirk that was worse than any dagger she might have plunged into his chest, he said goodbye and waved her away.

He didn't see her leave, or turn once the door closed, too preoccupied on his first of many drinks.

Edward spent the evening in the company of friends and associates at a gentlemen's club. At home the next morning he woke with Karina who would remain there comfortably ensconced until leaving for the airport on Sunday.

From his bed she watched him dress and pack his suitcases for the honeymoon and when he left her she went about her day sunning and swimming.

Vera's bachelorette party was not very different from her groom's, her mother and Florence discreetly declining the invitation to join in. The younger women of the Riley legal department had taken charge, all of them in agreement that the most popular ladies' club in Houston was the perfect venue for a girls' night out.

She woke too few hours later to the gentle nudges of both mothers. Her day had arrived.

Vera's wedding was different from what she had dreamed of as a young girl. She knew a handful of the 400 plus guests, though she hadn't invited anyone from her side save her parents despite Florence's encouragement to do so. Nor had she thought to invite anyone from school. Although she did have relatives, she scarcely knew them and didn't see the point in tempting human nature.

Despite her age and notwithstanding her groom, she had nurtured a respectably low opinion of humankind throughout her legal studies.

Her father gave her away, leaving her in the care of another. Or so he believed. Her mother, too unnerved by everything that was happening began weeping, sitting with her hands laced into his. Her bride's maid was Katie Lands, the principal co-conspirator of the previous evening and a young woman fast becoming a good friend. She neither wanted nor needed anything from Vera. She was already an established attorney with an enviable professional profile at Riley Corp. with no one's help.

The bride was stunning in a simple A-line, sleeveless dress, a tiara dotted with diamonds and low-heeled pumps, paid for by her father who could now easily afford that kind of simplicity.

The ceremony was simple, held in a church for reasons of social propriety, the minister understanding the Riley family's disinclination towards higher powers. The bride and groom exchanged rings, kissed, and were man and wife till death would they part.

Or so everyone presumed.

The reception went on until the early hours of Sunday, man and wife retiring to their hotel room to officially consummate their union free of pretence. They undressed, acted out their respective roles and went to sleep facing opposite walls.

Vera knew about Karina. Not a big deal. She was more interested in the father of her first child. She hadn't expected in her wildest dreams that she would be a wife at twenty-two and a mother one year later. Not once since her first year at law school did she think to miss taking a single

186

pill. Her career was all too important.

Nor had she ever thought to become a millionaire overnight. The best lawyer in any top ranking law firm, yes, but certainly not all the aforementioned at once.

How many times had her most recent ex called her since she'd met Edward, pleading with her to reconsider? She snorted. He was probably already on campus for his final year, along with the other two exes, hunting, competing for the younger first-year students, hoping at least for second or third before settling for fourth-year girls who were older and more jaded by their years on the campus merry-go-round.

Edward was thirteen years her senior. She assumed Casey would go first, followed by Florence in fifteen, maybe twenty years as a worst case scenario which would put Edward at fifty-five and her at forty-two. She would be young and attractive, even more so if things worked in her favour and what couldn't she then do with her accrued experience and 100 million.

She drifted to sleep smiling. For all she cared, Karina could move in with them.

*

They woke separately Sunday morning foregoing the eager caresses of newlyweds. He was already dressed. She woke shortly after, showering and dressing as he ordered room service.

When they were finished eating they left holding hands. They stepped into the taxi holding hands and walked to the airline ticket agent holding hands. Once they passed security they walked farther apart, albeit pleasantly.

The flight lasted three hours, Vera by the window, Edward taking the aisle seat within an arm's length of Karina.

The Caribbean resort was adults only, a party place for singles and open-minded couples, some young, some fearing the onslaught of their forties, divorcés searching for something years younger if not nubile, and divorcées hoping for a chance at one last memory of handsome and virile before nature ridiculed them. Not quite the honeymoon destination they had described to their parents.

The island paradise was an escape to one's dreams where names didn't matter. The common consensus being that mutual hedonism was far less expensive than divorce. What mattered were bodies and not trading the one you were with for another of a lesser quality.

Edward Riley wasted no time reconnoitring the compound searching for a man reasonably fitting his description. To his surprise he came across a few, chuckling, thinking he would give Vera her choice. Why not be magnanimous, since he had Karina?

Sex with twenty-two-year-olds in a shared dorm room on a single mattress as old as she was, Vera discovered, was no better than getting laid in her parents' unheated basement. Nor were a few guys squeezing her breasts like sponges or sucking them like beer bottles the same as several hundred strangers seeing them bare at the beach.

Her shyness didn't matter. A deal was a deal. She pulled away her top, very aware of all the men nearby paying particular attention to her. She was up for grabs, Edward suggesting perhaps he should stand her on a platform and start the bidding. She ignored him, resisting her temptation to flip him the bird.

Two of the men were married, at the resort with their wives. Each was willing, as were the wives. Two others were single, on the hunt, hopeful. They were equally willing once seeing Vera oiled and glistening, though Edward was abstaining, smirking. He wasn't into three-guy foursomes, however if she wanted to play doubles that was fine. Besides, he had other plans.

So did she, she walked away.

Vera chose the first couple, not the least bit wary. He

was late twenties and, she justified, she would have had another boyfriend for the current school year anyway. The guy was good-looking, svelte and he seemed easy-going. His wife was pretty with a nice body, her age, as naked as she was, and why not?

The man suggested dinner together, expecting he would leave with Vera, anxious, the woman expecting she would leave with Edward, curious. That's how things worked. Both surprised to hear otherwise over poolside drinks.

The four were at the resort for two weeks. Edward wanted the man to do Vera every one of those days as often as possible. Go for bust. She was practically insatiable. She could never get enough and he wanted her to enjoy her vacation. The more the merrier with one proviso: Vera would be his single diversion apart from his wife whom Edward might enjoy once in a while. Variety was, after all, the spice of life. In addition, if they agreed to exclusivity, he would give them ten thousand dollars on their last day.

They looked to Vera who nodded. He was telling the truth.

They agreed, Edward arranging immediately for suites in the same villa, after which he went to spend his evening and night with Karina, not surprised that Vera wasn't in their bed the next morning when he walked in to change for the beach.

The couple with Vera woke late, Vera sandwiched between them. The evening was a success, early morning coming too soon, Vera gradually blinking her eyes open to the young man's gentle thrusts and heat of his wife's mouth on her breasts, the man reminding her in an easy voice that Edward had said 'as often as possible'. Yes, he did. Didn't he? She closed her eyes, forgetting Edward and time.

The women kissed and touched while the man showered. Not kissing seemed somewhat silly. When he was dry they showered, sitting on the veranda with towels knotted at their hips to enjoy a morning coffee.

Of course the couple was curious, Vera answering that they quite simply had an open marriage and that her husband was at the club with another woman who was known to her. She wanted them for the entire two weeks, she added, because she thought they were a good match and she didn't want to spend her time being hassled. Nor was she disappointed.

That was the extent of her explanation over the two weeks, by which time she was as uninhibited with the woman as she was with the man, surprised by how much she would miss them when they kissed goodbye their last morning. Time had passed so quickly.

Edward hadn't once visited with them to try the man's wife. Nor did Vera ever tell him how dynamic the couple was with her, or that she was as good with women as she was with men. He had Karina.

The couple was reluctant to accept the ten thousand after such an unforgettable vacation with Vera; never aware of what they had accomplished beyond incredible and seamless sex with a beautiful woman they called by no other name than Vera.

Eight weeks later, home for the weekend, at dinner with Florence and Casey, she made the announcement. Edward's surprise was real. The kid would come in early June. In the meantime Karina was nearby in a downtown condo, convenient to his office. She was finding herself, thinking to reinvent who she was. She wanted a restaurant and with Riley's influence she would certainly do well.

Vera left home at New Year's escorted by her husband. She wouldn't see Houston for five months and her husband only on weekends, never enquiring as to how he spent his weekday evenings. She knew, and supposed not always with Karina whom she felt no malice towards. They'd even spoken together during the flight home from the honeymoon. Business was business. Her body was a means to an end and she was being well-paid for the ruse.

She was set up as promised in a luxury hotel apartment with a live-in housekeeper and a limo driver paid to make her schedule his. She was the envy of the most affluent students whose résumés either had not yet been accepted or were destined to commence their law careers as clerks.

Each day she woke expecting to refuse yet another request for a special favour, her sense of people proven and unwavering.

She graduated in early June at the top of her class, her parents and the Rileys sitting front row centre for the ceremony. A week later she was a mother with her nanny appointed, her office at Riley redecorated with her name etched into the glass panel of her door. Her dream had come true, many years ahead of schedule.

Edward had no idea whether the boy resembled him in any way. How would he? He'd never before seen a live infant up close. That it could grow into a reasonable facsimile of him or any other man seemed unlikely. More unthinkable was that any woman would willingly endure such a lengthy malaise for no better reason than to create a likeness of what was, more likely than not, below average, substandard. So what was the point beyond a careless disregard for the future?

He wanted out and left to spend his night with Karina.

Once at home Vera spent her summer recuperating, riding with Florence, working out with a trainer a few hours each day and occasionally doing lunch or Saturday shopping sprees with Katie Lands who also kept her current on the office politics of Riley Corp. By September anyone seeing her semi-nude would not believe for a moment she had a three-month-old at home. She looked magnificent, anxious for her vacation.

She and Edward chose the same resort once more, in part hoping to meet up with the couple from the year before, disappointed when they did not.

This time they displayed even less pretence, occupying

separate suites, Vera free to do whatever with whomever and whenever once the participant was selected. He just wanted her pregnant.

His suite he shared with Karina.

The first afternoon they spent searching for a suitable lover, an unwary donor while Karina infused herself with the heat of the midday sun, stretched out naked for the most part on her chaise-longue, savouring each admiring glance and envious stare.

This time Vera took the lead when she saw a couple she believed would prove compatible. She didn't need him negotiating for her.

They were mid-twenties, not married and had come in on the same plane. They had noticed her, they admitted. No kidding. Who wouldn't? The guy was thinking maybe, uncertain because Vera exuded the good life. The girl was occasionally bi- and beautiful. That's why they had come to the resort, hoping for a single woman with no strings attached, willing to include another guy if need be.

They came from a small town, saving all year to pretend they were someone different, like in the magazines they bought each week in a neighbouring town. Their vacation would last two weeks before returning home to teach English and math in a local high school.

Vera explained that she was alone. She and her husband were open, preferring to vacation this way instead of cheating. They had rooms in separate villas. He wasn't a problem, nor was he interested in joining them. He had other plans.

She was serious, she assured them. She liked them. They were sexy. They were her kind of couple and she thought they could have fun together with no pressure, providing they spent the entire two weeks with her. She wanted a commitment. She didn't want a different guy each night, or have to hunt until she found another couple with a willing woman.

The Fatal Diners' Club

They were perfect for her. So here was the deal. To ensure they would not abandon her midway through her vacation she would give them a gift of twenty thousand dollars cash with ten of that sum up front. She was somewhat of a nymphomaniac. She was addicted to girls since her first time a year earlier, she admitted, touching the girl's hand, smiling. She liked what she liked, completely free of guilt. She liked what she was seeing, and would give as much of herself in return.

They giggled. They thought she was joking or crazy. She wasn't one or the other. She was dead serious, dropping a small bundle into the young woman's beach bag before removing her top. The deal was done.

They had a first-floor room looking out onto a garden. She had a third-floor suite overlooking the ocean. Not a difficult choice to make.

From then on she waved at Edward and Karina on the beach or at dinner or from the poolside bar. She had to admit Karina was a looker from head to toe. Although she hadn't changed her opinion about Edward, so that little cozy triangle would never happen. Not that she had neglected her husband in their bed since the marriage.

She had played the good wife on several occasions in the sense she was fulfilling a contract, nothing more. He didn't expect gleeful yelps, anything out of the ordinary or depleted bodies collapsing onto dampened sheets. He got what he wanted, what he agreed to in writing, something to carry him over until his next visit with Karina or someone equally outstanding: Mundane marital intercourse preceded by the mandatory ritual of snapping on latex irrespective of when she might be properly and permanently protected against any future child-related incidents. She didn't mind that he was fucking Karina, the woman was exclusive. He wasn't.

She didn't care who he screwed or how often as long as he came home clean and she was quite certain Karina imposed the same restriction. She chortled. He was thirty-seven and dressing for sex like a teenager.

At the end of the two weeks she paid the young couple with a second ten grand as though thanking them for a small favour with an inexpensive trinket. Having a better time with them would be impossible. She couldn't imagine. She was with them most hours of the day, often alone with the girl and, although she enjoyed them somewhat equally, she considered him as pragmatic; the girl was the fun part. She kissed them each goodbye at the airport shuttle before stepping into a taxi, not once acknowledging them once onboard the return flight.

She was friendly toward Karina from a distance. They each had a purpose in his life with no reason for one woman to dislike the other. Karina felt the same, that in another time and place they might have been friends.

Vera began at Riley October 02nd '89; not once disappointing Casey throughout her first eight months, not once taking time to lament or bemoan her coming child whom she knew would be good-looking and charming. What better memento of a wonderful time?

Nevertheless, as was expected, office politics blossomed with fresh gossip and supposition. She worked as hard as anyone, harder, assisted by Katie Lands whom she had requested specifically one day over lunch with Casey, making very clear to her immediate boss not long after that she need not be reminded of her exclusion from family status when at the office.

Neither, she was certain, need he be reminded that she had graduated first in her class at Columbia and really did not need Riley Corp. She was more than willing to show him the letters she'd received from the country's many highly respected law firms, many of them in Texas, many of them at odds with Riley over various issues. However that would mean leaving Riley...with her children. And what would Casey and Edward think of that?

They understood each other.

The following June her son was a year old, her daughter missing the birthday party by less than a week.

Florence and Casey were elated, delighted with their granddaughter. They remained at the hospital most of the day cooing over the child. The Riley Corporation now had a choice of heirs apparent.

Edward made an appearance for a few moments with flowers once his parents had gone, leaving soon after to attend a dinner meeting, Vera asking him to be certain to offer Karina her fondest wishes. He would, of course.

Despite having seen the girl's father on several occasions at the resort, he couldn't distinguish the resemblance and didn't care. His father and mother would be blinded by their inordinate love for Vera. She could do no wrong. So how would they possibly think to consider the truth of what she had done to deceive them?

Vera's parents spoke to her from Italy. Despite their windfall, or because of it, she didn't see them very often. Either likelihood wasn't much of an issue.

Katie Lands stayed the longest with her, taking the day off work. Vera wanted her best friend near and Casey saw no reason why that shouldn't happen. The women's immediate boss agreed.

*

Vera retuned to work in late September after weeks of demanding sessions with her fitness trainer and the vacation she had planned to relax, to show off her new body and test her resolve.

Edward left her at the airport. He and Karina were departing from another gate where Karina was waiting for him, maintaining the utmost decorum until onboard.

Once Vera was certain their flight had departed she cancelled her flight, stayed one night at the airport hotel and departed the next morning for the island resort she'd become accustomed to with the same agenda in mind as with the couple who fathered her daughter the year before.

She had ironically discovered through Edward what would make her time with him tolerable. She was excited, turned-on by the prospect of another young woman, yet willing to appease her husband or boyfriend if need be.

The need never arose and the blissful experience was far from what she had imagined in spite of her past indulgences. This time money was not a consideration. Nor did she or the woman have to clean themselves before making pseudo-love for an impatient male audience. This time they simply gave themselves over to hedonistic release without spectators unless at the pool or the ocean, neither woman expecting more than final warm embraces at the airport.

Their time together was over except for fond memories that would fade with time. For the wife of Edward Riley to even contemplate approaching a photo lab with such brazen moments frozen in time was folly. The scandal would ruin Casey's family, in spite of which she had memories and plans for many more vacations without him.

Her contract with Edward stated that she would be faithful as a wife until divorced, the clear implication being that she would never fornicate with another man once her children were born. No mention was ever made of women who were now an intoxicating diversion well beyond an acquired taste. She was discovering who she was and for that she thanked him.

In retrospect none of her ex-partners were any good. She understood that for the first two she was purely a receptacle, her status for the three at college not much better, simply more accessible. She was one of many and probably forgotten. Her children's fathers were much better, she admitted, eager to please her, attentive and lustful. However with two young and naked women in his bed what guy wouldn't feel the pressure to perform well.

That's why they frequented such resorts, to prove themselves, satiating their egos.

As for Edward, she didn't understand what Karina saw in him. He was average at best, no better than her other five, most times Vera waiting until he was asleep to finish the job for him. There had to be money involved, she believed. The larger question was: How could she spend the next eighteen years focused on vacations while having protected sex with a husband who cheated on her as well as Karina? She couldn't. Nor would she, not after what he'd virtually forced her to recognize as her true self.

For the better part of a year she'd wondered, doubting herself. The girl was beautiful and beautiful was a non-negotiable requisite. She'd been spoiled by her holiday romances. Yet Katie didn't have a boyfriend. Vera didn't believe so. She never spoke of anyone special, always attending company functions alone and leaving early.

At any rate Katie was her preoccupation throughout the homeward flight. She was determined to know, arriving home a day late. She was resolved, anticipating the inquisition. She would no longer be the on-demand vessel for a despotic liar and general SOB.

Edward met her at the door, waiting for the chauffeur to place her luggage. He wasn't pleased; she didn't care.

"Your flight arrived yesterday, Vera. Care to explain why?"

"I made a last-minute change. My flight arrived today and, before you get stupid about it, I had an affair."

"Did you, really? I can't say I'm surprised." He closed the door. "You do realize you're admitting to a breach of contract."

"I'm not any such thing. What I am is a lawyer. Remember? I spent the entire two weeks with a woman, a very desirable and attentive woman. Where I did so is not your business. I will tell you, however, that I do plan to continue my vacations without you each year for that very reason. Our agreement stands as drawn up by you and your legal counsel without any mention of other women. That, Edward, is a legal loophole…your oversight." She chortled. "What? You didn't think for a moment that women would find me attractive? Well, they do. What's most amusing is that I have you to thank for the new me."

"You're overlooking your marital obligations as agreed to."

"No, I am not. I'm telling you outright that until you stop fucking around on me and your girlfriend you're SOL in this house, although I never did understand why you would want to spend more time pulling on a condom than using one."

"That was your rule."

"Rules change."

"You're telling me you're a lesbian, just like that. It's a little sick, Vera."

"For 120 million, yes, I believe I am a lesbian, or could be. At the very least I have very much enjoyed my few departures from disappointing male prodding, yours included if you must know. Five boys and three men, yet I'm zero for eight on the Richter arousal scale. I'm not good with that. As for sick, sick is asking your wife to seriously fuck two strangers and waiting for your parents to die so you can dump her kids without ruining your future. That's sick, really sick."

Edward filled a snifter generously with cognac. "And I'm not good with you fucking other women."

"Then we'll have dinner tonight with your darling Karina. In fact, I'll call her myself. You simply promise each of us exclusivity and, fine, I'll settle for you. I'm sure Karina will be very pleased."

"That won't happen, not in this lifetime."

"Then we're done here, aren't we? You have your two kids, a very lovely girlfriend, who knows how many younger girls on the side, and a wife you will divorce in a few years after discovering her deviant indiscretions. That's a pretty good life, the one you wanted. Further to which, in my view as well as legally, what I choose to do with another woman or women is not your affair."

"You're a mother."

"I'm a child bearer whose resultant offspring will have the best of everything now and after the divorce with as much affection as I can honestly provide so that they will grow normally into adulthood. Do I love them? No, I do not. To expect that much is unreasonable when they were borne of debauchery and profit."

"Pleasurable debauchery and mutual profit and now you're setting new rules."

"I'm modifying yours within the spirit of our contract so that we each survive the coming years. You're stuck with me, Edward, and thank you for offering me a drink…how gentlemanly of you."

She went to the bar, silence reverberating across the room.

"My apologies, I was remembering a girl stripped naked a few feet from the doors of her alma mater fucking me on the grass for a thousand dollars. That, Vera, is a whore by any definition."

"That's right. I was fucking you, not the inverse. For 120 million and a career, get it right.
Anyone's a willing whore for that kind of payback, Edward. You included. Or do we tell your parents about the origin and raison d'être of their grandkids? " Vera sipped her cognac, easing onto a sofa. "I didn't believe so."

"I could divorce you now. I've got the 100 million."

Vera drifted to another time and place for a moment without realizing she was smirking.

"That wouldn't work, husband. First, what reason would you give? Adultery would cause me to lose my job and your parents would insist that you maintain custody of the children. We're too early into this situation to claim

199

irreconcilable differences, not after playing the happy couple so well, and that would lead to a custody battle, shared visitation, and you'd never be rid of me. I do however agree with the concept of an early divorce. So in accordance with this unexpected codicil of yours, we will from this point forward maintain separate bedrooms and sleep more peacefully without the needless awkwardness of this ridiculous charade. No one needs to know except, of course, Karina who I'm sure will welcome news of your self-imposed deprivation." She put up her hand. She wasn't finished. "In addition to which, assuming your parents, whom I really do adore very much, will live at most another twenty years," she glanced at her watch, "and considering you have the funds, I will expect annual deposits into my personal account of five million dollars each year on the 25th of September beginning tomorrow. In consideration of how warmly I have come to feel towards Florence and Casey, I cannot now possibly think to gain by their deaths. That part of our contract must change. Should they pass on earlier than expected I would expect the balance in a lump sum. Should they endure, which is my sincerest hope, I will have been paid in full."

Edward coughed his last gulp of cognac from his throat. "Fuck you. That would mean anywhere from one-fifty to 200 accrued, not at all what we agreed."

"You'll be inheriting billions, poor you." She lounged into the sofa. "We'll make the changes contractually tomorrow, in exchange for which I will maintain the ruse and you can spend as much time as you wish with Karina and your bimbos. Hell, you can even divorce me secretly and marry her for all I care. I mean, really, what would be the difference?"

"And if I don't?"

"I'll go to your father explaining my version of the truth with irrefutable documentation. You know as well as I do he doesn't like you very much, Edward. No shit. In addition to which I will sue for divorce and custody, the house and half of everything notwithstanding the prenup claiming mental abuse, sexual abuse and adultery. Imagine the press. Of course you could certainly fight for custody, explaining to your father your version of my first twenty million and our side-bar contract. I'm certain he would be extremely delighted by your expectation of his and Florence's early passing, almost as much as Karina's delight at becoming a stepmother."

Edward refilled his glass, not measuring. His blood pressure alone would burn off any ill effect. His parents could well endure into their late nineties.

"Four million a year, take it or leave it. No discussion, no bullshit with suitable adjustments when they die. I will live with Karina except for family dinners, visits and any other family obligation I have to tolerate with my parents. I will spend the occasional night for the sake of appearance...happily in the guestroom and maintain a wardrobe here. As far as the spawn are concerned, daddy dearest works a lot. I'll do the occasional weekend and special occasion so they don't inadvertently fuck us up and how you explain your aberrant appetite for pussy to them is your problem. Are we agreed?"

"I believe we are. Shall we say your counsel's office tomorrow at nine? We'll take separate cars, of course."
*

Monday afternoon, holding her breath, Vera stepped into Katie's office inviting her friend to dinner. She wanted to feel excited. Instead she was burdened throughout the rest of her day with worry.

They left Riley Corp. late and drove together discussing their day. The restaurant was elegant, serving French cuisine and chosen by Vera because she wouldn't be recognized by staff or guests. The wine was delicious, enjoyed by one woman and much needed by the other.

"Thanks for the invite, Vera. It's been a while. I was beginning to feel ignored and about to invite you out somewhere to ask what was wrong."

"I wasn't ignoring you, far from it, and nothing is wrong. But Katie, I do have a reason for tonight."

"What's up?"

"I have to know why a stunning woman who's young and successful is continuously alone and never talks about the man or men in her life. Or you can tell me to mind my own business."

Katie was relaxed, not in the least put off by Vera's forthright curiosity. "Simply put I have no man in my life, Vera."

Vera sipped her wine, grinning. "You're not lesbian, are you?"

"Yes, I am, albeit a single one right now." She paused. "Now what happens? I hope we're not going to sit here all tongue-tied and uncomfortable. And please don't ask me what it's like, Vera. Besides, I haven't had a date in years. I'm not into one-nighters, dykes, or the lesbo club thing. And I promise I won't hit on you."

Each woman sipped her wine, each woman certain of what the other was thinking.

"I don't have to ask, Katie. I know what it's like to love a woman." She gulped a mouthful of Bordeaux. "Three times, actually…while vacationing. I virtually shacked up with them, especially the last one." She forced a smile. "So, you see, I'm not into one-nighters either."

Katie put her goblet on the table. "You're bi-? No kidding."

"It's complicated. Edward and I have an agreement. I was bi-curious after our marriage and until yesterday. Now, for a number of reasons, I'm taking out a full membership. No qualms." She giggled, feeling better about herself, "and no male residue."

"He knows?"

"And he doesn't care as long as I'm discreet. Like I said, we have an agreement, legal and binding. Anyway, let's forget him. I'm not at all surprised that you are and, that being the case, not to mention how good friends we are, I was wondering. I've been wondering for a long time."

"I have to admit you have put me to sleep a few times, Vera. If you're interested, you're pretty hot stuff."

"So I've been told. So are you, if you're interested."

"Shit, Vera, we work together."

"He'll be around on a needs basis as part of our agreement. If he screws up he'll lose all chance of inheriting Riley. If I do, which I won't, I'm still set for life. I could open my own firm tomorrow on the top floor of any building in any city."

"So...?"

"So let me sleep over tonight. We should have things figured out one way or the other by morning, if we haven't already. I want at least to try. How else will we know?"

*

Vera and Katie woke together the next morning. They weren't the least bit timid, ashamed or remorseful, simply more honest with each other about each other. They never separated.

By the time Vera's son was six he was prepared for private boarding school. His sister followed a year later. From which time and throughout their secondary educations Vera saw them on special occasions and over the summer months with good reason. She wanted them prepared for their destinies in a not too distant future.

In the final year of the boy's private primary education, his grandfather celebrated his eighty-fifth year, still vital, whispering in Florence's ear each night how much he adored her. A few evenings later, without the slightest indication, Casey Riley passed away peacefully in his sleep without ever discovering Vera's secret or that his son's vile deception was nearing completion.

Not five years later, Vera called her son home from his first months of higher education in Europe. His grandmother was dying.

At the precipice of her final hour Florence wanted a few moments alone with her lawyer and Vera, dismissing her son from her bedside, kissing her grandchildren farewell before shooing them away.

Vera, thirty-nine, was speechless. Florence, together with Casey, had decided not to trust Vera's future to an unfit husband and father. Edward, they knew, had met the very minimum of his familial responsibilities. He was a disappointment to them. To that end she, as much as her beloved Casey, was bequeathing to her before an officer of the court the sum of 200 million dollars. The money held in trust for her with the lawyer since Casey's death to avoid estate tax difficulties.

Florence loved her grandchildren dearly. They would be provided for separately, the more modest funds held in trust until age thirty-five. They were more humble than their father, though Florence did admit to Vera with a weak smile that she and Casey never did quite see the Riley resemblance.

She summoned her son, Edward arriving moments too late. His mother was dead, mother and son as distant in death as in life, Edward turning to leave without a single tear of regret.

*

Florence Riley was laid to rest two days later without much ceremony in accordance with her wishes. No one would any longer gain from knowing her. She was an era gone by. So what was the point?

Edward Riley was fifty-two, already ensconced as chairman of Riley Corporation for several years and heavily involved in politics with Karina standing faithfully by his side.

The following morning he filed for divorce taking full possession of his and his parents' homes, livid at legally owing his wife forty million when he'd just been made aware of his mother's hypocritical largess towards Vera which he had no legal recourse to reverse. He formally disowned and discredited her children without their knowledge, removing Vera as well as Katie Lands from Riley Corp. for which the women each filed a successful suit claiming wrongful dismissal. Weeks later, on the advice of his counsel, he chose not to appeal.

Instead he married Karina Montoya who chose to keep her name.

Vera Batten and Katie Lands moved to New York to open the top-floor law offices of Batten Lands amidst the daytime madness and nighttime glitter of Time Square, their client list a virtual who's who registry.

They had too much in their future together to plan, too much to anticipate without wasting precious moments reliving the past. Not until 2010 when Vera's son returned home with his sister did the children discover with little or no remorse from their mother that they were Battens with no claim to the Riley Empire.

Vera explained their origins, that they were half brother and sister, that their two biological fathers were deliberate holiday trysts unknown to her. The men were a means to a selfish end that culminated five years earlier with the passing of Florence Riley.

She would certainly be available to assist them with whatever situation required a mother's guiding hand if need be, though, in truth, she hoped they were sufficiently educated and prepared to manage their respective futures without her influence. They were, in fact, very close to the age at which she had first met Edward Riley and, most certainly, more privileged.

The girl wept openly, the young man sat stoically cold.

He never did like Edward Riley, his always absent father. He took his sister's hand. They had each other. Mother could go to hell for what she had done. As for Riley, nothing too horrible could befall him.

Vera understood, insisting they remain a while longer. Despite what they might believe, no doubt as a result of sudden shock, she was not a bad person if not a good mother. She was not finished. She gave them each a cheque for ten million dollars, sufficient funds to begin their lives together or apart. She added that Florence and Casey Riley were unknowingly never their grandparents. They were lovely people, never aware of the truth, and loved the children they believed were their grandchildren.

At age thirty-five they would inherit a financial gift from Florence, thirty-five so that they might have time to make their way in life without the crutch of someone else's wealth. Until then the bequest would be managed for them.

Her son asked with what firm and how much.

She didn't know. She never asked. Nor was the question appropriate. Suffice it to say Casey and Florence lived their lives as Thatcher and Betty Riley would have wanted, for the betterment of the world around them. In that way Edward Riley was an aberration. As for the firm, they would be advised in due course. He was twenty-one with a small fortune. What else need he know?

Her daughter asked whether Vera had ever loved her.

Vera answered truthfully. Her affection towards them assumed the form of preparedness against present and future hardships, their present now confronting them. She harboured no misgiving regarding their readiness to meet the real world head-on.

The girl persisted, wrenching the colour from her hands.

Vera was blunt. Subterfuge would serve no purpose. Her marriage to Edward Riley was a sham, a business arrangement for which she was well-paid. Both requisite and subsequent children resulted from prearranged adulteries. The fathers were chosen for their suitability and handsomely compensated for their service to ensure sufficiently frequent coital interaction and a guarantee of success. Neither man, nor their wives who participated in the encounters, was ever aware of her true purpose. They did however know of Edward Riley, without the knowledge of his name, who at the time was playing his own games with Karina Montoya somewhere not far away.

The separate experiences were far from a disagreeable mandate. Each father was educated and kind, as were the wives who unabashedly and tenderly brought her to the gateway of a new existence each time the men had nothing more to give. As for her children, no, she could not pretend to love them per se.

Her son scoffed. Did she ever love anyone?

Yes. She loved Katie Lands unconditionally. She had for fifteen years, tenderly and unabashedly once through her gateway to freedom.

The young man jerked to his feet, accusing her. She was loathsome, disgusting. His sister followed his lead, not as certain, lost for words, appalled by the revelation, each one feeling cheated and mistreated, neither one thinking to embrace or kiss the cheek of the woman sitting impassively and calm across from them. They had lived as sister and brother for twenty years, apart more often than together, stunned to learn that all they had was each other.

Neither did he or she consider for a moment to thank their mother for what Vera had done, each one believing they were deserving of more. Nor did they say goodbye. They simply walked out to forget her behind a closed door.

Vera understood their emotion, fully aware she would never see them again. She was fine with that. Nor would she ever think to question her life choices. She had Katie whom she likely would never have dared to love had she not known those men and their wives or the third woman who'd convinced her not to waste her life in loneliness.

Quite possibly the children were borne of debauchery, or possibly of a heightened pleasure most parents whether ordinary or wealthy could never fathom. Either way, she hadn't once forsaken her responsibility. She was content with the role she had played in their conception and their lives.

There was no part of Thatcher or Casey in the boy to infuse him with self-determination, no part of Betty or Florence in the girl to instill in her the courage and single-mindedness of Riley women. More to the point, no part of Edward Riley existed within them to make the world a worse place.

They would make their way in the world without the impediments of their fathers' inherent flaws or the presumption of success due in part to the men's abilities merged with hers. They would have no one to blame or commend but themselves. In that they were fortunate, if not yet sufficiently wise or worldly to be grateful.

She was content to believe she had done her best for them, certain Florence and Casey would understand now that they might have discovered the truth.

19
Priscilla Vendôme

Whereas Thatcher Riley was breathlessly smitten with Betty until his death and thereafter, his son's love for Florence no less consuming, Edward Riley's love for Karina was as deep as his need to share the bodies of women belonging in marriage or wishful thinking to other men.

Unlike his granddaddy in Thatcher's formative years, he had no good reason to fear God. He didn't gamble; he didn't wear twin revolvers on his hips and whether or not a woman might be a whore was solely a matter of interpretation.

He didn't fear God because he became increasingly wealthy from the day preceding his first marriage to his chairmanship at Riley, though he never denied that God did have purpose in his life. Despite the enlightened era God was essential for effective networking, a primary contact for meeting the right people with similar beliefs, motives, and practical faith.

Of course he funded charities, goodwill homes and summer camps so that he would not fall from God's grace during his frequent absences from his front row pew, never giving credence to what people thought, said, or believed of him. He was what he was. He was neutral with the means to do whatever he pleased for or against whomever.

He had never killed anyone, not directly, despite indifferently guiding many to their real or perceived ruin, once overheard postulating at a former associate's funeral that the meek would only ever inherit the earth by being buried in it. Nor had he ever saved anyone or encouraged anyone's potential. That was neither his life's mission nor his concern. If you were not already exceptional he didn't want to know you.

Pricilla Vendôme, however, to whom he was introduced in 2012 when she was thirty-one to his fifty-nine years, was exceptional in the seductive appeal of her body and her brilliant mind.

He didn't care about foreign affairs, wars or tribal conflicts in remote villages, though she did. Let the State Department, Congress, the military, arms dealers and journalists fight for whatever each one could gain from disputes in oil-rich countries. War was requisite to their commerce and reputations, no less than superior strategies were to clan chieftains, generals and disposable combatants.

That is how Edward Riley understood God: Requisite. Despite history's most enlightened era God was paradoxically essential to his acceptance in circles he viewed as crucial. Not that he cared or imagined that Thatcher and Casey might be turning in their graves. They were dead, forgotten. He had a strategy, a plan for which he needed God's good grace to make the world a better place, which he would undertake for what he judged was a reasonable price. Although, in his mind, God was indeed the servant.

War would always exist. His concern, his mission was his homeland. The country was not going to hell in a hand basket the way many believed, they were already engulfed in flames with their hands and feet shackled by false morals, engrained social mores, and the delusory belief of a mindless child that somehow God would smite them for doing what was right.

They'd gone too far, blindly mocking their futures like an emaciated cancer victim smoking a ten-inch Cuban on his deathbed.

He had no visible or confessed interest in active politics; his preoccupation was the ever weakening state of politics and the ill-conceived, ill-motivated direction of politics driven by men and women with more money than vision. He was neither Democrat nor Republican. He was Edward Riley, puppeteer, maker and breaker of men…or women, as the case may be.

He never knew the need or the urgency to lobby or beg for funding to get things done, very much the inverse. Notwithstanding his offshore accounts, he was the wealthiest man on the continent. Others begged him, prostrating their dignity unashamedly before him in the guise of mutual advantage while washing down lavish lunches and dinners with bottles of 300-dollar wine in posh restaurants and exclusive clubs.

He was the last Riley. His legacy would not be the Riley name preserved by someone else's bastard children, nor the corporation built on a foundation of gold dug from the frozen ground by weathered and bleeding hands. No. His legacy would be the first female president of the United States and what they would accomplish together. He had a vision.

Seeing her in person for the first time, he knew.

*

The world saw Priscilla Vendôme as charismatic, unruffled and forthright. She was attractive and charming, though never swayed by another's captivation of her, never drawn in by the practiced or effusive hyperbole of those years older than her and decades more jaded. She listened when others ranted. She argued when others were less well-equipped or adversarial and she never cowered in the face of belligerence or disparagement and scorn.

Edward Riley never watched television. Who had the time? He paid others to keep him current with world and financial events. He also paid them to maintain Riley Corp. as an elite paradigm in the business world. For that reason he listened to his VP of Marketing who just happened to room with Priscilla Vendôme throughout their four years of college.

He had no idea who she was or what she did, though he trusted his executive staff implicitly until they disappointed him. He watched her New York morning news show throughout an entire month before concurring with the marketing executive.

He believed the Vendôme woman was what he needed to head up his Communications Division headquartered in Chicago, from which point her past became decidedly less private. He saw something in her. She was undoubtedly Riley material and was summoned to Houston by his personal staff, Priscilla Vendôme excited by the prospect of a rare and exclusive interview while disappointed that cameras would not be permitted for the one-on-one.

She didn't come from money, working hard at whatever she did to compensate throughout her college years, bearing the weight of selfishness at throwing her parents into debt in order to graduate from Yale with honours at twenty-one.

Nothing in her past lingered to haunt her. Her slate was clean excepting a small number of fortunate hopefuls who could actually boast or remember that they had once screwed the host of a national TV show. She had no current boyfriend, hadn't for some time, nor was she a lesbian. She drank socially, didn't do drugs and her health was excellent. She wasn't in debt and she had begun amassing an enviable 401K portfolio.

She was pristine in 21st century terms. What failed to surprise him was that she vacationed at an exclusive island resort as part of her perk portfolio at the network, a retreat designed and available to the most affluent and discriminating guests. With good reason, he believed, which he ascribed to good negotiating on her part. She was undeniably eye appealing. Her body was one thing, from what he could imagine. However, put Priscilla Vendôme in a thong or without her top on a beach anywhere else in the world and she would become front-page news worldwide in a blink.

He was anxious to meet her. Her credentials were impressive, recorded for posterity in network archives. He'd viewed her in war zones amidst bombardments and hostile fire, though he didn't doubt for a moment that she'd pissed her khaki pants on more than one occasion. Who wouldn't?

She'd seen strife, poverty, death and hunger as much at home as abroad. She also had deep-rooted social goals, though she wasn't an activist. He believed because she knew better, which he viewed as a huge plus. No one liked or appreciated activists. They were taboo, trouble, single-minded zealots who could never see past their own narrow visions of a perfect world governed by them.

She'd paid her dues. She had balls. That's what he needed. That she might be the ultimate bitch was inconsequential. That she had disappointed her parents with her career choice was inconsequential. Middle-class she was not. What they thought or believed didn't matter.

He had a heads-up. She had arrived, driven by his chauffeur from the five-star boutique hotel where her suite was reserved for her convenience through the weekend. Riley interviews were rare and arduous undertakings not meant for the weak of heart, which was not his concern.

He had to admit he was taken aback. Most potential female executives came through his door in navy blue or black two-piece suits and low-heeled pumps. Not this one. Priscilla Vendôme was dressed in a bright yellow A-line skirt falling to a hand's width above her knees and a white silk blouse over a yellow camisole. She wore three-inch yellow Gucci sandals and her handbag was a snow-white Carolina Herrera. She had excellent taste and a fashion sense that had not fully come across on his inlaid flat screen.

Though what really surprised him were her stature and her voice. She was petite, topping 5'7" strapped into her Guccis, her soft voice and feminine allure far from what he expected, the absolute antithesis or her televised persona. She was authentic, completely delightful and quite impossible to imagine as a hard-ass news correspondent and indomitable morning show host.

He stood to greet her. "Good day, Ms. Vendôme. Thank you for coming all this way." They shook hands. "Welcome to Riley Corporation. Please, make yourself comfortable."

"Thank you for inviting me. However not having my crew with me is very irregular, Mr. Riley. I haven't done this since my school days. Taking notes, I mean."

"Is your suite to your liking?"

"Yes, thank you, a little piece of heaven that has unfortunately spoiled me."

"Which I suspect is somewhat of an overstatement, but thank you for saying so."

"I was stunned to hear from your office so unexpectedly, Mr. Riley, since you're such a private person."

"You may thank Ms. Corey, your once-upon-a-time roomie at Yale. She recommended you to me. I took the liberty of inviting her to join us for lunch."

Priscilla Vendôme's astonishment was real. "I haven't seen Pauline since graduation. We must have cried all that day. We were pretty close, until careers got in the way. Is she doing well?"

"Her office is down the hall from us. So yes, I would say she is doing very well. I'm sure you will have much to talk about this evening."

"Thank you. I will drop in to see her, though the interview shouldn't take longer than an hour or two. I appreciate your busy schedule and won't waste your time." She straightened her skirt, reaching into her handbag for a microcassette, pen and a notepad. "Shall we begin?"

"We already have, Ms. Vendôme. I did not ask you here to interview me. You are here so that I might interview you. I want to offer you a position at Riley Corp. Chicago. There are, of course, certain formalities, which is why I would prefer if you would remain in Houston over the weekend. I want you to leave here with a clear understanding of my expectations as well as your own and would expect a reply within a week."

She displayed no surprise, leaning forward. "Sir, thank you. I think, because I don't see a man of your calibre wasting time playing silly games. I appreciate your interest. However I have a job, a good job, which I was led to believe was the purpose of this appointment."

"You have a current position, Ms. Vendôme, a job as you say which has led you to Riley for a flourishing career. Which I believe in your case might well be a stepping stone to greater endeavours and much more significant accomplishments. You see, I know about you, Ms. Vendôme. We share common beliefs as we do uncommon misgivings. Please hear me out. Listen to what I have to say and take sufficient time without distraction to consider my offer."

"Sir, to say that without this interview my current standing will be a good deal less credible would be an understatement, unless you're the calf offered up for slaughter. On behalf of my team, let me thank you for making them work overtime this weekend. I'm sure you have heard about ratings, and my viewers do not like being cheated. They also have expectations that are more important to me than yours." She stood matter-of-factly, calm and collected. "Your personal assistant might have been more to the point on the phone. She's wasted your time and mine. Good day, sir. Please tune in Monday for the slaughter."

He stood, supressing a smile. He'd never been reprimanded by such a compelling woman. Most mortals, whether male or female, had trouble looking him in the eye.

He remained seated. "Would you have come…had you known?"

"No."

"Then I shall have to think of a suitable gift for my secretary to reward her collusion and, once again, encourage you to remain over the weekend. We have much to discuss and you will have your interview regardless of your considered response to my offer, which I will expect in a week's time."

"Listen, Mr. Riley, I'm good at what I do. I've worked hard to become the highest paid morning person east of the Mississippi at thirty-one. I'm at the top."

"I am aware of your remuneration, Ms. Vendôme, as well as your vertical success. Money is not an issue. Unless you believe a very substantial increase is problematic. As for being at the top, I believe you have underestimated yourself. Why would you choose to measure yourself by year-end salary negotiations based on uncertain ratings from those who are still in their pyjamas at nine AM?"

*

She had nothing to lose.

The interview lasted through the morning, with a luncheon at an intimate setting where old friends could reminisce while Riley looked on in quiet judgment, the more formal exchange of information continuing in his office until dinner when Edward Riley left her in the care of Ms. Corey so that she might bring a woman's perspective to the corporation and the Chicago position.

Saturday Priscilla Vendôme flew with him in private luxury to the Windy City. She saw the top floor, lake-view corner office that was waiting for her; she visited the lavish and expansive high-rise condo that could be hers boasting a guestroom, cinema room, personal gym with a full spa for the days she worked at home, and a panoramic view of

Lake Michigan, replying when asked that she would more than likely select a Vantage S Roadster. She preferred quiet luxury...with a kick.

He was good with that, a good choice reflecting her character.

She was good with six weeks' vacation and First-Class travel, still with a hundred questions whirling and colliding in her head. They met halfway. He drove her to the Aston Martin dealer to choose a colour, agreeing that the Chicago office would confirm the sale in a week's time.

Sunday Priscilla spent the day in Houston at the Riley Ranch whose stables Karina had converted to luxury parking spaces for her several vehicles.

She had long since accepted her husband's penchant for newness. She never questioned him, never worried over whose company he might keep or what he might do with any of them. She didn't have to. She knew: Young and beautiful. Despite which she welcomed young and beautiful Priscilla Vendôme into her home with genuine warmth.

What would be would be. She also knew that he always came home to her, not once ignoring her, not once making her ask for attention.

Sunday evening they dined out in Houston at the city's premier hotspot for fine cuisine and after-hours encounters. Reservations weren't required, whereas anyone else would reserve weeks in advance or chance to stand in line for a table at La Montoya.

The entire three days were impressive; daunting for a woman whose life was a repertoire of cataclysmic events and others' tragedies. Those were different. She was a spectator first on the scene deciding what others more fortunate would see and hear. This she was unprepared for. They were talking about her life, Edward Riley trying to reshape her future without warning.

She had no scriptwriter, no cameraman to record what she might have missed or forgotten, no editor to help her see through the maelstrom she was experiencing for the best ratings, the most impact.

Priscilla Vendôme knew inherently to miss her flight. Neither Riley nor Karina were finished talking. When they were she was dropped off at the airport and flown to New York by Riley Corp.'s private transportation.

The next morning she called Edward Riley on his private line. His interview would air the following day.

A month later the nation woke to hear the sad news. They would no longer wake to hear Priscilla Vendôme's undiluted perspectives of world events. They were selfish; most people were self-centred when faced with loss. No one cared that she was driving away from them in a cream-coloured Vantage S, not even her parents.

Part Two
20
Madam President

The first year at Riley Chicago went exceedingly well for Priscilla. Most Americans held a much better view and possessed a much better understanding of the far-reaching and shy corporation due to the hard work of the very media friendly and visible Priscilla Vendôme.

She was down to earth, a compassionate face on the body of Goliath. When head-on with business journalists she was believable, unshrinking and indefatigable, proving she hadn't lost her talent for ratings. They loved interviewing her as much as the public loved seeing her. They trusted her, believed in her. Even humdrum, terry-clad housewives tuned-in to news they could not understand.

They wanted more of Priscilla Vendôme who understood them and she quickly became a regular Friday morning favourite. They loved her.

She met with Edward Riley twice each month in either city, always alone for dinner, though often with Karina, irrespective of which their conversations invariably focused on their shared perspectives of the failing global and local human condition. They were of one mind on most social issues, Riley's most secretive thoughts increasingly unrelenting in their autonomous resolve to urge him forward the more he spoke with her, the more he understood her.

That he and Priscilla were occasional lovers was neither here nor there. He was attracted to her. Who would not be? To see her naked was to stand gaping at a flawless, laser-sculpted hologram. He was captivated by her smell and her texture. Quite apart from her willingness to be a team player, he often teased her.

In truth he began loving her as much as he loved Karina and wanted her more frequently.

Had the women been of an age, he often mused; his life would be enviable beyond the avaricious wishes of common men who dreamed of wealth and eternal youth. That was the difference: He reflected while other men chose to waste their time dreaming.

As it was he had them both in the short term, Priscilla entertaining him in her home when needed for mutual and convenient satisfaction, Karina on his arm as a showpiece and in his bed as a quintessential lover who never questioned his adoration.

Priscilla had no man in her life, though many had tried. Most of whom were married or significant to some other woman who didn't know better, lending credibility in their debilitated minds to the male myth, when unequivocally deprived of a one-nighter, that any woman as successful as she was invariably fucking her boss somewhere near or on the proverbial ladder.

That was not Priscilla Vendôme. She was pragmatic. She worked eighteen-hour days, she did not love Edward and she would not think for a moment to ruin Karina's home. Nor did she want complications. Men were possessive, no better than wolves, constantly obsessed with the need to piss protective rings around their packs and prized bitches, thinking to ward off pretenders to their hard won and newly coveted vaginas.

Edward Riley was a safe release. He was fit, more attractive than most men several years his junior and he performed well in bed, above average from what she recalled of her previous and increasingly vague experiences.

He never stayed over, he went home when nothing was left to discuss and he never spoke out of turn. They understood each other's boundaries until the evening he confessed his true motive for bringing her to Riley.

"I want you to become the next president, Priscilla."

The news didn't shock her. She'd learned years earlier to absorb good news and bad with the same analytical composure.

"Edward, I've scarcely been with you a year. I appreciate your confidence. I do. But I believe that might be a little premature. Don't you? Not to mention somewhat disruptive to the corporate intrigue and jealousy quotients." She whirled a chemise over her shoulders. "Not good to make executive decisions in a warm bed, Edward."

"You misunderstand. My executive personnel are fine the way they are. I'm talking about Washington. It's time for a change and you're it."

She was stunned, at first giggling, her composure spraying through her nose mixed with red wine. She abruptly stopped, wiping the back of her hand across her nose and mouth. She was horrified, her eyes unblinking, piercing his, the smooth lines of her face impassive. He wasn't joking. Not that he ever did.

He palmed her into silence with both hands before she could utter a single word.

"Hear me out. This country's too deep in their own shit to shovel out. What we need is a new era. We need to seed the manure that's suffocating us. We need to tear out dead stumps and plant fresh roots. There's a silent disquiet of mounting poverty in this nation that won't be quiet much longer. We're ill at ease as a nation. The whole country's on edge. Jane and Joe Nobody are afraid to go shopping. They're afraid to go to the movies and to school. Teachers are afraid of students, parents are afraid of their kids. That has to stop. The most dangerous part is that we block those fears from our conscious minds, those of us with minds, our everyday thinking, and we get brain-fucked when our worlds cave in. That makes you a potential victim as much as anyone else, Priscilla, even more so because you're female and a definite target because you're a beautiful female." He ignored her smile. "Don't think to make me believe for a moment you're not tired of the media constantly claiming to report the impartial facts while their sole intent is to blatantly promote violence and indifference towards so many of the nation's ills without ever telling the real story beyond a self-serving urgency for higher ratings and ephemeral shock value. You know better than me how photos of dead bodies are always more riveting, more entertaining and newsworthy than the drama of grieving families. The masses love the gore. They eat it up, fresh fuel for the nine-to-fivers at the water cooler. That is until something happens to them."

"Edward, you care about grieving families? That's a news flash. And, let's get something straight here. I never made dead bodies theatrical. Have you ever even seen a corpse, or smelled one up close and personal?"

"I wasn't talking about you. You're the exception, Priscilla, the exception in many ways. And yes, I viewed my parents in their coffins, though I fail to see how being an on-site witness, dare I say live, to a bullet-riddled or otherwise mutilated corpse would make me a better human being. You're quite right, though. I do not grieve for strangers. What would be the point and who's got the time? Why one and not the other? But you do, Madam President. The nation's gone to hell since you were sticky wet and your daddy, who probably did your mother more to prove to the world he wasn't shooting blanks, had not the vaguest idea what he was doing or what kind of world he was bringing you into. He was getting off, pure and simple, without considering the consequences of his actions, probably placating your mother who needed meaning in her life. Think about it."

She retorted, "I take it you mean consequences like a higher education and an incredible career...two incredible careers. And I would rather not think about my parents getting off. Thanks for the graphic nightmare."

"That was you, not them. They may have helped pay your way, increasing their debt load and reducing their comfort level. Good for them? No, not really. What choice did they have? That was the price they paid for having you beyond their means. And that should be where the gratitude stops. You did the rest. You were meant to join me at Riley as much as you're meant to reshape Washington and the country. Your parents may yet come to forgive your career choices."

"The debt was repaid some time ago. And don't worry about their comfort. They're doing fine. So am I without them."

"Yes, they are repaid and comfortable because of your success and your ethics, not theirs. And because you're an only child they skirted poverty instead of drowning in misery. Had you listened to them and not your heart's wishes you would be a nameless grain of sand on an ever-widening beach. You're an exception, Priscilla, on both counts. The truth is we're living in a quagmire of human rights which serve no purpose other than propagating the myth that we are all created equal when we are decidedly not. The laws are outdated, intended to protect the masses that confuse aimless lives with living until dying without the slightest concept of their shared responsibility or of the damage they have each wreaked by the unconscionable remnants of their existences that we're left to cope with. Instead they go about their days fucking like indiscriminate monkeys, making babies they can't afford, overspending and living either in squalor or in homes they can't afford until the repo man comes. In short they leave us with the only things they are capable of producing." Riley swung his

feet onto the floor, standing. "That's right, dependent welfare clones. The end result never changes. The circle never breaks. We, the few, literally end up burdened by hereditary welfare. We have to feed them, clothe them, feed their kids at school, kids who will inevitably drop out to emulate their ne'er-do-well parents because they've been preconditioned to fail. Then what? We foot the bill for feeding the mother, the daughter and the baby who, within a very few years, will do exactly what grandma and mom haven't stopped doing. She'll screw some punk in the backseat of a stolen car or an alley where she's living and end up spewing out a futureless kid at our expense. Then when she's all fixed up she'll spew out another and another that you and I will have to support because the guys have either buggered off, are in prison living the good life at our expense, or are too stupid to find work. That condition has to stop now." He checked his watch. "We can do this, Priscilla, you and me. I saw something in you from day one, something worth shaping, moulding into an unexpected force for them to reckon with. And I wasn't wrong. You aren't at Riley because I needed another executive. That was mutually good timing, but not your true calling. I had a vision. I have a vision. One I believe in. Think about it beyond the context of the absurd, when not going forth would be the unquestionable absurdity. Just don't wait too long. The fuse is lit and the clock's ticking. Believe me; we're in for one hell of a shit fest if something isn't done soon."
*

He was right, of course. Wasn't he always? So much had gone wrong since her youth and babies having babies was the root cause, the precursor to most social ills from poverty to crime. The nation had gone to hell and no one was doing anything about the spread of flagrant social disease because those who could were unwilling. They were afraid, morbidly afraid of the next election, the irreparable marring of their pristine reputations as just and God-fearing men, and the scripted perversion of the six PM news in the name of audience share.

He was right. If nothing else she agreed with him. What he believed, what he vented was incontrovertible.

When he left, she left with him. They flew together to Houston where the limousine was waiting to drive him home. She flew on to the Caribbean, to an island where her complete privacy came at a worthwhile price.

She spent the entire weekend alone, her phones turned off, deciphering his logic, trying to find fault where none existed except that what he proposed was ridiculous, truly absurd.

She couldn't possibly accomplish in four years what others had spent a lifetime striving to achieve, most of them failing. And her platform was another matter. None but the wealthiest few would vote for such draconian reform, most would certainly retreat to the safe harbour of status quo because they wouldn't recognize the need through rose-coloured Serengetis, their luxurious sanctuaries too far removed from day-to-day living.

Hear no evil, speak no evil, until it's too late. Then blame someone else. That was the politics of one forgotten century leaching into another that was too preoccupied with the here and now to see the future. Simply put, no one gave good shit and the blatant indifference pissed her off.

She loved her job, not regretting for a moment that she had abandoned the glamour of television. However he was right about one thing. She would not be happy much longer unless she followed him to Washington. She was shortchanging herself, he knew. So why didn't she?

She had nothing to worry about. He'd told her a hundred times. The squabbling of the Senate and the complacency of Congress was beneath her. Not only could he circumnavigate her way past that with his resources and influence, he would guarantee her the most prestigious Electors. That's how much he believed in her, how much Karina believed in her. Besides, what good was vast wealth if he couldn't buy what he wanted?

The questions were: What did she truly want from her life? And, in return, what was she willing to give of herself that would, in fact, alter her life? She had to decide. She had to make an irreversible and binding commitment. Once stepping into the fray she could not recant without irreparable damage to her reputation and his. He had to know soon, whereas she had to be certain, convinced. Three years was not a long time to prepare her or the nation and he wanted her in. At least they agreed on something.

Priscilla Vendôme did want in, she decided, smiling. She was dressed in a thong and wide-brimmed hat, reclining on a chaise-longue perfecting an even tan and sipping a daiquiri. At the very worst she would have tried and failed like so many others. She would be in good company. At best she would become the next President of The United States, the first Madam President, standing alone, and not a single affluent person frolicking in the turquoise sea between her and the setting sun had a clue.

Two unresolved issues remained: Were she to accept, believing she would, Edward would agree in writing to immediately buy her an island with a suitable airstrip. She would not forsake her right to privacy for any reason or anyone. As for her requisite husband, she would choose the man herself and Edward would no longer expect her affection once she was married.

A female president would be difficult enough for the country to embrace, a single woman would be impossible to even contemplate. As for kids, not a chance in hell would she ruin her body. Not for her mother, not for her country, and certainly not for Edward Riley.

That was not an issue, simply a fact.

All that apart, he was right. She would call him once

onboard the jet; tell him that she did want more than a corner office in Riley Corp.'s Chicago ivory tower looking out over a city and a nation in turmoil.

She did. She cared. She wanted to make a difference. She did want more and Edward Riley, provocateur and boss, had forced her to rethink her ambitions beyond the narrow dreams meant for others who covet rank, titles and money over real triumph.

She had travelled the world enough to know the planet was not plagued by lack of food or shortage of water. Sufficient supplies existed for everyone, or could exist. The problems were short-sightedness, lack of vision and uncaring, nor did the world lack oil or gold, diamonds or silver. Those were the real controlled substances, controlled by governments and greed.

Africa had more than sufficient rainwater each year to irrigate fields and harvest crops, to feed the poor who were dying of starvation by the thousands each day on a continent otherwise flooded with wealth. But keeping Africa distressingly starved and dry gave the world purpose, a sense of righteous benevolence. What other reason could explain or justify an abundant, precious life-source left to dampen sun-baked earth each day as wells and oases went dry on a continent boasting thirty percent of the planet's mineral reserves, forty percent of the world's gold, sixty percent of cobalt mined and nine-tenths of platinum, the most precious of precious metals?

Greed.

They were, and had been for years, a world power in the mining of precious minerals, indiscriminately squandering the most precious resource of all while funding self-serving civil wars and chaos. Of greater importance to them was that the humanitarian West was content to worry about a few Somali pirates and provocative, money-making images of emaciated and afflicted children. Children who should never have been born in the first place, children who were likely as not covered over in common graves a few days or a few weeks after the posed photos were taken and the photographer had cashed his four or five-figure cheque.

Africa was all about the West feeling good, not wanting to step on feet or injure feelings while, at home, parents sent their kids to school hungry to learn from half-hearted teachers who thought more about pedagogical days off and getting home earlier than their students.

Africa, though, was the tip of the iceberg.

The real plague was people, heedless masses exploding a global population beyond Earth's ability to contain them, with Africa, India and China refusing to relinquish their competitive surge towards disaster.

The outdated tribal customs of Africa were callously usurping prosperity while in India the narrow-mindedness of religion and regressive ancient beliefs, no longer relevant in any imagined world, continued more imperative than food. At least in the unseeing eyes of those endowed with the power of influence and wealth sufficient to live lavish lives above the filth and famine of abject poverty.

And despite their smugness neither one was better nor worse than China who, no longer able to contain its own population, had for decades swarmed across the Pacific and Atlantic to face Western inhospitality so they might proliferate with the characteristic uncaring of their ancestors.

That did have to stop. Change was crucial. Immigration of that widespread mentality into her country had to halt soon. Someone had to tell the Third World not created by any God, rather by ceaseless greed, that enough was enough. Let the West follow suit or not, though they likely would. They always did.

With his backing and influence she would run for and win the 2016 bid for the country's highest office. The incumbent was out, denied a third term by law and she had something no other contender could hope to compete with.

She had the country in the palms of her hands. They loved her. The women loved her. She smirked, sipping her cocktail. Think women didn't take voting seriously? Think again. They would for her. She would become the next president.

She had three years with limitless funding to prepare her mind for remedying five decades of neglect. Edward was right again, she believed. He could not have chosen a better time to meet her. She needed to meet and mingle with the who's who, gain favour without ever owing a favour. That's what he told her, what she'd known for some time.

She had to quickly learn who was right and who was wrong to speak with, trust, lure into the fold, who could help her win and who could not or would not. The concept of trust, he embedded immediately into her mindset, existed nowhere but on the reverse of a dollar bill in small print as an intangible and condescending relic of times past, times remembered or recounted by damaged or blurred minds as more innocent when they were not.

Times do not change. We are today what they were then, simply in far greater numbers, he told her. Trust has no purpose beyond the most intimate and exclusive circles, and then for as long as the circle remains intact. Trust without the warranty of mutual gain has no substance or purpose. Better to beware. Better to make apparent enemies than form untrustworthy allegiances.

*

Priscilla Vendôme dropped her straw into her glass, easing her way from the chaise-longue. She stood stretching.

She dropped her hat onto her seat, concealing her top. The sun was a half-circle of blinding gold light, a gentle sea breeze wafting its warmth across the white sand. The few couples bobbing in the shallow swells were lost in solitary worlds, light-years apart, loving, kissing or both. She was entirely alone.

The Fatal Diners' Club

Priscilla tugged at the ribbon tied loosely on her left hip, pulling at the one on her right, letting the single triangle fall between her ankles. She knotted a towel at her waist, sauntering to the shoreline. The sea was neither cool nor tepid as she stood ankle-deep wondering how long she would remember that very moment in time. She hoped forever.

She skipped backward. She would miss her favourite island. She tugged gently at the towel, dreamily. She didn't care. She never had before and she didn't then. No one cared. No one knew her. Privacy and seclusion were uppermost on the minds of guests, not her.

She strode in as far as her waist, her belly and breasts glistening from gentle splashing. She dived in, kicking, surfacing, twisting onto her back, floating, closing her eyes, depriving her senses of light and sound, her body weightless, caressed, searching her mind for her future, for the first time the President of The United States would swim naked in the sea.

Try to stop her.

21
NO WAY!

Artic blue is a colour we feel. It's frigid and bitter, and dry, sucking warm breath from our lungs through chapped lips and wet noses. Artic blue burns our skin and blinds our eyes. Artic blue is cruel, for all to test or challenge at our peril.

February13[th], 2024 was a vicious day, a Tuesday, a day better spent at home.

That no snow was swirling in the relentless winds wasn't a consolation to anyone caught in the tempest. Coattails were whipping, stinging the nylon-clad legs of fashionable young ladies, pant legs furiously flapping at the knees of au courant gentlemen, faces were raw, noses were dripping, eyes squinting, teary with cold, hands shoved into pockets to thaw the tips of frozen fingers housed in stylish leather gloves.

For those who were fortunate.

Winter is a good time, the best time to distinguish the rich from the poor, the Haves from the Have-nots. Fur coats and hats complementing snug boots and gloves are as much a statement as the white ridges of frostbitten ears and thin nylon shells accenting tattered sneakers, threadbare flannel pyjama bottoms and reddened hands clenching large coffees-to-go in paper cups to keep at least the palms from chafing.

Very few are able to disguise who they really are in the

midst of winter's harshness whether they wish to or not and Lorie Wilson didn't care either way. She was warm in her short leather skirt and cashmere sweater nestled into her lover's arms the day before Valentine's. She didn't need long-stemmed roses, lingerie or chocolates. She had him. At last she had a Valentine's to remember.

Invisible winds were howling, threatening to vibrate the floor-to-ceiling bevelled panes of her 23rd-floor penthouse from their frames, to ruin her day, to blow out the flames and consume the heat of her raging fireplace, to quell the soft music. She loved him so much, more than she ever believed, more than she loved her sapphire earrings and pendant she had adamantly refused, that he'd firmly insisted upon, that she'd finally and gracefully accepted in lieu of a sweater best forgotten while celebrating their first week together over a romantic dinner.

She kissed him. Whether at his home or hers, they had decided, they would never talk business. In that way they were not like other people. "Honey, I'm home. You'll never guess who I killed today?" would never quite set the tone for an evening of intimacy and romance.

She pinched each earring gently between her forefinger and thumb making tiny circles, holding the pendant into the orange light of the flames.

"Sweetheart, I've never worn anything so elegant. They're lovely."

"Like you. Hard to believe we've been together six weeks. Imagine if you'd been honest and told me upfront how much you adore me." He sipped a ten-year Bordeaux. "We wasted an entire week of lovemaking."

She reached behind her feeling for his cheek, smacking him. "No. No. Not a week. You wasted three years because you were too intimidated by extreme beauty and brains in the same body. I saw how you gaped at me when we first started working together. I thought you were such a pig."

"I was in shock. I couldn't believe anyone could be as stunning as you."

"Liar. You were undressing me. Admit it. A woman knows. You stood there like an idiot for a full minute ogling me."

"Guilty. At least now I know you keep your weapon in your purse."

She jabbed an elbow into his ribs, snuggling closer.

"We are certain about this. Aren't we, Dwayne? I feel like I'm in a dream, hating the thought of waking one day without you. No regrets? You're certain? I don't want you wake up one day to see a mistake instead of me."

"Before The Agency I had split seconds, not even, to decide whether to snap some guy's neck, cut his throat, shoot him in the head or let him live…which didn't happen very often. You had as much or less time to weigh your life against Vendôme's. So, yeah, we're certain. I am. I know that much. I was a long time before you mesmerized me at the gym and I've had weeks since to think about you, us, a virtual lifetime. So, yes, I'm selling. Done deal, my mind's made up. Besides, now that you've had me… think about it, where would you possibly find, you know, another me?"

Lorie reached for the travel brochure. "Maybe in France, sweetheart, in my thong, stretched out on a Riviera beach. Aren't most Frenchmen good lovers?"

"I wouldn't know. I suppose possibly the ones who aren't gay or gigolos. Anyway, I speak French. So what's your point? You've got a French lover."

She twisted, facing him. "No way!"

He shrugged. "Yeah, I do. French was cool for hitting on girls at college. I wasn't fluent, but they didn't know the difference. Then this one girl I met, she was French. Hot, I mean really hot…sizzling. We spent our final two years together before graduation, pretty much campus celebrities. Where one went, the other followed."

"Thank you, sweetheart. I get the picture. You've always been an irresistible pig. What happened to her? Get her eyesight back, grow a brain?"

"She was a Psych student, very brainy, really deep into criminology. Anyway, she had her pick of the litter. Everyone wanted her, all the big city PDs. She chose Detroit. That's where we celebrated her graduation. The next morning she crossed the street on a Green to flag a cab. The guy was on a cellphone drinking coffee. He was late for a meeting." Dwayne sipped his wine. "Then they were both late. He went to jail. She went to the morgue and I stayed an extra week for the funeral. A few days later I took a call from my uncle and left for the coast to join the navy. Not long after the SEALs adopted me, made me fluent in two dialects apart from other skillsets. The rest is history."

Lorie shivered "Dwayne…"

He squeezed her. "What's done is done: History 101, dream-girl. Now I'm all about you. I have been since I undressed you that first day. You're very right. I did, and every night since." He kissed her forehead. "You make damn sure you always look both ways or I'll be totally pissed."

"I would never have met you. This, us, wouldn't be happening. You'd be somewhere else, still in the navy."

"Who knows about tomorrow? So we are doing the right thing? You tell me differently."

She kissed him. "Yes, sweetheart, we are…just one thing."

"What?"

"Your first rent cheque will be three-point-two million, plus condo fees. You were a bit off on the math. Sorry. Can you handle that? I don't want a hapless drifter in my bed even if he is reasonably good-looking."

"Does price include parking?"

"Yes."

"Then I'm good for it."

"This is so weird, you and me... sweetheart, dream-girl."

"I like weird, soft and sexy weird, breathtaking weird, you learning to be a good cook weird. That's why I want out. I have for a while, Lorie. Deep down I believe I stayed because of you, which has nothing to do with your recently discovered insatiable charms. I know I did. Someone had to look after you. So now what's the point? It's not like we need the money. These Gourmands, who really cares about them? I don't. You don't. Hell, they don't care about each other. So in the end we euthanize them when they decide they've eaten enough, or when they decide death is less painful than life. Or they implode and we truck them to the butcher shop the way we did with Horn, all to save Priscilla Vendôme a few billion in healthcare costs each year."

"She's doing a good job, dropping to 280 billion from 350 in seven years. She criminalized Gourmands, essentially making them public enemies. In 2017 they accounted for half the population, now they're at a fraction of that number. That took guts and I never think of myself as killing them, sweetheart. We put an end to self-inflicted and irreversible torment, pure and simple. That's no different than when she legalized specific assisted suicide. The end result is the same."

"What she really wants is Hilary Basil. You have to wonder whether the guy really exists. Maybe he's many guys. Maybe he's a name without a face, or not." He paused. "You know what? He's protected."

"You're getting worked up. We promised. Remember. We're supposed to be playing touchy and saying nice things. It's our first Valentine's."

He put aside his glass, twisting their bodies in unison, lying facing her, kissing her, fondling one breast then the other. "I love you. But, you know what? Kill Basil and goodbye Gourmands. They'll self-annihilate."

She wasn't impressed, pushing him onto the floor.

"My point is we're not doing enough. We're at ninety-one percent so what? That's still over twenty-eight million Gourmands with BMIs over thirty. Then come the forties, fifties and the steadfast sixties in the top ten percentile of that. How do we get rid of three million incessant feeders? You tell me."

"We don't, sweetheart. The sixties take care of themselves, most of them living in low rent squalor to maintain their habit. That's their choice. They are not the issue. They've got an incurable death wish and Priscilla's edict to help that happen. They'll suffocate in their sleep or wait for the inevitable massive coronary. Or they'll choke on a day's worth of food lodged in their mouths. That's their choice. They aren't our real mandate and let's face it. The ones over 1000 pounds are history. We take care of the ones with sufficient funds to pay Basil for their treats and the younger ones while we wait for the oldest and the fifties to call us for a quick fix. That's what we do. Without us, sweetheart, without Priscilla's courage to make things right, the entire country would be royally screwed. We wouldn't be at nine percent remaining, more like seventy-five, much higher than when she got in. These people don't care. Most people don't care. You should know that more than anyone. We will get Basil one day. He'll screw up. He'll get lazy or over confident. Or one of his cronies will."

"Then he's got ten months to share with Vendôme before she vacates. And what happens then, when she's gone? It's not like she'll be re-elected. She's had her kick at the cat. She had her two terms, which means what for us? We'll be disbanded. Frankly I'm surprised we're not doing time in federal prison for covert activity, irrespective of Vendôme's personal Crusade of the Scales. We're the front line and not on the books to justify what we're doing. That means denial for them and sacrifice for us and I am not about to self-medicate with pentobarbital. Or does the next guy in her office secretly endorse us? I'd say probably not.

Riley's seventy-one. He'll lie down one day. No Riley. No Agency. He's the one pulling her strings, dream-girl. There's a link. Trust me."

"She has no strings, sweetheart. She's stand-alone and I've seen her face off with more than one military big shot. I was assigned to her for five years. She's good people. She requested me personally for the '16 campaign. She is good people. She's had a remarkable seven years and she's not finished. Did I also mention she's my friend? I believe so. And I believe in her."

"Seven years because of you. You saved her ass."

"I would again, the same way I would for you." She patted his cheek. "If I'm not on my period or otherwise upset with you."

Lorie stood to stoke the flames.

Dwayne stood, making a show of smoothing his slacks and sweater.

"I can't see myself doing this much longer with you. It's not what I want for us. What I do want are those three bars: North Miami, Miami and Key West." He went to her, kissing her, peering past the window. "I've also had my fill of winter and I'm starting to see dead Gourmands in my sleep when I should be seeing young naked women, you know, in a line." He kissed her again, "behind you."

She pursed her lips, raising an eyebrow. "Now it's three bars, not one. You'd go broke in a month, sweetheart. I've seen the way you serve drinks. And let me guess. Every night would be Ladies' Night, I suppose?"

"Three bars, that's what I want. I've been doing the math. Three because having one is nothing special. Anyone can open a waterhole. Also, one turns you into an on-site alcoholic therapist and with two you end up playing favourites. With three you're a businessman. We're business people, you and me. And why shouldn't every night be Ladies' Night."

"You have more experience with that than I do,

sweetheart." She closed the glass shields. "You haven't told me what I'd be doing in these bars. I am not waiting tables, Dwayne Michaels."

He beamed. He had an epiphany. "You could dance. Choose the location you like best. You would be the premier performer. Top billing, I promise." He took her in from her painted toes to her tousled dark hair. "Who wouldn't pay to see this upside down and naked on a pole?" He shrugged, smirking. "I'm thinking out loud."

"And I'm thinking I've got a brass poker in my hands." Sparks burst from the hardwood logs, spitting and crackling. "So please stop thinking of any woman upside down and naked, especially me."

"So last night, what, you didn't like?"

She shook her head, giggling. She conceded the point, replacing the poker, standing to face him, wrapping her arms around him.

"So this isn't a remnant, lazy bathtub talk brought on by a double scotch?"

"The dream isn't new...and I have the resources. Nothing's stopping me...I hope not."

"You're serious? I mean really. You are?"

"About marrying you? Yes, I am."

She stumbled backward. "Dwayne, that is not funny. Don't say things like that."

"I don't mean to be. What I'm thinking is this. Boyfriend girlfriend doesn't work at our age and you know as well as I do women have this security thing about marriage, about not being married. It's a big thing for them. Besides, if I'm writing you a cheque for three million and change to secure sleeping privileges, what's another fifty bucks for a marriage licence? That way you get a husband and you get everyone's respect; I get an extra four floors of view until we move to the Southeast and a contented woman. A win for you, a win for me, though not until summer when we can do things right. That's the thing. I've always wanted a June wedding."

Lorie's mouth was frozen open, her eyes unblinking, waiting for him to say something more stupid than he had. She knew she wasn't dreaming. She hadn't once seen him wearing such a ridiculous grin in her dreams.

"You want a June wedding, Dwayne Michaels. Well you be sure to invite me. In the meantime I'm taking a sweat, alone."

"What about me?"

"Oh, I don't know. Why don't you look into the bedroom mirror for me, Dwayne? I was under the impression that I had lost something, now I'm thinking you can find it for me in there."

He knew. Oh yeah, he knew.

"Like what, dream-girl?"

"Something resembling a genuine, self-centred jerk in remission, that's what."

He was right, again. He read her like a book.

Lorie left him standing, gazing out at the darkening sky, satisfied with himself that winter's frosty chill had permeated the room.

When she was gone he chuckled quietly, refilling his wine. He thought ten, or possibly fifteen minutes would suffice before he would risk joining her, albeit sadly not for a sweat. She loved sex in the sauna, often as a prelude to sex anywhere else.

He cleared his mind. Vivid memories aside, he had more important things at hand. He had to look into a mirror.
*

Lorie was sitting on a thick towel, protecting her legs from the heat of the dry wood. Her hair was swept back, knotted into a tight ponytail, her face and body deliciously coated with eucalyptus-scented sweat.

Dwayne Michaels peered first through the tiny window, scanning the four-person cedar chamber from corner to corner, avoiding eye contact, grinning, silently announcing himself before stepping into the doorway fully dressed in a black suit and red tie, a white shirt and ruby links lacing his French cuffs together. The creases in his pants were razor-sharp, his shoes polished to a high gloss.

He was so damned good-looking, she thought. And she was going to hate him for as long as she could. What was he doing?

He ignored her, his head lowered, seeing her arms cross over her breasts, one leg cross over the other, a perfect foot decorated with glossy, prune-coloured nails keeping rhythm with her current frame of mind. He understood. Being miffed with him was difficult at the best of times. All the more so now that she was naked and vulnerable. He understood. She wasn't being demure; she was defending her female sensibilities against his superior attack strategy.

Her fate was in his hands. She was the moist clay, he was the sculptor.

He placed the ice bucket between them, avoiding her eyes. The champagne was perfectly chilled, uncorked, two fluted crystal glasses held by the stems in one hand.

When he was ready: "Lorie, you look divine, the envy of all women."

"I'm soaked in sweat, Dwayne. Thanks. Remind you of something recent?"

"I'm reminded of a beautiful woman staring at me from between two amazing legs, which is not to say I overlooked her spectacular ass, which is precisely why I can't come any closer. You know, because of your shameless appetite for me and I have to look my best for you this evening at dinner. I made reservations for eight with limousine service, but not for Valentine's. So you have a while to pamper yourself. I took the liberty of preparing your bath."

This situation, very quickly, was not going her way. He was so damned confident. She refused to be impressed.

"We were supposed to cook a romantic Valentine's

dinner together at home, Dwayne…our first."

Dwayne. Ordinarily Dwayne might not have been good, not after so many sweethearts. But 'Dwayne' came from her eyes and her heart, not her mouth. They were telling him 'sweetheart', that she was disappointed. He was good to go.

She was unwavering, stoic. She would defend her position. She was right and he was wrong. She would not crumple. She was curious, though. She had to admit that much, accepting the empty glass with as little arm movement as possible.

"We don't need Valentine's to cook a romantic meal when every meal with you is romantic."

Okay. That was good. "I thought you went to look into the mirror. What, little Dwayne too afraid to see something creepy staring back?"

He tilted the lip of the bottle to within an inch of her glass, without stepping too far in, reaching, his hand steady, retreating to the doorframe.

Kneeling went against the grain. He wasn't that chivalrous, not to mention the precision crease in his pants he'd meticulously achieved.

"Miss Lorie Wilson, I did look into the mirror the way you asked. Sorry, no jerk. He's gone. However I did see your loving and devoted future husband. That would be me. I also found this, which I hope is yours."

Lorie stared at his open palm. She drained her glass, her eyes glued to the tiny felt box. She waited, time exploding in her ears. She wanted to hear words, to hear him say something, anything at all. Her heart was pounding, her chest heaving. She eyed the ice bucket, too catatonic to move. This wasn't happening. No way!

Dwayne slipped the little box into his pocket, startling her, more concerned with her empty glass.

Bastard!

He reached forward.

"Forgive my rudeness, Lorie, and allow me."

He refilled her glass with deliberate slowness, a narrow fountain of titanium bubbles crowned with white spume rising in her glass inch by inch. He met her pursed lips and furrowed brow with an annoying smirk, retreating with his own glass untouched.

"Dwayne, what is going on here?"

"We are...you and me."

He extracted the box, flipping the lid with a single flick of his thumb. The simple diamond glittered brighter than any perfect star she'd ever seen against a dark sky.

She gulped, her mouth instantly dry. "Dwayne..."

"If I may start over, Lorie, because you really are not cooperating here." He cleared his throat for affect. "Miss Wilson, will you marry me? Please. I've waited three years for this moment, six if consider the first time I laid eyes on you at the White House. So have you, and we're good together. You know that." He wasn't worried. He knew. He was confident, counting the seconds until finally, "I would like to drink my champagne sometime soon, dream-girl, and we do have a romantic corner table waiting for us." He raised his glass to the light, studying the continuum of exploding effervescence. "Something you'd like to say, dream-girl...anything...now...later?"

No way was this happening. She shook her head. "No way! Sweetheart, you're serious? We're getting married?"

"That's sort of what I'm waiting to find out. I chose the ring a few weeks ago. Thought today would be good timing since you girls put so much into this Valentine's thing. So yeah, we are. I think, maybe. Don't quite know yet. I'm sort of waiting for confirmation." He sipped his wine, thinking he might die of thirst before hearing a 'yes'. "I believe this is where you say yes, or no, and perhaps think about dressing for dinner."

She flew from the bench under a burst of champagne, a naked angel, beaming, glistening.

He caught her in mid-flight, legs wrapped around him, arms wrapped around him, so much for the suit.

"Is that a no?"

She painted his face with kisses. "Give me my ring. And we're getting married in September. I hate June weddings."

22
Percival Penny's 9-1-1 Call

The night before and a few hundred miles away Percival Penny arrived home from The Diners' Club Valentine's evening as he would from any other Gourmand feast, in one of Hilary Basil's dark green trucks.

He was strapped into his articulated lift chair in the vertical position, the most practical and most comfortable for him, before being fastened the bulkhead of the cargo area behind the drivers to avoid disrupting the vehicle's centre of effort.

He wasn't feeling well. He hadn't for a while and being alone in the dark, his head bobbing freely with the sway of the truck, made him feel worse.

He had barely managed to finish his meal and for the first time that he could remember since becoming a member he had been the first to leave.

He was forty-nine. He hadn't weighed himself in years and the last time he hadn't seen the digital reading on scale with his own eyes. He couldn't, relying on the doctor whose face he remembered wanting to slap from her head. He was then forty-two. She was much younger, twenty-eight or thirty and real easy to remember. She was a true bitch, superior, the last doctor he'd seen and far more interested in her designer clothes and her shoes than him.

She mocked him with undisguised candour. She might

as well have laughed in his face, were she not more concerned with combing her hair with her fingers, displaying her half-covered tits through her silk blouse and making certain the world, his world would admire the few inches of her legs she kept hidden under her skirt until she sat, each time she sat. Thinking what, that he'd go home and jerk off when he hadn't touched his dick in years?

He was tipping the scale at 345, she told him, on his way to an early grave. At 350, for his height, and factoring in his bone density, his non-existent muscle mass and his fat content, he would reach his ideal BMI of fifty or more. So why, she asked, would he possibly think to squander 2400 dollars each year to maintain medical services when he had the option of refusing while gorging himself towards sixty.

That was the added cost of caring for people like him, those not satisfied with merely being morbidly obese, more obsessed with gorging themselves than living.

The option was mandatory refusal of any such care, which, in any event, would become automatic when achieving a BMI of sixty, which simply required an additional seventy-five pounds, which he could manage easily over the coming year if he focused. Of course then he would be denied health care and insurance irrespective of the urgency, which didn't leave him much of a choice, she added without the slightest trace of care in her voice, standing so that she could sit.

He had to lose 100 pounds as soon as possible or risk dying anytime soon. And was there something about that he didn't understand? Wouldn't he once like to see his penis? Or use it for something more than a free-sprinkling hose?

He never saw her again. What did she know?

He remembered his humiliation the following year, first being weighed, then being asked for his credit card. He'd gone past 400. He weighed in at 435. His BMI was sixty. The bitch had been right. He was a No Assist. Fuck her. He didn't care. He remembered their shrugs. The law was the law. Sorry. Buy a scale. Come back when you see a three. That's what the intern said.

He remembered leaving, feeling their condescending stares assailing his back. He remembered the chill that he felt travelling the length of his spine and how he forced one foot to follow the other. Despite which he wasn't alone. Everyone he knew had refused to pay the penalty for being who they were. He'd saved a fortune. BMI was pure bullshit conjured up by the bitch in Washington who wanted a perfect world, a world of Vendôme clones, voted in by egocentric doctors in short skirts and open legs.

He hadn't felt well for a while; though sleeping in his chair helped to alleviate the discomfort somewhat.

He didn't tell his friends at dinner because they wouldn't care, the same way he wouldn't care about them. Of course they would have commiserated with him, saying what they had to, forgetting him soon after he was gone, dead, the way he and they had forgotten the others. How many friends had he lost, absent from the table without notice? He couldn't remember. Nor would they remember him.

At his home the drivers began unloading him at the dark entrance to the building's garage off the rear alleyway from where he could make his way independently to the elevator. Access from the front steps was impossible.

Basil's trucks came with an expert team. They worked efficiently unstrapping his chair, attaching the winch to the transverse bar above the wheels, watching him roll to the platform, stopping, waiting for them to complete the procedure without noticing him. He was invisible.

He took the service for granted. He never cared to know their names or to thank them for their professional attentiveness. He never thought to offer them a gratuity, unaware that, in the case of his death while in transit or upon his arrival, they were to deposit him in a convenient place or simply leave him outside his home. Basil's list of services did not extend to final courtesies.

Keeping the cable taut they chocked him in place, lowering him to street level, releasing him, letting him take control of the chair once again before leaving him without a word as they closed up the truck and drove off.

Inside his apartment Penny put himself vertical near the bathroom door. He stepped from the chair, barely squeezing his bulk through the doorway, hobbling to the toilet where he fished with both hands for the tie-strings to his velour sweatpants.

Each time he urinated he thought of her, the bitch doctor who was probably pleased to think he was dead. He told her that day how he pissed, hands-free, that he didn't need anyone to hold his dick. He choked out a laugh, coughing thick phlegm, thinking of the shock twisting her face when he told her that he pissed naked, that if he didn't hear it he felt it, in which case he would stay naked until he was dry.

He remembered how she remained sitting, mortified, the sharp sound of her knees snapping together.

He stepped back, first blowing a green clump from his mouth towards the bowl, missing, not feeling any better for the loss. When he finished urinating he tugged at his pants from the sides, letting the terry fabric absorb the usual errant droplets.

He lived modestly, like most Gourmands. His living room and bedroom were fitted with unattractive mechanical furniture meant to raise and lower him as well as to seat him in questionable comfort, though he hadn't been comfortable in years and his landlord refused to accommodate him by allowing structural changes to doors, the bathroom and the kitchen.

Nor had he worked in years, living off the substantial sum of money his dead parents had bequeathed to him in liquid cash, 401Ks and insurance that he had wisely thought to bank in safety deposits boxes where interest in the form of his reduced monthly welfare cheques, reduced because of

Vendôme, would for his lifetime far exceed the taxable dribble the banks would pay out.

What would the good doctor say about that?

He ached. His ankles ached and his hands ached. He looked at his bed through the doorway afraid to sleep, believing the night before he'd stopped breathing. He had reached for the phone, his body drenched in sweat, his heart palpitating. Then he laughed. He'd forgotten that grossly fat people were better off dead in Vendôme's perfect world.

Instead he tilted his bed to a few inches from vertical, waiting for his breathing to stabilize, for his heart to calm its erratic beating when he felt he was able to make his way to the kitchen.

But now his craving for food was somehow gone. He knew he should eat something, yet he couldn't. He felt weak, nervous. What if he had stopped breathing in his sleep? What if he did again and didn't wake in time? Yet he was incredibly tired.

*

Sunday morning when he did wake, Percival Penny was on his living room floor staring at the ceiling, living his worst nightmare. He couldn't move, couldn't roll over. Even if he could his arms were too short and too weak to push his weight onto his knees. And then what would he do? How would he possibly pull himself to his feet? Did he even know how? He hadn't been on his knees in years, hadn't needed to stand under his own strength in years. Nor had he once in his lifetime thought to lift a weight heavier than a full plate.

He rolled his head to one side. His chair was at the bathroom door facing the wrong way. Could he manage to crawl? He didn't know. Anyway, once there, what would he do? The brake was on, the digital control on the armrest too high to reach. Everything was too high to reach.

He was on the first floor at the corner of his building

with no one below him. The closest neighbour was annexed by the bedroom wall, but what if his body became wedged in the doorframe? Even if he succeeded the journey across the floor would weaken him. And what if they weren't home? What would he do? How would he turn to make his way again through the door? Screaming? Calling out for help? Screaming was useless. People were too afraid. Even honest people were reluctant to involve the police. What a fallacy that was: To protect and serve. Pure bullshit dressed in one-size-too-small uniforms or like commandos for the purpose of instilling fear and inhibition. He knew the truth. What they protected was each other. What they served were their own interests.

What they wanted, all they wanted was as much information about everyone everywhere. That was their true purpose. The very reason they wouldn't come. They knew about him. They would know within seconds that he was obese, a persona non grata disavowed by state and country. He was a No Assist.

Neither would Hilary Basil respond, nor would any of his friends. Basil wouldn't care and his friends weren't capable.

He tried to roll over, feeling pathetic, his fear mounting, wasting his breath, his energy.

He had no watch. His only timepiece was a clock on the wall that he couldn't see. Time had no meaning other than the foreign sounds penetrating outward from his stomach. He'd never known hunger, not for a day or an hour, accustomed to eating regularly on the hour or for an in-between snack. Eating was survival, his life source suddenly beyond his reach, too far and too high. He'd never considered putting emergency nourishment within reach of the floor. Why had he not done that? Survival.

His head began to ache. His neck was throbbing, his back beginning to stiffen with nothing to put under his head for support. Everything was too far away, beyond hope. He made a mental note. If he lived he would make immediate changes. He would store food near the floor, put door handles near the floor and emergency lights in every corner.

Daylight was fading. The darkness he feared was invading his space, stealing all sense of time. He wanted to cry, though to what end when no one was near to see him, to hear him whimper?

How many hours had passed since they brought him home? He'd spent the entire day where he lay, inert, the cold from the floor seeping through his flesh to his bones. He felt numb, wiggling his fingers and toes to help his blood circulate. Could he survive another night? He didn't know. He didn't think he wanted to. He didn't know what to think. Strange though, he thought, struggling to clear his mind of desperation, that he could see as clearly in darkness as during the day.

He began counting the seconds, each time starting over. He began a hundred times. He didn't know, abruptly stricken with the realization he needed to urinate.

At that moment he wanted to kill Priscilla Vendôme for her inhumanity, flooding his mind with despicable images of how best to hurt her, to punish her, to punish the bitch doctor for what they had done to him, how she had humiliated him. What right did they have to laugh at him, to deride him, to make the world see him as vile and loathsome?

Screw them. Neither one was pure. How could any female, let alone one her age, become president without screwing someone with deep pockets? And how many senior colleagues did the bitch doctor fuck in order to make her way in life.

He had to do something. He couldn't be found dead, drenched in a puddle of his own piss. The country owed him that much respect.

He ransacked his mind for a way to survive the long winter night. He was starving. He felt nauseous. He hadn't eaten in twenty hours, maybe twenty-four. He didn't know. He hacked once, twice, his entire mass reverberating. He felt his face tighten under the strain, forcing his head sideways in line with the floor, hawking the green ball as far from his face as he could.

How many times had he done that, a dozen, two dozen? What if he choked? What if he fell asleep and choked? If only the man had killed her that day. He wouldn't be splayed on the floor; a victim of his country's uncaring. If only he had killed her.

*

Morning doesn't come early during the endless months of winter's grip. That it did come at all surprised Percival Penny as his eyes fluttered open once again to muted daylight, laying there, a prisoner on the verge of pointless hysteria.

He realized no one had called him since he'd come home, not since Hilary Basil's people called to confirm his dinner reservation. He had no friends. He never spoke on the phone. He could scarcely remember whether he spoke with other diners or, if he did, about what. All they knew was food. They never asked about him, about what he did or where he lived, more interested in sauces, rare or medium, succulent desserts, recent and aged vintages of red or white.

He reached for his phone, strumming the casing with weakened fingers through his velour top. He had to try. The least they would do is help him into his chair where he could eat to regain his strength and think more decisively.

He prayed not to drop his one link with life, gripping the slim plastic case with one hand, and the other, barely able to bring his hands close enough to his face to fumble with the dial pad. He waited, concentrating, patiently filling his lungs with new air, dreading that he would cough, lose the phone and waste his one chance.

He was so close. They could arrive within minutes. He pressed the nine, pausing. He pressed the one, calming his excitement. He pressed one again afraid to bring the phone to his ear, not trusting his weakened fingers. Instead he remained as he was, waiting to hear the faint voice.

He knew she was there, that someone was there. Now they would have to come. They must.

He said, in the strongest voice he could force without coughing, "They're killing me! They're killing me! Please, help me!"

He dropped his hands to his chest, the phone to the floor without pressing END. They were coming. Now they must. They wouldn't be long. He didn't have to hear the words. What was the worst they could do? He chortled, spittle spraying from his wide-open mouth. They were coming to help him.

*

Penny didn't have many rights. He really didn't deserve many. He collected welfare, lived in subsidized housing and hadn't paid taxes in years. He did, however, retain the right not to be murdered, at least not once he'd called, and for that reason alone the police arrived within what he believed were a few minutes. He hadn't thought to count.

He heard their voices, demanding, the door crashing in with surprisingly little sound, two uniformed men, then two more rushing in, their arms outstretched, yelling, their weapons waving, scaring him. Then he heard one man yell "Clear!" then another and another, the fourth man staring down at him, holstering his weapon.

The dramatic scene he hadn't expected lasted under five seconds. His heart rate quickened.

"I didn't know what else to do," he tried. "I've been like this for almost two days. I didn't know what else to do."

The three others came to where their partner stood, closing in on Penny from different directions as though he'

252

been rigged with a bomb set to detonate at any moment, his torso framed on either side by an abstract border of greenish splatter.

"So, I'm thinking no one's tried to kill you." the first one said. "Do I have that about right?"

"You're right, and I'm sorry. I just need to stand. I need you to please help me."

"How do you propose we do that? We're not equipped."

The cop called in the false alarm, explaining, cancelling back up, cancelling the detectives and requesting an ambulance. He couldn't do anything but shake his head. He didn't have to speak. Penny could read his eyes.

"Please help me."

"We can't help you. We're not trained to help you. Besides which we would have to arrest you and, quite frankly, I don't know how we would do that. So you're much better off where you are until the paramedics get here. They're en route."

They turned to leave, disgusted.

He begged them. "Please, bring me some food, something to eat, anything…something to drink."

They couldn't do that either, each man pondering the same question: How would he eat flat on his back? How would he swallow? No way were they touching him. And how could he possibly drink without drowning. In any event he would just piss himself again.

"My head, could you please lift my head, put a pillow under my head to stop the pain?"

"That won't happen. We came here to prevent a murder, not commit one." He studied the glutinous gobs on the floor. "You'd choke to death in five minutes. Sorry, buddy."

They weren't authorized to touch him. Not that they would. Each had seen corpses that didn't smell as bad. He reeked of decay. The first cop wished him good luck matter-of-factly as though telling the time to a passing stranger.

They wanted nothing to do with him, the adrenalin coursing through their veins not yet subsiding from the thought of rushing into a murder in progress, of killing or being killed because of him.

They had done enough. They wanted to breathe fresh air.

They left, closing the damaged door behind them.

Percival Penny wanted to scream. He wanted to cry. The ambulance wasn't coming, he knew, not even for 2400 dollars. He was listed as a No Assist, already dead until he was buried.

23
February 14th, 2024

Lorie Wilson rolled over onto her fiancé ignoring his grunts and groans. She didn't care. She was elated. She wanted to talk. He was tired, exhausted, drained. He wanted to sleep. His agenda for the day was clear. The Agency could do without him at least until noon.

At dinner the evening before she'd worn a sheer black, mid-thigh dress glittering with black and silver sequins to disguise that apart from her patent leather evening sandals, all she was wearing was a black thong, black push-up bra and a diamond ring.

Everything but the ring was strewn on the floor.

Dwayne Michaels wore a blue suit and silver tie no one thought to notice.

Throughout dinner all she could talk about was her wedding. They would be married in September. Everyone got married in June. She wasn't everyone. That way she would have seven months to learn French for their honeymoon in France and seven months to get in shape for the beaches of the Côte-d'Azur, which meant tanning her breasts to the same golden hue as her ass. She had never gone topless. Well, not publicly, not exactly, or unless by herself as usual on her private rooftop garden. Of course, there was…No. She wouldn't say a word.

He was okay with topless, learning French was optional. The rest was too important to rush. The Agency and his dream of becoming a bar owner would take time. Until then they would maintain status quo. She agreed. At the very least she would do her best.

Though once at home she couldn't stop loving him, all but ripping away his clothes the moment he took her hand helping her from the limo. She was getting married to her dream…and she couldn't tell a soul excepting her parents.

She had no close friends; not really, not since leaving the Service, and the one woman who was her friend wouldn't be pleased.

Most of her relatives were either dead, retired or still in school and living with mommy and daddy. Besides she wanted a quiet wedding at the ocean without family she rarely saw and hardly knew, strangers flocking together for a free meal, booze and curiosity. Nor did she need or want gifts from bargain basements that she would never use or display because she had no plans to ever invite them to her home.

Dwayne, for his part, was happy to keep the secret indefinitely. He was a loner. The men whose friendship he'd once enjoyed he gave up when he left Black Ops, immediately becoming an outsider. Possible other friends, new friends would be too curious, too labour intensive, too troublesome to maintain. He would tell his uncle at some point, not feeling the least bit rushed. This wasn't a guy thing, strictly female.

No one at The Agency could know, not that he cared, nor would anyone he might pass at Riley think to slap his back or chance to say something suggestive about the very seductive and desirable Lorie Wilson despite their imaginations. He supposed the gun and badge on his hip was a deterrent of sorts, fairly certain.

He felt sad for Lorie. She had no one to tell other than somewhat straitlaced parents. He wondered what he could do about that.

As for her ring, she would never remove it. She was adamant.

He was cool with that. Their Primary never saw her, never came to the office, and he doubted sincerely that the Gourmands would care much.

He sat straight despite her weight, swinging his legs over the side of the bed, gently sweeping her into his arms with the same smooth movement. He carried her into the kitchen where he held her with one arm, hers clinging to his neck, her legs wrapped tightly around his waist. He poured a single coffee, black, no milk, no sugar, before hauling her on his hip to the bathroom where he set her down in the walk-in shower, kissed her, turned the dial to blue, side-stepped beyond range of the ice-cold waterfall and held her in place with an open palm pressed against her forehead.

His list of demands was concise: She would let him gather his strength, she would let him regroup his boys, let him dress and allow him to eat his breakfast in peace without being mauled. Or... he could stand there all day.

She capitulated immediately, agreeing to all four terms. She promised. She did. Dwayne! He believed her, moving in closer to soap her body and shampoo her hair once steam began rising from the floor.

She waited until she was warm and clean to forgive him, stepping out to give him space; sitting at her vanity wrapped in a towel to mentally script the proper words for her mother and father, uncertain that she wasn't somehow lost in a wonderful dream, unable or unwilling to wake into a real world.

Her father possessed a lawyer's learned inability to believe anyone at face value, though he'd never come up against a Black Ops guy with attitude. Her mother was no better, equally sceptical of the masses, believing a person's true nature could only ever be determined with a scalpel, Lorie knowing very well her mother hadn't once in her life come across anyone as disarming as Dwayne Michaels.

The Fatal Diners' Club

She could wait a while longer. Not telling them would somehow keep her dream alive and vivid, sensual and romantic. Telling them would bring a surge of predictable questions, a premature inquisition without current answers. She would lie, though. Whenever she would decide to call, she would have answered 'yes' to Dwayne the night before.

Where she had once hated her weekends, she now hated her workweeks anxious for her first business trip of the year for which she would pack entirely differently. Never before had she taken string bikinis, silk teddies and robes on her travels with him. Why would she? To tease and frustrate herself when she had always slept alone hating him because she couldn't love him?

Now she would. Oh, yes.

In the meantime she would have the morning with him.

The phone chimed. Dwayne Michaels stooped past the edge of the Plexiglas wall, listening, shrugging. Wednesday was Wednesday: Hump day.

Lorie scrunched her face into a grimace and stood, monitoring the first few words from their Primary.

Their Primary was local, their personal director and sole contact. He had three counterparts across the country, the four reporting to their Primary, unknown to Wilson and Michaels, who in turn reported to the president. Nor did Wilson or Michaels know or have contact with their six counterparts. And so The Agency went, cherishing anonymity and secrecy to avoid catapulting the country into chaotic hysteria.

As far as anyone knew or cared obesity was essentially outlawed. Beyond a 29.9 BMI Class to a maximum of 49.9 patients were obliged to pay a premium equal to the additional annual per capita cost of treating a 29.9 BMI Class or worse in the hope of discouraging them from achieving positive weight gain. The alternative was the No Assist list, a virtual death sentence. Yet the country was catching on, finally understanding. The system was working with increasing number of patients experiencing negative weight gain in each BMI Class but the 50s and sixties.

Those two were the incurable diehards who put food ahead of good health and longevity. The 50s were by far the worst, refusing to pay the premiums, falsely believing they were exempt from ever becoming a sixty or believing the event was too far into the future to worry about. However the concept of 'Live for Today' wasn't working for them.

The fifties, already on the automatic No Assist list, heedlessly gorging themselves towards sixty, believed they were too far gone to reverse their condition, or were too indolent to make the effort, or lacked the 2400 each year, or suffered from a condition The Agency irreverently referred to as LUT, 'Live until Today'.

They were, naturally, first given the opportunity to reverse their condition or to pay the upfront penalty equal to the added cost of their care. Beyond that point, beyond 59.9 BMI Class they were attached to the No Assist list and allowed to enjoy their perversions.

The Agency didn't care about illegal food, Gourmands or the LUTs. They were all potential links to what they did care about. No one, not the cops, not the DA, not the courts, not the president wanted Gourmands incarcerated in congested jails or prisons for any duration. They were too labour intensive, too costly, too problematic and too vulnerable.

The Agency was small, elite for a reason, chosen with the utmost care, their primary raison d'être: Hilary Basil. That was their mission. They were as covert as The Diners' Club was clandestine. In fact they were more so. Anonymity was paramount.

Lorie put her phone to her ear, listening to more. When she was done she said "thank you" and disconnected. Her morning was ruined.

*

The Fatal Diners' Club

The scheduled flight between New York and Boston would take less than an hour once airborne, plus an hour's drive to La Guardia and an hour of wait-time at the gate, plus another hour of disembarking and renting a car in Boston...if the flight left on time or wasn't cancelled or wasn't delayed. As well, getting out of Logan any day during rush hour was an absolute bitch.

Or the easy drive between the two hubs would take four hours on a bright and crisp day.

She had clothes she hadn't yet worn for him and restaurants in Boston where they hadn't yet dined together because, well, he was somebody else then. Best of all they hadn't yet shared a hotel bed, called down for room service, or watched any of the pay-per-view adult channels.

They drove, not soiling their dreams with reality, the principal topic of conversation the always elusive Hilary Basil.

Boston's South End was split by two demographics. One half was home to the young and upwardly mobile with high mortgages and heavy debt loads incurred by the high cost of education and leased European cars they each believed they deserved because of that as yet unpaid education. The other half was home to long-term residents who fought desperate battles each year against increased rents, low income earners living amongst subsidized welfare recipients who had long since forgotten what a workday entailed.

The two halves were distinct. Ruptured roads on one side led to smooth asphalt surfaces on the other, dull colours of flaking wood façades starkly contrasted well-maintained brownstones, broken-down and rusted Chevys and Fords delineated cracked and heaving sidewalks juxtaposed to shimmering rainbows of European colours displayed in driveways defining well-maintained front lawns.

The Fatal Diners' Club

A single and seasonal commonality existed. The broken sidewalks of one side and the manicured lawns of the other were inescapably equal under the brown-grey slush of an urban winter.

Lorie's new suede coat and hat were trimmed with fur made possible by a battered baby seal she'd never thought to consider. Her Cossack boots kept her warm to her knees, the outer edges trimmed with beaver. Her gloves were Italian kid leather lined with rabbit. Her defense was candidly simple when confronted with disapproval, difficult to debate: Absolutely no one cared about dead beavers, rabbits or goats. So get real.

And she held the same view regarding her current and decidedly more insurmountable confrontation.

She wasn't pleased about forging a path between two barely roadworthy wrecks or scaling the waist-high blockade of compacted snow barring her way to the front steps of Percival Penny's rundown building.

Dwayne understood. He went first, prancing past her, leaping, standing atop the mound, reaching earthward to her with outstretched arms.

She wasn't certain. She couldn't tell what he was thinking behind his glasses. He had that Dwayne Michaels look she didn't trust, though without him she would have to cross over on all fours. The mound was too high. She would look ridiculous and probably ruin her stockings or her coat.

Ridiculous didn't quite go with the 10mm in her handbag. She put her faith in him and told him so, her tone and expression more of a forewarning against whatever he might be thinking.

She trudged between the vehicles, taking his hand, surprised at how gently and effortlessly her feet left the ground. She wanted to kiss him, resisting the temptation. Then he was gone, standing on the sand-covered sidewalk, his arms once again reaching outward, beckoning her with gloved hands as though guiding an aircraft into the gate.

Like what? What did he expect? That she was supposed to throw herself into his arms? Jump? What? No way! She wasn't twelve. Her brow furrowed. She gaped at her feet. No! No, Dwayne! The snow beneath her gave way, Lorie disappearing waist-deep in a blink.

Dwayne rushed in, his face reddened with winter's bite, beaming with a bright smile, judiciously refraining from the faintest chuckle, laughter, or any sign whatsoever of amusement. The situation was serious requiring damage control, immediate assistance to those in need.

"Officer down," he yelled.

He was too late. Lorie's coat was bunched between the Alps and her shoulders, which meant, he was obliged to surmise, everything else was experiencing a cold snap. Not a time for selfish humour. She needed his empathy, to hear kind words. She was flustered, open-mouthed, searching this way and that for her missing waist, legs and feet. He reached for his phone.

"What are you doing, Dwayne?"

"Capturing the moment, you know, for workman's comp. We don't know how badly you might be injured."

She wasn't impressed. "Sweetheart, that thing I did last night. Did you like?"

She twisted.

"You know I did."

"Yeah, well, you enjoy trying to do that yourself from now on."

"I love you."

She took a deep breath, composing herself. "I love you too, so far. Now, would you please get me out of here? My bum's beginning to freeze."

She reached out. He leaned in, her face pressed close to his. His arms went around her easily, bracing his feet, tugging gently, extricating her inch by inch while ignoring her pleas to hurry.

Once she was freed he took a moment to study her. She

was a sight with her coat and skirt bunched to her waist, her bare thighs accented with the tops of her stockings, garter clasps and bits of icy snow, her boots stuffed to overflowing with half the previous day's snowfall.

He retreated, taking her in, capturing her for all time as she did a 360° checking for passers-by, held her coat in place, brushed her legs free of snow, swept icy crystals from inside the tops of her stockings, adjusted her skirt and coat and dug more coarse white crystals from the tops of her boots with both index fingers before curving her lips into a snarl with her eyebrows raised and leaving him to follow. Idiot! Her lips pursed into a tight grin: Handsome and charming idiot.

The wooden steps were concaved from years of natural wear and neglect. The wrought iron handrail that was once black was now reddish-brown and jagged with rust; the outer door was thick with ancient layers of paint. Inside between that door and the one that was barred were mailboxes, a mat, and a rubber refuse container missing a lid. Neither one cared to examine the contents. The odour was sufficient.

Lorie leaned her back into her fiancé whom she trusted more than Dwayne Michaels at the moment. She removed one boot shaking out the loose snow; the other boot was next without once touching her nylon-covered feet to the cracked and chipped tiled floor.

There was no camera to spy on them. No one stole from the poor. That's not how crime worked.

She changed her leather gloves for latex and kissed him. She hadn't kissed him since leaving New York, not quite on the verge of withdrawal but coming close. She dusted her coat free of persistent icy particles before becoming Agent Wilson and buzzing the concierge.

He wasn't a surprise. He was gruff, his language rude. He wanted to know who she was, what her business was.

Michaels answered "federal agents" in a way that

instructed the man to buzz them in as much as admonishing him not to get in the way. They weren't there to piss around with jerk-off janitors. Did he understand?

Apparently he did. The door buzzed instantly.

Wilson whispered, "I love you, sweetheart."

Of course she did. He went in. She followed.

The corridor smelled of people, pets, food, refuse and dampness. They'd seen and smelled worse. Televisions mumbled through a row of doors, with not much effort required to imagine what lay behind them, though poverty had changed for the better over recent years because of Priscilla Vendôme. Hate her or love her, one's economic hardship was increasingly self-directed as much as any other financial portfolio. She was helping those most willing to help themselves.

Penny's door was the first on the right, Wilson and Michaels forewarned of its condition. Michaels went in first, cautiously, without knocking, his weapon drawn. He always did. Despite Wilson previously being prissy, stuck-up and preppy, he would never let anything happen to her.

Wilson followed with her 10mm ready by her side. Despite how arrogant and self-infatuated he had always been, he had never once put her in harm's way. She knew that. She also knew then, as he did now, that she would kill anyone who hurt him.

The air in the apartment was noxious. They didn't have to imagine.

"Percival Penny, we've come here to help you. No surprises, big guy. Understood?"

"Yes. Thank you," Penny called out. "Thank God you've finally come. Please hurry. I'm here, over here. I'm in so much pain."

They saw the all too familiar lift chair, exchanging glances, understanding this would likely not end well for Mr. Penny. They proceeded slowly, exchanging telling glances. Because they had expected to find him alive they had left their respirators in the car. Instead they found him as the Boston PD had left him without a courteous heads up. That's why he hated cops.

Michaels had long since lost his humanity towards these people, Gourmands. The guy looked like shit, he thought with complete indifference. Penny's face was dull white, his jowls made gruesome by two days' growth of dark stubble. Circling his mouth was an aureole of thin, greyish crust. His hair was matted; his velour top had begun an impossible journey over a ponderous white gut spotted with patches of bristly dark hairs and moles. His hands lay almost flat by his side without his elbows touching the floor. The cuffs of his sleeves were wet, his velour pants entirely soaked from the waistband to his bare feet that were permanently swollen, discoloured with bluish-red skin that seemed painfully stretched, accented with hardened toenails that were untrimmed and yellow from lack of attention.

The seventies parquet flooring had erupted around him, swelled by the urine his clothing hadn't absorbed.

"Percival Penny," Michaels began, "good afternoon."

Penny looked first at Michaels who seemed absurdly tall. Wilson stood farther back, well beyond the field of hard and soft green fetid matter. As much as he strained, all he could see of her was her apathetic expression.

"You're detectives. I know what I did wasn't right. I know that."

Michaels holstered his weapon. "No. We are not detectives. Thanks for the insult, although we are here to help you."

"I don't understand. You're not ambulance people either. Who told you about me? How can you help me?"

"The police reported you, Mr. Penny, in a manner of speaking, and the ambulance is not coming. You're a No Assist. You do know that, don't you?"

"But this isn't my fault. This isn't medical. Please, help me stand."

"Unfortunately that isn't possible. You're triple my weight, dead weight, Mr. Penny." He scanned the floor to where the chair stood, prompting more questions. "How did this happen? On your own or did you have help?"

"I wasn't well. I fainted after coming home from dinner with friends. I don't know." He strained more, rolling his eyes to see Wilson. "Please, miss, get me some water, something to eat."

"I will very shortly, Mr. Penny, when we're finished talking. You will feel better very soon. We promise."

Michaels asked: "You dined with friends…at a home or in a restaurant?"

"Yes, we met at a restaurant."

Wilson cut in. "Mr. Penny, there's three feet of snow outside your building and steps you couldn't possibly negotiate with your lift chair. How did you manage your way to a restaurant?"

"My friends, they have a van. They took me."

"Mr. Penny," Michaels continued, "you must weigh close to a quarter-ton. Your chair weighs another two, two-fifty. Do your friends operate a delivery service by any chance? You're a good bit of cargo, Mr. Penny."

"I know what I am. So do my friends. They accommodate me. That's all."

"May we have their names, these friends of yours?"

"I don't know their last names. We're not friends that way."

"I suppose just friendly enough to transport you to…which restaurant was that?"

"I don't know. They usually invite me. I never ask, and then I was too busy with my chair to notice."

Without warning Penny hacked a dozen times staring into the ceiling, his glazed eyes bulging, his mouth wide-open, twisting his head, wincing, distorting his face, the surface layer of his bulk rippling to and fro as though in perpetual motion. He was beyond shame. He had little choice. He knew what people like them thought of people like him. He was weak, drained, this time the projectile falling short of its mark, barely escaping Penny's mouth.

Wilson averted her eyes, massaging her throat, regretting for the moment she wasn't deaf or wearing her respirator. Michaels stepped away until he was finished.

Penny lapped at his cracked lips with his newly moistened tongue, expelling a long breath, his chest heaving.

Michaels stepped into view. He wanted this over with. "We believe you do know, Mr. Penny, about the restaurant. Here's the thing. Help us help you. We'll go first with a few simple questions. Answer them honestly. That's all we want. Tell us what we need to know and we'll get you some water. We'll call some people to get you off the floor and I'll give you something to alleviate your pain. It's that simple. Believe me. We do not want to be here and we do not want to see you this way. So help us out here. Tell us something."

"Who are you?"

"We're people who know about The Diners' Club, about Gourmands, about Hilary Basil. What we need to know before we can help you is how you got to the restaurant because you were not with friends. We also need to know the name or the location of the restaurant. Then we get you off the floor and get you feeling better."

Penny's already viscid eyes began welling with tears. He had no idea who they were.

"I'll pay the 2400 penalty. Please, just get the fire department here. I'll pay you and the lady 2400 in cash. No one has to know. Please, help me."

"Have you ever met Hilary Basil, ever spoken with him?"

"No."

"However you do know of him. Someone has to tell you when and where to meet your Gourmand friends, someone has to get you there. No taxi will and your PMC won't get you onto a bus anytime soon."

"Somebody leaves me a voice-mail telling me when I should be ready. I'm never told in advance where they're taking me. It's always a surprise. I meet them at the garage."

"These restaurants, Mr. Penny, do you eat standing or sitting?"

His mind raced. "Sitting."

Michaels scanned the room. "Mr. Penny, where is your kitchen table?"

"I don't have one. I eat from my counter. I live alone. So what does it matter?"

"I'm curious. How do you pay for these meals, Mr. Penny?" Wilson asked.

"I pay for what I eat. I don't steal from anyone."

"Hilary Basil does," Wilson corrected. "He also kills. He's killing you, Mr. Penny. You do realize you're dying. Don't you? He's also making a fortune off you people. The more he feeds you the richer he gets. That is how it works, isn't it? Eat first, die and pay later. He's your beneficiary, isn't he? Who's your lawyer, Mr. Penny? Or is he or she Basil's lawyer?"

"I don't know what you mean. I don't have a lawyer and you don't have to make me afraid, miss. I already am. I've been terrified for two days."

"Have you planned another dinner?" she asked.

"No. I wasn't well. I told you."

"How will you contact them when you're feeling better?"

"They'll call me when space is available. When I don't answer I lose my place. I can never call them. "

"Have they called you," Michaels broke in, "since you arrived home?"

"No one has called. Not yet. No one else knows about me except you."

"I'm curious, Mr. Penny. How can you possibly afford these dinners?" Wilson asked. "This place isn't quite the Hilton and you subsist off reduced welfare. These dinners, they don't come cheap, from what we hear. It's top notch all the way. And you'll excuse me, Mr. Penny, but you don't appear very affluent."

"I have a nest egg. The dinners are my life, my one small luxury. I need them. Why do you care?"

"We don't care, and that's not a small luxury, Mr. Penny," Michaels added. "We've seen a menu. If it's true, you're eating extravagant meals while collecting welfare. Give us a name, the name of one other Gourmand so we can put this Basil guy where he belongs. Help us out here. He isn't doing you or anyone else any favours. The lady is quite correct. He is systematically killing you people and making a lot of money doing it. You and these other Gourmands might want to wake up to that sometime soon."

You people, these Gourmands? Percival Penny escaped into his darkening mind. He loathed them. Fuck you and people like you. Fuck the lady who's afraid to come closer. In another day or two he'd be dead. The day before he did want to die; now he wanted to live. He wanted to eat and drink and feel better. So fuck you and fuck her.

"Get me help first, whoever you are. You call for help and get me up. Then I'll give you a name. That's what I want."

Michaels turned to Wilson. "Please call the nearest team. Get them here ASAP." She stepped away. He turned his attention to Penny. "In the meantime, Mr. Penny, what do we talk about?"

"I have nothing else to say. I don't know anything. None of us do. But, please, give me water."

Wilson stepped into view. "The team's been dispatched, Mr. Penny," she advised. "They're coming from New York. They've got the right of way. That's about three hours, tops and you're not getting water until you're vertical. We can, however, give you something to make you feel more comfortable until then...once we have a name."

"I could be dead in three hours."

Michaels resisted a deep breath half afraid he would pass out, though in retrospect he believed the sight of them wearing their respirators would have caused Penny to have a brain aneurysm.

A deep soak in a Jacuzzi followed by a swim in a heated pool with Lorie in a string was definitely in order, after a glass of wine delivered to the room with a side order of spirits of camphor and a steaming kettle to clear their sinuses of Penny.

He was blunt. "Quite frankly I'm surprised you aren't already. Your floor looks like a spitball derby. We all have choices, Mr. Penny. You might want to start rethinking yours. You've got three hours, not twenty-four, not even twelve without assistance, and we haven't come from New York to watch you cough up balls or expire. So please give us a name. We'll verify the data and if you're not bullshitting us we'll give you something to ease your breathing until our team arrives. If not we'll wait outside where the air is less scented with your various flavours because right now, really, I am on the verge of puking because of you."

"You promise? They'll help me into my chair?"

"It's what they do. They're pros and we aren't accountable to the No Assist. We don't care who's on the list and who isn't. What we care about is getting Hilary Basil."

"What will you do when you find him?"

"We'll arrest him and his cronies."

"And us, what about us?"

"What about you? I mean, really? What would you expect? The Diners' Club is illegal, pure and simple. You'll no longer have a food source or transportation. As for individual Gourmands, we don't care. Why would we if you don't?" Michaels checked his watch. "The reason you're not all in prison is that, as a group, you're too much trouble. Simply put, Mr. Penny, we know you're all up shit creek and much less costly to the system as LUTs. The acronym means giving you certain freedoms of choice regarding your lifestyle. So, Mr. Penny, before we contribute to your mess on the floor, what do we do? Do we make you all nice and comfy or do we wait outside?"

There was no hesitation.

"Her name is Angela Bangles. She's in the book. I think, I don't know. But that's her name."

Michaels glanced to Wilson. "Please get a pillow for Mr. Penny and may I borrow your scarf."

What! No way. Wilson couldn't believe what he was asking. No way! The scarf was pure 200 dollar Italian silk. Screw professionalism.

She surrendered, only because now she loved him. "You owe me...big time."

"A debt I look forward to repaying. Thank you."

She unravelled the bright red silk, reaching out, not budging an inch closer to the green minefield. "You are not at all welcome."

Michaels masked his face, tying a knot at the nape of his neck, squatting behind Percival Penny as he tucked his coattails between his calves and his thighs, balancing. He reached into his suit pocket, removing a pre-measured hypodermic needle. The 60ml syringe was one-third full; the delivery would be fast and effective.

"No offense, Mr. Penny, simply a precaution. Whatever you've been decorating your floor with, I don't need. This is a muscle relaxant as well as a sedative. You should feel the effects almost immediately, a little euphoric. It's a very pleasant sensation, very calming."

He repositioned Penny's head indifferently to one side without warning, precipitating a gasp. He needed the skin as taut as possible, pressing a gloved palm hard against

Penny's temple to ensure compliance. With the other hand he injected the needle into Penny's external jugular vein without the slightest pause.

Penny twitched once, whimpering, his head held firmly.

Michaels emptied the syringe and stood.

"I feel drunk."

"Do you feel any pain?"

"No. I feel sleepy. I feel, I don't know... content."

"That's good, Mr. Penny. That's good. Goodnight."

"What?"

Percival Penny's brain ceased to function almost immediately. He had no reality, no past, no present or future. A minute later his heart stopped its useless struggle to keep him alive. Percival Penny was dead, euthanized like a household pet.

Michaels and Wilson searched through the apartment unhurried. For the most part they knew where to look and what to look for. They wanted his Personal Measurement Card. They found two. They wanted his membership card and banking information. They wanted anything they could glean about other Gourmands and Hilary Basil and found nothing.

Their Primary at The Agency would do the rest, contacting lawyers, bankers, family, whomever.

Their job was done. Michaels and Wilson had no reason to stay longer. Their assignment was successfully concluded. They turned on the radio and left, easing the door closed into its broken frame. The team was en route with instructions. Lorie Wilson had told them about the garage.

Penny would be removed efficiently, taken away, disposed of and forgotten. Whatever might happen after was not their concern. He was simply dead, injected humanely with single-phase pentobarbital. To anyone else, including the team, he had succumbed to massive heart failure.

Gourmands by law were neither eligible for nor subject to autopsies. No one on the No Assist list or exceeding 39.9 BMI Class was eligible. The cost was too prohibitive, the frequency too burdensome.

Outside the sun had disappeared over the rooftops. The earlier crisp air was damp and penetrating. Dwayne hugged Lorie close, not because of Penny. Because he wanted her close; she wanted him close. He wanted that swim. He wanted to see her in a string, to take her out for dinner, to show her off.

He gazed at the damaged mound of snow, smirking.

She punched him. No way! He could either carry her across, as any gentleman would, or drive to meet her at the first open space if he was so uncertain whether he could manage. She stood waiting, impassive, staring him down. She was daring him.

Big mistake, Miss Wilson.

Normally he would have stepped up to the plate, taken the dare, proven his prowess. However he saw the imminent dangers, he explained. What if he tripped? What if he dropped her? Or worse, what if he hurt her? He would never forgive himself for injuring the woman he was going to marry.

Still, he conceded, she was a woman, delicate and vulnerable, much less able to endure than a man. However he was unquestionably a gentleman and, with that in mind, before she could react, he left whistling, bouncing his way along the sandy sidewalk with Miss Lorie Wilson bundled and snug in her new suede coat slung over his shoulder.

She wasn't impressed. He didn't care, greeting curious and suspicious passers-by with a curt "she's being arrested for soliciting, thought you should know," though he had not the faintest idea where hookers in Boston hung out.

At the car he eased her to the ground. She punched him before straightening her coat, her hat and her dignity, stepping past him to the passenger side where she opened the door herself. She'd had her fill of chivalry for one day.

At the hotel they booked adjoining top-floor rooms. They ordered bottles of premium scotch and vodka from room service.

With the first glass they stripped, filling the same laundry bag before calling the concierge. No way was Lorie putting the clothes she'd worn on the job into her suitcase as they were. Neither was he, she insisted. She felt contaminated.

Most Gourmands dead or dying were as closely related to offal as Percival Penny.

When the man was gone they showered until Lorie's skin was pink, until she moaned in his ear to put her down, until a heavy mist filled the room and a layer of thick fog covered them over in the mirror. She felt clean. She felt like a woman. He felt as though he'd seen her naked for the first time, as though he had touched her for the first time.

He filled their snifters midway, which meant more than half-full. He was intrigued. He was anxious, declaring his preference, watching her decide between blue and red Rios or silver and gold thongs: A collection of tiny triangles, alluring ribbons and bows, sensual and feminine.

He hadn't yet seen her in a string bikini or the thongs she believed might be inappropriate for public consumption at a hotel pool. He disagreed vehemently. Why had she brought them, he argued, if not to show off her gorgeous ass? Really, most women in their twenties did not have buns anywhere near as tight.

Well he would certainly know, wouldn't he?

He sidestepped the issue, the apparently still active issue. Go for the gold!

He did have a point, she conceded, wavering. She wanted to. She was proud. She had waited a very long time, too long, so many years to feel sexy for and with her man, him.

The gold won out before she could change her mind. He was, however, forewarned: Pull at your peril, sweetheart. I will miss you, because I will kill you.

They didn't swim. Dwayne waded, Lorie floating backward in his arms. They were alone, apart from cameras in two corners and a mirrored wall which they suspected made them a Happy Hour attraction at the bar. In the sauna she steadfastly refused to undress, which he thought was moot, if not a little selfish.

Because they couldn't see a camera did not mean one or two were not zoomed in. Poor baby should know better, she pouted, empathizing with his misery. Or had he really ever been a Black Ops SEAL guy?

She readjusted her strings, teasing him with several "Oops! Sorry, sweetheart," until she leaned into him.

He settled for her weight against his chest, her head nestled close to his, streaks of mahogany lip gloss on his cheek.

Later, dressed for dinner, walking into the dining room, heads turned, prompting him to ask in a low voice how many of the business types sitting alone did she think saw her practically naked in the pool.

She responded, "All of them, sweetheart. That's why they're staring. I hope so, anyway. Don't you?"

He chuckled. He wasn't into one-upmanship, moaning disappointment when she guided his hand from her ass to her waist.

Once seated, the hostess was the first to see Lorie's ring. The waitress was second and the sommelier third. Each one equally and sincerely impressed, each one congratulating the future groom on his discriminating taste in beautiful women, the most beautiful of women the sommelier declared.

"Shouldn't we stay a few days longer, sweetheart, to check out this Angela Bangles woman?"

"No real reason to waste time, Lorie. Not yet. She's here

or she isn't. We'll do preliminary work on her from the office. If she does exist we'll have some sort of data on her, some idea of what to do with her before tracking her. I'm really hoping she isn't a lost cause like the last few. Penny's lucky I didn't glaze him over with chunks of yesterday's chowder. I was that close. Then again, he didn't seem very particular. He might have asked for seconds. The guy seemed about ready to devour his own arm…yummy."

"Sweetheart, we're eating."

"Sorry." He savoured his wine. "Thanks for the scarf, by the way."

"You're welcome, by the way. Just don't forget bright red, Italian silk, in a box, and nothing under 200 dollars. Gift wrapping is optional. More importantly it has to be mine; I do not buy other's try-ons, and sometime before summer would be nice." She gazed into her ring's glitter. "We're getting married, sweetheart."

"And we're moving to Key West. Let's not forget thongs and sand, sand and bare breasts. Now that's yummy."

"My father will absolutely freak. He'll believe you're kidnapping me, stealing his little girl."

"I will, if that's what it takes. You wouldn't be my first kidnapping. But here's the thing, dream-girl, for you as much as for me. September gives us six months, maybe a week or two more to get this Basil guy. I want that SOB. During my time with SEAL Team Two, we never once came home with our tails between our legs. We got our guy. We always got our guy… zero exception. We did the job, got it done. Once we got the name, the location, he or she was considered dead, or whatever we had to do. Without, I might add, a single piece of innocent collateral damage. Here, wherever here is, seven years later, who the hell is this Hilary Basil? I'm telling you, Lorie, the guy does not exist. Or, if he does, he's either a fucking smart magician or he knows someone who is."

"Sweetheart, we'll get him."

"I want to believe that. I need to believe that, and we've got six months. So I'm thinking this female Gourmand better be our guide dog or I'm about ready to start blowing off a few toes, hers or anyone else's. It's not like they can walk anywhere, or want to."

*

They left the next morning, late. Lorie, now that she was Lorie, was difficult to refuse.

However by Friday her dilemma remained bothersome, to him. Not her. She wasn't aware that he cared; she simply knew she did not.

Well that was total bullshit. Women cared. It was part of their female condition as much as periods, imaginary PMS, mood swings and cattiness. He knew.

At the end of business most days they each filed a report. At the end of each week supporting documents pertaining to their case files were forwarded by courier from their New York office to their Primary for Pick-Up, although not every day involved a measureable conclusion.

This time the decedent's papers in conjunction with the coroner's report filed at the crematorium were sufficient proof that progress was being made by The Agency, by Team Michaels and Wilson. That was the voice-mail response. Thing is, Michaels didn't think so.

Friday Dwayne asked Lorie to dress in something a little more feminine for the office, like a hot, desirable woman. Not her usual drab attire.

She smacked him. Pardon me?

Just do it. And we need to be at the office by nine.

Manhattan rush-hour, was he joking?

No. He wasn't, and could she please do something with her hair.

Lorie thought surprise lunch, or dinner. She didn't think asshole jerk because each day she could see quantifiable improvements in him.

She combed her hair to one side, sweeping the silky strands over one shoulder, holding them in place with a barrette. She pierced her ear lobes with her sapphire studs, draping her neck with her now favourite pendant, far from simple baubles.

She wore dark blue tights under a dark blue tweed micro skirt and blue suede boots meant for show, not winter. Her cowl neck sweater was cashmere and pale blue. That was it, apart from the blue satin bra strap highlighting a flawless bare shoulder. He was satisfied. Good work.

At Riley they parked in his space, stepped from his Jaguar, not the company SUV parked to one side. He took her coat, tossing it into the trunk, passing Lorie her matching blue Herrera hand bag before taking her arm, escorting her to the elevator that would carry them to the main- floor lobby.

Some Riley employees had arrived earlier, doing their hour behind the glass wall. Others would work out later, lining up to fill elevator cubes that would deliver them to their respective offices.

Their elevator was filled with woman as were most of the eighteenth floor offices. The door closed. He was alone in what once would have been his utopia.

He looked at her, turning her, cupping her face, kissing her fully and torridly on her lips. He released her; he was beaming, she was red, bringing her left hand to his lips, kissing her fingers.

He faced a backdrop of amazed faces, grins, smiles, smirks and open mouths.

"Ladies, please excuse me. I am not a predator. I'm in love. This beautiful example of female exquisiteness has very recently agreed for some inexplicable reason to marry me."

Lorie thought she would die. Better yet, that he should die.

Dwayne had expected some sort of applause, which didn't happen. Chatter happened until the eighteenth floor where he was pushed out by a female flood and ignored.

Lorie walked into their offices thirty minutes later.

"Thank you, sweetheart. It seems I'm going out for drinks tonight. Sorry."

"What did you tell them, about us, the Special Functions Group?"

"That we work for Washington solving federal cold cases, the fancy cars are part of an act…and that you're not a conceited jerk."

24
The Prenup

Priscilla Vendôme returned from her brief vacation completely tanned and completely confidant with her decision, although she was not at all well-rested. Nor would she be for a very long while.

Edward Riley met her in Houston, anxious to hear much more than she had a good time. He accompanied her to Chicago, delighted to hear over cocktails that he had a candidate for the presidency, whereas she had the promise of a private island with a runway suitable for landing a 747.

After dinner they enjoyed cognacs in her condo as a prelude to mutually satisfactory sex devoid of unnatural endearments. When they were finished he dressed, she slipped into a silk chemise and lounge pants before joining him in the living room.

She needed to establish certain guidelines.

She would run for the 2017 presidency. And she would win. That was her commitment. As for her marriage, she would marry two years earlier. The man, whoever he might be, would agree contractually that in the unlikely event she would lose the campaign, or whenever she might be called upon to retire from office at the end of her term, he would not contest an immediate divorce. That point was not negotiable. She would not live her life with someone whose love would essentially be a negotiated fabrication purchased at a very high price.

The Fatal Diners' Club

She had two plus years to find a respectable man, become engaged and get married. Getting married wasn't the problem. Who wouldn't marry Miss Priscilla Vendôme? Not that she was self-infatuated, she was not. She was realistic, as well as young, physically appealing beyond beautiful, inherently sensual and very successful.

Furthermore, once serious about someone, casual sex with anyone else would be out of the question. As much as she enjoyed their shared moments, she would have to put herself out there. She would have to be available, which meant fewer evenings at the office and more of her weekends seeing Chicago from street level instead of peering out over those streets from her ivory tower perch.

Edward Riley concurred without feigning the slightest regret which she would have seen as insincere. Despite how much he desired her affection his interest in her, exclusive of her future and his personal gain, was strictly carnal. She was possessed of boundless energy in bed. So, yes, he had to agree. Somewhere out there some man would soon become extremely wealthy and extremely fortunate.

They understood each other.

*

His name was Frederick Vega. He was touching forty; he was unmarried, slim, athletic, and well-educated with a degree and twenty years' experience in International Affairs.

Born in New York to a Belgian mother and Spanish father he'd lived and worked in that city since graduating. He would be ideal for his intended role, good for the Spanish-speaking vote and the Black vote. His adopted sister was not only Black; she was the National Co-ordinator for The Council of Black Women.

They met over drinks at a Riley Corp. spring gala in 2013, Vega at once smitten by the unexpected flirtation of a woman far too appealing to reside for the briefest time solely in his dreams.

Two weeks later Edward Riley slept with Priscilla for what they had mutually decided would be the last time, hoping she would make the occasion memorable. She did, Riley denying vehemently throughout the evening that he had played any part whatsoever in the selection of a possibly suitable husband.

She didn't believe him. However to what far reaching extent he did lie she would never be aware. He had perforce done what many others would soon do. Upon hearing she was committed to her future, to the country's future, he simply had to ascertain beyond any doubt whatsoever that he had chosen the right woman.

*

He had to learn everything about her, not simply what she had chosen to tell him, or what his HR people had not proven, merely verified. He had to know whether videos existed of her in bed with ex-boyfriends, photos of her kissing or fondling another woman for real or on a frat house dare, skinny dipping or flashing in a mall or other public venue on a dare.

Was she ever photographed while drunk? Was she ever caught DUI? Did she binge drink? Were her parents sober, religious or hedonistic, law abiding or rowdy neighbours? He needed facts. Was she in debt, were her parents in debt? Was she ever pregnant? Was she ever raped? Did she ever abort? What was her true medical history? Did she ever protest against the police, the government? Was she concealing the slightest character flaw? Would anyone, anywhere appear from nowhere on or before January 01st, 2017 with photos of a once topless or naked lady president prancing on a Spring Break beach?

He pressed the ten digits into his personal cell. The call was answered immediately.

Ned Michaels was an ex-navy SEAL, honourably

discharged from his unit some years earlier in a uniform he'd seldom worn decorated with polished medals attesting to a memorable career. The lies, guns and righteous killing had become too easy. He wanted out before he was carried out; somewhat dismayed that he hadn't convinced his young nephew to choose a path less dark. Now he ran a private organization known for getting things done.

He was unlisted, preferring word of mouth advertising, his comprehensive repertoire of services justifiably and prohibitively expensive. He was discreet and effective. His team got things done and he wasn't interested in peering through windows to see whose wife was fucking whose husband or wife or both. Or, for that matter, whether the husbands were doing the dirty with each other.

What Joe Blow did to make it through another day wasn't his concern. He serviced the needs of big business and government when government didn't trust their own to investigate and report on themselves.

He was acquainted with Edward Riley, had been for some time. They were in each other's private contact list, on each other's speed-dial. They met that afternoon outside the office to speak candidly at length. Ned Michaels' assurance not to neglect or discount her minutest infraction or seemingly innocent breach of proper conduct was all Riley required.

Riley enquired as to how long the investigation would last. Considering the background data thus far compiled in the dossier Riley had given him, Michaels suggested meeting once more in ten days' time.

Riley agreed matter-of-factly, neither pleased nor disappointed. There was one other matter, one Frederick Vega whose current file was less complete, a man already known to Riley in business if not personally. He was well-spoken, educated and had an elegant presence, the kind of man the nation would want to see standing by their president.

Riley passed Michaels the man's medical file, requisite data required of any and all aspirants to Riley Corp. He wanted confirmation. The Vega investigation would also extend to his parents as well as the woman they raised as Vega's sister.

If any of them, for whatever reason, perceived or real, were not completely beyond reproach Edward Riley expected to know precisely why with corroborating documentation.

The meeting was over. The men stood, shook hands, and left in separate directions.

Ten days later, moments before his secretary was ready to serve lunch at his desk, Riley's cell buzzed once. Disruptive tones and chimes which the marginally intelligent masses touted as cutesy forms of self-expression were forbidden at Riley Corp. A onetime polite warning from PR to those persons and corporations seeking to do business with Riley was standard protocol as a single chime or beep would end any meeting on a negative note as quickly as any fire alarm.

Don't think to err twice.

His personal phone was no exception.

He met Michaels that afternoon at a park on the far side of town. They walked for over an hour along winding paths, retracing their steps, dodging couples too engrossed with each other to see or to step aside, Riley barely speaking, preferring to hear Michaels' verbal report before delving into the in-depth written exposés of Vendôme, Priscilla and Vega, Frederick.

When they were done the men once again shook hands and went their separate ways.

That evening he stayed longer at the office reading each word, studying each video clip, replaying each one, seeing Priscilla Vendôme as recently as the previous evening working out in the corporate gym after hours, leaving, driving home, stopping at a grocery store for her week's supply of ingredients she would eat alone.

Incredible, he thought. He was seeing her grocery items up close and personal in her cart and she didn't have a clue. He saw her leave, loading her car. He saw her drive into her building and from the lobby he saw her stepping from the elevator to check for her mail.

The clip ended, Riley half wondering why Ned Michaels hadn't managed to film her in the shower or on the toilet.

The data was comprehensive, more so than he'd anticipated. He had chosen the right woman for the job. Nothing in her past or her family's was remotely problematic. No personal videos or photos of Priscilla Vendôme naked or otherwise compromised existed in any of the exes' homes in any format on any device. What amazed him most was Ned Michaels or his team infiltrating their homes, their computers and files. Nor was she ensconced in perpetuity on the internet or on long-forgotten social media sites.

She had not so much as a single filling in her mouth, which he had personally determined on several previous occasions, her body no less perfect from a medical standpoint as previously and personally determined.

She was pure; the Virgin Mary reborn as far as the country, the world and her voting public would be concerned.

Vega was equally conspiracy-proof. He was clean, video interviews with his past lovers ostensibly researching him for a high-level position confirming how well the women thought of him. His colleagues spoke well of him, respected him, believing the background check was related to his potential future dealings with Riley Corp. Vega was approved, good to go.

His parents were a non-issue: White picket, typically suburban. As for his sister, she could not have chosen a better brother to one day endorse.

The single glitch was Priscilla's views on family. She

would have to rethink her mindset. If Vega were good for the Black and Mexican vote, what would a new mother be worth?

Riley was pleased, calling Ned Michaels to commend him. They would certainly be speaking at some point in the future.

*

The next evening after a dinner show and a romantic stroll along the shoreline Vega had no idea he was sleeping with the next US president or that he was a key figure in that becoming a reality. Instead he believed he was incredibly and irreversibly in love with the most intoxicating woman he'd ever met and through the weeks his feelings for her grew stronger.

In June they travelled to Europe for a month-long vacation. Priscilla was already functional in Spanish. By 2016 and her first campaign she would be fluent. Returning for Riley's Fourth of July barbeque in Houston, Vega was anxious to tell the world.

He tapped his beer mug with his knife, requesting quiet. He was calm and collected, beaming, his face smeared with pride. Riley and Priscilla exchanged glances. He didn't ask. He didn't have to. He simply smiled and whispered the news in advance to Karina. He was pleased with his choice. Vega was spotless. He'd come out from under the microscope clean of the faintest smudge, rare for any a man his age.

His one fault however was not merely acceptable, rather highly requisite to their shared futures.

Riley was first to stand, applauding the couple. They were ideal together, meant for each other. Indeed, Vega's one flaw, if anyone would consider such a minor condition a flaw, would be easily rectifiable when the time was right. The date fixed in Riley's mind. He was happy for Priscilla, pleased with Vega.

The Fatal Diners' Club

Riley's life was enviable by the wealthiest of people. What he wanted he bought without restriction, his lifestyle crowned with a magnificent yacht that he took pleasure in with a wife whose body continued to complement the most daring thongs, on-demand mistresses, and a state-of-the-art jet that carried him in luxury from one woman to the others. None of whom would ever compare to Priscilla.

What he did not possess, what he had come to believe he required as a matter of pragmatism, was an heir.

Did he want one? He did not, though the reality of what he had denied for so many years was looming increasingly larger. The corporation was too vast to be broken asunder by his eventual demise, squabbling and greed. Riley Corp. needed ensured longevity, whether male or female, and he had already chosen the mother.

*

Priscilla Vendôme was all-woman. No one who knew her or saw her thought otherwise. What she was not was neither coy nor bashful. She would not be anyone's blushing bride.

She stood on her own cue, kissed his cheek and smiled. She was centre stage, effortlessly assuming the persona of the contented and future Mrs. Vendôme.

She would not under any circumstances take any man's name. How archaic was that? Nor was the issue open to discussion, particularly given the staggering divorce rates. Better he should know sooner than later without sugar coating and that evening in the Houston guesthouse she stole his moment.

"Freddy, please serve us each a stiff drink and sit. I have something to tell you, something you don't yet know about me."

From the bar he silently studied her, curious as to what mystery was about to unfold, until he realized. "Ah, yes. I suppose this is the inevitable "my sordid past" conversation. If so, you are definitely not to worry, my darling. Midlife jealousy is futile at best, if not somewhat juvenile. I've had my fair share of lovers also, you know. I understand completely."

"Good for you. Lovers, that's nice, and who said anything about fair share? That is so inexcusably sexist. As it happens my few experiences were ejaculate-driven automatons. This is not about comparing numbers. This is about me. Please, sit. I have something to say that's got nothing to do with my private past."

She took her drink, resting the glass in her lap. She did not require stimulus or a veil for what was coming. She needed her hands free.

Vega sat quietly, not quite certain how best to survive his unkind indiscretion. She had every reason to feel affronted, of course. His remark was inconsiderate of her sensitivities given the euphoria of her day. He should have realized from experience that from the female perspective such innocent quips were generally misconstrued as explosive character assaults on members of her gender.

He was perplexed by her tone, finding her body language and facial expression difficult to interpret. So enamoured of her, he hadn't yet discovered that she possessed neither. She had learned years earlier to always appear body and face neutral unless she intended otherwise. She was, in fact, expert at nonchalantly selecting her demeanour the way she might select a blouse or skirt from her wardrobe.

He reclined, crossing one leg over the other, waiting. "I'm sitting as duly instructed, madam, your humble servant and captive audience."

"Madam, that's good, very insightful. Listen, Freddy, I have no easy way to tell you this. I didn't tell you previously because I was not expecting to marry you…at least not this soon. In any event, irrespective of your decision, which may understandably change, I will be the next president."

He expelled a breath, grinning, leaning across to pat her hand. "Is that all? My goodness you had me worried for a moment. He has a great deal of faith in you, your Edward Riley. The news is scarcely earth shattering, my darling, albeit wonderfully exciting and richly deserved. We shall have to celebrate. Congratulations."

She took back her hand without pretence, raising her glass to her lips, scarcely sipping. Her eyes spoke volumes. She despised condescension.

"Yes, you're right. Edward does have faith in me, to the extent that we have decided together that in 2017 I will become the next president of the United States." She paused, her thin smile meant to challenge, not surprised by his blank expression. She was pleased. "Which means you will become the First something or other...the very first whatever they will invent to call you."

He heard the words, taking a moment to assimilate them into his memory of their recent and intimate history, their vacation, his proud announcement. He knew instinctively not to laugh, searching her face for the faintest glimmer of humour. What he saw was Priscilla poised and confident. She wasn't joking.

He sat straight, gulping a mouthful of Riley's finest cognac. "You're serious, Priscilla. This is real. You're telling me you have designs on the presidency."

"I can't imagine anything more real. This country needs someone with bigger balls, and I've got them."

He snorted, perhaps too loudly. "In which case they are extremely well camouflaged, my darling."

Her smile remained tight, her bright eyes tersely admonishing the spontaneous gaffe.

He felt dazed. He felt unprepared, trapped beside her on the sofa. He wanted her to say more, to break the silence.

She did.

"That's your second untoward remark, Freddy. Know much about baseball?"

"I'm sorry, Priscilla. That was rude of me. I'm understandably stunned. I was expecting a somewhat more intimate conversation with you this evening. Not this. The implications are staggering."

"I'm giving you an opportunity to back out, Freddy. Edward and I share a certain vision of this country which we intend to implement in four years. Edward has limitless funds and well placed friends; I've got three friendly networks that would hire me in a blink and weekly national coverage irrespective of my female anatomy."

He drained his glass. More silence.

"Correct me if I'm wrong, Priscilla, or if I appear somewhat probing. But do our presidents not require spouses for appearances sake, despite their historical proclivities for the occasional dalliance?"

"Marriage is requisite, yes. I was expecting to marry someone provisionally in two years, provisionally meaning he would receive ten million up front in cash to support his role as the good husband and ten more at the commencement of each four-year term on the condition he would willingly sign a document agreeing to divorce me immediately upon my defeat at the polls or upon the expiration of my terms. I had no intention of condemning myself to a marriage of convenience once the purpose was served. However I had no idea at the time I would meet you. You should also be aware that, irrespective of my political ambition, I would have insisted on the divorce clause in our prenup. I do not believe in the concept of fighting to make a marriage work, counselling or couples' therapy. The notion of fighting to circumvent fighting is a gross absurdity. If, as they say, marriage is a partnership, then when it's done it's done. Shake hands, walk away and get on with life. Start over... with your own name. I am Priscilla Vendôme, Freddy. I have too much vested in that name. Nobody will know Priscilla Vega. And that is non-negotiable."

He stood. His glass was empty.

Priscilla understood the need for more silence.

"Are you possibly thinking I will now desert you because of this unexpected revelation?"

"I'm not certain. How can I be? I do love you, Freddy. However in four or eight years with what I'm intending, who knows? Marriage, in theory anyway, requires mutual exclusivity, not our right to metamorphose apart from one another. In spite of which you will shortly receive a gift of ten million dollars in a Swiss bank account...untraceable. Of course, you will be required to sign the prenup and, in the event you leave the bride standing at the altar or any time before, Edward will expect you to return the ten million in full. Conversely, in the event I fail at the polls the money is yours to keep. Please excuse my frankness, but the harsh reality is that a woman unmarried at thirty-five is perceived as a random whore, as opposed to men in their forties like you who are considered as ladies' men, cavalier and confirmed bachelors."

He straddled the arm of the sofa.

"Meaning that, had I not met you, you would soon be actively seeking someone of certain qualifications to marry as a matter of political necessity...provisionally." He sipped from his snifter to moisten his lips. "I'm not asking. I'm merely stating an apparent fact...apparent to me in any event."

"Yes to both: The American version of an arranged marriage for which I do not apologize. I want that job. I also believe weddings are an eventual necessity for people in love. The presidency is added-value, or possibly not. All presidents share a single commonality, Freddy. They all look like shit after their first term. After the second term no one believes their age." She took his hand. "Are you ready for that?"

"I adore you, my darling. What more need I say? If you don't believe that, you will believe nothing. What I find troubling is the ten million. I felt until now that I had won your heart, not the lottery."

"I am not a lottery. And the money is not a gift in the truest sense, more like an honorarium. In the year preceding the election you'll be required to resign your position in New York in order that we campaign together. If I lose you'll be between positions for the better part of two years and very likely subject to political bias when searching for work as in the case of Riley Corp. where you will never be invited to work. Conversely, when I do win you'll receive a salary and expenses as my First whatever. This is not a bribe, Freddy. Think of it as a nest egg, something put aside for a rainy day. As for you and me, we're a pleasant coincidence. You walked into the right place at the right time. I'm glad you did. I just don't know what else I can say."

Vega was accustomed to making good decisions quickly. He loved her. He touched the crystal rim of his glass to hers, decided. She loved him. That's all he needed to know.

"I shall never call you Madam President, Priscilla. Nor will I ever walk behind you. In bed I will continue to prefer the senior position, unless otherwise persuaded by the president's youthful athleticism and, in public, you will be my wife as much as the nation's mother. You are my darling, now and forever, irrespective of your foreseeable big plane and fancy office." He smiled widely. "If you concur with these irrevocable demands, as I agree with yours, I see no valid reason to disrupt our current plans or our evening." He stood, reaching out for her hand. "I believe we have spoken sufficiently for one night, my darling. Can we agree on that as well?"

25
The engagement party

The engagement party hosted by Karina and Edward Riley was held on the first Saturday in August at the Riley Ranch. The who's who of Texas, California, Illinois, Florida, Washington and New York State were invited, expected to attend, amongst them were the three networks, the press, senators, congressmen, business associates and those who had once or often asked a favour of Edward Riley.

The future bride was glorious, stunning. The world knew her; they remembered her. They loved her, missed her and wanted to know more about her.

Frederick Vega was a backdrop in black tie, apparently charged with entertaining her parents whom she had never forgiven for their intolerance and lack of support when she had first declared she was leaving home to pursue a career in journalism; his parents who were unaccustomed to such extremes of high society, and his sister who needed him not at all. She was doing quite fine on her own which didn't go unnoticed by Riley.

He might have been a caterer for the attention he garnered.

He didn't mind. The day and the evening were hers, though he had been cautioned the timing was not right for the real announcement. That speech would come a year later. They didn't want to tease the world for three plus years with thoughts of Priscilla Vendôme as president. Nor did they want lesser female pretenders lining up behind her to soil or dilute her chance of succeeding.

Then came Thanksgiving and Christmas in rapid succession, the bride-to-be and Vega enduring separate lives for reasons of requisite propriety made easier by distance except for infrequent intimate weeknight dinners, escape weekends and a ski vacation in Vale. In truth, Vega was more disenchanted than Priscilla. She cherished her freedom. The wedding and his live-in status would come soon enough

When they were together he was a passably good lover, neither ardent nor unimaginative, never quite stealing her breath away, though never cause for disappointment.

Her reciprocity was real, lending credence to what wasn't. She enjoyed sex for sex, not for any deeper meaning.

He was deeply in love, as was Priscilla with him. She never refused him, whether taking his calls, accepting a luncheon date or turning this way or that in bed. No more or less than she had for Edward Riley.

Once married, she would be the unimpeachable wife. He would have no reason, not the slightest inclination to appear less than incredibly blessed with good fortune when scrutinized by the unblinking public eye.

That he would be relentlessly scrutinized was understood, though to what extent was not.

Each rare morning she woke in his arms she saw true love in his eyes, quietly wondering at the extent of that truth.

What he saw was her eagerness for Sunday, June 01st, with no such lingering doubt.

Priscilla Vendôme knew how to captivate when needed, and how to distance herself when required.

26
Cupid's Trinkets

Edward Riley sat stretched out in his study with the lights dimmed, staring at the chandelier, his feet planted on his desk crossed at the ankles. The flat screen built into the wall was black. The nightly financial report was over. The week was over, at least for those without much of a future.

He was pensive, appreciating the quiet. Karina wasn't home. She rarely arrived home on peak evenings before midnight when they would usually enjoy a nightcap together before retiring.

She hadn't once asked, or accused him for that matter, though she had always known there were others. He wondered whether she had ever thought of Priscilla, of him and Priscilla in bed together. He believed possibly so, though if she had, she hadn't once betrayed whatever emotion she might feel. Not to him, not to Priscilla.

Ten months had gone by, ten months of faithfully loving Karina notwithstanding occasional and selective diversions to lessen the tedium of business travel. They were all perforce young and beautiful and fitted with certain intelligence, none with the slightest idea of who he was. He could have chosen any one of them to impregnate, to make them independently wealthy for life. Yet he didn't. Despite their good looks they were not what he required beyond their willingness to open their legs and keep them open for as long as he desired them.

For which they were paid well, most of them single, some attached, some married and out on the town to escape the monotony of narrow lives they had rushed into without thinking. How many wives, all of them young, had he fucked in the last ten months? How many had he sent home well-fed with enough in their purses to buy their freedom?

He chortled. He'd never thought of himself as a philanthropist.

He toyed with the deep-green jewel, staring into the open felt box, glancing at the grandfather clock, mimicking the tick, tick, tick. Valentine's would dissolve into another day in five, four, three, two and another minute. Gone.

Through his window he saw the blue-white of the halogen beams in the distance flickering like bright stars along the unpaved road. Valentine's was amongst Karina's busiest evenings of the year, her regulars likely reserving their prized tables a year in advance before leaving.

Cancellations were expected, though Karina forbade special favours. A name did not guarantee a table unless the name was Riley. When the restaurant was operating at capacity, which was most nights, you stood in line or went somewhere less notable regardless of celebrity status.

He loved her. He always had more than any woman, more than Vera Batten whom he hadn't seen or thought to remember in years, whose bastard son was twenty-five.

He wondered how the kid and his sister had evolved in life. It wasn't uncommon for those who began privileged lives with the hard-earned money of others to die of drug dependency or in poverty, trading fine homes for tenements, fine wardrobes for the ragged fashion of homeless street dwellers. At least the girl, if remotely like her mother at that age, would have sufficient charms and attributes to ensure a passable existence until such time as her aesthetic value would inevitably wither by virtue of neglect or the indiscriminate abuse of those charms.

He laid the emerald pendant into the box, snapping the

lid closed. His personal secretary had enviable taste. She never disappointed him on such special occasions.

He stared at the clock. Whether he did or did not the cursed tick, tick, tick would never stop. He would be dead 100 years, a cluster of dried out bones clad in tatters lying amongst shards of rotting mahogany and disintegrating silk, and the well-oiled grandfather would continue tick, tick, ticking without aging a single day.

Edward Riley, unlike Casey and Thatcher, resented that he was aging despite his good health and disarming younger wife.

Her car's lights sprayed across his study walls. Karina was home. The engine died, the lights with it, as would he one day. What he needed was twenty-years. What he hoped for was thirty and more with his senses intact.

He stood, waving a palm across the light switch, leaving the room in total darkness. Champagne was chilling in the bedroom where he often waited to greet her. He laid Karina's gift on her pillow. He expected nothing in return. Valentine's was a woman's day. He twisted the bottle from the cork, preparing the fluted glasses, resting Karina's on her bedside table.

The front door opened and closed. He followed her every movement in his mind. She was pressing a fingertip onto the keypad by the door, the green light dying, the red light flashing. She was kicking off her shoes, crouching, taking them with her. She was climbing the stairs in her stocking feet, nimbly, like a cat. She always did, never once seeming tired or depleted by long and arduous days.

They had unshared secrets, each one. Everyone harboured secrets, save the worst of liars, though he believed she hadn't once thought to cheat. She was content with the trade-off, preoccupied with her restaurants when she wasn't with him or without him to worship the sun on the yacht in the Gulf or flying from city to city to make certain La Montoya would continue as the finest dining experience in the capitals of the country.

She looked better, lovelier than most women half her age. She worked regularly and intensely with her trainer to ensure that would never change. Where patrons of La Montoya paid dearly to delight their palates at lunch and dinner with succulent creations dribbled with decadent sauces and creams, she ate salads for lunch and prepared simple dinners for herself off to the side of Houston's most enviable kitchen where most times she ate standing.

Where other women her age went under the scalpel to disguise the haunting ill effects of childbirth, or laid unconscious while overpaid surgeons sucked half their body weight through a tube into a bucket, she went shopping for clothes the others couldn't imagine wearing. She was complete. She had a full life. She had no reason to either need or want children. Case closed, her views of motherhood and ego-driven reparative surgery were well-documented and not without certain injured emotions amongst the finest of Houston's families.

Simply put, Karina Montoya would never be any couples' first or last choice as godmother. Though, much to her credit, for each baby shower she had ever been invited to as a matter of protocol she hadn't once succumbed to the pressures of social responsibility. She quite easily said "no, thank you," bluntly changing the subject to something she was interested in.

He'd always known of one surgical procedure in particular that she did however condone. Nor would she hesitate for a moment. The planet was already overflowing with an unsustainable population. Of course, she was right. The world's indigent and uneducated were without question the worst offenders, using their bodies as affordable entertainment centres and momentary release without the slightest concern for social responsibility.

Nor were middle and upper-class Americans with four and five kids any better than welfare mothers and coffee house waitresses. In fact non-mothers, she had always believed and argued, were discriminated against for not worsening the world's condition while forced to carry the financial burden caused by women too stupid to comprehend that not being able to feed two kids probably meant not being able to feed three, four or five.

Then what of education, what of the future? How many brain-dead waitresses and open-legged welfare recipients could the world tolerate before imploding?

Karina padded into the bedroom smiling, unbuttoning her blouse. She almost always smiled. When she wasn't, that was a good time to leave wherever she might be. If you were trapped, that was never good.

"Good evening, mi corazón. Forgive me for being so late once again. Lovers are always the last to leave and tonight La Montoya was home to many of them."

"Happy Valentine's" He nodded towards her pillow. "I thought you might enjoy champagne as more appropriate for the day." He glanced at his watch. "Or more precisely… yesterday."

She kissed him and hugged him. That was her MO each night. She loved him.

She twirled and went to her bed. She loved surprises. The gift was unwrapped. Edward never wrapped her gifts. At Christmas they celebrated what she called 'The White Man's Christmas', boring, when he would give her one gift unwrapped. He wasn't into bathrobes, hot toddies and presents piled high under a non-indigenous tree when he could buy anything anytime he wanted and usually did, including negligees, peignoirs, jewellery and cars, or anything else that might catch his eye or imagination. Her gift, however, was always opened under the bright Caribbean sun on the foredeck of the yacht.

Karina was his drug, his life's crutch. What he would not do for her had never crossed his mind.

"Mi corazón, muchìsimas gracias. It's lovely."

"Lovely until adorning your neck… when it will fade against true beauty as everything does."

She patted his cheek. "And did Mary have specific instructions or was she left to decide for you what would look best at my neck?"

"She had full authority, I admit. Better to designate than disappoint is an appropriate axiom when one is in doubt or without requisite qualifications for a specific purpose."

"Then you must kiss her for me," Karina proposed with a smirk. "Or I will. She has excelled as always."

He agreed. He would. Mary was twenty-nine, single, and drop-dead gorgeous. Karina had no doubt he would.

He watched her undress. She was exotic. They drank their champagne as she showered away her day and slipped into silk to sit by the fireside. They held hands, talking in low tones to hear the soothing music of another era, neither one tired, each body and mind acclimated to long days and short nights.

When the flames began struggling to flicker, shadows fading into the muted lighting, they went to bed, ending their evening as lovers ever youthful. Words were wasted; the occasional few smothered with heated kisses before climactic release, before the agony of withdrawal, exhausted bodies and fevered minds yielding to peaceful dreams worlds apart.

What better proof of love than to wake hungering for more.

He laid by her side, studying her, her skin tanned with a natural amber glow, her contours the embodiment of femininity. What he had decided was not about love, were she ever to discover the lie. Not in his mind. Karina would always come first in his life, irrespective of past or future betrayal. That was an undeniable truth. He kissed the soft flesh of her shoulder.

He couldn't imagine his life without her, though Riley was clear in his mind on the eve of his failure. He would proceed with what he had begun ten months earlier. He was determined and would suffer no sense of guilt for his decision. Guilt was the bane of lesser men. The timing was propitious if he was to circumvent irreparable and concurrent miscarriages borne of what would certainly be his single most indefensible error in judgement. If he were ever to create an heir his eleventh hour had arrived and, despite her outspoken personal conviction, he would compel Priscilla Vendôme to understand the nation would not embrace any president devoid of strong family beliefs.

*

Halfway across the country Chicago was in the throes of another barren, colourless winter.

The night was bitter. Her windows were frosted, white against the dark sky beyond.

Priscilla Vendôme lay in bed. She was naked, yet she was warm, her dishevelled clothes strewn across the carpet. Vega lay beside her, sleeping contentedly, facing away. He always faced away.

She studied her wrist. The gold charm bracelet was an empty band with a single trinket: A tiny heart fashioned from gold, which gave her a clue as to what she might expect as impromptu gifts over the next several years, from a man she'd recently made a future millionaire, if there were several more years. She didn't know. He wasn't uppermost on her mind.

The diamond pendant she received by courier earlier in the day had graced her neck at dinner, Vega commenting on her impeccably good taste, Priscilla accepting the compliment without feeling the need to explain the jewel's origin. She knew twenty-nine-year-old Mary. They spoke on a regular basis. The discreet young woman had excelled once again and probably twice on behalf of her boss.

She propped herself onto an elbow. Ten months and Vega's effusive attention hadn't once faltered, yet she seldom thought of him throughout the many days and nights they spent apart. She did think of Edward, though, which she didn't for a moment consider strange. How could she not think of him?

In a few months she would marry the man lying beside her, whom she was certain Edward had placed in her path. But for what reason when she was more than capable of finding her own husband? Edward wasn't widely known for his big heart. His sensitivity quotient was something less than zero. He did nothing, nor did he endorse anything which he did not consider personally or commercially gainful.

In three years less six weeks she would be lying in bed somewhere inside the White House. Or would she? She wondered about that. Or would she be in the War Room? Or was there a War Room? She didn't know. How often had she raised her hand, standing to face him in the James S. Brady Press Briefing Room? Who would soon stand to face her? How many would she know by name? She thought most likely all of them.

Of one thing she was certain. Her personal security detail while inside the White House would be comprised solely of women. She would not sacrifice her inherent femininity or her privacy for anyone. Nor would she allow herself to transmute into a greying hermaphrodite like the countless genderless females on Capitol Hill who desired so much to compete equally with men that they failed to see how they had irreparably mutated into one of them in every way except squatting to pee.

Then what of Mr. Vega who in ten months hadn't once mentioned children? What was up with that? Love them or hate them, no man was indifferent to them. What guy would not want to know upfront what was expected of him, of what would alter his future very possibly or probably for the worse? Thanks for a good time, my darling. I do love you very deeply, but... Or, better yet, how wonderful to have such a precious little girl created in your image as proof of our undying and unquenchable love?

Barf. Beware of that one. That's what she had expected, though not a single word in ten months, not that she cared. She didn't. Nor would she ever broach the subject.

She raised the duvet, studying her body. She was pleased. What wasn't to like? Nothing sagged. What had to be tight was tight, would remain tight, and the only contraction she had any desire to feel was the man she was with pulling out.

She was proud of her body, as Vega clearly was. She wondered what was in his mind as he slept. He hadn't once mentioned the ten million he would soon receive or that very soon he would enjoy a private island, a private secretary and personal aide. That alone was bizarre.

She darkened the room, the windows becoming backlit screens.

She wriggled to lay on her other side, facing away before curling into her pillows, wondering. Who would she not marry because of Vega, because of Edward Riley? Who had she not met that she might truly love? Would she ever see him and know, see him and regret what she had done? Would the first female president ever think to cheat on her husband?

She closed her eyes. She didn't believe so. Then again she had yet to meet him.

27
The Wedding

Winter transitioned into spring. Priscilla's special day was a week away. She had nothing left to do, not that she had done much beyond listing a few names, selecting her gown and choosing a sunny honeymoon destination.

Her secretary and the planner did the rest to ensure the 500 guests would never forget the event.

May 26th Edward Riley flew to Chicago. Karina would join him on the Thursday. She and the female executives at Riley Corp. had an evening planned for Priscilla on the Friday that would not include him or Vega.

Vega's stag would follow on the Saturday, for which Mary had forwarded his sincerest regrets. He was previously committed.

Priscilla was in her office when he arrived. Throughout the day not a word was spoken about the wedding or Vega. Riley was all business when in town, though when the workday ended he invited her for cocktails and dinner which was not unusual. She read nothing into it. They often dined together when time allowed. She wasn't cheating. Their past was their past.

"Thank you for joining me, Priscilla, at what must be a very hectic time."

"Thank you for inviting me. Freddy sends his regards."

He ordered the drinks, waiting for the waitress to leave.

"How does he enjoy not having to look at prices?"

"He bought a Maybach Exelero." She chuckled. "He's adjusting quite well, quite possibly too well."

Thirty-one months and counting, nineteen until a tsunami called Vendôme strikes our political shores."

"I'm ready."

"More importantly so is the country, whether or not they're cognizant of the need. It's time for a female at the helm, at least one of your ability. If I were a betting man I would predict a record turnout, a record number of you ladies scurrying to vote as much against a man as for a woman. You are, as a group, inherently mean-spirited." The waitress came and went. "By the way, your running mate is from Alabama, Bradley Duncan. We have to secure the Southern electorate and he's the state mascot, their golden boy: Princeton, class of '87, but hands-on, a self-made millionaire, athletic with outspoken views regarding the nation's health and a moderate married with two kids old enough not to get in the way. Mr. America with a drawl running alongside the nation's darling."

"Does he know?"

"He does not, nor will he for another year, leaving him sufficient time to prepare. I harbour no doubt whatsoever that he will accept. I mention him, Priscilla, to drive home a point."

"Which is?"

He leaned forward, cupping the old-fashioned between laced fingers.

"Simply put, when we're done with this political business, after whatever number of terms you win in Washington, I wish you to take over control of Riley Corp. Karina has no interest in the corporation other than its perks and rightfully so. She has her own career and is in full agreement with my thinking. Should we fail in our bid for Washington, I would expect you to relocate in Houston immediately to assume a larger and more significant role until such time as I fully relinquish mine."

She was astonished. "You're serious."

"Very. Should you agree, which I do not expect of you this evening, I will have my will rewritten to reflect my wishes. Furthermore, upon my unfortunate demise my child will inherit forty-nine percent of the company's holdings; you will receive fifty-one percent which you will agree to bequeath to him or her upon your death or retirement. As well, I will stipulate that on the day you assume the responsibilities of your new role, 100 million will be transferred to your offshore account."

She wasn't surprised. "I don't have one."

"You will."

Her lips curved into a curious smirk. "I see a small glitch there, Edward. Namely, you don't have a child and Karina isn't about to ruin that gorgeous body of hers to supply you with one. Nor do I blame her."

"My first wife was a bit of a casual whore, and not a very careful one, burdened with the remnants of two escapades in particular that I'm aware of with men previously unknown to her. Needless to say such a scandal would have destroyed my mother, leaving me with little recourse but to raise them as my own until my parents' kind natures could no longer be injured by her thoughtless actions. The boy and the girl were immediately thereafter disowned by me with sufficient funds to ensure their permanent absence. The fathers were somewhat less than average and my wife, well, I suspect she most likely earned her law degree on her back. I could not for a moment imagine her offspring one day at the head of Riley. And you are quite right about Karina."

"Are you planning a surrogate, Edward?" She chortled. "Somehow I don't see you alone in a room with a little cup and a girlie magazine."

"That improbable experience would be uncharacteristic to say the least. I would be hard-pressed to recall a single episode in my life of that particular desperation." He signalled the waitress for more drinks. "However due to my longstanding neglect the need has become somewhat urgent. I'll be eighty-two or possibly dead when he or she is twenty-one and still without sufficient experience to share your control of Riley. That is why you must assure me that you will guide him or her toward that destiny before and after I'm gone and that after your political career you will legally change his or her name from Vendôme to Riley to ensure the corporation's continued family history. Otherwise, once I'm gone, Riley will scatter into inconsequential little bits, which I see now as an affront to my forefathers."

She blinked once, massaging her glass between her palms. "You're losing me here, Edward. You want me to have a baby with Frederick then give it your name and forty-nine percent when you're dead?"

He didn't respond. "Do you love Vega? Be truthful with me."

"Is he my heartthrob dream guy? No. He is not. Neither are you, Edward. I like him enough to sleep with occasionally. However like most men he believes he's better in bed than he is. Enough said. He's respectful, and he knows not to expect guarantees. I made that very clear to him. Will I divorce him at some point? Yes, I believe I will. I'd hate to think I'm disappointing someone more deserving."

"That isn't entirely true...about his being respectful, I mean. Having said that, what I want is for you to have my son or daughter by me and not from a little cup." He chuckled. "If memory serves, Priscilla, you are far more stimulating than a glossy page and you would not be the first bride to bid her illicit lover adieu on the eve of her wedding."

Silence.

"What you're suggesting is completely ludicrous. Those days are over. We agreed. And don't you think Frederick might want the first shot making me a mother?"

"He doesn't. And heretofore neither have you. Despite his sexual prowess feigned or real, imagined or practiced, which I don't for a moment doubt since you are the one in bed with him, and regardless of how you might feel obligated not to stray from his bed, and no matter what size gun he may have on his person to shoot with, he will never hit your particularly alluring target as he must."

"I don't follow."

"The man shoots blanks. The daily ritual you adhere to in order to ward off the evils of childbirth is not required. Your pharmaceuticals are wasted as result of his deceitfulness."

"You're saying he's sterile."

"Vega's as sterile as a hospital bedpan and, I assume from your expression, that he's relying on your once firm opposition to family as a means of maintaining his virile status with you. In short, the man's a liar. I wish I had known earlier. I'm deeply sorry, not for his inadequacy, rather for his lack of honesty towards you."

"You had him investigated?"

"I had you both investigated, to ensure your future, which is why I would prefer that you not tell Vega about our Mr. Duncan. I would also ask you not to tell him about your future at Riley or your bonus. At this juncture we have sufficiently good reason not to entirely trust the man."

"Thanks. He's about to become my husband."

"Indeed, a fine husband, husband to the next president who will one day soon be burdened with incalculable secrets worse than what we're discussing. Nor will anyone discover his inadequacy, beyond which his background is impeccable. You, however, and not surprisingly, are pristine."

"How much of a secret is a pregnant woman?"

"He'll be delighted with fatherhood, to the tune of ten million dollars every four years and I've taken measures to ensure his false pride. As for our child, you must. You really must. We're practically assured of every demographic except the millions of women who believe flooding the planet with their spawn is their sole purpose in life. We need that vote, I need you at Riley and I need Riley to continue as Riley."

"I don't want children, Edward. What don't you understand?"

"But you do want an island which will be yours during and after the presidency, you want Riley and one day, without him, while you're young enough to enjoy life, you'll be amongst the wealthiest and most influential women in the country with a generous head start. What don't you understand?"

The waitress stood discreetly to the side, Riley waving her in to order dinner, Priscilla Vendôme taking the few moments to quell the shockwaves reverberating inside her head.

"What about Karina?"

"She won't be told. I love her deeply, though I see no need to intentionally create a possibly volatile situation, women being what they are. I imagine she'll be happy for you and probably arrange a shower. This isn't about love or deceit, Priscilla. This is about me, you, Riley Corp. and the presidency. The child is simply a means to a necessary end, a veritable saviour. How many of us can say we exist to save a mega corporation and a country from pending disaster?"

"Shit, Edward. You had to wait this long, a week before my frigging wedding?"

He swirled his drink. "Not unintentionally. You will deliver nine months after your wedding. Ten months later we tell the world about you and Duncan. You can't buy that kind of sensational press for any money, not even mine. You know as well as I do, Priscilla. They'll eat you up...and little whatshisname."

309

"What will I tell Frederick?"

"Tell him nothing. Let him tell you."

"And when he asks who the father is?"

"Having discovered his natural deficiency, which is true, you regrettably did what you must in accordance with your timeline, which is also true. He thoughtlessly misled you with the full knowledge he might very well ruin your single most important ambition. He had a choice, you do not. And names are meaningless in such sordid situations, though I dare say the end product will one day become an enviable human being."

"You do realize this might not work out? That's a lot to expect from one night."

"I've taken that eventuality into account, for which reason I am staying through the week. I took the liberty of booking you a room at my hotel. I would like to suggest afternoon and evening encounters through to Karina's late arrival Thursday evening. We can meet again Friday afternoon and Saturday morning prior to your spa treatments with her."

Priscilla unconsciously tapped her fingertips on the table. "You want to do me nine times in a week. Escorts don't work that hard."

"We should view nine as a minimum requirement in the light of our possible failure, albeit gently, without our previous dedication to the moment. I'm sure you wouldn't want to spoil the groom's first official incursion."

He grinned, leaning slightly backward as the waitress approached with the wine. When she was gone he raised his glass.

"A mother...shit."

"The extent of your motherhood will be whatever you determine and Vega will have no claim. The kid will have nannies, nurses and a private education, possibly offshore. You'll have the best care, extended leave from Riley and a trainer paid well to reshape your body to its current thought-provoking condition." He touched the rim of his crystal goblet to hers. "Are we agreed?"

She filled her lungs to capacity, exhaling a slow stream of air through pouted lips. She nodded. "Yeah, we're agreed...about this and about Riley. I will need a copy of that will and a witnessed document regarding the 100 million, though I'll believe 'gently' when I can walk down the aisle without crutches."

He chortled. "Of course, you will have my arm the entire way as we pass through the admiring horde. I wouldn't think of giving away damaged goods."
*

Saturday evening Priscilla Vendôme joined Riley and Karina for dinner, neither woman caring to comment on the activities of the previous Ladies' Night. The conversation was all about Priscilla, her future at Riley and her assault on Washington. Little was said about Vega who Priscilla hadn't seen for a week.

As it turned out 'gently' wasn't good for Priscilla. The slow and deliberate motions of perfunctory intercourse with her bare ass in the air made her feel ridiculous, as though he was intentionally teasing her. She gave him a choice. The least he could do, she told him, was fuck her with a little enthusiasm or send somebody in who could.

However by Sunday morning she believed she might have been too demanding. The sex was good, very good; more importantly each thrust was a deep stab at Vega.

The morning was idyllic, which she spent with Karina refining details with the planner before dressing with Karina's help more for an elegant dinner party than for a wedding. She didn't want to be seen as a blushing bride. She was a woman in control; far superior to the man she would stand beside. Submissiveness had no place in her current or future plans.

Her cinnamon hair was pinned with a jewelled barrette

into a chic updo; her ears and neck adorned with emerald drops and pendant, her lips glossed with deep maroon. Her shoulders and arms were bare, the swell of her breasts accentuating the deep cut of her deep green fitted gown falling to a discreet few inches above her knees. Her shoes were two-inch green satin sandals.

She wore no gloves and no other jewellery, her hand resting on Riley's forearm.

"Thank you for doing this, Edward. I wouldn't want anyone else to give me away."

"What did you tell your father, if I may ask?"

"That I am not a forgiving person, taught well by him. He came for my mother, who came so that she might have something to tell her friends and neighbours. That, my dear Edward, is the essence of family life. We are each other's disappoint and he's here serving the same purpose as Frederick"

"Irrespective of which you are divine...in so many ways. How could I possibly think to refuse you?"

She squeezed his arm. "We've certainly had a week to remember. I officially qualify for handicap parking. I do hope you're happy."

"I am indeed. The week was extremely pleasurable and no less requisite. Seriously though, despite the arguable nature of the past few days, Priscilla, we have reshaped the future by our pleasurable actions."

"Actions, and all week I thought we were... He's looking. I wonder if reading lips is another of his secrets."

"You really are too good for him. Thank goodness for your contract...very forward thinking of you, a brilliant move."

"He's temporary, particularly since he's shown himself as a liar. In the meantime he'll serve a purpose. He travels for business and I work late. In two and a half years we'll see even less of each other and I do intend to invoke the contract when the timing is right for me. Until then he's a necessary prop and occasional release, possibly…on my schedule."

He kept a solemn face. "We're closing in on the Gates of Saint Peter, whose lesser guardian seems much more agreeable than I remember. Could I be wrong in assuming he's pleased with his new vestibule and organ whose current cacophony I find particularly annoying?"

"This was my one concession with future public opinion in mind. Perjury and pretence for the sake of his aging parents was not. Thank you for showing the priest his options."

"Or for showing the community that Priscilla Vendôme cares about them. More importantly, thank you for this, Priscilla. Thank you for Riley… for whatshisname."

"I'm thinking Edward. K. Vendôme for a boy, Karina E. if it's a girl. I love Karina very much, Edward. It's the least I could do given the circumstances, though I haven't worked out the initials yet."

"Why bother? Be unique." He patted her hand. "We have arrived at your future. We'll talk more when I dance with the bride."

Priscilla and Karina exchanged long and warm smiles. She ignored Vega's parents and her own. The mothers' shocked expressions hadn't gone unnoticed.

Priscilla's bride's maid took her place before the priest; Riley stood the bride beside her, bridging their thoughts with piercing glances.

Stepping away he acknowledged the Vegas with a slight nod, Vendôme and his wife with equal dispassion. He didn't like them. He was a firm believer in first impressions; as much as he was proficient in concealing them when need be. He'd seen the horror in the women's eyes at seeing Priscilla's gown, whispering an overt critique to their husbands behind gloved hands.

He could well imagine how Vega had put his people into a five-star at his expense, whereas Priscilla left her parents to arrange their own accommodations since her father hadn't seen the need to contribute to any portion of his daughter's wedding which was truly their unimaginable loss.

As for Vega himself, the ten million wouldn't last long, not with pompous generosity and a rash craving for luxury imports inconsistent with his current lifestyle. The one thing Riley did like was the Black sister. She was captivating in her appearance and in her convictions. That was good. The masses thrived on beauty. He made eye contact and a mental note to speak with her.

The wedding service was simple. The bride was sophisticated, youthful, unruffled in the face of adversity. The priest was humble, a self-deprecating man of God. Forgiveness came easily to him. The groom, for his part, was relieved and grateful the two hadn't killed one another.
*

Weeks earlier God had not been invited. In fact the bride had asked that He stay away much to the priest's theatrical irritation and Vega's disquiet as the son of devoted Catholics who would attend the wedding, despite which Priscilla was as adamant as she was calm.

In addition she would not convert because she had nothing to convert from. Why hadn't Vega forewarned the cleric? She felt as though they'd conspired to lure her into a trap. Strike two.

That would not happen. She was not a believer or disbeliever. She was who and what she was. Live and let live. Amen. She was the bride. Case closed. The only higher power she would consider would be a justice of the peace in a courtroom, in a civil union without spectators, followed by a reception.

Opinions were not welcomed. As for children, she didn't see the question as any business of a celibate priest or the future in-laws she had met once a short while earlier and had forgotten.

Vega simply shrugged.

She did not believe in all things bright and beautiful. She had witnessed too much that was dark and ugly in a world burgeoning with kids, most of them starving because they were small and that which was great around them did not care. So where was the wisdom in over population? She failed to see, though what she had seen too many times were the fly-infested wide-open eyes of imploring, emaciated children. And what was wonderful about that, Padre?

She suggested that he preach from within his realm of local experience, not from an ancient and outdated text, the world's first anthology of ordinary events recorded in a time and in a world of simple minds. Those combined books were, she argued to disbelieving ears, fanciful tales embellished to forever instill fear in the minds of the small and ignorant by those who once thought and those who today think themselves great and wise.

Enough was enough. The year was 2014. So let's everyone get real.

She faced Vega, explaining curtly that the Spanish Inquisition was at an end. She excused herself and left, calling Riley from her car to vent about a priest whose head was stuck in the mud of the Middle Ages and Vega whose head was stuck somewhere, she didn't know, ecclesiastical.

He listened, of course, commiserating; refraining until he could share the humour with Karina. He'd quickly learned that not listening to Priscilla Vendôme usually incurred a worst-case scenario.

Things would work out, he promised, disconnecting. He would make certain. A church wedding was an absolute requirement. Nothing less would suffice. Things would indeed work out.

Priscilla waited for Vega to exit the church, driving to her home where he'd parked his car. She didn't want to speak, Vega feeling quite content with the quiet and subsequent drive alone to his hotel room in the downtown core.

The next morning the priest called Vega. The cleric had reconsidered his fiancée's beliefs. He now understood her unsettling dilemma and agreed to make certain, heretofore unimaginable, amendments to the ceremony to assuage her distress.

*

To that end love, honour and obey became love, though she did agree to mutual respect, at least until she began to show. For as long as we both shall live became for as long as our lives endure, which went over everyone's head except Karina's and Riley's because no one close enough to hear the vows was paying attention and the groom had earlier told his mother, whom he'd told about the Priest and Bride, that 'endure' meant their shared lives lasting forever.

Besides, Priscilla reflected, had God been invited, He might have stood in protest and stormed out. What would He possibly think of a woman who had essentially bribed a man to marry her before spending a week fucking her boss more times than she ate in order to get pregnant for political and financial gain because her new husband wasn't up to par and that she would dump him once his Spanish heritage and Black lobbyist sister were no longer needed?

The priest cleared his throat.

"Oh, yes I do…Father."

She was married.

The worst part was over, next would come the mandatory "you're such a lovely bride, so very lovely," countless handshakes alongside Edward Riley, the head table and the inevitable time-honoured clinking for the amusement of those who had run out of things to talk about with people they didn't know.

The Fatal Diners' Club

She assumed Frederick would only be notable to his family. No one else would care much about him other than the bride's parents who themselves had no one to talk with.

She kissed her beloved husband, blocking out the polite applause, retracing the tumultuous week she'd spent on her knees and on her back, on her side and bouncing on Riley's lap, or clinging to the side of the Jacuzzi suspended in the warm swirling water with Riley's hands clutching her buttocks to keep her afloat.

She pressed a palm to his cheek. She could scarcely imagine how greatly her fall and winter would differ from her summer.

28
Miss Angela Bangles

April 05th, 2024 was a Friday.

Angela Bangles sat reclined in her lift chair in front of her flat screen without the discomfort of the canvas belt holding her in. Her favourite ice cream was butterscotch ripple topped with cascading dark chocolate and a crust of crushed walnuts.

She was treating herself, intent on eating the few remaining spoonfuls of the volcano as sparingly as possible. The commercial had just ended and the cooking show's season finale would last another ten minutes before she could sit upright and make her way to the kitchen.

The abrupt symphony of obnoxious, high-pitched tones startled her. She wasn't expecting the call that early, though she couldn't see the wall clock. One hand was clutching the smeared bowl against her chest, the other was glued to her spoon with chocolate and she was facing the wrong way.

She groaned without words, smothering the profanity. The call was interrupting her show. Why were they calling so early? She wasn't ready.

She dropped the bowl to the floor, flinging the spoon away from reluctant fingers.

She reached blindly to her right with both hands, grabbing at her muumuu, twisting the side pocket toward her front and up, tearing the side seam, bringing the pocket and her phone to within reach. She was panting, fumbling with both hands held at eye level to press the green button too small for her swollen fingertips. She was anxious, excited. She knew who was calling, afraid they would disconnect. They never left messages.

She could see by the screen she was connected, calling out to the person to wait as she fumbled for HANDS-FREE. Raising the phone to her ear was not an option for fear she would drop the small casing and be isolated until her housekeeping service arrived the following Monday.

She couldn't kneel or bend. She hadn't in years. She was too afraid. The one place she could sit when not strapped into her lift chair was her custom toilet, a rigorous ritual requiring several minutes of preparation if she were to avoid embarrassment and several more minutes when she was done.

The room accommodated her lift chair from which she could manoeuvre herself into a harness attached to an electric winch operated by a control box always within reach. Once securely held in place she was free to gather her dress inch by inch into her hands without fear of falling and, when ready, control her descent onto the seat. The toilet itself was low and wide, fully automated, allowing Angela to cleanse her private orifices without the need to step from her chair into the shower more than once a week, the very reason she was never able to leave home except to attend The Diners' Club.

She beamed, squealing her delight. The man was answering her.

Her transport would arrive at nine the following evening. She should be ready. That's all he said before disconnecting. There was never any banter, never any pretence at caring. Gourmands were a business.

She never knew whether to expect the company of men, or women, or both, though vanity was not a Gourmand issue. Dress was casual, one's appearance secondary. Narcissism confronted with global contempt wasn't a worthwhile mindset. Their common interest was good food and good wine in quantity, expertly prepared and served. She was more likely to hear the muted sounds of masticating, swishing, slurping and swallowing more than anything resembling congenial conversation.

Gourmands were not adept at conversation. For the most part they were recluse, shut-ins, uncaring of a world overtly uncaring of them. Current events had no meaning.

Camaraderie was ephemeral, groups of like-minded diners seldom exceeding ten. The commonality was simple. The Diners' Club existed to provide a service that each member was incapable of performing on their own and in a venue that would cater to them, not refuse them as repugnant as long as contractual obligations were respected.

Angela Bangles had been welcomed as a Gourmand because she met the primary criterion. She was able to pay for the privilege of excess, for what she could not do herself, and not by any cheque or credit card.

She could not cook for herself, the danger was too great, too worrisome beyond the packaged foodstuff destined for her microwave and what she could consume while vertical, sitting or reclined in her lift chair. Nor was she able to dine out, not like acceptable people. For years the nation's restaurateurs had come together to outlaw anyone beyond a 49.9 BMI Class from their establishments due in part to Priscilla Vendôme's sweeping strategy to curb what she claimed was the nation's catastrophic and threatening disregard for good health. They were too expensive to feed, too costly to seat or to maintain services for such as washrooms, waiting areas, parking and foreseeable medical assistance.

What the government could no longer accept, restaurants were able to no longer accept.

Angela Bangles was forty-five. She was single and lived alone. She was accustomed to solitary living. As a young girl her father had ignored her, not certain what to do with her, until one day he chose not to come home. Her mother was no better.

Most days and nights her mother was gone, working two jobs, though Angela was never quite certain what her mother did for a living except that many nights she would come home late and fall asleep in her clothes smelling of smoke.

Throughout her early teens she had no real boyfriend. The boys did like her, though she was never invited to dances, believing she wasn't pretty enough, but often when her mother was at work she would bring boys home so she could be like the prettier, more popular girls. She could even remember how at times the boys would fight over her, how they argued to be first, until she got pregnant, until her mother made her leave a comfortable home.

She had no choice, and nowhere to go. She dropped out from school while in grade ten to live on the street at a time when college was a minimum requirement for any decent entry-level position.

She had one skill which became less appealing with each passing week, forcing her to panhandle for dimes and quarters to pay for a bed at the mission until she became too much of a burden and no longer welcome, taken by ambulance with what little remained in her purse to a clinic for what she believed was the best solution.

She was months too late, she was told. What was she thinking? She didn't know. No one had taken the time to counsel her, to tell her what she must do. She didn't know. Her mind was in a shambles. Maybe she would leave it at a church or a hospital or something. She didn't know. Maybe she would leave without it, walk out and run away. What she did know was that she couldn't earn any money with it and whatever money she could earn she would need for herself.

She didn't know. All she could do was cry. No one cared. No one had time for another stupid girl bringing another unwanted mouth to feed into the world, until another nurse came to her bedside on the second night to prep her.

The woman was much older than the others. Angela didn't know, maybe thirty-five or forty. She was soft-spoken and gentle, making Angela feel as though she had a friend.

Two days later she lost her child to strangers for twenty thousand dollars through the nurse who knew a lawyer who knew someone who knew someone. In return for which Angela paid the nurse five of the twenty.

The remaining fifteen she put in the bank, wasting no time to find a real job, from then on spending her days punching holes into doughnuts and, eventually, her evenings and weekends filling her mouth with indigent men who couldn't afford anything better or prettier. She was making do.

More importantly she had a home of her own.

That was her life from sixteen to thirty, until the day her mother died, when the lawyer gave her the best free advice he could: Gold and oil. Then bury her mother the least expensive way and live as modestly as she could. Not as though she'd been given over a million dollars out of the blue.

He was frank. She had no education, no inherent ability, no skillset to offer the business community, no chance at all at a new beginning. She should accept what she was and not risk losing the windfall. Nothing was wrong with filling doughnuts, he told her.

She took his advice earning 425 dollars a week that was taxed and another three that was not, four during the more lucrative spring and summer months and into the fall. Homeless men had no need of her dead-end charms throughout the winter to satisfy their fantasies with closed eyes, their minds filled with images of the long legs in short skirts they ogled each morning sauntering into office buildings or climbing onto buses as they sat crossed-legged praying for a quarter as much as a breeze.

But those good days were over, relying on her two investments to sustain her.

She hadn't worked in twelve years, at least that long. The doughnut shop had fired her stating health reasons; afraid she would one day collapse at her filling station. That was the bitch's fault. Everything changed for the worse the day Vendôme was allowed to take over the White House.

Nor had she seen a doctor in that many years. She wasn't allowed. She was a No Assist, deemed proscribed by the system, by Vendôme. She was a leper without a colony who not long after was rejected by her own kind, forced to retire as the affordable release of desperate, unclean men.

She had become unattractive to the worst of them, her lacklustre performance challenging the most vivid imaginations when so many younger runaways, dropouts, and doughnut fillers were prettier for the time being and desperate for the money.

The last night, she remembered, the man refused to pay her. He'd pushed her away when she was done. She hadn't serviced a man since. The thought of reaching out to touch any man anywhere existed nowhere in her mind. Urine-scented washrooms, dark and fetid alleys, cramped backseats, the buckles and zippers of soiled pants leading to his pleasure before and after shared bottles of cheap booze wrapped in greasy brown bags would never resurface.

Since her mother's death she'd risen above the unwashed vermin she'd once known. That was her vile and forgotten past. She had no intention of regressing to her former self. She was content with her life despite what she had learned to live with. Who did not have a cross to bear, a price to pay for living well?

She gazed into the screen. The show was over.

She made her way to the kitchen, leaving the bowl and spoon where they lay. She didn't care very much about such things. She never entertained. No one ever knocked at her door.

At the fridge she reached for a medium all-dressed. The dough wasn't frozen. Thawing would take too long. In that way she was a good planner, taking time each evening to consider her needs for the coming day.

At the microwave she pushed the buttons and waited. She didn't look. She didn't like to see her reflection in the black glass.

Her hair was pulled back into a dishevelled tail tied with elastic bands she saved from the flyers she took from her mailbox once each week. Her style never changed. Nor did she ever receive mail. Apart from the bank, her phone provider and Hilary Basil, no one knew she existed.

She had a dime-sized mole on one cheek, a brown plateau that was home to unmatched black bristles. On the other cheek she had a birthmark that entirely disappeared on the rare occasions she blushed. Angela never wore make-up. She never had. She didn't know how and cosmeticians were expensive when she could better spend her money elsewhere. Besides, why be ridiculed and scoffed at?

She was the most petite of the Gourmands she had met, though she was neither proud nor embarrassed of her 385 pounds. They might well have accepted her as an honorary member if not for her 4'9" frame whose shape from any distance was unrecognizable as Earthly.

She was fat and she was unattractive. She was homely; a troll stared at and held in contempt by the beautiful people, which is what she deserved. She knew. She wouldn't dispute what she was. She knew how she appeared to others, why she didn't have a single mirror in her one-bedroom home on the first floor.

The microwave beeped. The time was 10:55. She opened the door, warmth and tantalizing aromas escaping to assail her. The pizza was steaming. The three cheeses were thick, bubbling, erupting slivers of pepperoni and green peppers to taunt her. She inhaled deeply, eager to touch the hot crust, fearful of burning her fingers, of dropping her treat onto the floor. She waited, salivating, perplexed. She was missing a delicious feast prepared on her flat screen.

She reached in, recoiling, twisting sideways as though expecting to see someone, an intruder, someone who didn't belong there.

No one had buzzed her apartment from the street in a year, perhaps two. She wasn't sure, maybe longer. She didn't know. She tore a wedge from the pizza, a bridge of cheese trailing behind as she went to the door to listen.

She didn't know what else to do.

29
We know you're in There

Three months, and she wasn't acclimated to having him in her home each evening, loving her each night. She was living a dream. She was right about one thing, though. Her father did freak about a month earlier as her distraught mother sat quietly listening to her daughter explain that she was getting married and already living with the man she more than loved.

She wasn't confessing. She was stating a fact, which didn't do much to appease old dad.

And Dwayne wasn't much help, telling Mrs. Wilson with his arm around her that if he'd seen her first instead of her not-too-bad-looking daughter, they would be living together or at least meeting secretly for fleeting moments of wild abandon.

Mr. Wilson wasn't impressed, remaining silent throughout most of the evening until dinner was over. They were in his home and he didn't like this Dwayne Michaels fellow who appeared from nowhere with his unworldly daughter whom he had obviously deluded with overpowering charm and calling her his dream-girl.

Dwayne understood. Years earlier he'd learned to discern when he wasn't liked, about the same time he'd learned not to give a shit. Instead he gave his full attention to Mrs. Wilson who hadn't yet prepared dinner. He offered to assist her in the kitchen, taking her hand, assuring her that he was a reasonably capable sous-chef.

Lorie advised her mother with a nod to accept and within minutes Mrs. Wilson was melting as quickly as the butter, the meal not at all what she had planned, every so often mouthing silent and secret "wows" to her daughter who couldn't believe she was in her parents' home with a real man...particularly a Dwayne Michaels kind of man.

He was so charming and charismatic with such flair and impeccable manners. He certainly must be a very good salesman she later confided in Lorie. She could certainly see why he would want to open a restaurant and why her daughter was so infatuated with him. Good things certainly do come to those who wait.

Lorie rolled her eyes and sat by her father who wanted to know why, if he was such a good salesman, he wanted to live in Florida, open a restaurant, and risk going broke. That was no life for his daughter and living together before marriage wasn't proper, Mrs. Wilson hum-humming, reminding him at the table as Dwayne served dinner that they had lived in sin for three years and only spoke of marriage when thoughts of Lorie began to flourish. And apparently he'd forgotten that he had once called her hot-stuff.

Dwayne commented that she was still very hot-stuff, garnering a pinkish hue from mom, a giggle from the daughter and an annoyed humph from dad who found Dwayne's grin annoying, his daughter's wide-open eyes somewhat theatrical and his wife's self-satisfied expression very condescending. He stared at the creation. No one but his wife had cooked his meals since moving into the house before Lorie was born. She knew what he liked, what he didn't like.

They ignored him.

He waited, forced by social etiquette as much as by hunger to reluctantly taste the baked salmon, first examining the morsel on the tip of his fork, disappointed.

Nothing was raw, wet, or overcooked. The second forkful took a while, his mind and palate searching together for something to find fault with as his eyes selected the next delectable mouthful. The third and fourth went somewhat more willingly past his lips, Mr. Wilson conceding when the plate was empty that the meal was surprisingly quite passable, if somewhat rich for his taste.

He wouldn't want his daughter eating like that every night and he did not like that someone he did not know was living with his little girl and thinking to take her away, though he would admit that at least Mr. Michaels didn't smoke and had passable good taste in wine. That was something, though the true test of a fine meal was the digestive served after and he went to his cabinet for a bottle that was older than Dwayne, which, Mrs. Wilson whispered, was the closest he would come to eating crow. He was an old fool thinking his daughter wouldn't call him as often or drop by unexpectedly for dinner.

Dwayne promised in a whisper that she would. Nor was he finished, waiting for Mr. Wilson to fill the ladies' snifters and his before standing to toast Lorie, his soon-to-be wife and Mrs. Wilson for her gracious hospitality.

Lorie, he went on, did not deserve her father's disappointment.

Lorie lurched forward from her seat, her sensually hoarse voice failing her.

"My disappointment, Mr. Michaels, is a family matter and justifiable. My daughter is wasting her life. The subject is closed."

"No, the subject is not closed. Did you vote for Vendôme?"

The older man hesitated, displaying his frustration to his wife. The question had no place.

"I'm asking you, Mr. Wilson, not your wife. Did you vote for her, yes or no?"

"I did, on the two occasions. I'm proud to say."

"The second of which because she wasn't assassinated that day in North Carolina, the day after your daughter might have had dinner with you and her mother for the very last time."

"I don't like your tone, Mr. Michaels, and you're certainly not making sense."

"I don't like yours. So we're even. That night after dinner your daughter didn't return to Washington to review notes for the Speaker. She flew out onboard Air Force One, assigned to protect the president, your president. You know, the president, the one you voted for that makes you proud, more proud than your own daughter."

Mr. Wilson coughed a laugh. "My daughter is a government office worker, a veritable clerk, when she might have enjoyed a fine career in law here in New York...or anywhere else."

"You're not listening, Mr. Wilson. Your daughter lied about what she does. She lied out of necessity. She's now a federal agent reporting directly to the president. She does important, dangerous, and very secret work."

"I don't believe you. Look at her. She composes letters when she might have been a lawyer of some repute."

Dwayne went to Lorie's purse, not asking permission, extracting the Beretta and her shield. He laid the blue and gold leather-encased badge and her chrome-plated weapon on the coffee table.

Her mother gasped her shock.

"No, she does not. She works covertly for Priscilla Vendôme, something a little more important than plea bargaining some rich guy's parking ticket or putting some punk in jail."

Lorie met her father's blank expression with a shrug, putting her hand over her mother's.

"We work together, Mr. Wilson, because your daughter could no longer remain in the Secret Service after killing the man who attempted to assassinate the president in North

Carolina. Your daughter did that while you believed she was writing letters in Washington. That was her fabrication so she wouldn't worry you. But I must confess. How you were blind enough to believe her boggles my mind." He sipped his cognac, acknowledging the exquisite taste and aroma. "You owe her an apology, Mr. Wilson, and I am not asking you. Understood?"

"I don't believe you."

"Then believe me, dad, for once. I did kill the man and I would again. Dwayne is telling you the truth, and very much against the rules. I was forced to leave the Service and we do work covertly for Priscilla Vendôme." She looked to her mother. "That was me you saw on the news. She's also a very special and close friend and, dad, if you tell anyone about this you might get me killed. So please understand. This is not a joke and you are not entitled to ask questions."

She held out her hand for her gun and her shield.

In that short space of time Dwayne Michaels altered the Wilson family forever. Two weeks later, out of the blue, the old man called Dwayne on his private line inviting him to a tennis match and lunch at the club.

That evening Lorie was the one who freaked.

*

They had waited too long for a perfect spring day to waste the day sitting in an airport and breathing stale air onboard a crowded jet. They drove. As much as Lorie enjoyed Boston in the winter, she adored the smaller city even more in the spring and had planned a long weekend once the workday was over.

She was convinced the love of her life had let her father win.

"I didn't. I swear. He beat me hands down. The old coot's fast on his feet."

"You're lying."

"He knows I love you."

"I don't care, and I know you're lying." She pulled to the curb. "But I think he is beginning to soften since you freaked him out."

The engine stopped purring. The building was three stories, the brown façade dotted with six black balconies used as storage bins for barbeques, bicycles, garden chairs, broken furniture and stained mattresses.

"Can you believe this?"

"I can't believe anyone would want to live this way by choice. I'd be afraid to sleep at night, afraid something would crawl into me."

"Something does."

He chortled, pleased with himself.

"I meant something big, sweetheart."

Touché.

"Keep telling yourself five more months until au revoir. Believe me, one day of Florida sunshine and these Gourmands won't exist."

They exited the car. When working Michaels never opened Wilson's door, not often.

The snow was gone. The air was scented with the sweet fragrances particular to spring. The sky was Mediterranean blue; the sun was a yellow disk: Their first spring together as them. She couldn't imagine how much more wonderful her summer would be or her honeymoon in France.

At first she thought he would laugh. He didn't, not once as she became more functional in French every day, every night sitting in bed with her earplugs and textbook. She'd already begun shopping for thongs, sultry beachwear and dresses. She would be the sexiest bride in France, the envy of every Frenchwoman. She hoped.

He had no doubt.

Since January, since loving him without hating him, she had adapted the habit of telling him that she loved him prior to each interview or intervention. Telling him brought perspective to a job entrusted to an elite few across the country.

They were aware Angela Bangles lived at the rear of the building. They knew everything about the woman including her unwanted child. They didn't care about that. The kid was living a much better life. Nor did they care about Bangles who, like the others, was fixated on self-destruction. They cared about Hilary Basil.

The front steps were uneven and cracked, though Michaels was learning to measure his wit while on the job. Wilson wasn't always inclined to share his humour. The entrance was small, the doors far too narrow for... another near miss of spontaneous wit. The once white buttons on the wall panel were grey, Michaels commenting that number 108 for some reason was cleaner.

He pressed a gloved finger onto the button. He always wore gloves on the job, so did Wilson. They could never be certain.

"Think she'll take the offer?" Wilson asked.

"No, I don't. What I think is that she belongs under a bridge. What I believe is that she'd be quite happy to. What I don't understand is why, and this low esteem stuff doesn't work for me."

"Guess we'll find out. I love you, sweetheart."

He acknowledged her with an indifferent nod. Despite the decorum of the job, knowing what Lorie Wilson wore under her clothes each day was a priceless perk.

He counted silently down from ten. No answer. He pressed 108 again, from to ten. The third time he maintained pressure on the button for that many seconds.

"Ms. Bangles, we're federal agents. Open the door. We know you're in there."

No reply.

Wilson tried. "Miss Bangles, please open the door. We're not here to bother you."

No reply.

"Ms. Bangles. Open this door now or the next noise you hear will be a Boston PD battering ram. The second will be your cell door clanging shut. Open the damned door...please."

Wilson confirmed. "We do need to speak with you, Miss Bangles, and my partner is serious about the police. We simply want to talk with you. Then we'll leave you. I assure you, you are not in any trouble."

The buzzer buzzed. Doors never chimed, chirped or jingled. They buzzed, Michaels pausing to wonder whether anyone had thought to patent the unimaginative drone.

He went through first, Wilson followed. The hallway wasn't the worst he'd seen, though certainly not the best. He suspected the hallway was lit 24/7 as a means of janitorial time-management more than illumination. Still, the uneven carpeting might have been any dark colour, the walls were decorated with scratches, scuffs, cracks, mindless artwork and the ceiling was a patchwork of stained, broken and missing acoustic tiles.

Such places were never peaceful. The price of quiet was unaffordable to anyone living there. These were the homes of low-income mothers with whom came the constant wailing of malnourished babies, indolent fathers ineligible for full welfare shirking child support to afford a constant flow of beer; either one or both heedless of the cacophonies of daytime talk shows blasting through their walls, either one or both teetering on the brink of homelessness. Not to overlook ex-cons and yesterday's hookers whose bodies were now better suited to laboratories and first-year med students, nor to disregard the pungent smells of mould and mildew melded with disrepair, of grease, burnt food, cigarettes and legalized marijuana.

Poverty, Michaels commented before putting his fist to the door, was a debilitating state of mind more than an economic reality.

The door opened slowly, keeping pace with the reverse motion of Angela Bangles' lift chair. Michaels went through first, stopping, scanning the room and doors before continuing. Wilson followed, doing the same.

Bangles was instantly intimidated. She was accustomed to huge, shapeless men in sweatpants and sweatshirts. Some even wore muumuus without the slightest embarrassment, not caring whether they were difficult to distinguish from the women. This man had stepped into her private place from a glossy fashion page. He was well-groomed, not a hair out of place and clean-shaven, in a suit that was blue and expensive. She could tell. She watched all the fashion shows. His shirt was white and crisp. He was wearing cufflinks and his tie was red, the kind of red most men couldn't afford or wear. What she found strange was that he was wearing gloves, thin gloves made from expensive leather. They were blue.

That didn't make her feel bad. He didn't. The woman did. The woman made her feel bad. She was lovely, probably every man's dream. Bangles couldn't see a single flaw. Her complexion was perfect, her lips the colour of blood pudding, her dark hair pulled into a ponytail as lustrous as thick strands of mahogany silk. Her skirt was knee-length and fitted, olive green, her matching jacket was tapered, held closed with two brass buttons. Her blouse was smooth and silky, very expensive, the colour of creamy caramel. Her shoes and purse were a set, dark chocolate, not from a department store basement.

She was afraid. These weren't the police she saw each night on television.

Angela Bangles was strapped into her chair. Her muumuu was pink, ripped down one side. She wasn't expecting company. Her chest was covered, though the fabric was inexpensive and her coaster-size nipples weren't completely private. The corners of her mouth were wedged with chocolate she hadn't yet licked away. Her chin was smudged with chocolate, the thick fingers of one sticky hand holding the doorknob, the other a half-eaten slice of pizza. Her arms were bare from her shoulders, pasty white and picked at with certain fervour, dotted with reddish-brown miniature crusts. Her calves were bare from her knees, decorated with sore scabs, larger versions of her grotesque arms, layered and shapeless as though her thighs had oozed down toward her ankles that were wider than her swollen feet housed in cheap slip-ons.

Wilson stayed as she was, closing the door with a hand gloved in brown leather as Michaels checked the bathroom and bedroom. Then:

"Good morning, Ms. Bangles. Thank you for finally letting us in. Good decision by the way," he began.

"You said you were FBI. What have I done?"

"I didn't say FBI. I said federal agents. We're a more exclusive club, like yours. As for what you've done, or are doing, you already know. Don't you? So let's see how this plays out before we get all panicky. However, to answer what you're probably thinking, we are not arresting you because we cannot. In fact we're prohibited. I suspect you know that also. Nor do we have any interest in harming you. You're doing a good enough job of that yourself. So relax. Take a deep breath."

Bangles flushed deep red, her scar disappearing, her wart suddenly feeling darker and thicker.

"I don't understand. If I'm not in trouble, what do you want?"

Wilson answered. "You're not in trouble. Hilary Basil is. What we need is for you to help us locate him. You're a Gourmand, Miss Bangles. You're a member of The Diners' Club. You're aiding in a criminal act we can't charge you with for reasons you're aware of. The same does not apply to Basil. The thing is we're now on a tight timeline to find him and you can help us. We need answers, answers we believe you can help us with."

"I don't know him. I don't know any diners' club."

"Yes, you do."

"No."

Michaels interrupted. "Basil is your food source. What he's doing is illegal. What you're doing is illegal by virtue of aiding and abetting him. Simply put: No club, no Basil. You know that. So help us out here."

She was flustered. "Do you have badges or something? How do I know you're really the police?"

"We have ID, yes."

"Can I see them? Don't you have to show me?"

"No, you cannot see them. We're a somewhat private agency, not unlike your feeding club. Public knowledge of what we do would prevent our work, which is finding Hilary Basil and we believe you can help us do that."

"I don't belong to a club. I never go out. I can't. I'm confined here because of my condition."

"By your condition you mean the self-induced super obesity that put you on the No Assist list and self-imposed house arrest. Sort of ironic, don't you think?"

"That's not true. I'm being punished for having a glandular condition. That's what should be illegal."

He studied the pizza. "I understand your point. I see also that your gland's getting cold, Ms. Bangles. Don't let us interrupt you. Or would you like another wedge of gland from your microwave? We can wait."

She wanted to drop the half slice. She felt trapped. Her mind was too narrow, too dulled by lethargy to comprehend what was happening. How did they know about her? Who were they really? How could she make them go away? She wanted to scream at them to please go away.

"Why are you here? I'm nobody."

"Not at all, Ms. Bangles, you are extremely important to us. So let's cut to the chase. You know very well why we're here and this conversation is not working out for me."

"No. You're wrong. I do not know why."

"Listen up. Your friend and co-feeder, Mr. Percival Penny, says differently. He says you do know why we're here. Oh, by the way, he's dead."

"Percival's dead?"

Michaels nodded. "He died from acute embarrassment on the verge of starvation. Fell out of that contraption you're strapped into. He couldn't get up on his own and, like you, he was a No Assist. He died like you'll die one day, Ms. Bangles, with food caked on his face, splayed on the floor in his own mess. He'd been there for a couple of days, marinating. He was pretty ripe. And you know what the worst part was for him?" The question was rhetorical; Bangles thinking her heart would stop beating. She shook her head. "That he was still alive to feel the humiliation of my partner seeing him sopping wet. Me, he couldn't care less about. Her, let's face it; she's not the worst looking thing in heels and a short skirt. From a male's perspective, I have to believe he couldn't have died too soon. I mean, look at her."

"You're trying to scare me."

"No, I'm not. I'm telling you what we saw, what we see too often. However he did say you could help us. He seemed to think a lot of you. Doesn't that count for something, that he was thinking of you as he was dying?"

"I don't know anything. I never go out and haven't seen Percival for a very long time."

"Miss Bangles," Wilson continued. "Before he died he complained of a miserable life, of dealing with excruciating pain and discomfort. He couldn't sleep in a bed, I suppose very much like you. He couldn't support himself long enough to stand, let alone walk." She paused long enough for Bangles to interpret the compassion in her voice. "He wanted to die, Miss Bangles, though I don't imagine quite that way. Please don't let that happen to you. Please don't. We can help you."

"Tell me, Ms. Bangles," Michaels went on, "that thing in the bathroom. Would you care to demonstrate for us exactly how that works? You've got to hoist yourself up and down each time you've got to squat for nature. Is that for real? Tell me, what would your daughter think of that?" He waited. "Yes, we know about her. You did her a very big favour getting rid of her, putting her up for sale. She's an architect, lives in New York, a real beauty. Think she'd like to see you like this, strapped into a go-cart? Maybe she could design a better sling for you. We can get her here if you're interested. We can do that for you. The genetic thing would probably scare the crap out of her, though. Might be better that she doesn't see into her future."

Her lips were quivering, her eyes welling.

"You shouldn't be allowed to talk to me like that. I can't help you."

Wilson said, "Yes, you can. We can help each other. Please, do that for us, for you."

Michaels went to the bowl on the floor. "Is this another gland from the morning menu, Ms. Bangles? Were you thinking to retrieve it anytime soon?" He scanned the floor. "And what's with the spoon, too much to deal with while zooming your way to a yummy pizza?"

Wilson cut him off. "Miss Bangles, tell me honestly. Do you hurt? I mean really hurt, the way Mr. Penny agonized each day. Wouldn't you like to walk again after so many years in that chair, or sit on the toilet without help? Do you remember what it's like to sleep in a bed with your head on a soft pillow? We can do all that for you."

"Don't say what you don't mean. I'm not stupid. I know. Doctors won't even look at me."

"We have the authority to waive your No Assist status. We can arrange for gastric bypass surgery. We can offer you cosmetic surgery as well, a physiotherapist to retrain you and psychological help because what you're living is a reversible mindset. We can do that. And we'll foot the bill.

Not a bad offer."

"You're very pretty; I don't have to tell you. You know better than I do. I'm sure he does too. But I don't envy you, miss. You might think I do, but I don't."

Michaels broke in. "Ms. Bangles, tell us where to find Basil, how to find him. Tell us how you find him. Tell us where you Gourmands meet for your feasts, how you get there, and the day he's in custody I will personally accompany you to the hospital of your choice where I guarantee the best possible care and follow-up. I'll go one further, I will personally buy you whatever bed you want and personally tear out that thing in the bathroom."

"You can't do that. No one can."

"The president can. Priscilla Vendôme can, and we report directly to her. Think about it. This is not a fantasy. This is real. So don't be stupid too much longer. We're giving you a life here."

"He's telling the truth, Miss Bangles. We can do everything we've promised...once you tell us."

The few moments of quiet were a difficult eternity. Neither Wilson nor Michaels felt the slightest empathy for Bangles. She was their job, though they were telling the truth. They would and could help her.

Wilson hadn't moved, neither had Bangles as Michaels strolled through the small living room stopping at the television. The hostess on the flat screen was White, no shit, blonde and twenty-something, not a hair out of place, probably a mom with two perfect kids and a husband who loved her, who thought of her every time he was out somewhere bagging something a little prettier without kids.

She was baking cupcakes with white and pink cream-coloured icing. And, go figure, not a fleck of flour or sugar on her nose, her cheeks, or anywhere else. She was too pristine, too pure. Her teeth were too white, her eyes too blue. She looked like a 34-B, was probably a 32-A with padding, and probably wore full cotton briefs with

Scotchgard protection. Enough reason for her husband or anyone else's to fuck around.

He lowered the volume. He was losing patience. Not with the dumb TV blonde or Bangles, with Basil. He wanted the man. He wanted to marry Wilson and move to Florida.

"So, Ms. Bangles, a little nip and tuck and a better life sound pretty good to me."

"No. I don't believe you and I want you to leave…right now. Or I'll call the police."

"Call them. They won't come. Besides, we're federal. We trump them big time."

"This is a one-time offer," Wilson added. "Don't push us away. Would you like to speak with the president yourself? Would you like to meet her? Say yes and it's a done deal. We can arrange that as well. That's how serious we are. That's how badly we want Basil."

"Just leave, please. I don't want you here."

Michaels wasn't giving up. "Ms. Bangles, explain something to me. Something isn't making sense. You have three million dollars in the bank, yet you live in subsidized housing that smells and looks like fresh shit. You're a millionaire wearing a tattered sheet which, quite frankly, isn't doing very much to conceal your bountiful charms. You're breathing through your mouth, if you haven't noticed, so I'm assuming you don't while you're gorging yourself. You're going to die, Ms. Bangles, in filth like Penny. You all will, all you Gourmands, because your reason for living is the inevitable cause of your deaths. What don't you understand about that? Anything you'd like me to clarify…anything? We're giving you a second chance at living. Do not screw this up."

She ignored him, looking to Wilson. "Miss, please leave me alone."

"He's right, Miss Bangles, if not very polite. You have the resources to live a much better life. You do not have to subsist this way. We can help you start over. We will help you."

Angela Bangles powered her way to the door. She wanted to make a point; instead she succeeded in making herself appear more ridiculous. The sugar coated knob was difficult to manage and when she reversed her chair to swing the door open she had no choice, dropping her slice of pizza onto her lap.

Wilson walked out. She was done. She was sad and disgusted and disappointed. She was also trained to forget. Or had she become apathetic? Probably so, she thought. No. That wasn't true. Not now. Not in her new life. How could that even be possible now that she had Dwayne?

"Ms. Bangles, one last word to show there's no ill will here. You have no family apart from a daughter who doesn't know you're alive and probably wouldn't care if she did. When you're dead Hilary Basil will take your money without the slightest regret or thank-you unless your will dictates otherwise, which we doubt. You'll be shoved into a furnace where you'll stay at full blast for, I'm guessing, four hours. You won't be given any more ceremony than you gave your pizza. You'll be buried in a clay pot without a name, without a stone. Not even a wooden cross or a post. You will simply be dead, grey dust, gone and forgotten. Not one of your Gourmand friends will be aware of your passing and I doubt they would even care. From what I see you've got three years max, possibly four, a million for each year, tops. So at least live the good life. Don't cheat yourself. Basil does not need the extra cash flow and you are one of the lucky ones. You don't have life insurance, endowments or property and until you're dead he doesn't have access to your money. That's a good thing. Not like the others who pay posthumously from their estates when they've fed their way into a clay pot." He reached into his inner pocket. "Anyway, that's it. The oration is over." He dropped a business card into her lap, missing the pizza.

"You said you weren't stupid. Let's see if that's true. Call us when you change your mind, before the tow truck comes with a winch to haul you away, to drag you along the hallway and through the garage past the garbage bins for all your neighbours to see. That's how your food buddy Penny was taken out, dragged by a winch cable for everyone to gawk at and giggle. I didn't stay for the show, though I assume he was quite entertaining. That's no way to die, Ms. Bangles."

He tilted his head, turning to leave.

"You won't be back?"

"Not until you call and not if we find him first. Good day."

Michaels walked out, leaving Angela Bangles to close the door. He didn't hear that happen.

Wilson was outside waiting by the car. Her arms were crossed, one foot tapping the sidewalk.

He knew. He was in deep shit, female shit, the absolute worst kind.

"We're done, time to enjoy Boston. You drive."

"Not the worst looking thing in heels...thing, really?"

He chortled. "That was man-speak for affect. You are not only phenomenal in heels, you are way prettier than Ms. Bangles. She wouldn't have a chance with me, you know, given the choice."

Her mouth dropped open. He didn't care. He had years of experience being rude, weeks of experience teasing her. He opened his own door, sliding in, waiting patiently. Whenever. He wasn't in a hurry. He could wait. The weekend was hers.

Lorie didn't bother staring him down as she crossed in front of the vehicle: A wasted effort. Instead she slid in behind the wheel, tugging her skirt to her knees as punishment.

"Sweetheart, we didn't do very well. What did you say to her?"

"To get a life before it's too late." He pulled away his gloves. "She won't. She'll die like all the others."

"It's so sad. We could have helped her."

"Don't be sad. She's probably finished the entire pizza, which was a sixteen-inch if you're interested." He patted her right thigh, tugging her skirt in the proper direction. "The good thing about this job is that we don't have to care, because they don't. Imagine systematically and willingly killing yourself, leaving your estate to the guy who's loading the gun for you. That's what we're up against."

*

Angela Bangles stared at the white card without a name, a ten-digit number printed in black.

She closed the door, twisting the lock. The pizza slid from her lap to the floor. She was angry. The pizza would stay there for three days, taunting her, staring at her. She hated them. She hated the woman as much as the man. She hated herself for everything they had said. She hated being alone.

She took a deep breath. She did breathe through her mouth. When was the last time she'd used her nose? She couldn't think. She was too hungry. She glanced at the clock on the wall. Another show was about to begin. She chanced to the open door of the microwave.

She had time if she hurried.

30
The Revelation

The wedding was a great success, a one-time memorable social event for Vega's parents and a solid footing for a future event none could imagine. Priscilla's parents left the reception early without saying goodbye, lost in a crowd. Her father felt snubbed, her mother was anxious to speak with her neighbours and friends.

Although crystal stemware did clink to encourage the bride and groom, the bride was relieved that, for the most part, those gathered closest to her table were somewhat above the pedestrian practice.

Edward Riley and Karina waited until Mr. Vega and Mrs. Vendôme left their guests not far from midnight, leaving soon after, first excusing themselves to Vega's parents as a matter of social correctness, explaining they had an early flight to Houston.

The couple understood. They had no choice, they were intimidated.

The sister was not, accustomed to the wealth and reputations of others, unflinching when asked by Riley whether she might one day accept an invitation to Houston as his and Karina's guest. He would be delighted to personally see to her travel arrangements.

The young woman accepted graciously, believing the gesture was a matter of courtesy. She had never seen Texas. Nor did she expect to anytime soon.

*

The bride was exhausted, depleted after her week, her day, the evening, and morning would come early.

The groom understood. Or believed he did.

Their flight to the Caribbean departed late Monday morning, the young couple first enjoying a relaxed breakfast in the hotel dining room devoid of the previous night's guests.

The honeymoon lasted ten days in the private sunshine and turquoise waters of her favourite island. When privacy was questionable, when she strayed from their seclusion to stroll the beach alone or with him, she wore a wide-brimmed hat and her Serengetis. She saw no reason to endure the hard-to-erase blotchiness of white breasts when the rest of her was not.

Vega agreed. He was accustomed to most European and Latin women enhancing the world's beaches, more so than the average American female who would never think to… with good reason.

He was proud. What was the point of nudity if not for others to behold? Any woman deserving of admiration when dressed would certainly expect equal or far greater appreciation of her beauty once naked. And Priscilla was aptly appreciated throughout the honeymoon which all too soon dissolved into the reality of her first day back, her time at the gym, moving in together, groceries for two and the realization that her luxury condo, now half the size, would soon become a boarding-house.

Vega had never stayed over with her when he was in town, other than weekends in Chicago or when they met for a lover's weekend away: Her rule. Not until they were married. She didn't need to think of anyone she had recently met going through her drawers, discovering more about her than she wanted him to know. Now he would stay over, every night, and where would she put a nanny? Worse, relocating was impossible. In thirty months she would be living in Washington, in eighteen or so she'd be crisscrossing the country with him, Riley and Duncan.

She would suffer through. Once the kid arrived she would have less than two years to wait, ten months before campaigning, and she suspected by September Vega would travel more frequently, putting his ten million to good use. She hoped so.

Not surprisingly, her first day into the office, her secretary brought her a sealed envelope. In it she found a letter and a copy of Edward Riley's will which he would amend to include the child's precise name once born. She deposited the documents into her bank's Safekeeping before driving home.

And so her weeks went throughout the summer, comprised of long workdays, the gym and partial weekends with her dutiful and doting husband with whom she chose not to discuss the future. The campaign was too far away for discussion, for precise plans, she told him once. Too much was going on at Riley including that she and Edward were currently faced with the difficult challenge of determining who would be her successor.

He understood. Nevertheless, they had young lives to enjoy as well as demanding careers, lives they filled with occasional candlelight dinners and the theatre, dinners for business that she enjoyed, that he did not; paint chips and designers to make the condo a little less her and a little more them, though, without question, the boat consumed the better part of most weekends.

Despite her frequent protests, Frederick Vega wanted a yacht. Not one like Riley's mega-vessel that he hadn't yet been invited to, which he couldn't afford after any number of presidential terms or privileged lifetimes. His was a sixty-foot sport cruiser he couldn't pilot because he'd never been on a boat, an entertainment centre floating at dock at the edge of Lake Michigan that was often more of a bitch than the ocean and that might allow for a five-month season of weekends in a good year.

People were talking and she didn't need the rumours. She was Priscilla Vendôme; she was recognizable and held to a higher standard. What did he not understand about that, about her?

He claimed he was thinking of her. He wanted his wife to have the best of everything.

Not good enough. If she hadn't thought he was a fool before, she did then. From the ten million he was left with five, tops, after the yacht and his parents' new home for which he had promised to pay the property taxes and upkeep. If he maintained his present delirium, if he didn't wake up, if she didn't win the election, he'd be broke and unemployed before the divorce and his newly proud parents would be on the street. Not that she cared. She didn't care at all.

Priscilla loved the Caribbean for the anonymity, the freedom, for the same reason she loved her condo...or had until her new life. What she didn't like was walking on wobbly floating slips or trying to relax in her private space that wasn't private at all while squeezed between two equally monstrous boats where every word spoken was an intrusion.

At the marina she was a spectacle, everyone knew her or knew of her. Everyone wanted her autograph, souvenir photographs side by side with her that she couldn't refuse. Following her landslide victory the photos would become collector's items, despite which her weekends, the sunniest and the warmest, were her private hell until the Saturday of Labour Day Weekend.

That weekend was the best of the season. Every yachtsman worthy of the name was out on the water, most of who would raft together in secluded coves Saturday evening, eating, drinking and swimming through to Sunday morning.

The last yacht disappeared through the narrow channel, crossing into the lake, lost against a backdrop of moored sailboats painting the lake's blue water white.

Priscilla and Vega were in port, tied to a slip, one of the few times she was able to wear a thong with not much of a top once they were alone.

"So, Captain, how's the fuel situation? Think we have enough for the journey? Should I check the GPS, perhaps send out a Mayday on channel 16? Or is it Pan-Pan when you're stranded in port without champagne?"

"Good one, my darling. As it happens, you will be pleased to discover, I have come by the name of a commercial captain. He's retired and has agreed to tutor me beyond the norm. I should have my certification this time next year, far exceeding our neighbours' qualifications. Not that I'm interested in one-upmanship." He twisted the bottle from the cork. "Then we'll be out there on the deep blue sea rafting, skinny dipping, doing what they're doing and really enjoying this thing the way we should."

"This thing, is that what I heard? You paid a few million for a 'this thing'?" She swung her legs from the chaise-longue to the deck. "And, Freddy, when you wake up from your dream please tell me what makes you believe for an instant that I would swim naked with them, your dock buddies. They're twice my age and hideous. Not that I could see anything. Shit, their BMIs can't be less than fifty. I couldn't see their parts if they stood on their heads. And the women's tits, if you want to call them that, I can't imagine. It's bad enough I've seen the men's."

"I don't follow my darling."

"Well try. At Riley we're mandated to work out one hour a day. You know that. Let a BMI exceed 30 and you're gone. Why? No sick days. Not one sick day. Those people, your friendly hippos, they're screwing us over to the tune of 2400 a year to keep them alive when they don't give a good shit about themselves unless they're too far from the table or at the end of the line." She stood for a glass of lemonade. "This so-called 'thing' put you and, thank you, me along with you, in with the wrong demographic. The pretty people are in the tiny twenty and thirty-footers. They're also that much younger and having more fun. Then you might have had a chance seeing me in the moonlight, at least for rafting. And you seem to forget about 2017. I'm not about to show anyone the next president's bare ass, tits, or anything else. Get real."

"That's Riley's dream, and neither one of you is doing anything to make the dream real. You shouldn't get your hopes up. That's a high place to fall from."

"It's our dream, his and mine. And who said anything about falling? Because you don't know something doesn't mean it isn't happening. And let's not forget you took his ten million, Freddy, a good part of which you're floating on as we speak. That was a serious commitment. I would not piss with him."

"I intend to honour my pledge. I will do as agreed and act accordingly when the time comes."

She scanned the marina. She felt embarrassed, sauntering to the afterdeck. Sixty-foot yachts remained at dock on beautiful days for two reasons: The prohibitive cost of fuel or an idiot captain who bought something too big and drank champagne on sunny afternoons when other boaters drank beer. She stretched out onto the wrap-around bench, loosening the strings of her top, pressing a hand against her stomach, taking a moment. She couldn't imagine a more propitious time, rather than waking one morning feeling like crap and having to deal with his male indignation, his wounded sense of self. So, why not right then and there when she felt wonderful and more than a little vindictive?

She wasn't worried about his reaction. She was curious; about to flagrantly confront his lie, assail his masculinity.

"Freddy, the Riley gym is the best-equipped in the city. You haven't once joined me there for a workout and a sweat despite your spousal privileges and, if you haven't noticed, your suits are beginning to betray a certain relaxed attitude. Hundred-dollar belts are one thing, not seeing the buckle is quite another. It's time to trim a bit. And that is not a request. A good workout's a lot cheaper than a new wardrobe and better for you than champagne at noon. What I can do, you can do. The campaign we're heading into will be a stressful ordeal. Count on it, and you will not survive the year if you're not in the best possible shape."

He checked himself. She was right, and annoyingly self-righteous. The day was taking a bad turn. He had looked forward to a few drinks, a barbeque and a romantic night in the marina alone with her, convincing her to make love in the open air on the afterdeck. Instead he found himself a little miffed with her.

"I see your point, my darling. You're right. I have been somewhat self-indulgent of late. My single defense is that I was trying to please you. I believed I was pleasing you. However I also see that you have enjoyed the good life as much as I …if we're pointing fingers. Not that you're not the loveliest woman at the marina." He filled his empty glass with more champagne. "May I propose a truce as well as a brief extension of our indulgences? What I suggest is a pleasant evening of good food and wine befitting of a romantic mood and next week my regimen will begin in earnest."

"First off, I am the most beautiful woman here, despite the current vacancy rate, and not because I'm your wife. Second… I'm also very pregnant."

She waited, like a schoolgirl who'd just revealed a dirty secret about her best friend after crossing her heart and hoping to die forever.

Vega was a better liar than he was a thespian. At first he stood comatose, shaking himself awake, taking long backward strides to the gunwale. He was in shock, his eyes wide open and white, his brow striped with deep furrows, his mouth twisted with the agony of disbelief.

He stared at her, Priscilla intercepting each rampant thought from behind her dark Serengetis.

He drained his glass. His body relaxed, a deep-pink flush smothering his face with fabricated relief. She could see he wanted to choke from the elation of such unexpected good news.

"Darling…how… when?"

"We know the how, Freddy. The when was the honeymoon, I suppose."

"Priscilla, this is glorious news. Am I the first to know, my darling?"

"Yes."

He wasn't.

"We must call my parents. Mother will be delighted." He went to the wet bar, refilling his glass, the white foam spilling over. "And all the while I believed this current fascination you have with soda water and lemonade was related to this upcoming campaigning business, wanting to appear your best. How long have you known?"

"I wanted the right moment." She looked around. "This looks pretty right." She smiled. "You're going to be a daddy. Congratulations."

"My heart is about to explode with wonder."

No shit. Not to mention your brain. "Isn't this when you're supposed to put your hand on my belly and kiss me."

He jerked forward. She raised an open palm between them.

"Please, don't. I was joking. Let's not be more mommy-daddy than we have to. This is too new."

"We're pregnant, my God."

"Do not ever say that again. I mean, really, how stupid an expression is that?" She was serious. "Grow a pair, Frederick. I'm the one who's pregnant, not you, not

351

us…and I fully intend to be a complete bitch about it with you and everyone else."

"You could never be."

"Don't think so? Watch me."

A single thought flashed across her mind. Priscilla Vendôme was in the grips of an epiphany. She despised him. She loathed him instantly and thoroughly, more than she had previously. What was going on? She'd seen his original medical records. The man was as dry as burnt toast. He would know there was no way. Yet he was standing facing her as though some other man, a complete stranger, had not fucked his new bride before or during their honeymoon.

She knew what was festering in his mind, pleased with the destruction she was wreaking, relishing the moment more than she could have imagined. He was rapidly creating images of who, how often, where and when. Vile images of her naked and open body gyrating over or under another man, her heated body glistening, dripping with beads of oil and sweat under the midday sun, her and her lover heartlessly mocking him with cruel laughter.

She blew a stream of air from between pursed lips. Ooh, not bad, she thought. She would definitely have to try that someday…with someone she hadn't yet met.

If only he would dare for a moment to suspect the truth, and for what purpose. Then he would fully understand that with ten, twenty, and possibly thirty million the expectation of, if not his forgiveness, his compliance was certainly requisite and expected. However the truth was too unreal. Instead his imagination was feverishly creating scenes of torrid adultery, recalling each afternoon fishing trip, his morning scuba diving and his hour-long massages by the seashore, her time strolling alone or her escape into self-indulgence at the spa

His eyes were on the verge of betrayal, his voice belying his sense of joy.

"I can think of no better way for you to express your true love for me than with this child." He reached for his sunglasses, raising his glass in a toast. "My most ardent wish is that he or she will resemble a beautiful woman more than a fortunate man."

31
The Heir

Edward Riley was first to hear the news. He would soon be a father. Karina and Riley together were second.

What Riley had not expected not long after was the revelation of Vega's pride at becoming a father. He concurred with the expectant mother. What was going on? However the question was rhetorical.

A month later mother and father met in Chicago.

The day was over, not the rush-hour. Dinner reservations were made for eight.

Riley stood to stretch, walking to Priscilla's private bar. He poured a double malt scotch into an old-fashioned, shaking his head, disguising a smirk with pursed lips.

"I wish I had been with you to see his face. I enjoy so little levity in my life these days. You acted so incredibly and blatantly unfaithful at the very moment any normal man would eagerly prance around like a peacock boasting that he and no one else had taken possession of such a lovely specimen as you, the very moment he was conditioned to believe you would be his and his alone forever. At least until the anticipated boredom of monogamy would likely manifest into the seven-year-itch phenomenon when the intrigue of newness cannot be refurbished without the most outlandish fantasies or the inclusion of third parties." Riley took in Chicago from her office window, smirking. "Imagine the depth of his dilemma. The very deception he engineered and maintained preventing his confession and your shame as a harlot. He knows the truth. Yet he must believe that in your mind the child is his since you did in fact celebrate your nuptials with a degree of believable enthusiasm. The instant and cataclysmic convulsion he must have battled to contain within a mind bombarded with lewd images of his immoral wife spread wide under another man, listening to her unwittingly expose her debauchery while revealing what should have been his second proudest achievement, is beyond the scope of my limited imagination. I suppose one might say he did indeed reap what he sowed," he chortled, "and somewhat more."

"He was comical. At first I thought the back of his head would blow off. Then I thought he was going fall overboard trying to appear so damned cool." Priscilla Vendôme coughed a laugh.

"If he'd been honest we could have done the in vitro thing," she paused, smirking, shaking her head, "or not. We would have parted company. Instead he knows I'm a cheat, if not somewhat of a whore, and he has to live with the lie. Not a good beginning, not that I care."

"In fact it's an excellent beginning to a predetermined conclusion. He's the cheat, not you. The man's an inconsiderate liar. How he imagined he would possibly conceal such a defect would boggle even the most average mind, particularly given his future role as the president's husband." He chuckled. "Perhaps you should tell him that he's been corrected. At the very least that he's the source of our evening's amusement."

"I'm more concerned with him screwing around. I don't want anything dirty in my bed."

"He will. Of course he will as a predictable response to his injured feelings, his affronted masculinity. It's human nature at its finest."

"He's been very quiet since I told him, though he's still attentive, still doing the flowers and lingerie thing, and he's started travelling with a gym bag."

"He has little choice. You virtually threatened him. If he leaves he's into me for ten million which he no longer has and I assure you that his life would quickly become very unpleasant. He also knows he has to keep his boat afloat for appearance sake and a roof over his parents' heads, which he won't manage with a paltry few million. A fool and his money...That's what you must remember. He's going nowhere without you. He's adapted nicely to his new life, Priscilla. Not completely without some encouragement, I'll admit, and that he's discovered you're unfaithful is of no consequence whatsoever. Whether he believes in your chances or not, he wants the second ten million and a third. I have no doubt he'll respond obediently to your firm tugs on his choke chain, none at all. He'll continue as the ever-attentive husband and once in the public eye he'll become your premier advocate. That he'll enjoy other women in his travels as a means of alleviating his ill-feelings towards you is not an issue." He smiled. "Neither is your loyalty to him. Feigning headaches is quite unnecessary. He's a prop and occasional release, your words. Why burden yourself with worry over exaggerated pretence? After your second term he'll be set for life and divorced. Ten years that will come and go in the blink of an eye, ten fast-paced years to reform the country's mindset. As for Vega, you'll hardly know he's alive."

"What don't we do for money?"

"That particular list does not exist. Or if one does its purpose is to deceive. No one is that pure of heart. Or have you forgotten the venerable man of God who presided over your blessed union? How did you put it, as long as your lives endure?" He glanced at his watch. "Dinner awaits us."
*

Throughout the fall and into early winter Priscilla endured the complications of childbirth-related misery and discomfort, thankful her body was misshapen when thongs and suntans were not an issue.

Nor did she exempt Vega the weeks he was in town from said misery or the classes she attended with other young mothers who saw her as a role model. She had no intention of relenting, of soothing his wounded ego or moderating her obsession with humiliating him. Quite the opposite, she was intent on adding copious amounts of insult to injury. What did she care about masculine pride? The man was a liar and a fraud. Where was the pride in that? How could she possibly forgive or condone what he'd done?

She enjoyed sitting on the carpeted floor with her feet spread wide apart, huffing and puffing with Vega's arms wrapped around her hugging the plump results of another man's fruitful work. That alone was worth the nausea, the cramps, her aching back and the sense that her swollen feet would split apart.

That energy she transferred directly at him. She was every bit the supreme bitch she had cautioned him to expect, putting extra effort into making his decision to travel as often as possible and return home later, rather than earlier as the eager new husband and father, much easier. For all she knew he'd always had a whore in New York or wherever else he travelled.

He had no reason to rush home, despite doing so most weeks with a gift intended to make his role as a loving husband easier to act out. Although he shared her bed, she either made a casual excuse or he did. She simply assumed he was coming home satiated and didn't care.

He presumed neither did she since his prowess or lack thereof had led her to fornicate with a stranger as his new bride. Though, as much as he despised the thought of playing father to a bastard, he was relieved that with each passing week her body was becoming less approachable, less desirable. Regardless of how he felt about her the pretence of willingly abstaining from sex with a woman of her good looks was shallow at best.

The weekends were the worst, Priscilla encouraging him each week to leave her to work on his boat or to study with the wiry and weathered skipper he'd come across. She knew a true mariner always had something in mind to make the coming season more memorable than the previous year, his vessel more seaworthy or more conspicuous to neighbouring boaters.

Christmas and New Years were spent in Houston with Karina and Riley, Karina's invitation sincere from a kind heart. She believed Christmas alone in Chicago would prove unnecessarily difficult on Priscilla given her responsibilities at Riley, a new husband and the pending stress of motherhood.

Riley concurred, for different reasons. Christmas would indeed prove difficult for the mother of his child.

For her part Priscilla was overjoyed. She had no great love for winter and no love at all for Vega. The chance of escaping both for ten days was too appealing. Vega agreed, the dread of what he would do with her over the festive week when all else was closed was alleviated. At the ranch he could get lost, be alone or spend his time meandering between invited strangers, whereas Riley would provide no diversion at all. He was too infatuated, too preoccupied with his darling protégée. The two men were worlds apart, linked solely by now questionable business ties and her.

As for yachting, the extent of Riley's seamanship was instructing his paid captain as to where he wanted to go.

Karina made Christmas Day special with colourful Mexican flair. Her one stipulation was that they exchange a single gift for the person whose name was drawn from a box. They were far too privileged in life to adhere to the concept of commercialism engendered by guilt when the thoughtfulness of one gift brought more meaning and required more inspiration.

Friends were invited as were neighbours, Priscilla taking advantage as she always did with Karina to improve her Spanish. After dinner the women separated from the men, Karina serving her guests while Riley served his, most leaving by ten or eleven without receipts for their generous donations to Karina's personally funded food bank. She didn't need the government's money, intervention or scrutiny, nor did her friends and neighbours require receipts to prove their good will.

New Years was celebrated in black tie and long gowns with good wishes for 2015 abounding amongst millionaires and billionaires, throughout which Frederick Vega realized he did not exist when separated more than a few feet from Riley, Karina, or Priscilla. He was out of his league, better suited to staying in the marina when others went to sea.

11:59 brought relief. He could soon leave; go home to Riley's guest house to sleep with his back to the wife who hadn't stopped dancing and talking all evening. It was impossible to him that a network has-been could maintain such a degree of popularity.

Three, two, one and a not so happy New Year to live through with a pregnant whore who'd lived up to her commitment of being a complete bitch about it. How would he possibly survive the coming twelve months, predictably the twelve worst of his life? In spite of which he felt no infringement on his manhood.

In a year he would quit his job. A year later he would either be a well-paid pawn or divorced and free to breathe. He harboured no doubt about the divorce. The marriage was a ruse. As for child support, that wouldn't happen. Not unless she wanted the world to know the details of her honeymoon.

She looked good. She was beautiful, the belle of the ball, Houston's Cinderella. He half-believed she could become president. What he found peculiar was that not a word of a pending campaign had been discussed in his presence. No doubt the affront was intentional. He was being excluded. He wasn't one of them.

He snickered. What would her proud mentor and benefactor think of her to know that she was a shameless whore, that she was carrying another man's kid?

Confetti burst from the ceiling, balloons drifting this way and that, elusive targets for the palms of drunken men and giddy women. Karina was the first to hug him, to kiss his cheek as he watched Riley bring Priscilla into the New Year, kissing her cheek and whispering into her ear whatever else he wasn't privy to.

Another man stole Karina's attention. Protocol mattered, he didn't. She walked away. He felt stranded: A pauper floating naked in a sea of affluence and influence. He was being snubbed. His wife was ignoring him, standing by Riley's side, shaking hands with yet another man he didn't know when she should be standing with him, kissing him, wishing him a happier New Year.

She was lifting the puppy's paws from the floor, his paws, training him, teaching him what he should expect over the next two or six years. Not a chance would she ever be re-elected. Not once the nation saw who she really was, a whore, that she was in fact the face of the Riley presidency.

He sat smouldering, waiting; staring into the crystal of the gold watch Riley gave him at Christmas. Not only had she not bought him a gift, claiming she didn't want to contravene Karina's Christmas tradition, she had refused his.

The man they were with bowed to her. What kind of man would do that? She was smiling. All three were smiling, parting. She was coming towards him. Her face flushed against the golden shimmer of her gown and her shawl. He wanted to smack her, to wipe the snide grin from her face.

"Priscilla." He hadn't called her his darling in weeks, not since the day on the boat when she shattered his world.

"You remembered where you left me. I wasn't certain you had."

"These affairs are always partly business, Freddy. Sorry. A girl has to do what a girl has to do."

"I understand completely," like fucking a stranger in the sand and hoping the result isn't mentally deficient. "Who was the man, the one Edward introduced?"

"He's a friend of Edward's from Alabama. His name is Bradley Duncan. He's very charming, a true Southern gentleman. Such a rarity these days in most men, don't you agree?"

"I noticed. And, yes, I do agree, as you must agree that gentility is wasted on most women of the day."

"He asked about you."

"And what, may I ask, did you tell him? Since I was too far from the private conversation to hear for myself, or respond for that matter."

"I told him you aren't feeling very well, that crowds aren't your thing and that you're not really pouting because you believe everyone's ignoring you, which isn't the issue. I know. It's the baby. You're not ready to become a daddy. You think you're too old for what's coming our way and you feel neglected because you haven't been getting any, which is no way to begin married life." She patted his cheek. "I understand. I do. However I did warn you and until this baby thing is over, until I'm tight everywhere and perky once again, I'm off limits. Just so you know. It's only right that you share the pain as well as the glory. You are after all the one who did this to me, Freddy."

"You're the one who was careless. That's not my job. You should have taken the usual precautions. In fact someone with a more suspicious nature might believe your pregnancy was intentional, a key to the White House. And, on that note, what did Riley whisper in your ear that was so private? Or shouldn't I ask?"

"That I have 731 days of private life left. One year

before all my warts and blemishes become public. That goes for you as well."

"I'm missing your point."

"I'm telling you it's alright for you to screw around. I understand that you're frustrated by this protracted abstinence I'm going through and your resultant celibacy. I will absolutely understand if you pay for it by dinner or cash. Not, however, by credit card or with your real name, and not after December 31st of this year. You are a virile man, after all, Freddy. So go ahead, get your rocks off."

He was sincerely taken aback.

"Thank you, though I have to admit I'm shocked. The proposition is interesting, very open-minded of you if not a little disturbing coming from a new bride on her way to the White House."

"I'm talking about temporary release, not long-term complications. I understand what you're going through because of me," she patted her stomach, "because of this. Let's face the facts. You're going to screw around irrespective of what I say or think, if you aren't already. So we might as well be upfront with each other. All I ask, demand, is that you don't come home with a smile on your face or dirt in your pants. And don't be stupid about it, in which case we'll tuck you back into Pandora's Box and make you disappear. Do we understand each other?"

"And who might 'we' be?"

"All of us who, unlike you, believe 2017 will happen." She coughed a laugh. "So, really, Freddy, make her as young and as dumb as legally possible."
*

Whether he did or not, would or not, didn't matter. She didn't care. All she wanted at the moment was any man's nuts in her tight fist.

She was naked, a thin sheet of cotton they had the audacity to call a gown draping her from her shoulders to her knees. Why they even bothered she had no idea when her feet were elevated, anchored in cold stainless steel stirrups, and some arrogant asshole whose first name was Doctor had his face buried under her shroud while playing peek-a-boo inches from her dilated vagina that, heretofore, was a tight and perfect pussy, her on-demand source of pleasure and ecstasy.

She would never feel those delirious sensations again. The thing was ripping her apart.

She didn't want to take deep breaths or push down and she sure as hell didn't want to relax. She wanted to reach out. She wanted to rip his hairy head from its neck, wrap it in barbed wire, shove it up his ass and tell him to relax.

Miss Karina E. Vendôme was not cooperating. She was being rudely evicted a week earlier than anticipated by everyone but her creators. She wasn't ready to leave the warmth of her home on the whims of strangers who, for some reason, thought her little head was a handle.

She was resisting with all her will, determined to stay home. She was not pleased. She did not like the cold and the brightness. She wanted familiar warmth and darkness, screaming her discontent. Why couldn't they understand? Why weren't they listening to her?

"What?" Priscilla grunted through snarling lips, her red face lined with blue veins, her glaring white eyes streaked with red, her black pupils locked on him as though on a target. "What?"

Priscilla sank into her pillow, her body drenched in sweat, her hair matted. She didn't hear them. She was more concerned about the nation's network sweetheart and next president laying spread apart for the entire world to judge with her feet in the stirrups and her legs wide open as though displaying her blood splattered vagina and buttocks like the crown jewels.

What was it with medical people that they didn't understand propriety? How would Doctor like walking around a women's locker room with his shrivelled dick exposed?

They finally did understand, whenever, however long they'd taken to make her comfortable, to pat her face with a warm cloth, to cover her with a warm blanket. She had no sense of time. A nurse was coming towards her. This was her moment. She was a mother. What would she think? What would she say? She expected it would look like an alien. How would anything look once rescued from a flooded ditch after nine months? What would make hers look any different, smell any better?

Miss Karina E. was bundled in a blanket and dressed in a tuque. She was tiny, pink and severely wrinkled. She refused to open her eyes to the bright light. She was so pretty. She was so cute, the nurse told the mother.

Was that right? Priscilla opened her arms, taking the package, smiling because she had to, agreeing because she had to, because the new baby was hers. Yet, see something like that six feet tall coming at you, screaming wildly, Priscilla thought, and who wouldn't run like hell to search for a weapon or a cliff to jump from?

She knew differently. Little Karina E. did very much resemble an alien, certainly not Vega, certainly not Edward. She had no idea who the girl resembled. Who would? Such was the clichéd hyperbole of friends and relatives with nothing original or truthful to say.

Her eyes brightened, her lips curving into a wide, seamless smile. The nurses believed they understood why. They didn't.

Karina, Riley and Vega were in the corridor. The grandparents were not.

32
Casual Friday

Frederick Vega never again asked for or expected marital privileges. The ground rules were set. The most he saw of her body was in a one-piece on the rare occasions she visited his boat that he refused to give up.

By mid-summer her trainer had transformed her body from the blights of motherhood to the contours of a model while Karina E. gradually shed her extra-terrestrial appearance and began assuming a more human exterior.

Vega restricted his role as a loving father to public appearances, his time in Houston with Riley and his own family. At home, when he was at home, he made no effort at all, preferring the relative quiet of the guestroom.

Weekdays the girl belonged to the nanny whose hours reflected Priscilla's. The young woman, who had likely forgotten things about herself that Riley had uncovered, had been in the right place at the right time. She had a two-year contract with an enviable compensation package which included a luxury apartment in the same building so that she would be available 24/7 and a European car that was the envy of any woman her age. What she was not given was any idea whatsoever where she might be living within in two years.

When the nanny's days were over, or on her weekend day off, the kid was entirely Priscilla's problem.

Throughout the spring Vega had kept busy with his

seamanship studies, throughout the summer the yacht was his single escape despite remaining at dock unless his weathered instructor was with him to guide him from the slip and into the channel. He didn't yet have his papers. Nor would he anytime soon for having underestimated the depth of what he'd taken on in a moment of truly regrettable impulsiveness. He had wanted to prove himself to her, and he most assuredly did.

He would sell the boat one day. He was reconciled to that. However not until the first female president's yacht would demand a much higher value than what he had paid. What better proof could he offer of his confidence in her? Until then he at least had a retreat, a safe haven from her.

The trip to Houston came out of the blue where he was concerned. He never knew what to expect with her, though, think what she may, he didn't care. He had become accustomed, if not immune, to her last-minute news bulletins.

He saw no reason to accompany her. At the moment he had nothing to contribute. Besides, he told her, he hadn't had a vacation since the wedding and she really didn't need him.

Riley's jet was flying in to meet her, the nanny was accompanying her and he had no intention of spending a week in the background dying of boredom, smiling on-demand for no reason while fully cognizant that he was an invisible fixture. He didn't need the bullshit. He was going to Spain for three weeks. He was booked. And yes, she had every reason to believe he would enjoy himself to the fullest.

She could make his excuses and stay in Houston for as long as Riley wanted her around.

Priscilla had no comment either way. More on her mind was Bradley Duncan.

*

The Fatal Diners' Club

The first week was a working vacation for Priscilla. She enjoyed visiting with Karina who spent the week doting over her miniature namesake. She enjoyed the ranch, the hotter weather and the relaxed Texas ambiance.

She also enjoyed the outcome of closed session meetings with Bradley Duncan who, by week's end, had agreed to run with her in the 2016 presidential campaign. They would see a good deal of each other over the next six months. They would have to understand each other's mindset, think and act in sync with one another and learn to trust what each other would and would not say, promote or promise.

They formed an instant synergy, each one fully aware, as was Riley, that their platform would work best under the guise of Guaranteed Better Education, (albeit with repercussions should the federal criteria not be adhered to and maintained by individual states), Guaranteed Health Care, (albeit with serious repercussions should the federal guidelines be ignored), and Guaranteed Reduced Poverty from her administration forward (albeit with severe penalties imposed on any and all parties found guilty of abusing or circumventing the system set in place to improve the nation as a whole).

Each had a lot to think about before the next scheduled meeting, Duncan returning to Alabama to speak with his wife in detail about their shared future, Priscilla boarding Riley's jet that would fly her to her favourite island for the last time and without the nanny or Karina E. to distract her.
*

The nation and the continent as a whole were increasingly becoming less educated, less healthy and overpopulated: A malaise which in itself was a repercussion that would eventually fester into the country's defeat and ruin by external economic and military forces.

The principal cause was known, at least by those old

enough to remember its inception: A revolutionary concept once wrongly embraced without much thought by a new and pre-middle-aged generation as forward thinking. They had no idea at the time what they had wrought, nor did they display the slightest remorse in later years before it was too late to reverse the trend.

Casual Friday had begun decades past by those who needed to leave their mark on society the way the 50s would always be remembered for rock 'n roll; the 60s for embracing the mini-dress, the British Invasion; and the 70s for rampant free love and a redefined freedom of speech inspired by drugs and social unrest.

Casual Friday: Self-expression allowed as a perk to those with little or nothing to express.

Once each week suits, ties, dresses and nylons were out, khaki pants and safari skirts were in with blue denim shirts, frivolous blouses and bare legs promoting a relaxed work environment which all too quickly metamorphosed into a deteriorating dress code and a correspondingly slothful work ethic migrating from work to families to schools.

The most prime example of the human condition: Give an inch, take a mile.

If management didn't care why should the workers who were parents? If men could begin wearing jeans and sweatshirts to work on Friday, why then couldn't the women? And then what made Monday different from Friday? From which point the distinction between men and women deteriorated to a state of androgyny. If a woman chose to dress and comport herself like a man, why then would a man choose to treat her like a woman?

Either no one thought to ask or no one thought to say and the mentality was literally brought home to stay, eagerly adopted by minds not yet sufficiently developed to distinguish right from wrong, who themselves became parents, too often prematurely, and the mindset became the entrenched norm without anyone stopping to consider that we all develop, study, and eventually work in the way we dress. No exception to the rule.

Self and mutual respect was gone, historic remnants of a society no one could or cared to recall.

No one would dare to wear a two-piece suit or a silk dress to a garden barbeque, yet the same majority began wearing cargo pants, sandals and baseball caps to work, in restaurants, to weddings, funerals and courthouses. And no one took the initiative to say go home. You're being disrespectful to yourself and everyone else.

People grew into a state of uncaring, discovering that not giving a shit about themselves or their kids was easier. Being a non-argumentative friend required less effort, less thinking than acting as an authority figure and mentor, someone to look up to. Being a good boss at work meant not being reported to HR as an overbearing tyrant. Being a 'good guy' or 'one of the guys' when wearing Capris pants and flip-flops was more apropos to a happily functioning workplace.

Kids began attending classes in clothing better suited to sleeping because their parents wore the same clothes to work as they wore on the weekends to cut the grass or wash the car. And if the kids were expected to learn in their jammies, why were the teachers expected to wear suits or dresses? They didn't, and as a result more respect was eroded from the system.

Sir and ma'am became you, so what, if not a direct 'fuck you, asshole,' without any penalty because teachers had become afraid of guns and knives and parents had come to live in fear of overly spoiled, out of control kids who knew the phone number of Child Protection Services. The threats were real, the parents' shameful accomplishment for having engrained in their kids that they were special, miraculous gifts to the world when they were nothing special at all, when they would not for some time prove themselves worthy of high opinion, if ever, which was unlikely.

The Fatal Diners' Club

What was one six-billionth of anything, but nothing?

So what could anyone expect other than 'be home for supper' would become 'don't be late'. "Don't be late' would become 'leave a number' which would evolve into 'don't wake us when you do come home' which led to mothers and fathers sitting alone at a table with nothing to do after except wash the dishes and fall asleep on the couch. So why not eat out?

The wife wouldn't have to plan meals, slave over a hot stove or wash the dishes alone. Nor would she have to plan lunches for next day. That's what Styrofoam doggie bags were for, filled with all sorts of glutinous, trans-fat saturated goodies that began insidiously converting the country from slim to chubby to fat to morbid to super and to super-super obese troglodytes. And if he was getting fat, why couldn't she? Not to the exclusion, of course, of state-approved vending machines spitting out soft drinks and junk food to feed and fatten, or power drinks meant to energize sleep-deprived minds housed in shapeless and sluggish bodies slouched under high school desks and in university auditoriums across the country.

When had humans begun adapting to sitting on their backs and not their buttocks when working, studying or driving?

That had to stop. The mindset had to reverse soon. Bosses had to become bosses, teachers had to regain their forgotten respect, and earn that respect. They had to start doing their job, understand that teaching involved more than pedagogical days, snow days, holidays, and summer-long paid vacations.

After-school sports had to become more important than turning teenage girls into mothers. Parents had to become parents who would make certain their neglected sons weren't going to school with loaded weapons on the off chance the teacher would say something to set him off or that their daughters weren't sexting or stripping on their webcams in search of a better self-image expected by the boys who wouldn't date them twice otherwise.

Casual Friday and its woeful legacy would stop. It would stop January 06th, the first Friday of 2017, in all federal offices. Its immediate obliteration would be mandatory for anyone seeking to work for or with her administration, or for anyone seeking federal funding which would include state-run institutions from hospitals to prisons.

That was the tip of the iceberg. The nation would learn the hard way to respect itself, not merely brag about itself for the sake of appearances between neighbours when the rest of the world was ridiculing them.

That the current administration had begun dismissing destructively overweight soldiers from the service was not enough. That too few corporations had begun seeing the need to trim the waists of their CEOs was not enough.

Discharging or dismissing someone for being obese would not prevent his or her obesity, or stem a national crisis. Very much the inverse. Given the primary human conditions of self-pity and denial in the face of condemnation, the affront would certainly foster profound indignation irrespective of intellect, thereby cultivating further self-destructive behavior, thereby worsening the debility and increasing the burden on the system as a means of reprisal.

Why were soldiers trained to defend their country then allowed by their command to degenerate into hazards to themselves and their squads? Where was the command? Where was the authority? They were the worst offenders, the most responsible and most culpable, as were the parents. Nor was the corporate world any different. Neither were the police, doctors or nurses who no longer deserved the smallest modicum of respect they had once trained for.

That had to stop. The rhetoric had to stop. Everyone was talking, no one was doing. The country had become too selfish, too introverted with the advent of comfort food and the nurtured belief that we're better than we are when we're not.

Accountability would become the new aspiration, the new norm. That was Priscilla Vendôme's mandate. That would be her lasting legacy and Bradley Duncan stood ready to support her.

Blind disregard was no longer acceptable. Obesity was no longer acceptable, could no longer be tolerated as the norm and the Riley Corporation was no less committed to the cause.

From the days of Casey Riley casual dress was forbidden throughout the corporation. Working at Riley Corp. meant men dressing like men and women dressing like women, each one dressing for respect as much as sought-after careers. Dealing with Riley Corp. meant arriving properly dressed for meetings and doffing your hat once inside the main doors, or not being admitted past the main-floor reception desk.

Furthermore, standing in the presence of ladies entering the room was not merely viewed as polite and respectful, but essential to a gentleman's code of conduct.

*

The dress code for Priscilla throughout the two weeks followings the meeting was nude on the veranda, nearly nude on the beach, at times entirely when she was completely alone, and seductively dressed each evening she chose not to dine alone in her villa.

The other guests had no idea who she was under her hats and sunglasses. Nor was she alone in her expectation of privacy. Nighttime was no different. Cameras were forbidden in the dining room and the vivid images anyone might wish to savour would soon fade despite their best efforts.

She had so many details and concepts to consider, the

mechanics of which were the domain of Edward Riley.

The campaign was five months away. In the meantime she would attend increasing numbers of luncheons, dinners and events so that by design, person by person and mouth by mouth, her candidacy would become common knowledge. People who counted would talk, rumors would flourish. However the press was off limits despite what they would inevitably be fed, uncover, misconstrue or fabricate until such time as she deemed appropriate the admission or denial of their facts and fictions.

She had established in her mind who would win the first interview and who she would favour with the last: The two most crucial.

What she would miss most was a real man by her side. Vega had fast become a disappointment despite her firm belief that Riley had known all along, that he'd intended from the very beginning to have an heir to the Riley throne and that she'd been chosen as the mother, the mentor and future guardian of the corporate princess.

She didn't mind, not really, though as she sipped her fruity cocktails by the ocean, her silky skin glistening, she couldn't help peppering her thoughts of the presidency with thoughts that he had known since bringing her to Riley, waiting for the perfect moment to impregnate her for the good of the country as much as for the future of Riley Corp.

She giggled with no one to hear. She doubted whether mother or father would ever forget the week of intensive focus they had dedicated to each cause with mutual and unbridled enthusiasm.

But those days were now over. They did what was required of them without lingering regret or guilt. Nor did she believe she would ever forget Vega's audacity at continuing the sham.

She would tell him one day. She would when the time was right, thinking perhaps as he signed the Declaration of Divorce.

She wiggled onto her front, naked except for colourful thread-like strings intersecting the smooth curves of her ass to ensure her modesty when sitting, standing, walking or wading with others nearby, signalling a passing waiter for another cocktail.

Even if he knew he wouldn't care. She probably couldn't count to the number of bare butts and breasts the kid saw each year. Good for him, she thought, if not the most desirable substitute for a lucrative career.

She was invisible. Or she would be once he left to serve another near-naked female.

She wrote no notes, dictated not a single thought throughout the two weeks that were coming to an end. She was prepared, like a pianist performing a concerto she'd composed and performed in her mind and for music lovers over and over again, like a ballerina who knew that to leap she would not fall.

She knew, as did Riley and Duncan.

They would win after twelve arduous months of campaigning with compassionate half-truths. The nation could not know what would soon befall them with a sweeping vengeance to erase so many years of indulgence and neglect. They would not understand to what extent they had unwittingly and uncaringly eroded the cornerstones of their once-prized society. They would be afraid, encouraging each other's fear that was unquestionably the ugly and inevitable companion of change, transferrable between weakened minds, whereas intelligence and vision were no longer transferrable.

The country's mean intelligence had diminished to unacceptable lows. So few were endowed with a clear vision of what was right and what was wrong, the few who were remaining silent.

The lethargy of obesity and idle living not only deteriorated the muscles of the body but of the brain. The greater majority would refuse to acknowledge the need for substantive, draconian change. Nor would they readily or anytime soon embrace the remedy.

She reached for her drink, smiling. Resisting a smile was impossible. The kid was smiling; his teeth couldn't be bigger or whiter. Peripheral vision must certainly be an asset in his line of work, she supposed. Why not?

When he was gone she stood and went for a stroll along the ridge of sand and sea, pleased with herself that she knew what no one else did. She would have four, possibly eight years to flip the country on its ears and the world with it. In addition to which she had decided that as part of the Secret Service female contingent she would insist upon, unless someone from the boy's club was willing to bare his neck to the sword, she would personally interview and select the best-trained and most amiable as her primary shield.

Cruel to say, but they would protect each other.

The woman chosen would also act as her primary companion on the private island for occasional weekends and brief vacations as part of the female contingent, though the Secret Service boys wouldn't be left out. Some aspects of her new life she would have no control over. To that end the crew of Air Force One and the escort pilots could fend for themselves on the boy-side of the island.

Perhaps she would buy the women loincloths and archery gear and have an Amazon Day. Why not, because she was president or soon would be? Not a good enough reason. The Homeland boys would have to deal with it. If her historic male counterparts could cheat, fuck interns, secretaries and the not so diplomatic wives of diplomats, she could have Amazon Days. Besides, anyone expecting to suck up to the president while playing eighteen holes of brain rotting golf would have to wait for a future election. Golf was out. Bows, arrows and bikinis were in. Vega was also out, very out. He'd be busy somewhere else.

She lowered the brim of her hat. Silent beeps, silent smiles meant to compliment her. Good, she thought. Good for her. She put the guy passing her at ten years younger and the girl didn't seem bothered by his distraction as Priscilla made a mental note to send her trainer a personal gift once she returned home to Chicago.

She waved demurely and kept walking.

Part Three
33
The Presidency

November 08th, 2016 changed the world.

Her parents hadn't called her to congratulate her, nor had they ever come to see Karina E. which Priscilla interpreted as a cessation of family responsibilities, her father's defeat not hers, since he had years earlier predicted her failure. What must he be thinking now? Like she cared.

Through to the end of the year President-elect Priscilla Vendôme would continue daily meetings with the incumbent whose time was over, who soon realized he was surrendering the seat of power to a capable successor worthy of the position.

She would meet with economic advisors who quickly understood not to talk down to her. She was a graduate with honours from the Riley school of how to make the most money while spending what was necessary for the best and longest lasting ROI.

Initially skeptical military advisors would stand to attention with sincere respect once they understood the extent of her grasp of international affairs and government agencies such as Homeland Security and others somewhat less public. Once they understood she had experienced dozens of frontline war zones and not as a squeamish little girl shrieking, that she had helped more than once in triage without acting for the camera, caring for their soldiers who were now her soldiers.

She didn't have to wonder about the horrors of war, she told them. She'd seen ripped off arms and legs, smelled the stench and watched men die, some with tears, some without.

She was specific with dates, zones, companies and conflicts. She remembered the men's names, who died and who did not. The neatly uniformed officers weren't expecting her. They were expecting to guide Alice in Wonderland through four difficult years, difficult for them. What they got was a Commander-in-Chief in heels and Armani.

The darker agencies were no less accommodating for different reasons. Some even knew her personally; all recognized her as the once dogged newswoman. What Priscilla knew without the need for transparent subterfuge was that she would never know the half of what was in their combined minds. Covert meant simply that, a need to know, and she wouldn't need to know everything.

Nor would they know everything. After all, fair was fair, she reflected at her leisure once they had gone from her temporary office. Yet little did she imagine that, in the very near future, The Agency, her agency, would be the most covert of all.

She had believed at first that the search would be difficult, hampered by male intrusion, delighted to discover she was wrong. In fact the young Secret Service agent was practically given to her on a platter, as though the boys were happy to get rid of her, assigned to protect Priscilla throughout a year of campaigning. Perhaps, Priscilla once thought, the idea was to have her fail alongside an assassinated female candidate.

What struck her most about the woman was her youthful demeanour, surprised to discover her real age. She didn't act at all like her macho male, black-suited, silver Ray-Ban counterparts and she didn't drive a black SUV.

The Fatal Diners' Club

She wore au courant Gucci, Herrera and Serengetis in deep blues, reds, greens and black when required. She drove a candy apple red Corvette; she appreciated good wine, good food and had impeccable manners. She was well-travelled, had a law degree and was as expert with her10mm as with her feet, hands and a few weapons Priscilla had seen once or twice in B-rated movies.

She was also calm and unruffled. When she hurried she gave the impression she was measured, in control. The only time she ran was in the morning and late evening when Priscilla jogged with her for alone time. She never lost her temper, never raised her voice. Nor was she ever intimidated. She never said 'sir,' not to her superiors, nor to anyone else with the exception of waiters; fully aware she pissed-off Vega each time.

Nor did she ever take instructions from him. She answered to her unit chief and was assigned to Priscilla Vendôme, no one else.

As Priscilla's opponent crisscrossed the country counting his pennies onboard a tour bus most times, greeting his acolytes and shaking hands in three-piece suits, or polo shirts and slacks, or chequered shirts and lose-fitting jeans in the company of the recognizable men in black, Priscilla did not.

She travelled by private jet, distances under 100 miles by limousine stopping to buy ice cream for entire schools, helping the elderly cross at intersections and often strolling along sidewalks after breakfast, lunch and dinner dropping quarters into expired parking meters.

The cops didn't mind. She called them by name, most of the male cops visibly more interested in her very breathtaking security detail who was fully resigned, she once confessed to her charge, to never having another date as long as she lived. Men were too labour intensive. She planned on being a lesbian in her next life. At least then she could wear her lover's clothes and make-up.

Priscilla commiserated. She understood the logic, though none but a complete fool, a man or a woman, would let Lorie Wilson get away. She wasn't certain, nor was the question an issue.

Throughout the campaign Priscilla wore Armani suits and dresses, or khaki shorts with tee-shirts, bobby socks and dessert boots, or fitted jeans and cowgirl boots and a hat that actually smelled of horse and Lorie Wilson was equally well-dressed for each occasion minus the aroma of Houston. If not for the10mm under her jacket or on her hip the two women were perfectly matched.

When asked by candidate Vendôme one day at lunch near the end of the year-long contest how she was with a bow and arrow, Lorie Wilson genuinely surprised her. Priscilla Vendôme reciprocated in kind. She asked Lorie what she was doing for Christmas, not that Lorie had much of a choice.

Agent Wilson had been to Texas quite often, in fact she had travelled to every state onboard Riley's personal jet over the previous twelve months. That said, she had never been invited to a sprawling ranch, ridden a horse or strolled the beach of a private island protecting a president while wearing a weapon strapped to the waist of a clingy high-rise and décolleté swimsuit.

The nameless island was complete with a beautiful villa, guest houses, a pool, a sheltered dock for Riley's yacht and a runway suitable for wide-body aircraft and fighter jets. The name on the deed was Riley Corporation; the lease holder for the coming eight years was unnamed, the lease paid in full on December 31st, 2015 to avoid conflicts of interest the same day Priscilla Vendôme officially resigned from Riley Corp.

The six-day vacation was her first in over a year excepting the previous Christmas with Riley and Karina. She needed downtime. Presidents were not permitted the luxury of calling in sick, sleeping-in, leaving work early or vacationing in paradise alone. Apart from that, however, they could pretty well do whatever they damn well pleased.

The 24th and 25th were spent in Houston. On the twenty-sixth she flew to the island onboard Riley's jet with a single fighter jet trailing a mile off portside. An advance security team had arrived on the island the day before with dogs, guns, night vision goggles and all that cool guy stuff. Sadly, the female contingent was conspicuous by its absence. That team was strictly an in-house accommodation to a female president and that was non-negotiable.

She acquiesced without much choice, ending her fantasy of a fun-filled Amazon Day.

Riley and Karina did not accompany her. Karina was faced with one of her busiest days of the year and Riley was committed to year-end meetings compensating for a year largely dedicated to Priscilla. Karina E. was two months from her second birthday, as charming as her mother and partly responsible for the landslide victory. Despite which she would spend what remained of the vacation in a guesthouse with her nanny who could not yet believe her employer was the president, or that Priscilla was now ma'am in public, or that she had her own two-bedroom suite in the White House and a personal Secret Service detail.

Duncan would never see the island. He wasn't a friend, he was business and in Washington celebrating Christmas in his new home with his family. New Year's Eve he and his wife would attend the formal White House gala with Priscilla et alia including Vega whom he didn't particularly care for.

The man was officious and irritating, on one occasion deserving of reprimand and a succinct reminder that the role of vice-president was far more critical than that of husband. Of course Priscilla made the curt point in Spanish and those nearby were too preoccupied to overhear.

From then on Frederick Vega did what he was told,

though not spending Christmas with his darling wife was his decision for two reasons: He wanted to impress his parents whom he hadn't seen in over a year with his recently assigned security team and he wanted to escape the cheating bitch-elect one last time for as long as possible.

Her final words to him were not an endearment. She wasn't asking him not to go, to change his mind, to spend the holidays with her and their little girl. Not quite. She was lecturing him, chastising him as she would a child, her child.

"Do not fuck up, Freddy…literally. Or save my people the trouble. Find a river and jump in."

There was no humour in her voice.

*

The best parts of her vacation were the strolls on the beach with Lorie Wilson, the quiet moments talking woman to woman, swimming in the ocean and doing her best to hit the bulls-eye or at least come to within a foot of Lorie's arrows that soon went through the red dot that Priscilla claimed was way too small anyway, and probably too thin.

Lorie Wilson was undeniably her social equal, raised by affluent parents and remembered posthumously by loving grandparents. She did not need to work. She did not need to carry a weapon or be conditioned to take a bullet for the good of a nation that didn't know she existed. She was in the Service because that's what she wanted. She believed her work was important because, all things being equal, she was the best. Otherwise Priscilla had no doubt she would be a very wealthy and upscale lawyer.

If Agent Wilson felt peculiar the first day wearing her weapon strapped to a sexy one-piece, she kept the emotion well-hidden. She was professional. She was also to-die-for beautiful. On the second day, when her gun belt wasn't much wider than her bikini bottom, she didn't blink when the president was topless without a word of warning and suggesting they were both girls with no men in sight.

Yes, ma'am.

Their space on the island was private apart from the occasional Secret Service launch passing a mile offshore, when the women knew by the groan of powerful twin engines to face away with their bare backs draped with muslin shirts. They were more intrigued by the twice daily flyovers and the graceless refuelling tanker that came once to circle the island for an hour, quite certain the guys were putting on a show for the incoming POTUS.

During the return flight, nearing Houston where they would spend a night before continuing on to Washington with Karina and Riley, Priscilla Vendôme asked Lorie Wilson what she had planned for New Year's Eve.

Lorie sighed. She had an evening planned of dinner and drinks with a real man: A beef dip, a bottle of Grand Cru something or other and Humphrey Bogart.

*

New Year's Eve was a function in the guise of an elaborate gala: A function of being seen and noticed, of shaking hands and making promises. Mostly they were the who's who of Washington who wanted and needed to suck up to Madam President, many of whom had shunned her during the first six months of her campaign, many remaining uncertain as to what they should call Frederick Vega or whether they should speak with him at all. Most did not.

At midnight all eyes were on her. They expected a speech. They didn't get one. What they got was a toast and her gratitude to the out-going president who raised his glass to her.

If they hadn't already discovered that President Vendôme was a woman of few words they had likely made the irredeemable mistake of not taking her seriously. She was trained and accustomed to speaking concisely in front of a camera amidst the most threatening conditions while conveying the best and most complete sense of what was going on around her without the embellishment of transparent melodrama for the sake of ratings. That would not change.

Hyperbole required too much effort. State the facts and have a solution before you do or go find another job. That would be her protocol.

*

Meanwhile Lorie Wilson was in her condo pampering herself. The apartment smelled of pears and apples, her skin was silky smooth after her bath, her silk chemise was a Christmas gift to herself and the twenty-year-old bottle of wine on her coffee table was a gift whose card she would cherish.

The card read: Don't we all wish we had a Humphrey Bogart in our lives…or at least a better aim? Priscilla.

The roast of beef was almost done; the gravy was simmering and the bread was ready for the oven. The wine was delicious. She'd decided not to spoil its body and flavour with her usual pre-dinner vodka or two. Still, she was tempted. How else would she get through a phone call to her parents in New York?

She couldn't help thinking how much she and Priscilla really had in common, how much she liked the girl. Too bad she was the president and not the girl next door.

She dialled, believing in her heart of hearts that death by a butter knife would be less painful.

She loved them dearly, but weeks away from her thirty-first birthday she was finding it difficult to be her father's precious little girl and her mother's joy. She didn't want joy. She didn't want precious. She wanted Humphrey Bogart in full colour and without the five o'clock shadow.

She wanted too much. She wanted a real man on a planet where real men didn't…"Hi, mom."

Of course she was sorry. Of course she'd wanted to

spend Christmas and New Years with them. Unfortunately she had no choice. She worked for the Speaker of the House and her time wasn't her own if she wanted a decent future.

In fact she was still in her Capitol Hill office on New Year's Eve reviewing legal arguments for an upcoming committee hearing. Yes, she did meet the president in person, for a short while. Yes, she seemed like a really a nice woman. Yes. She would do her best to come home for Easter.

"Hi, dad. Yeah, I know. I miss you guys too. Happy New Year and, yes, I'm fine. No. I do not have a suitor, or a date. Thanks for reminding me. No, I'm working. Go figure. What's new? Absolutely nothing and, yes, I'm living alone. Yes, I do know I could work anywhere in New York, have an exciting career and six figures. I do know that, but I'm here. I'm doing what I believe is important, what I want to do even though…What? Yes, maybe one day I will make a big difference in Washington. Maybe then you'll be proud of me for what I'm doing. Or at least forgive me for not becoming a ritzy, high-profile lawyer. Either way, I am really on a timeline here and I do have to go. So let's say goodnight, dad. What? Yes, I will be home at Easter. I promised mom, didn't I? Goodnight, dad. I love you too."

Lorie pressed END. She did love her father, yet sometimes, often, he was a complete pain in her ass. She knew she would never stop telling her parents lies to spare them the worry. But, hey, everyone in Washington lied.

Maybe she would be a lesbian in her next life. Or was what Priscilla assured in whispers while returning from the island true. She didn't know. How could she? Perhaps one special man was meant for her, a real man, a man who hadn't yet found her.

34
The Oval Office

Priscilla's first day on the job was January 03rd.

She began with one rule: No kids in the Oval Office. She didn't have the time, the patience, or the inclination.

Her first guests were Karina and Riley who stayed for an hour before returning to Houston for a meeting later in the day, departing with warm hugs, Priscilla unaware his meeting was with Ned Michaels. Nor was she aware of the reason.

Her second guest was Vega.

"That was needlessly humiliating, Priscilla, being barred, being told you were in a private meeting with our friends. I would have liked saying goodbye to them."

"Take a taxi to the airport." She pointed a finger. "I didn't tell you to sit."

He didn't.

"So, you made it. Congratulations, though the mind boggles at how many of his millions your friend Edward spent to see you sitting behind that desk."

"I can think of twenty million you care about, Freddy. And if you're smart, which I find questionable at this point, and have for a while, you won't be as foolish with the second ten which may well be your last."

"What you're alluding to is that sitting behind that desk is forcing second thoughts." He smirked. "You know this is really Riley's office you're occupying. I know, and so does he. You can be sure of that. You're a pawn, Madam President. Without his money you would be in Chicago right now…if not reporting the six o'clock news."

"Over the next month I have meetings with the leaders of Israel, France, Mexico, England and Germany and I've met each one of them previously. I've interviewed them, spoken with them, had lunch with them, and even laughed with them. What have you done? Who have you met?" She didn't pause. "That's right. So don't worry about this desk. It's the perfect size. Furthermore they are my friends, not yours, and dare to call me a pawn once more and I'll ban you permanently from this office."

"I have no doubt that you would. I do apologize. In fact, if anything, I'm the more likely pawn in this charade."

"People have done worse for twenty million."

"People like you. It's very clear Riley wanted us married, but for what purpose I have no idea with so many wealthier candidates out there, men with more political minds and ambitions. Who am I but a six-figure nine-to-fiver?"

"You're good-looking, you're fit, your features are what were required and you're sterile."

He blanched, lurching. "What?"

"You're impotent. You shoot blanks and you know what I'm saying is true so stop with the faces. However, if you're wondering, I did have your file updated. You're in perfect health, a real man whose divorce is pending because I'm about to seriously piss off over a 130 million people who probably won't forgive me anytime soon."

"How so?"

"Read the newspapers and stay current. And let's get something straight here, Freddy. You're the wife. I'm the president. You don't get to know what goes on in this office. You get to do what I tell you to do…when, where and how. Play nice and in four years you're either free of me or another ten million richer. That's the deal. Until then be the adoring husband and father."

He nodded, too overwhelmed to move.

"So then, tell me. How did you feel, Madam President, fucking someone thirty years your senior a day before your wedding? That is what happened, isn't it? We are talking about Riley, aren't we, and little Karina E. who arrived a week early with such a beautiful name? Was that how you spent my stag night, fucking your aging boss?"

"Actually we were together throughout the entire week, if you must know, a few times each day. Not that I was counting." She smirked. "We had to guarantee results."

"I understand now why you were smiling coming down the aisle. I must have been quite the joke. He really was giving the bride away, after he was finished with her."

"We weren't talking about you at all. I did what I did for this office. So did Edward and who said we're finished." She taunted. "Did he set us up? Yes, he did, big time, because I'm younger than Karina and needed a baby for this job as much as Edward does for Riley Corp. Karina doesn't and she's emphatic about it, which I understand completely. The kid is a means to an end, as you are. She was born for two reasons, pure and simple. Edward knew you were deficient which leads me to believe you were one of many men he investigated. Remember who we're talking about here. So yes, he intended for me to be the mother of his child. Do I feel cheated, used or lied to? No, I do not. The truth be told, I'm very flattered he thought that much of me. Does he suspect that I know? He probably does not, nor will he. Am I clear?"

"I'm not surprised; though I'm sure Karina would enjoy knowing the origin of her cute little namesake."

"About as much as you enjoy living. You're talking to the President of the United States, Frederick. Threatening me is not a good thing. You were used, are being used. So get over it. Grow a pair. Go count your money, buy something useless. If you'd been up front with me in the first place I'd probably be married to someone else. So look in the mirror before pointing fingers. Edward took advantage of your being a fraud. As for Karina, I love the woman very much. She's a good friend and I don't believe she would mind if she understood the reason why. As for the sex, the arrangement was purely pragmatic, though I can appreciate now why Karina is always smiling."

"You needed a baby to become president. Well, as long as you enjoyed yourselves."

"That's right, as much as Riley Corp. needs a future president and chairman. And we did enjoy ourselves, actually, despite turning my vagina into hamburger."

He was becoming immune. "So... Priscilla Vendôme becomes the president or chairman of Riley Corp. in four years with her vagina open for business. Or something like that," he scoffed.

"I suppose something like that, Freddy. Or soon after because I expect to become the most disliked president in history very soon... or the most loved. The coming year will make or break a possible second term."

"So you said. What you didn't say is how."

"I intend to make obesity illegal."

Vega took a moment, his ensuing laugher difficult to control. "That's precious. That is truly precious, another Vendôme fantasy." He regained his composure. "This is what you spoke about while he was fucking you, putting fat people in prison?"

"I didn't say prison. I said illegal. Over 150 billion a year in health costs, 2400 each year per obese person beyond the norm. That stops now. So do you. Make one more snide remark about my body, about Karina or Edward, or the girl for that matter, and you'll be attending a state funeral...yours. Now get out."

35
The First Year

The truth was simple: Fat was expensive.

The reality was simpler: Already wealthy corporations were earning record profits by virtue of gross negligence; doctors whose single purpose was to heal were getting rich by condoning illness rather than condemning poor health. Parents were no longer parenting and teachers were no longer teaching.

Close to forty percent of the country was obese, some morbid, some attaining super-super status as though striving to win a perverse contest. Those they knew about. A significant number of others were just plain fat, uncaring, devoid of pride. And what of those they did not know about? That was the issue.

That had to stop, and not over several years, not by degree. Time was a diluent to most causes. The population had to relearn taking responsibility for whom and what they were for better or worse. She wasn't concerned about humiliation and human rights or even accolades. She was sick to death of seeing streets, restaurants and planes littered with lumbering and misshapen humanoid facsimiles waddling along in a state of oblivion while stuffing their faces. When did size eighteen and twenty become the norm and muumuus become fashionable? When did overhanging guts become trophies? When did women like her and

Karina and the women in her detail become minority freaks?

No one ever died of embarrassment from being healthy. They would relearn, forget and possibly forgive. Within four years the country would become a much healthier place or pay dearly for the pleasure of being obscenely obese.

By June 01st every man, woman and child in the country would be compelled to visit federal offices set in place for one specific purpose: To be weighed. Step on, step off, and sign.

The programme was not intended to make doctors more affluent or to over burden the system. Those refusing would be presumed obese by default. With them, those with a BMI exceeding 29.9 would pay an additional 2400 dollars per person in taxes equivalent to the annual cost of their self-inflicted disease. Be obese if you want. That's your right. Just don't expect everyone else to pay your bill, though a grace period through to the calendar year-end would be granted, twelve months for the country to shape up before the first yearly penalty would be applied to their new national health account.

Exemptions would be granted to those with pre-existing medical conditions once verified, as well as those with a life expectancy of less than one year and children under three. Welfare recipients and low incomes would not be exempt from the cost equal to a daily coffee and doughnut. Those weighing in under the 29.9 would require mandatory yearly follow-ups; anyone refusing would be automatically upgraded to obese irrespective of insurance or financial well-being and be required to pay the 2400 dollars each year until complying.

Effective immediately federal institutions, airports, schools, universities, hospitals and clinics would be forbidden to sell or promote soft drinks, power drinks or harmful junk from an extensive list agreed upon by her medical and health specialists. No exemptions. Businesses and all states would be encouraged to follow suit, as would municipalities, encouraged to ban legally harmful substances from city halls, municipal building, bus stations, sport complexes and the list went on.

Hotels and restaurants would be encouraged to reduce mega portions, eliminate twenty-four and sixteen-ounce drinks. Those voluntarily adhering to the restrictions would receive tax incentives and movie theatres were another target. They were as bad, if not worse than most restaurants, with outrageously priced junk food which only the most conditioned of the human species could consume without a violent reaction.

Doctors would be mandated to comply with a stricter code, to become doctors, to treat their patients as such and not customers, to tell their patients that being obese was not the new vogue; they were in fact costly to themselves and others. Nothing was cute about baby fat when transmuted over time into 30+BMI Class. Mothers could no longer blame motherhood for food-induced obesity. Fat was fat.

The country's parents had the most to lose at 2400 dollars per obese child. They had one year to prove significant change, two years for the child to attain a normal BMI or be confronted with legal action and possible separation by Child Protection Services. To that end, effective immediately, recess and Phys Ed would return to curriculums as would mandatory health classes and that was the beginning. Dietician was about to become a much sought after career choice and food was about to become a monitored substance.

She would also be talking with fifty governors, thirty-four of whom lived in death penalty states. She didn't understand why a man of 450 pounds wasn't executed because they couldn't find a vein in order to put him down by lethal injection. Obesity could not become a means of surviving the death penalty. She understood that electric chairs might be too small, that the trap doors of gallows might be too narrow, or that the possible inaccuracy of pinpointing the heart might preclude death by firing squad. She got it. She did. What she didn't understand was that a simple dose of pentobarbital or cyanide was overlooked as a solution to all four issues and the meting out of justice. Neither solution was particular about its point of entry, particularly when taken orally.

Priscilla Vendôme was an advocate of capital punishment; those who weren't had probably never seen someone murdered.

She was ready. Her personal physician was ready. The networks were ready for the Friday eight PM time slot. They just didn't know why. For the record Priscilla Vendôme was 5'4", she weighed 120, her BMI Class was 20.5 and Vega would stand with her.

*

Friday Vince Goodman sat in his office. He'd known for a while about the president's first news conference. He loved her, for what she was doing. He really did, though he'd never met her. He even went so far as to vote for her. He was compelled to do so and he encouraged most of his friends and colleagues to vote for her. President Vendôme was going to make him a very wealthy man very soon.

That she would likely be viewed as a draconian queen didn't matter.

*

Her speech shocked the nation, though she was steadfast. She would not relent. The pandemic mindset was too severe to ignore. Other administrations had failed them, she would not. Behind her was a montage of teenagers who'd died over the previous ten years from heart disease and others who had died alone in dark closets and behind bedroom doors from fear, fear of being ridiculed by their peers for being fat. Such mindless persecution would no longer be tolerated. To that end, effective immediately, bullying would be an indictable and punishable offense irrespective of age.

The speech was not given from her desk, rather in a school auditorium where the guilt-ridden and humiliated mothers of those children were assembled for the cameras to scan, many in tears for what they had unconscionably allowed to happen, realizing they were in a real sense being publicly reprimanded by their president for not caring enough.

As she addressed the nation the names and photos of their children were scrolled and read. Being there was a penance, their public admission of guilt and uncaring. No one had to tell Priscilla Vendôme how to face a camera.

By morning she was front page news around the world, no one applauding, everyone stunned.

And she wasn't finished. She expected a report on her desk prior to June 15th. She got it. All but a paltry fifteen million had complied: 4.6 percent.

The statistics were staggering, worse than she had imagined or was led to believe. Including the 4.6 presumed obese by default fifty-one percent of the country was obese, exceeding the most recent estimation by another thirty-three million.

36
The Second Year

People are sheep. Tell most of them with any degree of authority to cross the street for no reason and they will. Much of what she had hoped to accomplish was based on that human frailty since being told what to do absolves us of responsibility.

By December 31st three percent of the country had proven to Priscilla Vendôme that they were overweight but no longer obese, less of a burden to the nation and exempt from the penalty, most of them children. Whether they were healthier because their parents were suddenly afraid of losing them to the coroner or the parents viewed multiples of 2400 dollars as impediments to sixty-inch flat screens, a bigger SUV or a family vacation at an all-inclusive was irrelevant.

Her plan was taking root.

She had anticipated more debate, a stronger backlash which didn't happen to any great extent. Instead industry, commerce and individuals began seeing opportunities for financial gain, some within the law, others not so, which was anticipated.

Wherever good might endeavour to flourish, its nemesis would most certainly nurture its own deep roots: Human nature. And one such individual was Hilary Basil who hadn't taken very long to put his business plan into operation and she wanted him found.

The Fatal Diners' Club

Vega spent Christmas in New York with his parents. The president didn't care what the country might think, though he was instructed to join her for New Year's.

She spent Christmas on her island with her daughter and the nanny, currently en route to Washington at 45,000 feet to end her first year and welcome in another with Karina, Riley and several hundred invited guests.

She was tanned and relaxed from a week with Lorie Wilson walking and talking, playing Amazon and losing, swimming and staying balanced. In another time and place they might have been friends, the reality was that Priscilla Vendôme was Agent Wilson's job.

The evening came and went, people saying what they were expected to say as much as guarding lubricated tongues against what they shouldn't. Vega excused himself to her, retiring early. No one saw him leave. No one thought to ask where he might be. No one cared.

At midnight glasses clinked, 2018 was greeted and most were gone by one AM dissipating into the streets of Washington. Karina and Riley left as well, returning the next afternoon for a private dinner with the president and her husband.

Karina adored playing with Karina E. throughout the afternoon as Priscilla looked on and Riley kept Vega current with the business world while sipping a few well-aged cognacs. When the day ended the women hugged and kissed, the exchange was real. With Vega, however, Karina didn't feel any sense of closeness so she simply said goodbye. Worse, Riley shook his hand without looking at him while speaking with Priscilla.

He had three years left to endure.

He was certain. He couldn't believe the country would tolerate her for a second term, not the way she was treating them like children.

When they were gone he retired to his private bedroom. Priscilla had decided after his caustic remarks the previous year that he suffered from chronic sleep apnea. He would be better off sleeping alone, she told him. Her peaceful slumber was much more important than his.

*

Throughout the first week of the New Year mailboxes across the country were opened to curiosity and expressions of disbelief. No one understood the purpose of the electronic cards imprinted with their names and lengthy codes.

The nation was talking, wondering what was happening, wondering how far she would go. They'd forgotten how she warned them a year earlier that her programme was comprehensive, intended to make a measureable impact and would be implemented incrementally throughout her four years.

Friday, January 05th at eight PM, the nation's doubts were anything but assuaged.

Three percent was not good enough, not factoring in the birthrate. Effective March 31st all comestibles sold from whatever outlet would require that caloric values be attached to the bar code, each comestible purchased would then be accrued on the purchaser's Personal Measurement Card, an electronic card tied to his or her national health account and cross-referenced to residences measuring the total caloric purchase per family per year.

Eat as much as you want, she told them, just don't lie about it.

The draconian queen had arrived and she wasn't finished.

*

Six months earlier, during the first week of July, Dwayne Michaels had met with his uncle in a downtown Richmond bar. They hadn't seen each other in a while. The older man was interested in his nephew's life, his career, his state of mind after so many years with the SEALs. Twenty-nine wasn't too soon to consider retiring from the unit, Ned suggested. Life had more to offer than precision killing and spending most of his waking hours in the dark, or in ditches, or worse.

The conversation was theoretical. Dwayne Michaels was decorated. His career and future were set in his mind. He had a clear vision of where he was going, what he wanted from life. His uncle agreed and ordered another round. They had dinner together, promising to see each other soon, weeks and months passing quickly when time is not your own.

January 02nd, 2018, Ned Michaels called his nephew again. He wanted to meet. He wanted to discuss his nephew's immediate future. Dwayne replied that he had a future, serving his country, but he would gladly meet for a beer.

The next day Dwayne Michaels greeted his uncle with a man-hug. He ordered four Michelob; neither man drank from the tap. He listened intently through his two beers before leaving his uncle to return home to pack.

What he had expected was dinner with a man he respected more than any other. What he got was an instruction to do what was right, for him, not for anyone else. He was his own man despite chain of command. He didn't know what was going on, yet he didn't have a choice, not initially. That was clear. His uncle was vague. Yet the order came from the president. She wasn't asking.

What did his uncle have to do with Vendôme? His uncle replied "nothing." He felt cornered, unprepared. All he knew was that he was instructed to call his commanding officer. He was to request a leave of absence without explanation, which just did not happen in the navy. That was bullshit, despite which the CO agreed to his request without a single question as though he'd known to expect the call. What the hell was going on?

The morning of January 04th he stood alone in one corner of the visitor's entrance to the White House. He felt strange. He felt out of character. Something wasn't right, though he'd been instructed by his uncle not to wear his uniform. Why his uncle, why not his CO? He didn't know. Answers weren't coming his way.

Then he saw her. She was coming toward him as though she owned the place. He studied her until she was too close, believing he'd never seen a more beautiful, confident woman.

She strode toward him as though she could walk through any wall. She disliked him instantly. She thought he was an absolute jerk, arriving for a meeting with POTUS in leather pants and a bomber jacket. His boots gleamed like black crude. What the hell was he thinking and who was he? What did the president want or need with some guy who was so... She didn't know what he was, so absolutely perfect.

She stopped abruptly, addressing him by his rank. And why wasn't he in uniform? Jerk. He tilted his head, acknowledging her. She kept her hands by her side, disregarding his. She guided him along endless corridors ignoring him, turning left and right until he lost count, ignoring him, passing in and out of doors without glancing behind her to see that he was keeping pace.

He was following her. He believed he could spend an entire lifetime following her. He was checking her out and he knew she knew: The male-female thing, game, whatever. She knew. He couldn't imagine a more divinely sculpted ass, the way her perfectly straight mahogany hair swayed in rhythm to her hips. The last door led into a room sparsely furnished with four chairs around a coffee table. His fantasies were over.

"The president will be with you shortly. She apologizes

for the wait, Lieutenant Michaels. Good day."

He watched her walk out. Her voice was low, guttural and sensual. He wanted to say something clever. She wasn't wearing a ring. He wanted to invite her to dinner. If she looked so fantastic in her clothes, how great would she look without them? He thought, phenomenal. How would she feel? He thought, like the softest thing he might ever touch.

"What is your name, miss, if I may ask?"

"Excuse me?"

"I asked your name."

"I can't tell you that. Good day, sir."

She closed the door behind her.

Five minutes later the door opened. He was standing. She gave him a look as though she was having a bad day because of him and stepped out. He'd seen worse. However he didn't think he would ever forget her, not a woman like her, not very soon anyway.

"Lieutenant Michaels, good morning. I'm Priscilla Vendôme. I'm pleased to meet you."

"Good morning, Madam President. Please excuse my casual dress. I'm a SEAL, ma'am. I don't have much need for fancy suits apart from my uniform which I was specifically instructed not to wear. Further instructions were somewhat vague. In fact, I don't have the slightest idea why I'm here. I was simply told to report. So here I am feeling a little underdressed."

"Your ensemble is very dashing, Lieutenant. Let's not worry about the protocol of military dress code. I'm the one who suggested informal attire. Please, be seated. Did Agent Wilson offer you coffee or tea, a juice perhaps?"

Probably just as well she didn't. I think she might have spit in it. "I don't believe I made a very good impression, ma'am. I'm fine. Thank you."

The president surprised him with a light-hearted giggle. He remained standing.

"Lieutenant, I cannot conduct this meeting staring up at you. Please, sit. I won't bite you."

"Yes, ma'am."

"Good. Then let's begin. You come highly recommended. Your file is very impressive, a good deal more intriguing than any novel I've read. You've seen a bit of the world, Lieutenant, without the world seeing much of you, a SEAL for seven years."

"Yes. Team Two, based in Virginia." His smile was bright and disarming. "But you know that."

"I do, yes. I also know your BMI Class is 23.7 and you're here because I wanted to see you in person before asking you to work exclusively for me. As you know, I'm waging a war on obesity. Thus far I'm not losing. I'm winning a few minor battles but I am far from achieving a decisive victory. I went into this so-called war believing my enemy was a blind mindset embraced by half the country. That was fair. That I could deal with. However, as I'm sure you know, opportunity for good will always create potential for bad."

"Human nature, ma'am, it's kept me pretty busy the last few years."

"And that's why you're here. Last June the US Postal Service intercepted completely by accident and my good fortune an envelope addressed to a man in L.A. The man is what we now refer to as a Gourmand. His BMI Class was 56.8. I say 'was' because he's currently dead. The envelope was sent from The Diners' Club, though a more suitable name would be The Fatal Diners' Club because the intent of someone called Hilary Basil is to collect payment for what is presumably a gourmet meal served in a clandestine environment by way of the estates of these Gourmands once they're dead. Call it immoral; call it evil, whatever you wish. But it is not good. It's counterintuitive and this Hilary Basil is working diligently in direct opposition to my expectation of success. What he's doing is illegal and corruptive and I want him stopped."

"Ma'am, that sounds like other agencies' business. I think my uncle got this wrong."

"I don't know your uncle, Lieutenant. I specifically do not want to know him. He is strictly a facilitator whose work extends beyond you. On temporary assignment, if you prefer. That he's your uncle is coincidental and, suffice it to say, I was convinced by people I trust that your relationship is non-threatening to what I seek to achieve. In short, what you hear from me and read in this room is confidential and betrayal of that confidence will not be tolerated. Your uncle is employed by a third party who did not choose you. I did, after considerable deliberation. You beat out many others. Although I want you to work for me to find this man your role will be considered covert and you will work as part of a team. The system will recognize you as a federal agent with the implied privileges and then some. No one else will, including me. To your friends and acquaintances you will be whatever you choose, anything but what you are. Once you leave this room I will not know you. By way of example, did you happen to sign the registry when you arrived?"

"I did not. I was not instructed to and I did not ask."

"There is one, of course, without a Dwayne Michaels because he was not here today."

"That's sort of my life story, ma'am. And when I find this man what do I do with him?"

"I can't know that. What I can tell you is that you will have a partner, a woman, and that you are the fourth team assigned."

"Agent Wilson," he tried. "I could see that working, ma'am."

She smiled. "That would be in your dreams, Lieutenant. No. Unfortunately she's mine for three more years, hopefully longer depending how I manage the nation's grocery bill."

"Is she good at what she does, the woman?"

"She is. If you agree to the assignment you will have her file to review. She will also have yours minus information considered sensitive. I want synergy between you. Do you have a choice? No. You don't. However, like you, she's been put under a microscope and subsequently chosen by me after reviewing several others."

"Who do I report to, if not you, ma'am?"

"Someone we will call your Primary, whom you will meet rarely, whose name you will not know, whose name I do not know. He will in turn report to another whom you will never meet, my Primary if you will. The nature of this assignment is one of trust. A little melodramatic, I grant you, albeit necessary. I want a fourth team established ASAP to find this Hilary Basil. The three others in the Southwest, Northwest and Southeast you will never meet, each team working independently toward the same cause and in place since last July. This man is creating a small empire for himself at our expense, Lieutenant, and I want him stopped for which you will be paid a quarter-million dollars plus expenses each year with immunity from punishment should you become involved in something I don't want to know anything about."

"That's a bit more than a lieutenant's salary, ma'am."

"Because the assignment will last as long as I do, three or possibly seven years. After which you'll be unemployed unless another agency is interested in your skillset, although I understand you live quite comfortably at the moment."

He nodded. "I do, ma'am."

An imperceptible hesitation followed.

"Question, Lieutenant?"

"What happens to my commission, ma'am?"

"You will be honourably discharged with a personal letter of commendation from your president and you will receive your full military pension when the time comes." She reached for a glass of water. "You will be headquartered in New York, which is all I can say for the moment."

He wasn't certain. He was blindsided. His uncle hadn't told him any of this. He likely didn't know. "How long do I have, ma'am, to make a decision. This is my career we're talking about. You've read my file."

"I have, which is why we're talking. You have until you leave this room, Lieutenant. Take the entire day if you wish. Mi casa es su casa, so to speak. If you need me for anything Agent Wilson will be outside the door. If you choose to decline my offer I won't ask you to justify your reasons. I will respect your decision. Simply ask her to accompany you through to security. I will understand completely." She passed him a folder. "This file will explain in detail what we must accomplish, what this man is doing. I don't want Hilary Basil, Lieutenant, simply because he's running clandestine restaurants across the country. You'll understand once you've studied this information which is Your Eyes Only. Do we understand each other, Lieutenant?"

"We do."

"Good."

She leaned forward to stand. He was first on his feet.

"Thank you, ma'am, for considering me."

At the door she glanced over her shoulder. "Oh, I forgot to mention, Lieutenant, that should you accept, your PMC will be deactivated. NYC has so many fine restaurants... should you accept."

She reached for the doorknob, stepping out.

Agent Wilson stepped in. "Sir... coffee, juice, anything?"

"Nothing, Agent Wilson, not unless you're free tonight and would consider joining...."

"No, sir, I am not." Jerk.

She closed the door.

Ouch.

The Fatal Diners' Club

*

Three hours later he opened the door, peering left and right into the hallway. She was sitting across the hall, staring at him, unblinking, clearly annoyed by his antics. She was not enjoying acting as his babysitter. He could almost hear the "what took you so long?"

"Oh, Agent Wilson, it's you. Hi there. Remember me?"

She stood. She wasn't impressed. "Do I call the president, sir? Or do I walk you out?"

"I'm thinking Secret Service Trainee." He assessed her from her shoes to her knees to her...He inhaled a deep breath, smirking, tongue in cheek. "You know, the gun, the attitude."

Blood surged to her head. "The president or the door, sir? This is a busy place."

"The president, please...at her convenience, naturally, since I have no plans for dinner."

She glared, a hectic salvo of invisible daggers spraying the frosty air between them.

He'd never seen such piercing, liquid eyes. She moved a few steps to the side, pressing her speed-dial, speaking into her phone. Dwayne Michaels retreated, closing the door, grimacing. She was one frigid woman, definitely in need of a heat surge, and gorgeous, though he didn't think she would have any problem at all playing Ping-Pong with some guy's nuts or pulling the stick from her ass to beat him to death.

An hour later Priscilla Vendôme walked through the doorway. She didn't waste time.

"Am I looking at Lieutenant Michaels or Special Agent Michaels assigned to a non-existent task force?"

"Special Agent, Madam President. I studied the file. I'm in. Thank you for the opportunity, though I do have a few more questions and would like to meet my Primary as soon as possible with my partner."

"I will arrange the appropriate meetings and your discharge into civilian life. Remember, Lieutenant Michaels, you are now covert, more so than you're accustomed to. Effective immediately you're mine. Neither your SEAL buddies, nor your CO can know about this. You leave the details to me."

The president accepted the folder, shook his hand, thanked him and walked out.

Agent Wilson stepped in, holding the door open. He stepped past her into the hall, waiting, unsmiling. He remained three steps behind, easily meeting each of her shorter strides. He was enjoying the view. She had no lines, which meant thongs which had to mean thong bikinis in the summer and…And what? She wasn't interested. Life went on. It wasn't as though he'd known her for a night, a week or a month, not that he didn't have his favourite girls for balance.

Somewhere there was someone for him, waiting for him, someone a little less…He didn't know. Anyway, maybe Vendôme had given him a fresh beginning, a pathway to his dream of sunny climes, gaudy shirts fluttering in warm ocean breezes and serving margaritas, perhaps sipping a few. Besides, who was to say Agent Wilson wasn't a lesbian? She was cute enough, sexy enough, like the ones on his sixty-inch flat screen.

Yeah, she was definitely a cutie. No kidding.

Lorie Wilson knew why she disliked him, why she instinctively hated him. He was picture-perfect and didn't need anyone telling him so. He was a SEAL, a conceited macho asshole jerk.

Guys like that didn't get married. Why would they? They got laid and went home to gloat or to a bar after midnight for desperate seconds. They were full of themselves, as though she would date a penis-driven android for the sole purpose of him getting his rocks off. Good luck with that. She wasn't a sperm bank. Like she was supposed to believe his eyes weren't glued to her ass. Yeah, she knew exactly what he was thinking. No way! Grow up and get real, macho asshole.

Once through security she stopped at the door leading to the outside. She didn't say anything.

What he wanted was to lift her from under her arms, bring her in close and kiss her, inhale her and taste her. However the 'when in doubt' theory applied. Instead Lieutenant Michaels extended his hand, waiting, waiting until… He was right. Her skin was the softest he might ever have touched, would ever touch. Imagine her cheeks, her lips, her everything.

He wanted to say how lovely she was. He could definitely see himself with her and not for a night if she weren't such a hard-ass and, yes, prissy. Then strangely, strange to him, he was sad, his face a mirror of his thoughts: A rarity for a SEAL.

"Thank you for your time, Agent Wilson. I apologize for the trainee comment. That was inappropriate. Please forgive me. Good day, ma'am."

Lorie Wilson withdrew her hand, though not quickly, her fingers tracing the length of his without her permission. She hated herself. She saw something in his eyes, albeit much too late. How could she dissolve from being a complete bitch into someone he might like, would like? She couldn't. Then she was alone. He was gone without another word.

She watched him leave. His stride wasn't arrogant, not self-important like so many others leaving the White House. He wasn't glancing over his shoulder, nor would he. Most men would, not men like him. She wanted him to at least glance over his shoulder, please, to see her standing, waiting, when she would smile. She would. She could smile. She did often. She would walk out to meet him with a smile, though not too eagerly, to start over and apologize for being such a stuck-up bitch.

Agent Lorie Wilson blew a stream of warm air from between full lips moistened with rich mahogany gloss. She was somewhere else, in another place and time. She couldn't remember the last time a real man had hinted at taking her to dinner.

He hadn't done anything wrong. So he was flirting, big deal. She was worth flirting with. Perhaps if he had asked her once more, at least suggested... No way. She knew better. She would have refused, humiliating him more than she had, though she did believe men like Lieutenant Dwayne Michaels were immune to humiliation, immune to hurt feelings.

Why hadn't he met the president in his uniform? He was a naval officer summoned by the president and why did Priscilla appear so pleased when leaving the meeting when she should have been annoyed by his lack of etiquette.

He'd called her ma'am, ma'am as though she'd been neutered. That hurt. Why not hag, or matron?

Her life sucked big time. She sucked big time. If only he had asked her once more. Anyway, who cared? He obviously didn't. He was gone and she didn't have to loathe herself the next morning for being a desperate woman.

37
The Third Year

By December 31st of her second year the national dilemma was down a further six percent from forty-eight. Close to fifteen million healthier souls had accepted her challenge, which wasn't good enough. She wanted more and she wasn't waiting.

Affirmative action was happening, though the nation would not learn to what extent until the afternoon of January 01st when most everyone would face the same quandary: How much gravy was too much?

Very few missed the three PM event. She was good television. They knew something was coming their way, unstoppable, another Vendôme tsunami, this one striking from Dulles International.

The nation understood she wasn't camera shy, nor was she flamboyant or dramatic. She was straightforward and compelling, always dressed in fashionably short dresses, often seen in designer shorts and tee-shirts when appropriate, always making a subliminal point.

She was gaining support despite her many adversaries, most of them Human Rights activists or the obese exceeding 29.9 BMI Class: The border between overweight and obese.

Her best wishes came first, scarcely peeking at the teleprompter while assuring them that 2019 would be the best year in recent memory. They didn't care; they already knew that from her weekly press meetings. What they wanted to hear came next as the camera panned out from her face to include knee-high boots, a pleated skirt that would make much of the nation gasp and a high-neck cable sweater. She didn't care. She was very recently thirty-seven passing for a woman several years younger.

That's what she cared about. That's what she wanted them to see, to understand that clothes do indeed make the 'man'. Clothes are the front line of respect, for the simple reason that how a person dresses is a visible measurement of their self-respect without which so many other qualities are either undiscovered, forgotten or dismissed.

In her hands was a briefcase. Beside her was a suitcase. All told the President of the United States weighed in at 200 pounds. The ticket agent added 100 dollars to the cost of her travel.

The camera panned out once more.

The man standing beside her on a separate weigh-scale had no briefcase, nor a suitcase. He weighed in at 400 pounds and would travel at no extra cost, though for his willingness to help her make a point he was next in line for a gastric bypass without cost and exempt from that year's penalty.

From then on all passengers on all airlines would be weighed with their luggage. The need was long overdue. The airlines for decades had considered passengers as payload. The single difference between a crate and a human was that crates didn't order cocktails at eight bucks a shot. Now transparency would prevail, no hidden costs. Nor would anyone any longer have to fear the dreaded last passenger or the sandwich syndrome.

Airlines had begun installing wider seating at the rear of aircrafts for passengers tipping the scale. Now the country understood why. Once filled, any other passenger considered unsuitable for standard seating would be bumped to another flight, day or airline. The decision would be arbitrary, made by a weigh-scale, and the slightest hostile disagreement would mean immediate inclusion into the dubious and long-lasting No Fly club. Not a good thing. In addition to which passengers exceeding 59.9 BMI Class would, from then on, be prohibited from boarding commercial flights as a safety measure.

That, she told them, was her law not the industry's corporate standard.

Movie theatres, arenas and performing arts centres had also unanimously and willingly agreed with her third-year policies, further demonstrating how the country could no longer tolerate obesity at the cost of everyone else's expectation of comfort. Limited seating for them would be located in the last few rows, excepting corporate boxes and private balconies.

She went on, stunning a nation that would think twice about a second serving of mom's hot apple pie. Effective immediately the permits of drivers exceeding 59.9 BMI Class would be revoked. That meant getting someone to drive you home from mom's festive table unless a first-time fine of 5000 dollars wasn't a sufficient deterrent. Any second offense would mean having the opportunity to buy back your vehicle at auction.

Then she reminded them that the nation's police were already out in force checking for DUIs and, likely as not, somewhat more stringent in their dedication as a result of working overtime when everyone else was having a good time. Be forewarned.

A female reporter raised her hand. Acknowledged with a smile, she asked Priscilla Vendôme whether the most recent rulings applied to Air Force One and the White House theatre room. And wasn't she afraid of catching cold dressed that way? She should have known better. They knew each other from times gone by. They did not like each other. Then and now the woman persistently derided the president for how she dressed and acted.

The president replied that her aircraft as well as her home met the requirements of her friends and her guests. The Press Gallery, however, was being fitted with new seating despite which she would still clearly hear the lady's questions despite the greater distance between them.

Another reporter raised his hand. They too were old acquaintances. If she thought to try she couldn't possibly remember the many times Gregg Johnson had flirted with her, begged her on his bended knees to marry him or at least run away with him. She liked him. He was good people.

"Yes, Gregg. What is your question?" she asked.

"There is no question, Madam President, just a major thumbs-up on the hot look."

Cameras flashed capturing her wide smile and exaggerated wink. The press conference was over.

She stepped from the weigh-scale wishing the nervous man beside her good luck. She was travelling to her private island; he was going to the hospital. Lorie Wilson was two steps behind her, unsmiling, her eyes searching.

The six o'clock news reiterated what everyone knew. Vendôme was not backing down, she wasn't stopping. The next morning across twenty-four time zones the world chattered about her skirt, her legs and her brash flirtation.

The fortunate reporter's headline read:
PRESIDENT SHRUGS OFF COLD AND CHUBBY REPORTER WITH HOT LOOK

The chubby reporter who chanced to challenge her had a different perspective.
PRESIDENT DRESSED TO KILL (THE NATION)
*

It's what she wanted. Two points of view: One from a good-looking man who was erudite, well-dressed and respected by his viewers and readers; the other from a fat woman with a wart on her nose and whose dress resembled a tent designed to withstand hurricane force winds.

She read Gregg's report. The other she deleted from her tablet, tempted to delete the woman from the Press Gallery.

She was on vacation, a president's vacation which loosely translated into a few hours each day of R&R under the sun, in the sand and frolicking in the waves with Agent Wilson away from men, cameras and the world.

She was hitting the target each time, amazing Lorie Wilson once in a while with a direct hit. They had seven days together: Seven mornings in slingshots, seven afternoons without their tops.

Lorie Wilson had finally acquiesced the previous year. Calling Priscilla Madam President when they were practically naked did seem a tad ridiculous, no less so than wearing a 10mm on her bare hip. Where she drew the line was cocktails. Drinks could not happen, Lorie surprised one evening when Priscilla knocked on the door of her private villa. Priscilla felt like talking and the wine was too good to drink alone. Besides, she wanted more girl time with her friend.

That was a direct order. Who cared if the men would talk?

At the end of the seventh day business as usual reigned supreme. Vega was returning from a week spent in New York with his parents, Duncan was en route to Canada to meet with the still wildly popular prime minister. He would certainly convey Priscilla Vendôme's sincerest regrets; the man was charismatic and charming, the first world leader to congratulate her a year after his own historic landslide victory.

Lorie's vacation began the same week. She flew to Miami where she boarded a ship to cruise the Caribbean. She spent the week alone, strolling seven different beaches, disappointing seven different men after seven succulent dinners and sleeping alone after watching television while others danced to soft music, strolled on deck and made love.

She didn't need the aggravation. If a woman as lovely as Priscilla could live happily without a man, she could. Besides, what was so sexy about a man's sweat and body hair sticking to her body, his smell, his gentle touch? She couldn't remember if she'd ever known.

38
The Fourth Year

Priscilla Vendôme wished her fellow Americans the happiest of New Years. They had every reason to be proud. Obesity was at twenty-nine percent, down by thirteen points. Forty-one million Americans had dropped to below 29.9 BMI Class. Of the ninety million remaining the statistics were promising for a very successful 2020. Relatively few remained unconvinced.

Kids were healthier, their school grade averages much improved over previous years. The military and police forces were fitter, divorce rates were down, cardiac arrests were down and an increasing number of adherents were taking a stand in support of her, which she understood was often self-serving, taking advantage of her determination, as in the case of insurance companies.

Insurers were now refusing to insure applicants with 50+ BMIs, cancelling policies and terminating claims. Dressing had also become more complicated, a side effect she had quietly anticipated and personally wished for. America was slowly becoming a more attractive place.

With twenty-two percent fewer obese clients, clothiers were experiencing decreased demand for large sizes as were manufacturers who realized that size was a cost burden they were not willing to subsidize, in effect creating another deterrent to bulk feeding. The industry was forecasting as well as preparing inventories for another Vendôme year of smaller is better.

To that end Priscilla Vendôme addressed the nation from Dulles international once more.

No one recognized the man standing beside her on the weigh-scale. He wasn't the same man. He didn't appear lethargic or awkward. He was able to stand straight, not slumped over. His brow and face weren't glistening with sweat under the bright lights to make him appear wet or greasy. He was tanned, a reward from his thankful president, and seemed healthy. He was dressed in a new suit and shoes, a new shirt and tie to celebrate the occasion. They stood together on the weigh-scale, the stunning and intimidating President of the United States holding his hand in hers. There were no briefcases or suitcases and together they weighed in at 400 pounds.

The man was crying, unrehearsed and honest tears staining his new face. She'd saved his life.

No one had to tell Priscilla Vendôme how to work the cameras. For all intents and purposes the 2020 campaign had begun.

Effective the 31st anyone exceeding 59.9 BMI Class would be refused public transport on buses, coaches and trains unless wearing a medical bracelet and would be banned from such facilities as amusement park rides and ferries where they might pose a danger to themselves and others. Also, and effective immediately, medical attention would be weight-restricted, priority given to those whose ailments or surgeries were not weight-related unless previously exempted.

Gregg Johnson was front row centre, smirking. She knew what he was thinking. She was wearing oxblood boots, maroon tights, a stylishly short crocheted skirt, a bomber jacket and a maroon beret. He was an incorrigible flirt. They exchanged smiles.

"Yes, Gregg."

"Madam President, devastatingly breathtaking as

always, this is your fourth year. Are you satisfied with twenty-nine percent?"

"I won't be happy, Gregg, until all the men of this country look like you."

He chortled. "And how should all the women look…in your view, Madam President?"

"Not like you, Gregg."

"Madam President, how do you intend to enforce your transport restrictions?"

"Something told me you might ask that question, Gregg." She nodded to her Press Secretary. "Your BMI is 23.1, Gregg. This is your new Personal Measurement Card, hand delivered." The woman took the ID, crossing between them. "Yours is gold. Most are. That's good. Others are yellow, green and red designating the four BMI classifications. Think of a traffic light. As well, silver cards are being mailed out. That's not so good and I don't imagine anyone receiving one will be very pleased, either with me or themselves."

"Thank you. One more question, Madam President, if I may?"

"How could I possibly refuse my prime example, Gregg? Go ahead."

"Will you run for a second term? And, if so, will you continue your weight crusade?"

"Yes, I will run. And my weight crusade as you call it is far from over."

"It is truly amazing though, Madam President."

She was staring him down, waiting. She knew the look.

"Madam President, how is it at all possible that, after three years of living in the White House with all that implies, you have not aged a day? In fact, you are impossibly lovelier each day."

She shook her head, pursing her lips, a burst of air escaping her nose. "I lied about my age on the job application."

The Fatal Diners' Club

*

Her one failure thus far was Hilary Basil. He was invisible, if he even existed, and despite The Agency's investigations The Diners' Club continued to mock her. That had to stop. Hilary Basil had to be put down.

Her January vacation would be extended by a week. The coming year would be an absolute bitch and she wanted her R&R time with Lorie Wilson. She didn't have many real friends and Lorie was the closest thing to a girlfriend she could claim. They had so much in common. She loved the girl, believing any vacation without Lorie would be wasted time. She was so much fun.

Her second week would be with Bradley Duncan, his wife, Edward, Karina and at least one hour each day with Lorie for an early morning jog.

Duncan was in for a second term. He was popular with the ladies, the over sixty-five voter population and the South from California to Virginia. He and his wife were also the country's best ambassadors, liked by Mexico and most of the European Union.

Priscilla believed that whether in 2021, were she to lose, or in 2025 when she would quit politics to take over the helm of Riley Corp., he would become the next Secretary of State after her administration, though her thinking was focused on winning.

Edward Riley was no less committed. His pockets were deep, the deepest, and at sixty-seven he would be wherever and whenever she wanted him.

Vega was another matter, good for relations with Mexico and Spain. He didn't want a week on the island with her or the kid and she understood. She didn't need him.

Her platform was not the abolishment of obesity, not directly. Over three years she had saved the country billions in health care, money redirected to better hospitals, better doctors and nurses, better schools, better teachers and brighter kids.

Families were eating at home, talking. Mothers were relearning the art of cooking. Everyone was learning the taste of better food. Fathers were relearning parenting and juvenile crime was decreasing steadily.

Restaurants were closing: Collateral damage. There were too many in the first place. That was the temporary downside for which she had implemented a solution. The retraining of anyone out of work as a direct result of her programme was funded by the government from increasingly popular lingerie boutiques to gyms where memberships and attendance were at record levels.

That was her platform, not war, not the economy. America would always be at war and would always survive. That's who and what they were. The difference being that now the military was fit.

Priscilla chuckled, studying her body glistening with lotion, studying Lorie's. Anywhere else passers-by might take them for close friends or lovers. They were definitely becoming close friends. The woman was beautiful. Her body was flawless, any man's dream, and Priscilla wasn't the least bit timid about telling her so. She made a mental note. She would ask Gregg to stay longer after the next press conference, or she could have him arrested by the Secret Service for an evening of interrogation. They'd be good together once the ice melted.

Love had increased in the nation with the exception of the nation's capital by one, a situation which was not acceptable in her view.

They sat side by side, inches apart. She wanted to know what Lorie was thinking, feeling. She seemed so distant, unhappy. But who was she to know another's deepest secrets? She was the president, that's who. She couldn't count the secrets housed in her head, pretty sure she had room for one more. She draped an arm over Lorie's shoulders.

"Got a problem you want to talk about, girlfriend?"

Lorie laid her head against her president's shoulder. "Priscilla, I absolutely suck at life."

*

The campaign began in earnest February 01st, the premise being that what America didn't know wouldn't hurt America. She was the draconian Queen, a moniker she didn't like or dislike. She was what she was. More importantly, how many lives had she saved and how many had she changed for the better? She was doing what she was paid to do: Make America a better place.

Would she implement draconian measures in her second term? Yes. She would, once, on January 03rd, 2021.

Many were afraid to imagine, exactly how sweeping those measures would be creating as much disquiet as expectation.

*

She scarcely saw her husband, never thought of him as one. He was a prop, a tool. He was a political necessity as was Karina E. who was in her first year of private schooling.

The fresh scents of spring became the stifling heat of summer which blinked into the ambers, reds and browns of autumn, cities were names to read on Teleprompters and stadiums were drab, emotionless caverns no matter where they were. November 03rd, the day the world was waiting for, was seven weeks away and Lorie Wilson was not enjoying the few hours her president insisted she take to visit with her parents for dinner in New York.

Months earlier Gregg Johnson hadn't worked out for her. Not that she was ever made aware of the president's kind-hearted conspiracy. He was flattered that Priscilla had thought of him. He'd seen Agent Wilson on several occasions. She was gorgeous, easy on the eyes. No kidding.

However he didn't think his fiancée would quite embrace the idea of another woman. He didn't mind. He didn't. He would do anything for his country, but women were funny that way. She should know, with respect, Madam President.

One more word and she would have him arrested, she threatened, tossed into a dungeon. Instead she gave him an exclusive, a hug, her best wishes, and sent him home.

Her next stop the next day was in North Carolina.

*

That evening Vince Goodman took the call from his man in Charlotte, NC. The conversation was brief. The man's voice was calm, even. He wasn't afraid. He wanted his pain to end. He'd suffered for too long. He was dying from years of denial. What was another hour or a day, a week or a month? His once uncaring disregard for his health had metamorphosed into constant agony. He was committed. He would not fail. He wanted a better life for his wife.

She would understand. Her life would be so much better without him.

Goodman listened. He didn't care. What mattered was that Vendôme was out of control, her agency increasingly more of a threat. The timing was overdue to reshape her administration, to make them understand the country didn't need a nursemaid. Neither was she the nation's nutritionist. They needed a reality check. She needed to be put down. Goodman and his associates needed The Agency to go away.

Bradley Duncan had to assume the presidency. Once made aware, despite his convictions, Duncan would not condone the existence of the president's personal attack force. Nor would he appreciate having been kept in the dark. The country would vote for him. They liked him and life would go on irrespective of Vendôme's repressive Personal Measurement Cards.

Before disconnecting Goodman clarified a specific

point. The man's wife would get a million in cash the next day if he succeeded. If he did not, she would get a bullet. The Diners' Club was too profitable to be torn asunder by a despotic female.

Did he understand?

Yes.

*

Lorie's parents were surprised by her visit that she explained easily with a lie, saddened that she had a late flight out, omitting that she would be onboard Air Force One.

The 630 miles from New York to Charlotte lasted ninety minutes. From the moment the wheels touched down Lorie Wilson was all business.

Priscilla Vendôme was in her private quarters changing. She never wore slacks, encouraging the women of her administration to wear dresses with the exception of the Secret Service. The nation's women for too long had dressed like men, fogging the distinction. Women in cheaply made sweats, baseball jerseys, windbreakers and caps on backwards had no right to expect chivalry. Not that the men were any better. Happily the slothful trend was reversing.

Eighteen hundred guests were expected to attend for a heads-up on her progress. They would hear that an additional nine percent of the country had slimmed to below 29.9 BMI Class over the previous eight months. 100 million Americans had bought into better lives in three years and eight months, which wasn't enough. By January she wanted six million more.

501 South College Street was a busy place, crowded with onlookers who couldn't afford the 500-dollar seats. People were anxious to see Priscilla Vendôme. They wanted to see what she was wearing. For the first time in history teenage girls had posters of the US president on their

bedroom walls and thirty-eight wasn't old.

Lorie Wilson was first from the limousine, speaking into her sleeve, her open palm stopping her boss. She didn't like cheering spectators. She didn't like crowds and she didn't like the cacophonous clamour of voices or the thunder of clapping hands. She particularly did not like POTUS talking with the crowd, but she was more than the president. She was Priscilla Vendôme.

The afternoon was bright, the sun eclipsed by tall buildings. The conference centre had been swept by her detail earlier that morning. POTUS was good to go.

Lorie Wilson took the president's hand, helping her out. She always did.

The crowd erupted into a roar, flashes dotting the foreground, cameras and cellphones held high, eager hands clasping books and magazines reaching out for quickly scribbled autographs or to touch her.

Young girls loved her. Mothers loved her. Jeans and sweats were passé. Skirts and dresses were in. Fashion magazines were in. Priscilla Vendôme was in. She was wearing a simple A-line and sleeveless silk dress with closed pumps to match the colour. So were the girls she stopped to chat with, squeezing between them for a photo souvenir none of their friends would ever have, the men in the crowd equally intrigued by Agent Wilson.

The entire nation had opinions for better or worse regarding the president's female detail.

She didn't see them. She saw him.

In 2017 every second American was obese, noticeably disfigured by weight. Now less than one in five were set apart to deal with the new social stigma.

Agent Wilson was trained to determine height, weight, origin at a glance. She put him at 5'11", 380, American, probably mid-West. His face was chalk-white at the end of summer. He was wearing a dark coat on a day the beaches would be crowded. He wasn't moving. He had no expression. The rest of the crowd was smiling and waving dime-store flags. He was inert. She spoke into her sleeve. The instant cold permeating her body shocked her. The man stepped farther out. The gun was a Glock: Dull black steel, 9mm, seventeen rounds. A cop's gun. Lorie spun past POTUS, blocking her, the crowd scattered, the girls ran, cheers turned to screams, people were tripping, falling, the man was jerking, twisting, stumbling, his mouth wide-open, his eyes white, his chest ripped apart.

The man lay dead, splayed. Pandemonium. POTUS was gone. Lorie was alone. Standing. Feet apart. Arms stretched out. Body rigid. The world was quiet. Her gun was gone. She was running. Men running with her. Her arms held in theirs. She was flying. POTUS! Where was POTUS! Doors opening. Doors slamming. Sirens wailing. Tires Screeching. Pounding heart. Precious breaths. Warm hands. Comfort. What?

"POTUS is moving, unharmed. You did good Wilson. Goddamn did you *ever* do good."

The two-way radio crackled. A distraught voice. Urgency. Lorie slumped into the seat.

"Yes, Madam President. Agent Wilson is fine, not a scratch. The assailant is very dead."

*

The mood on Air Force One was sombre en route to Washington despite the furore. The work being done was instinctive. No one was asking. Everyone was doing. The world wasn't standing still. Duncan and Vega were being hurried home. World leaders had to be contacted. Rumors had to be quelled. Press releases were being written. The entire planet already knew to expect a live speech from the Oval Office at eight PM Eastern. The president would not be seen as a flustered female, simply a poised, elegant and feminine woman.

Until then her top priority was Lorie Wilson.

Lorie was in the president's personal quarters, sedated under the care of Priscilla's personal physician. She'd killed a man. She'd saved the life of the president, a woman she loved and admired, her friend. How would she explain that to her father? She wouldn't. She would never be identified, never recognized for what she had done. She didn't care. What she did was her job. She didn't need or expect medals or a promotion for meritorious behaviour above and beyond the call.

She needed Priscilla to be her friend and her president.

*

"…, thank you, ladies and gentlemen. However before I go I would like to ask Carmine and Ophelia to call me, the young ladies I spoke with this afternoon. We were not finished our conversation before the interruption and I would like to meet them next week in Charlotte. Good night."

She did want to speak with them, to meet them. She also wanted the nation to understand she had not forgotten the girls' names because of a little gunfire.

*

The assailant was a John Doe for the time being. He had no ID and his gun, with one round discharged into the air, was untraceable. Not so for his wife. She wasn't a Jane Doe. Her name was Nancy Jasper and her life wasn't better. Her life was over. She was dead in her home from two gunshot wounds.

She had no family, no friends, no life insurance or money in the bank which made her subsequent disappearance practical following her heart attack as stated on the misplaced ME's report.

*

Dwayne Michaels heard the news first on his car radio. Like everyone else in the country he was home for the

425

six PM news, glued to the screen. He sat stunned. He was seeing Agent Wilson whirling herself in front of the president in a single fluid motion, putting eight direct hits into the guy's chest. He reran the video report, eight times in under three seconds without hesitation. Then she was gone, swept away. Six seconds, tops, too quickly for the camera to follow. The men in her detail weren't pissing around.

He hadn't seen her in almost three years. He couldn't remember the last time he thought of her? Why would he? Why would he torture himself with impossible dreams? She was amazingly gorgeous. He tried to remember the smoothness of her skin. He couldn't.

He reran the video. Her face, her eyes were as though she was staring into a pinhole. He was impressed. She was one focused woman, albeit cold as ice.

*

Vega was at odds. He didn't love her. Anyone unable to see through the clumsy charade was either blind or chronically stupid, despite which he would sleep alone that night.

Nor did he need her. He hadn't for years. She was a whore. Her dirty little secret shared by him and Riley, though everyone had secrets and he would sooner file for divorce as a Christmas gift to himself than continue the ruse.

The pretence and the humiliation weren't worth another paltry ten million, not now. What he didn't need was the publicity. He was fine with following behind her, lost in the crowd.

That she was going to win was a given. He would get his ten million from Riley, tolerate the next four years with more frequent travel and laugh his way to the bank. Then he would be free, truly laughing at her, not simply mocking her each day.

Too bad the agent got in the way. His life would have been so much happier without her.

*

Lorie was sleeping in the infirmary, oblivious to Priscilla holding her hand. The young woman had instinctively saved her life. That courage would be rewarded and not with a piece of brass intended for the already crowded chests of pretentious generals.

She knew Lorie was well-off financially because of her grandparents. The woman didn't need to work, which was irrelevant in her mind. Neither did she have to carry a weapon or be expected to take a bullet meant for someone else. That part of Lorie Wilson was over and in the morning Lorie would become even more comfortable.

The president nodded, releasing her friend's warm hand. She would take the call. Edward Riley was en route from Houston with Karina Montoya.

*

Riley disconnected. He didn't love her. He loved his memories of her. In fact he believed Karina was more attached to her than he was. In spite of which they shared history, a young daughter, and a simple phone call would not suffice to express his and Karina's gratitude to the agent.

He hadn't yet fully recovered from the shock of the news, from the televised video report. How close had they come to utter disaster, to losing her?

She was ahead in the polls. She was popular, loved by seventy percent of the country and one child who could not accomplish the impossible without her mother by her side to guide her. The woman agent had not merely saved the President of the United States; she saved the future of Riley Corporation where he would soon need Priscilla Vendôme in place as much as he needed her now in Washington. Such service would not go unrewarded.

*

Vince Goodman called his angry associate who took the call on his private line. The man was dead, which was the plan. He was intended to die. So was the woman dead, by design. What wasn't intended was an ill-spent million. No trail. No connection. The target surviving was unfortunate, he insisted, not insurmountable, though any hope of killing her in the near future was unthinkable.

She would run for another four years. They would simply continue staying one step ahead of her secret agency.

39
Miss Wilson

The following morning Riley and Karina arrived at the White House for breakfast, invited to stay for lunch.

Priscilla wasn't seeing Lorie Wilson right away. She had a difficult task ahead of her, one she alone would undertake. First, she wanted to speak with Riley. She had a favour to ask.

Riley agreed wholeheartedly. He also agreed to double the amount suggested by Priscilla and wanted to meet with the young woman to thank her personally before leaving.

When he told Priscilla in private why, she showed no surprise.

*

Lorie was refreshed, not the least bit groggy after her lengthy sleep. A fellow female agent had gone to her home for a change of clothes, an overnight bag of essentials, and her infirmary room was equipped with a bath and shower. All she was missing was her weapon.

Not many Secret Service types were ever invited to a luncheon in the president's private quarters. In fact Lorie was the first and likely the last.

She had seen Riley on several occasions in Washington and Houston. She knew who he was, as much as anyone else in the country, possibly a bit more because she had on occasion been to the ranch. He was a frequent visitor to the White House, though she had never met him, was never introduced to him or his wife and had no idea Riley had read every word of her service record and personal profile.

Riley and Karina didn't stay long after lunch. Shaking her hand he congratulated her, wishing her well. He had assessed her without her knowledge, discreetly nodding his approval to Priscilla. Karina liked her very much as well, hugging her closely. Everything else had been said.

When they were gone Priscilla poured herself a double scotch and served Lorie a double vodka with a single ice cube, leading her friend by the hand to her sofa.

"Thank you, Madam President. You've been very kind to me, as usual. Ms. Montoya is very nice. I can see why you like her, though having lunch with them certainly was not what I expected. Thank you."

"She is very nice and, hey, I'm Priscilla when we're together. Remember? Here or anywhere, especially when we're sitting holding hands. Sometimes this Madam President thing is so pretentious." She giggled. "I pull my stockings on one leg at a time and I curse like a sailor when I get a run, girlfriend."

Lorie giggled with her. "This is so weird, me sitting here curled on your couch and getting drunk with the president."

"No one will blame you, not if they want to keep their job. I certainly won't. But, Lorie, I do have bitter sweet news that won't go away. So you tell me. You flip the coin, girlfriend."

"The bitter is always best before the sweet."

"You are no longer assigned to me. I have no choice in the matter. In fact, you are no longer assigned to the Secret Service. That was my call. You are Ms. Lorie

Wilson. I have to believe someone like you would not want to remain here as a paper-pusher."

"I did know to expect that, Priscilla. We're sort of like safety belts; once we're used we're discarded, no longer reliable. And I do hate paperwork. Thank you. I know telling me this wasn't easy, nor part of your job description. I appreciate that you did." She sipped her drink. "So what's the good news? Do I get fast-tracked to the unemployment line?"

"You're leaving tomorrow onboard Edward Riley's jet for a couple of weeks of pampering at a place I used to go for balance. That's my treat. I couldn't think of anywhere you would enjoy more." She smirked. "And you can be as carefree as you want without being hassled. I want you to relax and to recover. I also want to hear how you're doing each night because if not for this bothersome election coming up you and I would be going to the island together for some target practice. Not that you need practice."

Lorie was shaking her head. "No. A simple thank-you will do, Priscilla. I don't merit any special treatment. I really do not."

"The hell you don't. I disagree, Lorie. You do merit special attention because I say you do and you are special. You put yourself between me and a bullet. I could have lost a good friend because of who I am. So, that said, two million dollars is being deposited into your bank account as we speak as a joint thank-you from me and Edward Riley which hardly begins to express what I feel."

"Priscilla, I'm already very comfortable and a change of career is not a big issue for me. Will I miss you? Yes, I will. But I can work for any of a hundred companies, if I choose to do so. I don't need…"

"What's done is done. The matter is permanently closed." Priscilla handed Lorie a file. "We're on to other matters. I would like you to consider a one-time job offer while you're basking in the sun, knowing I'm thinking of you. It's not a career move, Lorie. It's an important job with a single four-year term if I win the election. You would be working directly for me, the president, with a select handful of others you will never meet. You would be paid by the Riley Corporation as part of a Special Functions Group and work with this man. The job is covert, Lorie, not even Bradley Duncan or dickhead are aware of this particular agency. This is strictly my deal."

"What is their function?"

"Specifically to find and kill one man. He's the head of a private organization I want shutdown. Of course, this is dependent on my winning the election. Should I not succeed The Agency will immediately dissolve. They will never have existed, which I cannot let happen. As for the agents themselves they are hand-selected by me, very well-paid for their work, and enjoy quite a few perks which is the sole Riley connection. They are, however, not recognized by me or this office and are separated from each other and from me by a small and invisible hierarchy. They don't know each other beyond a single partner and one contact whose name they don't know. What I mean to say is that, should an error in judgement occur, the individual would be disavowed by this administration and subjected to appropriate and permanent remedial measures. Do I make myself clear?"

"Yes. Hear, see and speak no evil."

"That's right, to the greatest degree."

"What happens after the four years, Priscilla?"

"This is confidential. This conversation stays in this room. Should you accept, not even your partner is to know about this."

It was Lorie's turn to grin. "Nobody knows about our skinny-dipping…girlfriend."

"Okay, that's a good point. So here it is. In 2025 after my second term, if not this January, I will incrementally take over full control of the Riley Corporation. Edward wants out. When that happens whatever job you want that meets your impressive qualifications is yours. You tell me what job, in what city, and it's yours. I haven't made this offer to anyone else, nor will I. If you decline an active role in The Agency after reading this man's file and what is expected of you by The Agency, the Riley career stands and takes effect immediately. I have no intention of losing my girlfriend."

"Mr. Riley is involved this agency."

"He is not, not actively. Riley Corp. is a convenience."

"You're sanctioning a murder."

"A rose by any other name...Yes, I am, and regardless of the need to distance myself you will be operating with full impunity from this office. Between us girls, Lorie, the man I want dead is responsible for yesterday. The assailant's name was Alvin Jasper, working for another man. His wife was also found dead this morning by the Secret Service, shot, though officially she had a massive coronary. No one will ever discover his name, or hers. They're being cremated as we speak. The irony is I can't tell anyone, not the FBI, not anyone."

"What's his name, the man who wants you killed?"

"I'll let your partner tell you, if you decide you want him as a partner."

"Will he try again, do you think?"

"I don't know. We do know he's not alone. He's somehow protected. We don't even know if the name we have is real. The Agency's been hunting him for almost four years across the country."

There was no hesitation.

"I'm taking the job. I'm in."

Priscilla patted Lorie's knee, squeezing gently. "What you're taking is your vacation. Read your partner's file thoroughly. Be certain. Then you tell me."

"What's his name, the one I'll be working with?"

Priscilla shook her head. "Not until you return rested and tanned. His name and personal data are privileged to me and two others, one of whom I don't know, intentionally omitted from the file. As will yours be."

"What happened to his current partner?"

"She got married a month ago and we retired her. The Agency recruits singles, no exceptions."

Priscilla stood to refill their crystal glasses.

"What was yesterday really all about? Why does this guy want you dead?"

"The election, what he believes is coming. He knows, or at least he suspects, that I'm not finished with my programme. And his fears are justified. Simply put, the more I succeed the more he'll fail."

"You mean the PMCs. There's another announcement coming."

"Yes, a very big one which will somehow directly impact him. How exactly? We haven't figured out. That'll be your job."

"The country's healthier because of you. So he's doing something which isn't healthy, I assume."

"You hit the mark, again. It's all about what is essentially the supply of illegal food, wine and money. I've told the nation they can eat as much as they want, gorge if that's what they want, just don't come crying to mommy with a tummy ache because mommy knows how much you're eating and drinking and she'll bill you 2400 dollars and take away your chubby children. He found a way around those penalties and now I've found a way around him and I have to believe he sees me coming. What he did not see, was you. So I imagine he's a little pissed right now."

"So this is about black market food."

"He's selling black market food and wine to his followers at a very high price and I'm selling narcissism to mine for free. The PMCs, they're more than about health. That's smoke and mirrors for the masses. The cards are really about vanity, Lorie, without which we learn not to care about ourselves and our self-respect flies out the window. Then we don't care about others, like our children, as we inevitably learn not to care how others view us and their respect for us is deservedly lost. That's what I've done. I've re-established the nation's sense of pride and respect and the results are in. Dress for the job, dress for respect and Riley Corp. is the premier example. Their caretakers go to work each day in clean slacks, shirts and polished boots. They also hit the gym along with everyone else. They don't have a choice. In return no one disparages them. They get the respect they deserve. No man in this entire country would ever have dared to make vanity an issue the way I have. Take you and me. I'm vain as hell, Lorie, though as Priscilla Vendôme the news lady I never wore jeans and safari shirts in the studio or short dresses and low-cut blouses in flood or battle zones. So are you vain. You want that perfect image, which doesn't mean we're a couple of stuck-up bitches. We're making a statement. We're proud of who we are and we demand respect. I mean, really. We're beautiful women and we are hot. Put us on any beach together and we would stop traffic dead, male and female, especially in those barely-there slingshots we wear. Talk about hot. That's hot, big time. Way too hot to share with a, I don't know…him."

"Don't get me started. At least you have one. If I don't find a man soon I'll have to start dating women." Lorie sighed, taking her old-fashioned. "I don't suppose there's any chance you'd be interested. I'd split the rent."

"Don't tempt me, sweetheart. I've endured a very long and dry four years with dickhead, I'm heading into another drought and I'm serving Russian doubles to a totally sexy woman who's already seen me naked and oily." Their glasses clinked. "So do not get me started."

"We did have fun…naked and oily."

"We will again, when this presidency thing is all over. We're friends, Lorie, girlfriends."

"On that note, Priscilla, I really should go. People will talk."

Priscilla Vendôme chuckled. "Who died and made you president. Besides, you're out of a job because of me and I'm taking the afternoon to spend with my friend to make her feel better. No more shop talk."

"But Mr. Vega…"

"Dickhead isn't permitted in here. Besides, I sent him to pick up a pizza…in Italy."

*

Lorie Wilson had accompanied the president onboard Riley's jet countless times during the 2016 campaign, albeit without the pampering and the one-on-one attention she was now getting from the attendant.

Priscilla was right, Lorie pondered en route to her vacation. She and Priscilla were good-looking. Lorie was right as well. The previous afternoon was weird. Two women, both attractive, both vibrant, one an assassination attempt gone wrong, the other saving her with a gun which would likely find its way to the Smithsonian, sitting in the White House overlooking Pennsylvania Avenue while drinking scotch and vodka with their shoes kicked off and curled into each other with their arms interlaced watching Fred Astaire and Ginger Rogers.

That was weird. Being driven home by her detail

after her dinner with Priscilla was weird and stepping into a private jet alone was weird.

Reality was sinking in. She was out of a job she loved, a job she had trained for and lived for, protecting a woman she had come to love as a friend and admire. She'd killed a man, turned his chest into a stew, which didn't bother her. He was dead as much for the gun as for what she'd seen in his eyes. What amazed her was how quickly everything was over; persistent and gruesome images of a far worse outcome keeping her up most of the night. She would never have forgiven herself if she had failed to protect her president and friend.

She promised Priscilla she would call her parents, deciding she would wait until the next morning. She had too much going on in her head. She called moments before departing for the airport, moments before checking in with POTUS who was already airborne.

POTUS, she groaned. More reality: Priscilla was no longer POTUS to her. That was more than losing her job.

Her parents weren't a problem for once. Although they had noticed a slight resemblance between their daughter and the woman who shot the president's assailant, they knew their Lorie was safe and sound in Washington after her visit. Besides, her father laughed, when had their Lorie ever done anything more life-threatening than baking cookies in her Grade Eight Home Ec class?

He was right, of course. She couldn't think of a single time and her mother knew Lorie would never think to wear such pedestrian sunglasses intended for roguish men or her lustrous dark hair in such an unflattering bun. Certainly not, she was far too lovely a lady, far too refined.

What planet were they from? She disconnected

without mentioning her impromptu vacation, sparing herself the inquisition. She told the taxi to wait, closed the door behind her and buried her parents from where they would not resurface for an entire fourteen days.

She wasn't wearing a gun. She didn't like the feeling. She felt undressed, incomplete. She always wore a gun or had one in her purse. Stepping alone into the jet felt strange, the pilot and attendant greeting her. What kind of money was required to live that way, she wondered, everyone following your schedule?

The flight was smooth, too early in the day for a cocktail until the attendant reminded her she was on vacation. She relented. She asked for vodka and soda an hour before lunch and sat with her feet up to read the man's profile and edited history.

She wondered whether he had been told, whether he knew about her or about what she had done. She wondered whether he was reading her profile. She believed so; pondering to what extent she had been edited.

Then they were landing, Lorie unaware the wheels had touched down, the pilot escorting her through the terminal, though Priscilla hadn't warned her to expect a limousine.

She wasn't intimidated. She felt awkward despite her inherent femininity. No man had ever opened a car door for her, not once that she could remember, nor taken her hand to help her step out, the chauffeur averting his eyes from exceptionally well-toned legs.

The resort was glamorous, her detached villa luxurious with a patio setting submerged in several inches of sun-warmed water where she was free to sunbathe or dip in absolute privacy. She decided she would do both.

Priscilla certainly did live the good life.

She didn't hurry to explore. Laying on her chaise-longue naked as an abrupt wave of emotion crashed over her. She felt drained, inexplicably depleted as though she wanted to cry without reason. She gave herself the afternoon to forget, coating her body with lotion, letting her mind drift as she basked, surprised when she woke.

She slid her body from the chair into the shallow water. She laid still, her legs far apart, her arms reaching aimlessly, her hair floating. The sensation was foreign: Naked, exposed to the sky and the sun, the gentle breeze and warm water caressing her with teasing ripples. She lay at attention, rolling, holding her breath, splaying her arms and her legs for one minute, two minutes, three minutes and gasping.

She jackknifed her body, her ankles touching, coming to attention, stretching, arching her back, her skin sparkling. She moaned. She felt good. She felt beautiful. So what? Beauty without admiration served no special purpose, had no special meaning.

She towelled, squeezing her hair into a slick tail, fingering a code into her door before tying herself into a thong, adopting the easy European mode of bottoms only. Priscilla had told her not to bother with tops. The compound was a Garden of Eden for a single woman: No single men. No hassles.

She zigzagged the length of the beach, no one shocked by her bare breasts. No one was staring. Women wore thongs, vivid and daring; their men wore straight-backs or thongs, which was quite alright with Lorie given their tanned and tight bodies.

Lesbian couples ambled along holding hands, smiling discreetly. Women alone, content, meandered in lost worlds, waving while passing. She wondered at that, at the couples and the singles, remembering her times with Priscilla at the beach and in the ocean, remembering what she asked her friend their last time together curled on the sofa.

How would she feel falling in love with a woman? Did Priscilla know? She snorted softly, shaking impossible images from her head and waving. Probably a matter of time, though she couldn't imagine where or with whom, maybe. Someone had to want her, want to love her.

Before dinner, while the sun lingered high in the sky, the yellow heat soothing, she showered at her patio and lay on her chaise-longue to dry and read his report once more.

No way could one man do what he was claiming in his file. No one was that perfect. He was Caucasian, 5'11", thirty-two, retired from the navy, a lieutenant, an ex-SEAL with more than a dozen kills. He had no family. He had a degree in phycology and the credits went on, Lorie studying twenty pages of citations and medals. He was a survivalist, a specialist in weapons and deep diving, a parachutist, Black Ops trained in unarmed combat with more black belts than she had skirts. No way at thirty-two. No way.

He had no family, lucky him.

She wriggled to her feet, slipping into a terry robe. Calling the president when she was naked didn't feel right. She reported in. Was she relaxing? Yes. Did she like the place? No kidding. Did she...? Yes, she did. Good. No mention of the file was made, no girl-talk, simply a promise that she was fine and would check-in the following evening.

She dressed for dinner in a tube dress that was white, strapless and short. Too alluring for dining alone, she told herself. So what? What the hell. Such was her destiny. Her life was shit. She was going to die alone in a rocking chair in a home for the old and forgotten with her mind too far gone to remember any good times. What good times?

She left before dessert was served and went to her

villa. She sat gazing at the moon alone from her patio, wondering whether her guy would be a thong-guy. She hoped so, whenever that might be, sometime before her breasts pointed to the ground instead of whomever, sometime before she required a crowbar to pry open her vagina. Though, if all else failed, she hadn't seen one woman at the beach or at the pool whose breasts weren't spectacular, whose ass wasn't perfectly tanned and flawless…if all else failed. God! She was so pathetic.

She woke the next morning cloaked by the warmth of the early sun, her new dress and panties submersed in the pool. No way! She loved that dress. She rolled to one side, splashing into the water, debating whether or not she should drown. She couldn't think of a good reason not to.

Throughout her vacation she stayed to herself. No single women, she noticed, were connecting. Some left after a few days, replaced. Others stayed for a week, no one giving the impression they had scraped pennies together for their trip of a lifetime. They were the pretty people, penthouse and Lamborghini people. Singles and couples wanted their space, though she seriously doubted anyone wading in the sea or laying out in the sun or in the shade of a palm tree had recently killed a man in broad daylight or was contemplating killing another one sometime in the near future.

She called Priscilla each night with never an enquiring word about the man's profile or her decision. On her last night she was invited to the White House for lunch the day after her return.
*
"You did enjoy. I can tell. You look wonderful."

"I did enjoy, very much, and I do feel wonderful. But I did miss your archery lessons."

"You didn't find anyone to play with?"

"With my love life, I was afraid to try. I've never seen so many beautiful women in one place."

"Imagine what they were thinking. And the patio, used to its fullest each day?"

"I don't think I like clothes anymore."

"And was the file good reading, Lorie?"

"Does he fly? I mean with a red cape and red booties."

"If he could I wouldn't be surprised. I told you he was good."

"Does he have my file?"

"Not yet. As previously mentioned, this is very secret."

"I'm in, Priscilla. I want to do this for you."

"Then he'll have your file this evening. My courier service is much faster than FedEx. It's so cool to command an air force. And I will want you living in New York ASAP. Find a temporary place, something nice. Riley will pick up the tab until I'm elected or the head of Riley when you will either stay in New York or choose another city when working with me at Riley Corp. However I am hoping you might like Houston." She sighed. "Who knows? Maybe we will end up splitting the rent, once I dump dickhead. In any event, it's adios to Washington."

"Thank you, Priscilla, for everything."

"Let's not get mushy."

"Sorry. I can be in New York by the first of the month. I'm always getting offers on my condo. It'll sell quickly. I do have to say, though, I'm curious about who this guy is."

"His name is Dwayne Michaels and, as I said, he is good…very good. You'll work well together."

Silence permeated the room transmuting into disbelief.

Lorie wasn't blinking, flashbacks illuminating her

dark eyes. Her mouth was gaping, words difficult to find, express. Blurting "No way!" was involuntary.

"That's right, girlfriend, the good-looking hottie in leather." She chortled, her voice musical. "Hey, even presidents have wet dreams. I am a woman, you know, in spite of dickhead. So, hey, good luck with him. All I'm asking is that you don't do anything stupid like fall in love or into his bed."

"That won't happen anywhere outside of his dreams. His kind jumps at anything moving in a skirt. I'm surprised he didn't hit on you."

Priscilla scrunched her face. "Thanks, I think."

She squeezed Priscilla's hands. "I meant because you're hot and, you know, the president...good for his résumé."

"Tell you what. If he hurts you, I'll have him buried alive. I can do neat stuff like that because I am the president. No problem."

"Then we have a deal."

"Come to think of it, I should have dickhead buried." Priscilla hugged Lorie close, kissing her cheek, smudging the gloss into a pink blush with her palm. "We're girlfriends, the best. Do not ever forget that, Lorie. I won't. You need me, you phone me."

Priscilla served a simple lunch of different pâtés and cheeses with crystal goblets of full-bodied Bordeaux. She prepared her lunches as often as her schedule allowed to stay balanced. She wouldn't always be president.

When they were finished they sat together on the familiar sofa to view Lorie's vacation photos. They would definitely miss each other.
*

That evening an air force colonel touched down in New York to meet with a man he didn't know. The exchange lasted mere seconds. The envelope made private and confidential by the president's seal contained two others which were not officially sealed.

The man drove to Manhattan where he met another who knew to meet him and where to stand. That exchange was much less time-consuming, the cloak and dagger theatrics of his wide-brimmed hat and dark glasses considered essential.

At home Dwayne Michaels dropped his keys onto the sofa table at the door. He was neither anxious, nor curious. What he felt, what he wanted or didn't want, didn't matter. The choice wasn't his. He went to the kitchen, poured a two-fingered Johnnie Walker Black, sauntered to his living room and opened the envelope.

She was a Caucasian female, 5'8", thirty-four, recently discharged from the Secret Service after meritorious service. She held a law degree from Harvard, graduating with honours before doing five years with the FBI. She was a markswoman with extensive weapons training. She had third, fourth and fifth Dans in three disciplines. She had parents, both living. The father: Lawyer. The mother: Surgeon. No other family of note.

Besides that her profile was pretty thin.

The final line was a caution to destroy the communication. The document was unsigned.

Dwayne Michaels studied the history, committing the details to memory. He didn't like what he was feeling. He went to the kitchen for a refill, then to his office to shred the few sheets and wait by the phone. He was pissed. They were giving him the president's hand-me-downs.

The phone chimed once.

"You read the file, Mr. Michaels."

"I did. Who is she?"

"Her name is Lorie Wilson. You'll be told very soon

when and where to contact her. She comes to us highly recommended from the highest possible person of interest. Treat her well, Mr. Michaels. That came to me as a direct order. Good night."

He was right. Lorie Wilson. Holy shit! The White House Ice Queen.

He downed what was left of his drink, inhaling a deep breath, exhaling. What were the odds? What the hell had he ever done to deserve this kick in the balls? He was pretty certain he could have loved the woman, would have loved her, fallen for her big time if she had been a tad warmer and more pleasant than a slab of beef hanging from a hook in a meat locker.

Now he would have to work with her. Shit! The highest possible person, meaning the president, meaning he was screwed. He wasn't pleased.

Okay. So she could probably defend herself in a situation with some guy hitting on her, or a pothead looking for handouts, maybe with a mugger or two. But her shooting, her kill hadn't been mentioned in her profile. Maybe the president had a reason. Or maybe Miss Wilson was a little brain-fucked after killing some guy up close and personal.

That was his guess.

Then again, he had time. There was always a chance, albeit slim, that Priscilla Vendôme would lose the election, or maybe he would get hit by a bus before sitting too close to Wilson and dying of exposure to extreme cold.

40
Love to Hate, Hate to Love

Dwayne Michaels was not impressed, not by Harvard, the FBI, or the Secret Service. All three equated to disciplined and narrow thinking, marginal team thinking. Stand alone, you're up shit creek. No excuses, dead. She wouldn't break the rules; never bend, most likely because of the stick up her ass.

He was at the hotel bar an hour early. Not that he wanted to drink, which he was. Two PM meant five PM somewhere. He was sitting on the barstool nursing his scotch because he wanted to see her arrive. He wanted confirmation. He knew what to expect. He knew what was coming.

She would arrive in a black Rav4 or a black Impala: Affordable penis envy. She would wear a black pant suit, neither tight nor loose, maybe dark blue, buttoned. Her shirt would be button-down, white, starched like her, maybe a tie, black or blue, one of those female bowties. She would wear pumps, two-inch, matched to her suit, polished, not shiny. Her hair would be wound tight, some sort of a bob or ball on the back of her head with a pin jabbed into it, a possible weapon for sticking some guy in the eye, maybe the next guy who doesn't do a good enough job getting her off. The make-up was easy: Green eye shadow under silver-coated stereotypical RayBans regardless of the pissy weather, prune gloss and prune nails inside black or blue unlined gloves. Jewellery: Diamond studs, a gold or silver flag on her lapel, no rings. No wonder.

She wouldn't saunter through the glass doors to the lobby. Not her. No. He'd seen her walking, watched her walking, each cheek of her phenomenal ass rising and falling in sync with his heartbeats. No. She would march in as though on a mission to kick some guy's nuts through his mouth and if she did join him for a drink, which she wouldn't because of that stick thing, she would order Perrier with a twist of lemon and side-glance him because he'd be on his second scotch.

That was Agent Lorie Wilson in a nutshell.

*

Lorie Wilson was ecstatic driving through Manhattan.

She'd been in New York three weeks where she had lived as a girl until leaving for Harvard and a life she had meticulously mapped out. She would join her father's law firm, fall in love and get married in her late twenties, probably to another lawyer, or maybe a doctor and she would vacation in exotic and sunny destinations twice each year, which didn't quite work out. So much for predicting the future.

The week before she hadn't thought for a moment that Priscilla would take her call amidst her jubilant celebration, surprised when asked to wait by one of the president's aides. She didn't know what to say, what the president would say. Hearing the familiar voice she simply said, "Priscilla, you did it. Congratulations."

They spoke for five minutes, both women saddened yet gleeful. They would not speak again or see each other for four years. Priscilla Vendôme had won the election by a historical landslide victory. Because of Lorie, Priscilla told her, her friend whom she would never forget. No way! The president had kissed her through the phone, wishing her well, thanking one last time for saving her life. How cool was that?

Lorie understood what she was driving toward: Mr. Hotshot commando asshole. That's what. She harboured no misgivings. She would spend the next four years being told what to do. He would always know best, he would always drive, he would always interrupt her, correct her, always have done something better or more dangerous than her. Well, no shit. And Priscilla thought she had it bad with dickhead. Now who would Priscilla confide in, frolic in the sea with, stroll on the beach with, or run holding hands with and laughing?

She'd known for a few days where and when to meet with Dwayne Michaels. The man had called her late one night, introducing himself as her Primary. She'd asked him when they would meet each other, the man responding before disconnecting that they had met for the first and for the last time.

She pressed END. All she could do was to believe and trust in her president and friend. She was doing something good for the country.

Michaels would be standing under the awning, waiting, leaning against the façade of the hotel, one knee bent, one foot pressed into the wall, maybe playing seesaw with a toothpick in his mouth. He'd be dressed in black leather: Black leather pants, black leather macho bomber jacket, black boots and black glasses on a day dulled with black clouds and thick rain.

She was also well aware of what he was expecting. Well he was wrong and if he imagined for a moment she was wearing sensible underpants and a boxed bra he was an absolute idiot. Not that he had a chance in hell of seeing her undressed, of slipping her silk thong from her hips to her knees to her ankles, of easing the thin satin straps of her three-quarter laced bra first from one bare shoulder then the other, caressing her, cupping her...

No way. Dream on. She was there. Why so soon? He wasn't. Why wasn't there more traffic? She was in Manhattan for God's sake. He would be in the lobby, wearing his dark glasses, full of himself, God's gift. Jerk.

Then he would suggest drinks. Oh, big surprise there. He was a beer drinker, definitely a beer guy. Not because he liked beer, he probably didn't, because in his macho mind drinking beer would make him look rugged, cool, like the frigging Marlboro Man who probably couldn't satisfy a woman because his ego was bigger than dick.

She pulled into the curb, checking her hair in the mirror, checking her eyes, her lips, her teeth, waiting for the valet to open her door.

*

Dwayne Michaels ordered his second scotch, his eyes fixed on the lobby doors. Nothing was happening. He checked his watch: 2:59. She was late. Not a good beginning.

The candy apple red hardtop Corvette pulled in slowly. Nice ride, he thought. Inside was either a tall, good-looking blonde with legs to her neck or a bald and overweight divorcé. He voted for the blonde. But he wasn't seeing Wilson anywhere.

The barman broke his spell.

Michaels shook his head. He was running a tab, thanking the guy, taking a sip, forgetting the possible blonde. His mouth was dry and he did not like people who didn't respect time. Mere seconds could save a man or get him killed and a drop-dead gorgeous body was no excuse.

*

Lorie Wilson covered her head with the hood of her cape before stepping from the car. She pranced across the wide sidewalk devoid of people signalling to the doorman to remain inside.

The lobby was cavernous and empty except for the Reception people and a few men sitting far apart reading the Saturday Times. She didn't see any women, which she thought was strange until understood. How silly was that? They were all at home getting ready for their dates. She was the only single woman in New York stuck at home on Saturday nights with a lover that came with batteries and personal hygiene instructions.

She walked to the centre, scanning the room. No jerk in black leather. She glanced at her watch: 3:02. He was late. He was making her wait, making a statement, teaching her a lesson. He shouldn't have bothered. She'd passed Jerk: 101 years earlier.

She wasn't impressed. And no way was she going to stand alone waiting for him looking desperate. He could search for her. He could find her in the bar.
*

Dwayne Michaels never lost his temper. Tempers got people killed before their time. He put his napkin over his glass. He would be a few minutes. He had a call to make and wasn't into others overhearing his conversations. How could he work with someone he couldn't rely upon? He couldn't, nor would he. President or no president, Wilson was history.

He eased from the stool. Passing through the doors he noticed her for the first time, the woman in the bright red rain cape and matching knee-high red rubber boots. She sparkled under the bright lights, her ensemble speckled with dazzling raindrops. She wasn't blonde, but definitely…Oh, shit!
*

Lorie Wilson twirled, brushing away the raindrops, untying and shaking her cape once before draping it over her arm.

What! No way. No way! He was coming towards her.

She couldn't believe her eyes; eyes that she realized were saucer-wide. She hated him for seeing her. She hated herself. She couldn't in her worst dream have shown her surprise more visibly. Dammit.

His suit was deep blue, single-breasted, buttoned, and custom-tailored. He was wearing expensive and he was wearing tasteful. Any fool could see that. His shirt was Mediterranean blue with French cuffs, his tie a rich yellow, almost gold. God! He was so frigging gorgeous. His shoes were blue, Italian, had to be, and polished to a matte finish. He had no rings. She hadn't expected any. He was single. Not a hair was out of place, except the errant lock she remembered that made him somehow manlier, more roguish. And could his eyes be any more chocolate? He wasn't smiling, neither did he seem serious.

God! How would she survive four years? No way.

*

Dwayne Michaels kept walking, maintaining his pace. She was coming towards him. He couldn't image anyone more beautiful. Her sweater was the best cashmere, bright yellow, a cowl neck, nicely filled out, the strap of her red bra decorating an alluring bare shoulder. Her skirt was A-line, bright red, short, six inches above her perfect knees. Her nylons were sheer. He thought pantyhose, hoping for stay-ups and any woman dressed like that would be wearing a thong, definitely a thong, red satin to match her bra. Her purse was red, made by Herrera. She had good taste. Her lustrous mahogany hair was a halo under the bright lights, straight; combed to one side, no bangs, just a perfect forehead and a flawless face that for an instant had flushed pink with surprise. She hadn't expected to see him. She thought he was late. She was angry. Not a good beginning. He hadn't been right about her jewellery either. Her ears and neck glistened with deep red rubies set in stainless steel. How could anyone be that hot and cause permanent freezer burn?

She stopped four feet from him: A safe distance, a striking distance. Good girl. He closed the gap by extending his hand.

"Good afternoon, Miss Wilson. My name is Dwayne Michaels. You may remember me from a few years ago at the White House."

She took his hand. She had no choice. Hers was lost in his. His grip was firm yet gentle, the way she remembered. He didn't have to prove himself by crushing her hand. He was too confident for showy excess.

Her grip was firm. Her skin was cool, smooth. Now he remembered, though this time the lingering message between fingertips wasn't conveyed. Why die twice?

No, I do not remember you, not this way. Want to go somewhere and strip me naked, ravage me till I pass out? "Yes, Mr. Michaels. I do remember you. Remembering faces was part of the job."

"I didn't see you drive up. Did you arrive by taxi?"

She turned from her waist. The Corvette hadn't moved, framed by the doors. The valet was taking his time.

"That's mine."

He wasn't keeping score. He didn't have to. He was losing big time to his expectations and the interior temperature was cooling to dangerously low levels.

"Nice ride…very red."

"Were you leaving the bar, Mr. Michaels? Do you want to speak with me in the lobby?"

"I have a drink waiting. I came out to see whether you might be waiting. May I take your cape?"

You're lying. You thought I was late." No thank you. I'm good."

I bet you are, though I'm curious. How does a frozen penis look?

He stepped to one side. "Then may I suggest an early cocktail?"

They began walking together. Anyone noticing might have thought that's what they were.

Passing the bar he reached for his drink and a plainly wrapped package.

She took notice. No beer. So what?

He acknowledged the barman who would follow once they were seated, Dwayne Michaels choosing a table in the farthest corner, closest to the fireplace, a private corner, taking her cape, pulling out her chair.

Big deal. So what? Not a word about how she looked after she'd spent the entire morning dressing and doing her make-up. The guy was either gay or lived with glaucoma. Her skirt wasn't her shortest, but pretty damned close and he didn't even glimpse at her legs as she sat adjusting her hem, pretending to. The first time in how many long years she was having a drink with a man in a bar and he was a eunuch, an idiot. She didn't care. Anyway, the barman seemed to appreciate nice legs. Nice? No way. They were fantastic. Maybe she would take him home. Maybe he would want to strip her naked.

"What's your pleasure, Miss Wilson? That information was omitted from your profile."

Great! Now the barman thought she was being interviewed. Jerk.

"I prefer Ultimat, neat, one cube, no lemon or lime. Thank you."

Strike number, what, fifteen, twenty? This was not the girl next door and his sixth sense was in serious need of repair.

He wanted to tell her she was stunning, because she was.

He wouldn't. She wouldn't care. She already knew. Besides, house rules were in place. Then again rules were made to be broken, occasionally forgotten, which posed an interesting question. She wasn't the type to drop her panties on a whim. Not women like her. So that meant dating and dating meant lying to some guy, maybe *the* guy, about who and what she was. Unless she didn't care, putting out for the occasional executive type in town on business or doing what was needed for casual release between extended dry spells while on vacation with the who's who type of people. That was more her style. She was strictly upper end. And who could blame her? She was attractive. Her body screamed for attention. And how does a woman liker her tell a prospective lover that her primary job is to die to save the president?

The barman came and went. Idle banter wasn't Dwayne Michaels' strong point.

He tipped his glass towards her, taking a sip. Wilson barely moistened her lips with hers.

"This is for you, Miss Wilson. It's a Beretta 92FS, brand new, silver-plated, registered to you. It's what we carry." He pointed to the package. "Don't expect to use it anytime soon unless you're on a bad date. This guy we're chasing, he's not going down that way. He'll just be tired with life that particular day and die of self-injected pentobarbital."

"What's his name?"

"Hilary Basil. He brokers food and booze at a price to a very specific clientele."

"Whoever he is, he must have warehouses, inventories, delivery vehicles, employees. He can't work the entire country himself. Somebody's delivering the food somewhere."

He reached into an inner pocket, passing her an envelope. "This is your agency-issued PMC. Don't lose it. None of your grocery, alcohol, restaurant purchases or charges will be compiled from this card. You can live the good life as long as you can pay for it. We're exempt from monitoring. See where I'm going with this?"

"Basil's transactions aren't recorded."

He nodded. "And his clients are tight-lipped, too afraid of losing a turn at the feed trough."

"And where that is we don't know."

"Bingo. All we know is that they're grossly overweight with BMIs exceeding forty, some way past sixty where numbers don't matter. If you think you've seen fat, Miss Wilson, you haven't. These Gourmands don't have anything visibly in common with the rest of us."

"We call them Gourmands. That does seem a little cruel."

"That's what they are: Gluttons. The way you're a woman, the way I'm a man."

Thank you for noticing, dead below the waist. "And we find them how, if we don't know where they are?"

"We don't. Not yet. They find us. We get ambulance or police calls. Those who qualify, those who pay the 2400 get help, waiting their turn. Those who don't, they die or live with what they are until they do, continuing their feeding habits in the meantime. It's a big deal for them, right down to their muumuus and fancy sweats. You see, Basil doesn't sell his food; he serves it in party style. Not only are the individual transactions not monitored by PMCs, these Gourmands who are virtually banned from restaurants have a night out, able to wine

455

and dine in relative comfort with others like themselves."

"So we find where they eat. How difficult can that be?"

"Very. We're eight searching for a few or several thousand in different cities across a vast country. Basil wouldn't be doing this unless they were worth his time and trouble. There's also a thing about warrants, arriving too late on the scene and no current law exists against eating food. What's illegal is defrauding the system, encouraging people to gorge themselves to death, and then cashing in on those deaths."

"So we wait. That's it, nothing proactive. We wait. How exciting."

"The Primary generally gets a call after midnight. These people eat late. They like the dark. You'll understand when you see one."

Lorie adjusted her chair, uncrossing one leg, slowly crossing the other, sipping her vodka.

He was dying. Her legs were killing him. Thirty-four was a typo; the woman was twenty-four tops and lethally good-looking. Seeing her again he wanted to take her home, rip away her clothes and defrost her. She was playing a game, and he understood why. She thought he was an asshole for visiting the White House in his leathers and now she was claiming her turn. She wanted him to see her legs, to see she was hot, feminine, not a Secret Service robot with a tight ass trained to kill. Instead he glanced at her boots.

"Your outfit is lovely, Miss Wilson, very chic…and not at all suitable for the job. I would suggest longer skirts or slacks. Gourmands are close enough to death. They don't require a catalyst."

Prick! You couldn't have said that. Tell me you did not say that!

"I wear my clothes for myself, Mr. Michaels, not you or anyone else. Nor do I require instruction from you or anyone else on how to dress appropriately for work. For your information I'm meeting someone for a dinner and theatre evening and I wasn't certain how long this meeting would last since you chose to meet with me at such an inconvenient hour. I am also coming to this job directly from personally serving the President of the United States. Enough said."

"I remember. You presented yourself and acted very professionally." Though I prefer your hair this way and you do not have a date. You're way too classy to wear those colours to dinner and a Broadway show. You are one exceptional woman, not to mention eight rounds in three seconds.

You're an idiot. "That's precisely what I am…professional." She exaggerated checking the time. "Are we almost done here?"

"No. We are not. However I won't keep you much longer. Like you, I have a date. I promised two young ladies I would take them to dinner this evening. They're very excited."

She raised her eyebrows. She wanted to stab him.

"Two young ladies, is that right? How very nice for you, Mr. Michaels."

He grinned. "I started seeing them a few years ago. To say the least they're becoming very good at what they do when they're together. I feel very gratified, though never quite as good when one's free and the other's working. In return I reward them once in a while with a Saturday night on the town to let them feel like ladies, to keep them interested and keep them coming back. Not to say they don't hamper the dating process. You know how women are."

"Mr. Michaels, good for you. However I don't know you and I'm not at all interested in your young lady friends. So unless I really need to be here…"

He reached into another inner pocket, passing her a magnetic key card.

"This key opens the main door of Riley Corp. New York. We're on the eighteenth floor, number 1800. Behind that door you have a private office, the same size as mine if you're curious, and yours is currently empty of furniture. You have a ten-grand budget for paint and furniture, better sooner than later unless you enjoy standing. We also have a private fitness centre strictly for us where you will be expected to work out two hours daily when we're not travelling. The real Riley people are mandated to do one hour daily in a facility almost as good. We get an extra hour because we're special. Everything is modern and complete including a dojo where you and I will not do Randori. I do not fight with women, irrespective of their sense of equality. They're no challenge. No pain, no gain, that sort of thing. However, if you wish, you're free to bring all your martial art toys and the place is expansive enough for your archery gear. Work out whenever you wish according to our workday. I generally arrive early. Two hours, Miss Wilson," he glanced at her legs, "not that I think you need more than ninety minutes. You will also enjoy a private locker room and spa when you feel the need to relax, decompress or enjoy a good sweat. That private girl space has a walk-in shower, washroom facilities, a vanity area and is fitted with a lock. We have a full kitchen, almost never used, a plush lounge area for after-hours or a drink before facing Manhattan traffic. And, no, we don't have a swimming pool. We're referred to as the Special Functions Group. We don't go to Riley parties. We don't participate in lotteries, showers, weddings, lunches, retirements or funerals. Nobody knows what we do. No one cares because no one ever sees us unless we're on the elevator when all they get to see is a luxurious foyer through our glass doors. No one knows what we do because we don't speak to anyone. They think we're a couple hoity-toity assholes too good for them."

You are an asshole. "When do I start?"

"We start Monday. Come in late. Buy a new workout outfit, buy a few." His head to toe assessment was imperceptible, except to Lorie Wilson. "Don't chintz. Buy something nice. Spoil yourself. You have a wardrobe budget. At times the job gets a little messy. Take the time during the week to set yourself up. Don't buy anything cheap. We have housekeeping and laundry services. What we don't have is files, Miss Wilson. No files, but we do have one damn big shredder which I would suggest not standing too close to unless you're not the shy type. Got my tie caught once. I liked that tie. Did I mention we fly First Class and stay in five-stars?"

Buy something nice. Don't buy anything cheap. She wondered how her stiletto would look sticking in his throat. "We're not working this weekend?"

"We never know. We're on call, though what we do is seldom urgent. So enjoy your date. We don't use sirens like you're used to, Miss Wilson. No glitter. We spend most days tracing wills and insurance policies. Some Gourmands don't look as though they've got spare change left at the end of the month. Others are millionaires and we have no idea how close we are. Despite my gut feeling that we are. This guy Basil will be put down and I'll be the one to do him. Sounds monotonous, I know. Believe me; what you'll be doing is far from boring." He sipped his drink. "And I believe we're done here." Unless you want to join us for dinner, spend the evening with me, undress for me, and make love with me. My girls would like you and have to be home in bed by eleven because they're relearning to respect their parents they once thought were like totally stupid, whatever. They're learning to live with new rules and new love. No? Okay. He didn't think so. He stood. "Enjoy your date, Miss Wilson." He helped ease her chair from the table, reaching for her cape, cloaking her shoulders. He wanted to smell her hair, to kiss her, to take her home and quit The Agency. Instead: "I look forward to seeing you on Monday, to working with you."

She was searching for words. She couldn't remember the last time she'd felt so angry with any man. Her date would have understood a last-minute business dinner. Things happened. This was New York. What date? She didn't have a date. She had dinner with her parents and he was having dinner and playtime with bimbos instead of dinner with her and perhaps dancing to soft, romantic music. She hadn't danced in years.

"Thank you, Mr. Michaels." Mr. Michaels, what was up with that? "I'll see you Monday."

"I'll walk you to the valet."

"Thank you. That's so very gallant of you," especially since you're a total jerk. "I'll be fine and I hope you enjoy your double date as much I will mine." She reached for the package. "We'll see each other Monday. Oh, and I won't be late."

Then she was gone. She wasn't striding like a man. She was sauntering, bouncing. He was counting down from ten. He always did unless pressed for time and five was more expedient. Such wasn't the case. If she glanced over her shoulder at him before he got to one he was taking her to dinner with a couple of good kids whose lives were turning around.

Nope, wasn't going to happen. Two was too quickly followed by the fateful one. He shrugged and walked to the elevator. Life would go on.

Lorie Wilson felt him watching, staring. No way would she give him the pleasure. She felt good, she was in New York. She was going on a dinner date with a handsome gentleman who loved her and she would walk away from him as though it wasn't complete bullshit.

She hated him.

At the valet station by the door she turned, thinking maybe. He was gone. She breathed a sigh of relief. Good. She was happy. He saved her the trouble. He probably ate with his fingers and used his sleeve as a napkin. Screw him and his twin bimbos.

Nothing was wrong with her mother's meatloaf.

41
The President's Final Phase

Gregg Johnson was front row centre for the president's first speech of her second term. Everyone knew he was the teacher's pet, a distinction he wore like a badge of honour. He gave her a thumbs-up as the entire gallery stood as she entered the room.

She got straight to it without preamble. She saw no point in putting sugar on acid. This one would hurt. However, barring unforeseen circumstances, these two bills would constitute her administration's final effort in support of health care.

Effective immediately a No Assist List would be implemented. Anyone exceeding 59.9 BMI Class or anyone not registered in the system would be refused any and all medical care other than treatment provided in private clinics and paid for in full by the patient. Pre-existing medical conditions were the sole exemption.

Rescue by any first responders of those individuals, by ambulance, firefighters, or police would now be denied except in those instances involving danger to other persons or properties. However those individuals would now be exempt from the annual penalty of 2400 dollars. Simply put, those wishing to ignore the system would in turn be ignored by the system.

She went on. The silence in the room was explosive. No one was writing. No one was recording. They weren't allowed, not until the question period. Everyone present had sealed copies of her speech, the president's single most effective insurance that she would not be misconstrued or misquoted.

The nation was growing beyond a sustainable population. Too many heedless people were having too many babies without considering the immediate ill-effects and future ramifications of their passions, plans, or lack thereof.

Families of three, four and five children could no longer and would no longer be tolerated. The math was simple: 5x5x5x5=625 unsustainables created from a single source and very possibly within that lifetime.

Nor would America continue as a breeding ground for other nationalities whose countries were already enforcing limited families.

Hence, effective immediately, any household currently with two children eighteen years or younger would receive an incentive of 1000 dollars per parent to encourage no further domestic growth. Medical procedures ensuring no further growth and paid for by the Health Reform Programme would be available to each parent.

Parents of one child would each receive 2000 dollars and each would enjoy free access to respective medical procedures in order to prevent a second child from occurring. Couples and individuals over the age of eighteen choosing to remain childless would each receive an incentive of 3000 dollars. However the corrective initiative would then be mandatory for both the man and the woman.

Those individuals exceeding the two-children limit after October 03rd of the current year, irrespective of divorce, remarriage or adultery would repay the incentive and be fined an additional 10,000 dollars per child. Parents of illegitimate children, irrespective of age, would receive no incentive, nor would they receive funding from any other national programme. In short, do not believe everything he says and don't play games you or your parents cannot afford.

The same would apply to immigration.

Effective immediately, only those families of two children or less would be allowed into the country, held to the same standards and restrictions. Those families currently not in the system and exceeding two children per household would be invited to leave the country immediately.

Individuals who were not yet formally American citizens would not receive incentives, yet would be held to the same restrictions, penalties and/or deportation.

The good news came last.

The nation was at twenty-four percent. She didn't get her six million Instead sixteen million over the last four months had dropped to under the requisite 29.9 BMI Class. The nation was catching on, supporting her, working hard at reshaping itself. The high school dropout rate had dropped to half the pre-2016 rate. University admissions were up by ten percent, divorce rates plunging and more families were talking together, spending time together.

And what was the net result? Teen pregnancies were plummeting. Girls were learning to respect themselves.

Thank you, ladies and gentlemen. That's all.

"Yes, Gregg."

"Madam President and, might I say in support of your programme, that you continue as the essence of youthful beauty and grace. Are you expecting, Madam President, a backlash and what's your take on the coming four years?"

"Gregg, how does your wife put up with you? Please convey my heartfelt sympathies to her and, oh yes, give her these." The president's Press Secretary took the two cheques, making her way to the journalist. "Congratulations on your first baby. Don't spend it all at once. As for the backlash, no, I do not. Seventy percent voted for me. That tells me something. I've accomplished what was long overdue and necessary to save this country. These final measures are intended to make the statement that your family, friends and neighbours are not responsible for you. You are. If you don't care, they shouldn't. As for my take, I won't allow five percent to assume precedence over or dominate ninety-five percent. That's my goal. By December 31, 2024, that's my goal. I can live with one out of twenty. The question is: Can they? And the answer is no. They cannot."

"Can you elaborate on the penalties, Madam President?"

"Gregg, you and wife have a little Gregg. So I can understand entirely that your darling wife might want a girl. No one in this room would blame her, and that's fine. You'll be great parents. You'll simply be asked to return half the amount of those cheques. However, cheat on your lovely wife after the little girl, knock up another lady after a few too many beers when we all look pretty after midnight and that will cost you ten thousand in addition to the cheque assigned to you. If it's the lady's first or second no problem. We don't care who's doing whom. However if it's her third the ten-grand applies to her as well as her incentive accordingly. So you be a good boy and drink your beer at home."

"Her brothers are cops, big cops. But Madam President, three kids, what happens if I don't have the ten thousand?"

"Buy a tent and leave your home in move-in condition for the next guy."

"Madam President, a final question."

"You never have a final question, Gregg."

The Press Gallery erupted in rumble of chuckles.

"How do you respond to those who accuse you of single-handedly ruining the pizza delivery business?"

"You just made that up, Gregg. You really are incurable. But to answer 'them', I order an all-dressed once a week from Frankie's. Pizza is my single vice. Now sit down and be quiet."

When the press conference was over an unsmiling man dressed in black went to where Gregg was sitting. The president wanted to see him.

He had been in the Oval Office with her before. There was a comfort zone. This time was different. This time she was pouring a cognac for him and she had gifts for the baby and his wife. They were friends, good friends.

As he was leaving they hugged. He'd always been a big brother to her, always looking after her, protecting her from would-be wolves as well as real threats, worried about her no matter where they were in the world together.

He was the sweetest, most charming pain in ass she could image. He was also influential. His viewers and readers took him seriously and he was on her side.

He understood 625 offspring in one lifetime was intolerable. He listened to the statistics, shocked.

The next morning the country would read that:

The President Declares War on Welfare
*

Lorie Wilson sat in her New York condo alone, watching the one woman she'd ever called a real girlfriend. The thing was she couldn't invite the president to her home to do girly things and talk about men because Lorie didn't have a man and she was confidentially aware Vega was window-dressing.

She missed Priscilla, only now she didn't have to worry about confusing Priscilla with Madam President when eager ears were nearby.

She felt sorry for Priscilla who was trapped. She felt sorry for herself. She had four years to go before deciding what she would do, where she would live, wondering whether she would ever again splash in the surf with her friend and pretend she didn't have a care in the world.

Her office was set up, the motif modern like her condo, and she did buy several new outfits for her private gym. So what, like he would care.

He wasn't alive and, quite frankly, she didn't care anymore. She had wasted too much time thinking about him, hating her days with him, hating that she had ever met him.

She knew one day she would find someone better than him, someone entirely more deserving of everything she was. She was almost certain she knew that. She thought she was, almost.

*

Dwayne Michaels left the bar early. The evening news was over. A couple of mid-life-crisis punks were shooting pool, jabbering to be heard above the melded murmurs of others regarding their views on Priscilla Vendôme, about how they wouldn't mind enjoying a little a piece of her, that she was putting herself out there so why not take a piece.

Others in the room, the men, chuckled. The couples ignored them. They didn't need trouble.

He walked over to them. He explained that he worked for the president, so in effect he was a little piece of her and he was happy to oblige. He crashed one head into the table; the other didn't see the eight ball. Surprisingly, the other men in the room were abruptly less amused.

He paid his tab and left. He needed more sophistication in his life. What he didn't need, or at least in lesser quantity, was the complication of dating. Women never broke up easily and now that she'd raised the bar, now that he'd seen her practically naked in blue and red body-hugging Spandex and leg warmers he was pretty well screwed.

42
Boston

June 12, 2024 was a Wednesday, leaving twenty-nine weeks to the day for President Vendôme to accomplish her objectives before handing over the reins to one of the current combatants, neither man thus far promising or threatening to continue her war.

In three years she had virtually eradicated welfare. In short, no one was getting a free ride. Having too many babies was no longer a good or acceptable excuse not to work. Teen mothers now had no right by law to keep their children. Federal prisoners were put to work for decent wages and paid taxes. No work, no special privileges, their choice. And Mom was no longer a title held in high esteem. You might work at home, but you would work and the abuse of Child Assistance cheques had long since ceased as a result of her family incentives.

Don't like the rules. Buy a metal detector, become a beach bum. Panhandle. Find a warm grate in the winter. Just not in Washington, D.C.

She would be a tough act to follow.

Her one frustration was Hilary Basil. The country had dropped to nine percent. Twenty-eight million Americans were obese down from 163 million when factoring in a decrease in total population of three percent. Of those, five percent were BMI 40s who had a chance. She wanted that five percent by Christmas. The others beyond 49.9 BMI

Class either didn't care or had done an excellent job eating away their lifespans. Of that four percent, most would be dead within five years to a decade giving her a perfect score.

She was forty-two. She had achieved a better America, a healthier place no longer ridiculed by the world. She had done her time. She was ready. She was anxious to take over control of Riley Corp. She wanted her life back and Vega gone while she was young enough and attractive enough to find a real man who understood the difference between attentive lover and deceitful fraud.

Whatever Vega hadn't squandered of his thirty million would be his severance for whatever he had actually done throughout her consecutive terms. Vaya con Dios. She didn't care, though she was certain Gregg Johnson would have a field day with the headline on January 02, 2025.

Karina E. Vendôme was nine. She was turning out well, though she had nothing to do with Vega and would learn the truth on some future date when Edward would inevitably decide he had lived sufficiently long.

The girl liked Priscilla, though viewed her more as a president and a face on television than a mother. Perhaps that would change, perhaps not, though currently her real attachment was to her nanny who was friend and teacher, guardian and confidante who would soon leave the White House with Priscilla to become an employee of Riley.

Edward Riley was seventy-one, anxious to abdicate his exalted position both at Riley and in life. He was tired. He wanted more time with Karina who had never discovered or never mentioned the girl's true parentage. She adored the girl and she loved Priscilla deeply.

The emotion was mutual. What else mattered? They were not like other people, those who envied them. They lived with daily burdens most others could not for a single moment fathom.

Priscilla did often remember Lorie Wilson, in her dreams and in her waking hours. She missed her, missed their special times together, their talks and their walks. She'd often thought of phoning, knowing full well she could not. Together they had made an irreversible decision. Lorie Wilson was the right choice, the gem of The Agency, the perfect complement to Dwayne Michaels, though any discovered connection between them would prove disastrous.

Her sole connection with The Agency until January 01st would be her Primary whom she selected personally, with whom she spoke quarterly for updates in conjunction with her National Health Programme.

Then she would rejoin Riley, bring Lorie onboard and definitely find a beach where they could lay in the sun discussing bonuses, perks and men. Or lie on the hot sand and not talk about men.

*

Lorie and Dwayne were at Long Beach. Lorie was soaking up the sun; Dwayne was soaking up Lorie, refusing to relinquish the camera.

They were alone. The nearest of the few couples scattered on the sand was a half-mile away. The weekend hordes were at work and school wouldn't be out for two weeks. Not that Lorie needed to work on her tan. She didn't. Their condo patio was private; however Dwayne had successfully and contentedly pleaded his case. Anyway, he was, after all, talking about her long-time dream. Did she, or did she not, want to romp naked into the Atlantic, make sand angels and see her penthouse condo thus attired?

She'd dropped her triangles onto the sand, remaining adamant about her thong. He could play with the strings. That's all. No way was he holding it for safekeeping, not until she reached for the sun cream. No way! He was quick, she wasn't, and the stage was set for more fond memories.

No one was passing. No one was coming or going, time cheating them, minutes creeping from midmorning into early afternoon.

They were good for another couple of hours. The sun was at its zenith, too blinding to see, the sky was more white than blue and the air was still.

Lorie lay on her front facing the horizon, her arms crossed into a pillow. The ocean was a sheet of black glass dotted with the dull colours of miniature tankers and freighters. Dwayne kneeled beside her, freeing his hands of the camera to fill them with her. She loved his massages. The wine could chill a while longer. Lunch could wait. She wasn't ready to move.

She was dreaming of September, her wedding and France.

There wasn't a sound, not a whisper, silent glints of silver hurtling through the sky leaving trails of pure white vapour.

How her life had changed in twenty-three weeks. The man she once loved hating and hated loving kneading warm lotion into her naked body in concert with her guttural purring. Not drifting into a deep sleep was impossible. Her eyelids fluttered, opening wide, closing, resisting, closing, closing, the world disappearing.

No way!

"No, don't answer that," she moaned. "Someone dialled the wrong number."

"It's Wednesday. We're working."

"Yes. And our work is too important to interrupt. They can call again."

He reached for his cell he'd placed atop the picnic basket, grinning, smacking the recently greased mounds of her spectacular ass. Her eyes flashed open, her reverie broken. He pressed SEND.

The number was restricted to those who understood that calling him would mean their escape from agony in one of two ways. Either way, nicety was not required.

"Yes."

First silence, followed by hesitation made loud with laboured breathing.

He waited, counting down from ten before pressing END

"I told you, sweetheart." Lorie groaned, pushing herself to her knees, from her knees to her feet. "I don't like whoever that was." She held out her hand. "May I please have my thong?"

He shook his head. "Listen, you've wanted to do this for years. So do it, right now. Run into the Atlantic naked, check out your, our condo and strut your stuff back here. Go."

"Ever heard of binoculars?"

He shrugged.

She waved him away, sauntering naked to the water, exhilarated, teasing him with an exaggerated sway of her hips. She waded to her waist, bathing herself, dunking herself to her shoulders, Dwayne's Nikon capturing every fifth of a second.

At the shore she stood glistening. She wasn't shy, not afraid of being seen from so far away, not in a hurry. She felt exotic, more so than on the island which was, oh yeah, pretty exotic. She was living every second she could of a dream while gazing at the distant skyline, her penthouse, their penthouse. Her body titillated by the cool ocean. She posed, stretching and bending this way and that, taunting him, threatening to close the half-mile between private couples, pausing a moment before she leisurely meandered her way towards him. She loved being risqué for him and with him. He was hers. Life didn't get any better than being with him.

"I'll have my wine now, and my thong, sir."

He reached for the wine, nicely chilled, filling her plastic goblet, smirking, passing her the wine and the bikini.

She wasn't impressed, rolling her eyes.

She kneeled beside him, kissing him, dropping the thong, sipping her wine. "If someone sees me it's on you. I'll smack you, sweetheart, very hard."

"No pain, no gain. I'm willing to sacrifice myself for the greater good. That's who I am."

"Whose good would that be?"

"Mine…of course."

The phone chimed. Lorie lurched with a scowl, spilling her wine, Dwayne reacting much faster once again, holding the phone away from her.

He sipped his wine, his expression superior, pressing SEND. He waited.

In his ear, a sudden deep breath, gasping. He hunched his shoulders.

"Good, I know you can breathe. Now how about saying something before I disconnect?"

"I'm sorry. I'm very nervous. Please don't hang up. Are you the man, the one with the lady who came to my place?"

"When would that be and why would I have gone to your home?"

"You gave me a card. You told me to call. The lady said you would help me. Was she telling the truth?"

"Where do you live?"

"Boston. I live in Boston. I didn't know if I waited too long. I'm really sorry. Did I wait too long?"

"Am I talking with Ms. Angela Bangles?"

He made a thumbs-up to Lorie.

"Yes, I am. I'm sorry."

"Why are you calling?"

"He called me this morning. I'm sorry I didn't tell you the truth. I was so afraid of you. I don't have any friends, not real friends."

"Who called you, ma'am?"

He knew.

"Hilary Basil, he called me."

"And you're calling me, why?"

"Because you said you would help me. And the lady, she said you would help me."

"Ms. Bangles, I'm a long way from Boston. Do not make me go there for no reason. Please do not do that."

"The lady said you would help me."

"The lady told you the truth. You're the one who was lying, not us."

"I won't lie anymore. I'm sorry."

"I hope you don't, Ms. Bangles, in which case we will see you this evening. Please be home. Goodbye."

He disconnected.

Lorie was keeled over, beating the sand with the edge of her fists.

"No way! Dwayne! She called."

"No shit." He drained his glass, stooping, tossing Lorie her thong. "Get dressed. We're leaving. And why are you lying around nude on a public beach? Have some respect, woman."

He leaped backward not a second too soon, grinning, watching her spring to her feet in a blur, ready to kill him. He was so pitiable, sad really, to think she couldn't close such a short distance with no effort at all to tap his nose with her toe. She shook her head, sighing. He wasn't worth her trouble. Why embarrass the simple man? Sorry, SEAL-boy. Instead she strapped herself into her metallic red eye patch in a way that commanded his fullest attention. Yes, so very sad.

"I am so glad you never stopped chasing me, dream-girl. It is true what they say. Good things are worth waiting for."

"You keep thinking that, sweetheart. Bangles, did she sound serious?"

"If she's not she won't feel the prick of a needle. It's the least I'll do if she's ruined my day."

"I had a feeling about her. This is fantastic."

"You people always think you have a feeling about something or other."

She smacked him, not hard. Then she kissed him.

"I hope she's wearing a thicker tent dress."

"Dressed or undressed, you be good to her. Let's not freak her. She could change her mind."

They dressed, gathering their padded beach throw and basket. Dwayne shoved her triangles into his nylon shell, wondering what her problem was. She was good for another ten minutes.

She hesitated a moment, deciding to humour the pathetic man. Besides, she felt sexy, not to say she trusted him. She took his hand, keeping her crocheted pullover safely away from him.

*

Ninety minutes later they were showered and dressed for business, en route to Boston. Dinner would have created too lengthy a delay. They were eager for the possible moment that had taken seven years, eating their picnic lunch with homemade lemonade as they drove.

Michaels didn't want to piss her off. He was wearing slacks and loafers, a sports jacket with an open shirt without a tie. The casual style wasn't intimidating; the Beretta under his jacket made the ensemble somewhat more business-like.

Lorie was dressed in a light-weight sweater, cuffed dress-shorts and open-toed sandals. The desired affect couldn't be simpler. Her purse was another matter, home to her Italian-made weapon, a ten-inch stiletto, her compact, her lip gloss and a pair of clean panties should the unexpected arise. A girl never knew.

They packed provisionally for an evening away and the next morning, choosing the black SUV for the road trip. Current year Jags and Corvettes weren't quite a good match for various other models and years parked or abandoned on Angela Bangles' street.

The façade of the tenement hadn't changed. Such buildings never would until abandoned or condemned, rezoned for the homeless, or incorrigible druggies, or runaway squeegees and their dropout girlfriends, a few of whom continued to exist as a reminder to others that freedom of choice was alive and well in America.

Priscilla Vendôme's land was better, much better, if not perfect.

The glass on both doors leading to the inside corridor was stained with layers of history. Some, Michaels was certain, he could remember from their previous visit. Tenements didn't employ concierges to maintain the buildings and smile at satisfied tenants. They had janitors who wore singlets stained with sweat and beer and lived rent-free for the least work they could manage on a given day and this guy seemed to be waiting for a time when a scraper might do a better job than soap and water.

Both Michaels and Wilson wore thick, disposable gloves. He buzzed Bangles' apartment, surprised, thinking Bangles must have spent the afternoon strapped into her chair by the door.

"Ms. Bangles, we're here. Please open the door."

She obeyed, not saying a word.

Wilson put a hand on Michaels's arm before following him through the open door.

"Sweetheart, I love you. Please be nice."

He nodded. Hearing 'sweetheart' from her soft, sensually guttural voice was strangely out of context amidst the filth they witnessed most weeks. He didn't like when she did that, touching him, saying that, but she didn't know. He would never tell her. He understood. What he actually didn't like was that he couldn't hold her close and kiss her.

The smells hadn't gone away, nor had the rude sounds of poverty. Michaels didn't need eyes to discern where he was. Smells and stench versus aromas and pungent sweetness spoke of who and what a person was. Noise on the other hand, or the lack thereof, spoke of respect, or the lack thereof.

The poorest of homes smelled of bacon fat, fried lard, the stench of baby shit in diaper pails and garbage. Finer homes carried the aromas of exotic spices, fine herbs, the delicate flavours of sauces simmering and disposable diapers went out with the garbage before the guests arrived.

The noise of the poor came from sixty-inch televisions, Black, Hispanic and White daytime hosts worth millions commiserating with the poor whose daughters were pregnant, whores with wailing babies, or druggies. The sons were either not available, which he understood, or ran out early once they had their fifteen minutes of fame.

You had to love it, whereas most noise emanating from finer homes was borne of infidelity, a neglected wife, a misled daughter or the melodic tones of crooners enchanting lovers dancing until the appeal of infidelity took root.

He knocked once on her door, not waiting long, preceding Wilson inside.

Wilson closed the door.

Seeing them again Bangles flushed deep red, her birth scar disappearing before their eyes. Wilson believed the woman wanted to make a good impression. She was wearing a muumuu striped with factory folds that she or someone hadn't yet washed out. Michaels didn't care either way. What he did know was that the beginning of his day with a naked and tanned erotic angel made Bangles appear all the more like a squat ogre.

If anything the condition of her body had worsened, though from what he remembered she didn't look any larger. The thought was fleeting, not a concern.

"Thank you for coming. I'm sorry. I didn't know if you would."

"Don't be sorry. You're the reason we're paid." He glanced around. Nothing had changed, except the bowl and the spoon were gone from the floor. He was certain the pizza was gone as well. "We have two questions that will save us a lot of time. We also understand, Ms. Bangles, that you are a little nervous about us. But here's what. We are the good guys and we are here to help you. The offer of a new bed stands, my treat, as does everything stand that we offered last time."

"Miss Bangles," Wilson interjected, "are you a member of The Diners' Club."

"Yes, I am. I'm so sorry. Really, I'm sorry."

"And are you now willing now to help us find and stop this Hilary Basil?"

She nodded, strapped into her chair in a semi-standing position, her arms pushed from her sides by her sides. She looked ridiculous, like a blow-up clown, Michaels wondering at the last time she might have managed to brush her teeth.

"You're saying you'll help me. I need you to promise me."

"We do promise." Wilson took a step closer, the extent of her conviction. "You will be in surgery the same day we arrest Hilary Basil."

"But if you don't find him, even though I'm helping you, I won't get better. I don't want to live like this anymore. I can never be like you. I know that, but I don't have to live like this. I know that also and I can pay. I'm not poor."

She tried staring at each of them. She couldn't. They were better than her. She could tell what they were thinking.

Wilson and Michaels exchanged frustrated glances. She didn't believe them. They were losing her.

Wilson said, "You won't have to pay, Miss Bangles. We will, for everything, as promised."

Michaels was more impatient, fully cognizant the ride home could well be somewhat tempered with a backlash of female sensitivity. He reached into a jacket pocket. "Ms. Bangles, this is a vial of pentobarbital in liquid form. It's primarily used for euthanizing animals and executing criminals. We prefer the term intervention. In this strength it's effective within a minute or two depending on health and size, that sort of thing. You fall asleep and you do not wake up. You're dead. It's painless, fast and easy with no official inquiry or autopsy because you're a Gourmand. So here's what we're going to do. You're going to tell us right now what we need to know and when you're finished we'll talk about how soon we can get you to a hospital. Jerk me around and you won't have to worry about a hospital. I can have you dead in sixty seconds. Then it's off to the furnace and you'll be a roast of pork by midnight."

Angela Bangles' mouth puckered, concaving her cheeks. She took on the appearance of a bloated fish sucking in its food, her chest was heaving, the pressure building within her head threatening to blow out her eyes.

Wilson didn't like seeing her man this way. She knew he wasn't like that.

"Miss Bangles, calm down. He won't hurt you. He's simply telling you that we're serious. Help us, and we will help you as soon as we possibly can. That's up to you. You called us. We did not call you. Please give us the opportunity to help you."

Michaels broke in. "Would you like some water, Ms. Bangles, maybe a good night's sleep?"

"I do want to tell you." She focused on Wilson who took a moment to glare at Michaels. "I do. But can I tell you, miss? Can he go somewhere?"

Wilson didn't say a word. She didn't have to; she was a woman, his woman. Michaels went to the window, peering out onto Shit Street.

Wilson waited with no intention of further closing the space between them. Nor was she thinking of sitting.

"I started seven years ago. They sent me a letter. Then they called me. I'm one of their longest members. Mr. Basil called me himself. I was afraid then, too. I guess people like me are always afraid." Bangles hesitated. "I don't know

479

your name."

"I'm sorry. You can't know my name. Do you have the letter?"

"No. I was told not to keep it."

"Do you remember the content of the letter, what they wrote?"

"They explained that soon the government would not allow us in restaurants, and that happened, but with them we could eat the best food, the best wine and nothing would show up on our Personal Measurement Cards. We wouldn't have to pay either, not if we agreed to put them in our wills and they would pay for that also and that we could be members for as long as we wanted without paying. They would also pick us up and bring us home for free. We could be with people like ourselves and no one would laugh at us or make us feel bad. I forget if I was told anything else."

How did he know you? Why did Basil think you would be interested or viable?"

"I don't know that. I'm sorry."

"How often does your club meet?"

"Three times each month. I go whenever they call me. If I don't they won't call again until the next time."

"On Saturdays," Wilson suggested."

Bangles nodded. "And weeknights." She shook her head. "Never on Sunday. I like the weekends because of my television shows. I take so long to get ready that during the week I would miss my shows."

"Where is this club? How many members are you?"

"I don't know. They come to get us and I don't always see the same people. I did like Percival." She flapped both arms a few inches, sighing or catching her breath. "He was nice."

"They come to get you, how?"

"They come with a truck. They always come after dark, even in the summer. I meet them at the garage because I don't have a ramp."

"When is your next dinner with them?"

"This Saturday. That's why I called you. They'll come for me at 9:30. I always leave here early. If they don't see me they won't wait."

"Then let's make certain they see you, Miss Bangles. I can also assure you they won't see us. Go have a good time. Enjoy yourself. How long do the dinners last?"

"I don't know. Two hours, maybe longer. Once I'm there they leave to bring someone to take my place and drive me home. We're never more than ten at one time and I never know until they call how late I'll be eating. They tell us ahead of time so that we can plan our earlier meals at home. They're very nice that way."

"Did you sign over your estate, Miss Bangles?"

She nodded, the fatty bellows between her chin and her neck squeezing out then in. "Yes. I think everyone does. Mr. Basil said if I paid cash each time he couldn't guarantee me a permanent place. He said credit cards are dangerous. The government is watching him, spying on him, but helping us, giving us dignity and bringing us together as friends is more important to him. He said the government is trying to hurt us. That's why Mr. Basil is my beneficiary. He told me it's the best way to hide from the government, that we could go to jail for what he's doing and that what he's doing to help us is very expensive. Because of my age he said I could live a very long time. Besides, I don't have any family and I don't want to see my daughter."

"What he's doing is illegal, not you. He's cheating the system and stealing your money, about three million if I recall. That's a lot of food, Miss Bangles."

Bangles' scar began disappearing.

"What will happen to my money now?"

"Nothing will happen. Once we find Basil his lawyer will be instructed to redraft the will. End of story and your money remains yours. If the lawyer doesn't comply he'll deal with us, which I can tell you will be extremely unpleasant. Remember, Ms. Bangles, we work for the president." She let Bangles catch her breath. "Do you have a copy of your will?"

"No. I suppose he forgot after all this time."

"Perhaps the name of his lawyer," Wilson tried.

"I don't know. I think I was very nervous. Will he know I told you?"

"He will not."

She seemed relieved. "Thank you, miss."

"Miss Bangles, thank you. You're doing something good. You won't see us Saturday. We'll just be here. Believe that."

Nothing was left to say. Michaels was at the door. He'd heard of a popular Asian restaurant he wanted to try. On the street he inhaled a deep breath.

"Make certain they see her. Good one."

She scrunched her face. "Yeah, like euthanize, execute and intervention. Whatever were you thinking?"

"We were losing her. She was prattling. We needed a spark of drama."

"Take me to dinner." Lorie shook her head. "Roast of pork."

43
Saturday

Lorie and Dwayne stayed over, barring Angela Bangles from their evening. They arrived home late Thursday afternoon after stopping at The Agency to put in their gym time and a few more hours at the beach. Hence the need for clean panties in her purse, Lorie losing to Dwayne's logic that they were working, not shirking. Like a painter who, once at home, didn't want to smell paint, like a doctor who, once at home, didn't want to hear about anyone's aches and pains.

Requisite balance, he explained.

He was no different. Once at home he needed to see something slim and beautiful and he was taking her to the beach, for balance, where they could plan Saturday night without distraction. Unless of course…

She smacked him.

Friday morning they hit the gym, worked out together, showered, and changed into casuals for the road trip and long weekend.

Dwayne's phone chimed at minutes before twelve. Their Primary was sending them to Baltimore. He hated Baltimore. Another near-dead Gourmand had turned up. The man had called the hospital complaining of severe chest pains, asking for help. They refused him, of course. He was a No Assist. When contacted by The Agency, asked whether he belonged to The Diners' Club, he sounded flustered. He began hesitating, repeating himself. He was a possible source.

Dwayne checked his watch, noting the address, disconnecting without mentioning Angela Bangles. He and Lorie had agreed not to until they had something concrete, not another dead-end.

They had time for both cities if they flew. He called the airline booking First-Class seats for Baltimore, returning that evening, also reserving seats on the first flight out to Boston Saturday.

At JFK they booked into the Sheraton, left their car and left their luggage. At the airport they showed their IDs, bypassed TSA and a line of already disgruntled passengers at the gate.

In Baltimore they took a taxi, Dwayne Michaels asking the man politely not to screw them over unless he wanted to lose his permit. They were federal agents with no time to piss around.

Arriving minutes later they were surprised, the driver's tip exceeding the fare. The Gourmand lived next door to the airport in a private home whose front was decorated with a wide and low zigzag ramp from the sidewalk to the porch. What surprised them more, the house was clean.

He pressed his finger to the doorbell. No response, yet the lights were on. Again, this time much longer, Michaels commenting that the man was either deaf or stuck on the can, that they couldn't be interrupting his dinner hour because every hour was dinner hour for them. He crashed his elbow into the narrow side window, twisting the lock from inside, the high-pitched squeal sounding instantly.

He told Wilson to stand by the sidewalk to greet the police.

She loved him. He knew.

Stepping inside, his weapon drawn, he called out. No response. The phone began ringing, the security company calling to verify. He didn't answer. Neither did the corpse in the corner of the kitchen sitting at the table with its face in a soup bowl, the sides of its head and the perimeter of the bowl splattered with a coagulated medley of vegetable bits and dried strings of pasta.

A few minutes later Wilson came through the door, smirking, rolling her eyes, ahead of the uniformed cops whose guns were drawn, held chest high, their heads pivoting.

He chuckled, commenting on their chivalry. He didn't like cops: Twin assholes in tapered shirts a size too small emulating their television idols.

They had attitude. They thought they did. To a SEAL city cops were the bottom feeders of law enforcement: Guys who failed the grade or knew not to try.

Who was the vic? Cool TV talk, man. He had no idea. He didn't care. Why were they at the house? He couldn't say. What agency were they with? He smirked. What didn't they understand about a gold shield and United States Government? He gave them a number, telling them to call for a pick-up.

One cop began scribbling on a notepad, not certain what to write. Nothing, Michaels retorted. The guy was a No Assist. Cause of death, oh, sorry. COD: Drowning. In effect, he didn't exist.

Michaels and Wilson left them standing by the corpse, making their way methodically through each room. The guy wasn't the largest Gourmand they'd come across. He lived alone. He was neat and he was organized. His lift chair was clean, stationed by the table, the pantry filled with enough food to last a normal person several weeks. The bedroom and the bed were equipped with steel rails and handles, the closet neatly arranged. The bathroom looked like a hardware store. The living room, Wilson commented, was free of dust, the depression in the sofa facing the flat screen leaving no doubt where the man spent his time.

He didn't work. He was on disability with fifteen dollars in his wallet. He had no credit cards, no driver's permit and a silver PMC, which likely meant he hadn't voted for Vendôme. What he did have was a silver and black Diners' Club card. What they had was another dead-end.

They were done, a wasted trip. They left with the cards. They weren't waiting for detectives. In fact detectives weren't invited to the party. He was a No Assist, not a homicide. The cause of death was irrelevant.

Michaels told the cops to close the door behind them, suggesting they not stick around for the retrieval team that might take a few hours. He didn't have to glance back to know that one white and one black middle finger were jabbing the air.

*

Lorie and Dwayne relaxed over a fine dinner in New York, a night of lovemaking and a late breakfast in Boston. Lorie had quickly learned when first travelling with him that he didn't eat meals in airports or in-flight meals prepared by wannabe chefs using hospital leftovers.

After breakfast they checked-in early to the Hilton, went to the pool and the sauna, had lunch and left. They had eight hours.

Dwayne Michaels was in his element.

The rear of Angela Bangles' building was no different than the front. The sounds coming from open windows were the same; the clutter on the balconies was the same and no one was sitting outside on a day that was sunny and warm, which he didn't think was strange.

Ego and vanity cloaked in suntans were traits of the middle-class and well-to-do.

They walked the length of the laneway lined with buildings cloned by the same builder forty or fifty years earlier, buildings separated with crooked fences, rotted mattresses, broken furniture and garbage bins full to overflowing. Both entry points fed onto two-way streets 1000 feet apart.

That wasn't good. Bangles' building was midway. Nor was the fact that no apartment in her building appeared vacant for them, nor did anywhere in the laneway allow for concealment and observation. Not even the garage was a doable option, far from it. The door would have to stay open, the interior would be lit and they would be spotted the moment they exited into the laneway whose entire length was unlit.

Lorie identified the complications, wondering why Dwayne wasn't saying anything. He had to realize. He was teasing her, being a jerk, a nice jerk, waiting for her to say something. She did, ignoring her best instincts.

He listened. Good girl, patting the top of her head. That's why he loved her. She had a great body and she was smart.

They would rent another car, black or dark blue, a Chevy or a Ford, unpretentious. He would observe the truck from his vantage at one entry point, Lorie from her end of the alley. Once ready they would leapfrog, maintaining radio and GPS contact. They would also buy meal replacement bars and bottled water. Dinner would have to wait until the following evening.

Lorie listened. What a man, her hero. Still, as much as she loved him, she would be having sex by herself that evening because, after all, she was a good girl.

They left with six hours remaining.

En route to the hotel they rented another Ford, blue, one that wasn't yet cleaned, taking a moment to dull the headlamps with a handful of earth. The other vehicle was brown with clean lights. They bought a second GPS, not trusting the rental, a second camera, and went to a grocery store.

At the hotel they checked their radios, headsets, the GPSs, their weapons and their SLRs. Dwayne had his own bag of gadgets as well.

When he was satisfied Dwayne called Reception for a wake-up call, set his alarm clock and went to sleep for two hours, leaving Lorie to wonder how he could do that.

He woke at seven, seconds before the clock's piercing beep, lifting and replacing the phone's receiver into its cradle. Lorie was already dressed in soft black boots, black jeans, a black tee-shirt and jean jacket. He showered, dressing in oxblood boots, dark blue jeans and a dark blue raglan sweater to avoid looking like twins or newlyweds.

Before leaving the room she hugged him and kissed him. She loved him. She had also reconsidered he plans for later in the evening, meaning he wasn't to do anything stupid.

At eight o'clock they were posted at opposite ends of the laneway, waiting. Nothing much was happening. A cop car passed by Michaels' vehicle, slowing. He advised Wilson, not surprised a few minutes later when she advised him. When he saw them again moments later, more curious, he flashed his shield, waving them goodbye.

At nine a cluster of giggling girls passed by in the semi-dark. He figured late teens, dressed for clubbing in flighty skirts and dresses that would be completely useless on stairs, boarding buses or a barstool, albeit very convenient from a male perspective. Yet those same girls would likely wear full swimwear at the beach and scream bloody murder if their brothers happened to walk in on them. Bizarre, he thought. Where were the parents?

At 9:10 the sky was darker, Angela Bangles backlit for a moment by the indoor parking lights as she was wheeling her way to the edge of the laneway, waiting by the garbage bins. What a life, breathing in the stench of rotting food scraps before going to a supposedly fine dinner. He spoke to Wilson who also saw her.

She was lowering herself into a sitting position where she remained until 9:25, making him think the truck was always on time. He spoke to Wilson.

9:29, she spoke to him. A truck was passing her, two men, turning into the alley: Plain, a fifteen-footer, dark green, unmarked. He saw them, their high beams. Shit. That wasn't good. Any photos would be Wilson's deal. She heard.

Wilson drove a few feet closer to the line, exiting her vehicle, stopping where the sidewalk met the lane. The men were of average height and build, nothing special, dressed in dark overalls. One was raising the rear door, lowering the hydraulic platform and lighting the interior; the other was guiding Bangles into position. Both men were securing her with wheel chocks and a cable, raising her, removing the chocks, waiting. Bangles knew what to do.

Wilson couldn't believe what she was seeing at five frames per second. Bangles was crossing the deck, one man maintaining tension on the cable, both men waiting until she was flat to the bulkhead before removing the cable, letting her turn 180°, strapping her to the wall in a vertical position. They weren't speaking. They were leaving her, in the dark, lowering the door, raising the platform. They were coming his way.

She was horrified, Michaels wasn't.

She returned to her car. Michaels was standing by the side of his vehicle with his back to the lane, letting the men see some guy getting into his car that fit in, looked like everyone else's.

A minute later Wilson trailed behind. They were headed downtown. That was good. The worst scenario would have been two cars driving into an abandoned industrial park after dark on a Saturday night.

The ride lasted twenty-five minutes with the right amount of traffic to make trailing easy. Once in the core Michaels and Wilson coordinated falling back, pulling into curbs, killing the lights for a few seconds, pulling into the traffic again and when to pass.

The building was three stories. The single-door front entrance was dark, the adjacent bay door remotely operated. That part of their evening was over. They waited, hoping Bangles knew what she was talking about.

Two more dark green trucks arrived by ten. Between a quarter and half-past the hour ten trucks departed. An hour later, within a few minutes of each other, the ten drove past them disappearing into the indoor parking, Michaels commenting, with the late shift of Gourmands.

Then ten left. Bangles and her co-eaters were going home, they presumed well-fed. At 12:45 the process was repeated. The late diners were going home. Michaels and Wilson followed the third to last truck to a street not far from Bangles, a few minutes farther out. Michaels drove by. Wilson parked where she could be seen. She stepped out, nonchalantly walking away, noting the address. Locating the Gourmand's apartment at a later time wouldn't be difficult.

Michaels circled the block, parking several car lengths from Wilson. The driver and his helper were working at discharging their load, not hiding, nor paying attention. How would one possibly hide while moving a quarter-ton of meat under a bright light at 1:30 in the morning? Anyway, he didn't need more photographs. He had all ten tag numbers and a few faces. No need for a slide show.

The men worked quickly, from experience, not from panic. By the time the Gourmand was safely in his garage the truck was reversing onto the street. They did a right-on-red and drove off. Michaels did a U-turn and followed, calling Wilson, telling her nappy time was over. He chortled at the wet sputtering sound blasting his ears.

At 2:00 AM they were in Salem, driving into a problem: an industrial park. He told Wilson to keep driving and to slow. He stopped, stepped out and hurried to the trunk. He reached for the tire iron and his black canvas bag, smashing his taillights, his headlights and parking lights.

Wilson's taillights were dim; those on the truck mere specks. He told her to stop, to pull over by the closest building. Above all she was not to activate the door locks.

She didn't. Seconds later she joined him, shocked by his face masked with night vision goggles.

The entire park was dark, deserted. The truck ahead was breaking, slowing to a stop at the top of a loading ramp leading into a one-story warehouse, waiting for the roof to clear the bay door. There was no other light. Michaels flipped up his goggles. They needed concealment. Not all the drivers had finished their deliveries. They could see sixteen sports cars, sedans, vans, and SUVs in the parking lot.

Hilary Basil certainly did not work alone and his guys worked very late.

The warehouse's bay door rattled closed, the goggles dropped into place.

Michaels was quietly in his glory, Wilson a little freaked by driving between and around buildings completely sightless. It was eerie.

When they stopped he reached to the backseat for his canvas bag. He got out, crossed in front of the car where she barely saw him, and went to her door. She didn't care about markswoman crap and martial arts trophies. She took his hand, not quite enamoured of his headgear.

Within the quarter-hour other trucks began arriving, all of them by 2:45. None of the drivers or helpers noticing the spectators sitting on a nearby picnic table eating granola snacks. By three o'clock the sixteen vehicles were gone. No one was sticking around for an after-hours beer, the last guy out testing the door.

Michaels waited ten minutes from the time the last taillight faded into the dark. They had time. Sunrise wouldn't happen for two hours. More importantly, noise travelled farther at night.

They scurried from one building to another, Wilson running blindly. At the ramp he left her to check the corrugated door. Within a few feet he dissolved into a shadow. The sensation unnerved her, hearing his voice before seeing him re-emerge as a life form she knew. The door was staying closed.

Together they circled the building. He was searching for the Network Interface Device and exterior alarm. The device was by the front door, the siren was directly above tucked under the soffit and well beyond reach.

He shrugged. The worst case scenario would be the local cavalry charging in with flashing red lights for five minutes of bullshit. The best case: No cops. He needed sixty seconds, 100, tops. So who would hear? A night-watchman who would either be startled awake or watching internet porn, by which time the night would once again be quiet.

He reached into his bag for Swiss-made wire cutters, a set of seven German-made lock picks and a mini-flashlight. He raised his goggles, giving Wilson the light, telling her where to direct the beam first, second and third. She understood.

Did she?

Yes.

Good girl.

She scrunched her face. They would talk later.

He separated the lock on the device box without another word. Next he snipped the ring and tip wires severing the link to the central security service. The shrill of the overhead siren blared instantly, Wilson jerking. Seven seconds.

She held the light to the lock, a standard tumbler model. She didn't know the difference. What she wanted was to get inside. He chose the proper pick, working with the precision of a dentist picking at a microscopic cavity, the driver and bottom pins separating, the shear line clicking, the tumbler turning. The door opened. Thirty-six seconds: A lifetime.

Inside, the keypad by the door was flashing red. Good. A second panel was locked, cheaply made. He chose a pick, complaining his tools were too fine for such common work. She cared. Fifty seconds. The panel jiggled open in seven, Michaels ripping the red and green wires from their sockets in three. The siren died. Sixty seconds. No way. She patted his shoulder, her hero. He kissed her, stealing her breath, counting to seventy, eighty, ninety and 100. He always planned for the unexpected.

He smirked. He wasn't losing his touch.

He did an inventory, everything placed into his bag. His goggles weren't required.

The interior was cold. He flipped the light switch. Whatever they expected wasn't this.

Dozens of institution-size freezers lined the longest wall, several more fridges and several coolers filled with desserts and pastries. They opened each one. One mystery solved. Most of the hundreds of wine crates hadn't been opened. A few were. In the middle were cutting tables under bright lights, and packaging equipment. Along two other walls was floor-to-ceiling shelving fully stocked with all manner of foods and beverages. Along a fourth wall was wine-making equipment with hundreds more bottles and label printing machinery, Michaels erupting into a fit of laughter. Apparently Hilary Basil was aware or convinced that not all Gourmands were enlightened connoisseurs, his five-week variety apparently as delicate to the palate as a fifty-year Paulliac grand cru.

The place was a veritable food mart.

What they did not have were cameras. Why? Who would they call to report the crime?

There were a couple of private offices with glass panelled doors, both locked, something for another time. The filing cabinets in each were locked indicating a trust issue, though nothing he saw was problematic. One other door led to a single washroom, another to a lunchroom. The garage was at the rear behind a heavier door containing the thick smell of rubber and the groan of ventilators. The ten trucks stood ready in a neat row.

His watch read 4:00 AM. They were leaving, though not without a few bottles of wine that were exceptional, taken from original crates. She'd done well for them, though he somehow doubted that Bangles and her Gourmand friends were capable of savouring the subtleties of finer wine. He imagined Basil understood that to his advantage as well. In any event she would be getting her ride to the hospital. That was the deal, though when Wilson asked why he was laughing he didn't answer.

She let him be. Wine was his thing. She had a more critical issue. She couldn't wait until the hotel and would not under any circumstances take off her pants in the dark and squat in the middle of an industrial park like a Spring Break teenager when a perfectly good washroom was available. He understood: another female thing.

She wasn't long. They were good to go, Wilson dying for a hot shower. The job was done, satisfactorily completed, Michaels closing the lights, testing the door without correcting the damaged lock on the box. No one ever looked at NIDs and the electrical panel would have confused most electricians.

The distant sky was dull yellow, encroaching on monochromatic greys. The new day was in its infancy promising high temps and blue skies.

Wilson was pleased with their success; more pleased that her day was over, looking forward to an afternoon by the hotel pool and bar service. Then she wasn't. They had shopping to do, and not for short skirts and sheer blouses. Good stuff.

Dwayne trailed Lorie into the city with their headsets on, Dwayne explaining that being a 'good girl' was a good thing.

44
Special Delivery

They slept until noon on Sunday, waking with a mission.

The first order of business was returning the damaged vehicle. He had no idea what might have happened. His best guess was bored punks. Anyway, what did it matter? He'd purchased full coverage, so deal with it.

The second order of business was a late lunch, then on to electronic and hardware stores. By four Lorie had her own night vision goggles, which she thought was sort of cool. By five she was stretched out by the pool sipping a tall vodka and soda in a bright yellow Rio to the chagrin of mothers and the envy of daughters. Dwayne was doing laps.

Monday morning Dwayne rose early. He didn't need her, as much as he wanted her. They needed to determine at what time the place opened, how much time they would have to work Tuesday morning without fear of interruption that would end badly...for Basil's boys. They had serious work to do without constantly looking over their shoulders.

He would maintain contact with her and expected to see her by the pool whenever that might be. No promises.

He arrived at the industrial park at 4:30 AM. He was alone, parking where he wouldn't be conspicuous or in the way later in the day.

The first car arrived minutes before noon, four others on the hour. He was surprised. He'd expected more personnel activity considering the size of the place. That was a plus.

For whatever reason they might be interrupted, if that did happen, he could drop five guys in a breath. And he would.

Throughout the afternoon delivery trucks came and went. Lorie was by the pool, updated hourly. She missed him. She was topless, slick with oil in her skimpy red thong: His favourite. The women hated her, of course, because a dozen men had proposed. They were very persistent. They wanted her badly. Oh! No way. She had to go. Another good-looking man was coming towards her.

Goodbye, sweetheart. Click.

A moment later his cell vibrated. "You don't do anything stupid without me." Click.

By five the park was deserted by dedicated hourly workers. No other outside activity excepting Basil's guys, one truck leaving at six most likely to deliver the evening's feast to the hall or the restaurant or whatever the place was.

He ate his last sandwich prepared by the hotel the night before, drinking minimal water.

At minutes before eight cars began arriving, the same sixteen and four others he anticipated. The four they hadn't seen early Sunday morning. Minutes later the truck returned. By 8:20 the five day workers were gone and by nine o'clock the first of ten trucks departed.

If nothing else they were efficient, though he wouldn't rely on noontime arrivals. He and Lorie would be gone by 6:30 AM.

By 9:40 that night he was greeted by Lorie in total darkness. For once he was at a distinct disadvantage, tracing her enticing murmurs, stumbling until her found her, her skin soft and warm to his touch.
*

Tuesday they departed at 3:00 AM, arriving at 3:25, parking in total blackness away from the building. They were inside at 3:30. Within a few minutes the office doors were picked open as were the filing cabinets and Wilson was left alone to do her thing.

The offices and phones were first, lenses and bugs strategically installed for optimum visual and audio quality. Bugs were concealed under the work tables, wide angle lenses in the four corners of the warehouse area. Another wide angle was installed in the garage with bugs under a desk he believed was a dispatch station.

He was finished at six-fifteen, no trace remaining. Nor had Wilson been idle. She had gone through the files meticulously, making photocopies of certain documents, transferring Gourmand and supplier information from their flash drives into hers in duplicate. She had the names and addresses of several hundred past, present and future hopefuls. Some dead, others waiting to replace those who soon would be dead.

On almost every document was the name or signature of Hilary Basil. They had at long last hit pay dirt, leaving with two bottles of exquisite wine and driving into town away from the park for breakfast.

*

They returned at 9:30 for ShowTime that didn't begin until noon with the same five cars. Good. A pattern was forming.

One man began his day by reviewing papers left on the desk in his office, papers Wilson had copied earlier. Seemingly satisfied, he shredded the sheets. The others were working at receiving goods, stocking shelves and preparing what was needed for the evening's meals.

They watched and listened to nameless phone conversations from the one office being used, writing terse notes before leaving to relax over a lunch in town and do some sightseeing. They'd seen enough for the time being, though what Michaels did want to see and hear was what would go on between 5:00 PM and six, then between 8:00 and nine that evening.

They already knew when the nightshift ended, arriving

unnoticed moments before five to continue the stakeout amidst the hectic scramble for first-place in bumper-to-bumper rush-hour traffic.

The men inside were packaging the food, bottles of wine, loading the truck parked closest to the ramp. No one was rushing. No one was talking. The one lead guy, the one with the private office was writing on a clipboard. A clipboard: Ancient and interesting. Go figure. Probably more fuel for the shredder. The door to the second office remained closed. So who was missing?

When the 6:00 PM truck was loaded and gone, nothing slowed. Clean-up began, wine tasted and approved before being bottled, and what appeared to be preparations for the next day.

8:00 PM. Cars began arriving, the truck close behind. Wilson was intrigued. She had never done surveillance, a stakeout, or a B&E. To think she was doing all that with her lover and fiancé was weird.

Four of the five day workers began leaving, each of ten nightshift teams speaking with the man in the office, taking envelopes Wilson and Michaels had seen him preparing earlier in the day. When all ten trucks had gone in search of their Gourmands du jour the man with the office was the one who tested the loading dock door.

Wilson asked what next.

Michaels answered, "A surprise, dream-girl, but not for you."

He pressed ten digits into his phone, not expecting her to answer, thinking he would have to knock on her door. She did answer, however, on the twelfth ring.

"Yes, hello, who is this?"

"Ms. Bangles, this is your friendly federal agent. Be ready at four AM in the back alley. That means in seven hours from now, Ms. Bangles. Understood? Be outside waiting. I will not call again and do not make me wait. This is your one chance, our thank-you for helping us. Do not screw this up."

"Where am I going, sir?"

"I hope to somewhere better, which is up to you."

He pressed END. He wasn't much for idle conversation. He checked his watch.

Wilson sat with her mouth open.

"We need clearance for Boston General ASAP. Think your buddy Priscilla is still awake?" Hesitation followed by disbelief…her disbelief.

"Who are you, and what have you done with my Dwayne?"

She snatched the phone, dialling from memory, identifying herself to the White House receptionist. Moments later, to Michaels' surprise, she heard a familiar voice.

"I'm well, Priscilla. Thank you. I've missed you, too, very much. I can't tell you how I've missed our times together. I'm always thinking of you, which is why I'm sorry I had to call you. No, actually I'm not sorry. This call is business. I need your authority to transport a Gourmand to Boston General for treatment on your tab. She deserves big time, Priscilla. Believe me. She does. I also need the Chief of Staff to meet with me at five AM tomorrow." A moment passed, Lorie smiling. "That's a date. See you in January." She turned to Michaels. "We're done. The calls are being made."

This time Michaels' mouth was open. "No shit…Priscilla, I missed you? I really missed our times together? That's a date? See you in January? Something you want to tell me, dream-girl?"

"No. I don't believe so, sweetheart. I did tell you we were girlfriends."

"She didn't ask why?"

"No. She can't, which isn't to say she's not thinking about us right now." She glanced at her watch. "But, sweetheart, remembering my times with Priscilla at the beach somehow makes me think a late dip would be cooling."

They were at the hotel in thirty-minutes.

*

Wednesday, 2:00 AM, the phone screamed in unison with the shrieking alarm. They woke in each other's arms, heads crashing into heads.

Lorie had preserved the sanctity and reputation of the presidency hours earlier in the face of extreme personal sacrifice. What she was doing, she was doing for her country, she told him, losing consciousness more than falling asleep before faced with the disgrace of betrayal, before her will was broken, draping his body with hers.

Of course, she still did want to kill him for wasting three years of her life. And he would never hear about...

At 3:00 Wilson stood watching at the bottom of the ramp, half believing what she was seeing, half believing the man who belonged to her as Michaels had driven out from the warehouse garage, had parked the truck, jogged back into the building, brought down the bay door, and was casually exiting from the front entrance. After all they'd done, now they were stealing a truck.

At 3:45 they arrived at Bangles' building. She was in the alley, waiting in the dark. She was flustered at seeing the familiar vehicle coming towards her, clearly afraid, Wilson stepping out quickly to reassure and console her.

Wilson wanted to remain with her in the cargo area, Michaels disagreed, which meant that wouldn't happen, which meant don't argue. An hour later Angela Bangles was a patient at the Boston General, the Chief of Staff personally taking charge. He'd spoken briefly with the president's personal physician, not knowing what to expect. Now he understood. The idea was for Miss Bangles to leave the hospital on her own at some point without her chair.

Angela Bangles couldn't believe what she was hearing,

that President Vendôme was taking care of her personally. She was nobody. President Vendôme was so important. She must be in a dream.

All this time she believed they were teasing her, making fun of her. She was crying. No one ever cared about her. Her face was glossy with tears, her red scar disappearing. She couldn't stop thanking them. She was blubbering. She wanted them to thank the president. They would. Could she at least know their first names? No. Would she ever see them again? No. What would happen to her? She would undergo all surgeries necessary for her to walk again, for her to sleep properly in a new bed. What she would not do, never again, would be to participate in The Diners' Club. In which case she would definitely see them again, Michaels assured her.

When he went to put ten 100-dollar bills in her lap, keeping his promise, she refused. She would buy her own bed, she told him, and find a more comfortable place to live. He placed the money in her lap. A promise was a promise, though he would forego the repairs to her bathroom.

He turned on his heels and walked out. Wilson followed a moment later: a female thing.

An hour later they left the warehouse, Michaels with a bottle of fine Bordeaux in each hand. Whatever they needed to see and hear they could do from their hotel room that afternoon.

*

After breakfast Dwayne and Lorie went shopping. They hadn't expected to remain in Boston as long. Their second to last stop was a lingerie shop, one of Dwayne's favourite and covert incursions since officially loving her. The final stop was Boston's DMV.

They ran the tags of all thirty-five vehicles. The trucks were registered to TDC, Inc. whose address was the warehouse. They had the names and addresses of the twenty-five men. None of whom was Hilary Basil.

Yet his name was on invoices and delivery slips, Dwayne and Lorie both certain the person as yet unknown in the second office was the missing link, Hilary Basil, who had to show sooner or later. The office was lived-in, used, not pristine. The question was: How much longer?

From then on when one was searching through the flash drives and hardcopies the other would be glued to the screen.

Lorie's pool time would have to wait until the last truck pulled out.

*

Weird didn't quite describe spying remotely, illegally breaking and entering, grand theft auto, or making dynamic love, talking about a French honeymoon or placing a personal call to Priscilla, not the president. She did have a point, he conceded, convinced he wasn't hearing everything about her times on the island. No way was that believable.

By Thursday at noon nothing much more had happened. They weren't learning anything new about Boston and nothing at all about the other cities. The nightshift had gone home and the dayshift was arriving. The dayshift was the key. The night guys were a bizarre limo service, nothing more, all of them identified and traceable as were the day guys.

So where was Basil, the missing link? He was on vacation, or in another city filling a second office there, wherever there was. He could be anywhere in the country. Or dead, soon to be reported as a Gourmand, a No Assist. How ironic would that be?

Breaking into the downtown location would serve no purpose. They wouldn't find Basil flipping burgers or sirloins and whoever was would eventually be rounded up with the others. Nor could they discount their Primary who would call sooner or later sending them somewhere or asking where they'd been.

They had a long leash, a lot of freedom and they wanted to maintain status quo. They did not want to rock the boat and they certainly could not mention Vendôme. Contacting her had gone against the chain of command, a major faux-pas. Above all they wanted Basil first. They were the closest, they'd come first and they wanted the gold star on the homework assignment. In fact they had no idea what the Primary did beyond reporting to Vendôme through someone else they had no idea about.

They went to dinner at nine, frustrated. Dwayne deciding they would return on Sunday.

They would not report Bangles' assist or the hospital. Then they would check the DMVs of each city in their quadrant searching for TDC, Inc., their single lead beyond which they didn't have much.

*

After breakfast on Friday Lorie was using half her screen reading the files on her flash drives, searching for the faintest clue, the slightest lead. The other half displayed the empty offices.

She understood Dwayne was frustrated, better left alone to make flight, hotel and car reservations. She knew not finding Hilary Basil was tantamount to failing a Black Ops mission. She believed she knew how he felt. The same way she felt that fateful day, consumed by the post-traumatic stress of thinking she might have failed the president, her girlfriend.

At first she had promised Angela Bangles hoping she could keep her word, hoping Priscilla would agree to reward the woman. Not really certain, relying on their friendship. Dwayne made that happen. He was making everything happen, shocking her with the 1000-dollar gift to a scared and grateful woman. She understood what he was feeling, that he wasn't doing enough.

He was wrong, though telling him would sound trite.

Now they were… "No way! Sweetheart, get over here. Now!"

He pressed END. Whoever he was talking with no longer mattered. The flash drive files were gone; the screen filled with the offices, two men meeting, shaking hands, unlocking and walking into the second office. Lorie enlarged the image, zooming in, staring at Hilary Basil. Who else could he be?

The two men sat, saying nothing of particular importance. But the voice…there was something about the voice. Dwayne zoomed in again, staring.

"Holy shit!"

"What, sweetheart? What's wrong?"

Dwayne swept up the computer. "We're leaving." He leaped across the bed for the camera, hurrying to door.

She grabbed her purse. She was wearing her weapon. "Sweetheart, what…?

"That isn't Basil, Lorie."

"Then who is he?"

"Our Primary."

45
The Primary

Dwayne Michaels hadn't once driven with sirens blaring or red lights flashing, zigzagging through traffic, not that he couldn't. That's not what Black Ops did. They were more sedate, patient, less hurried. They sneaked up behind you and slit your throat or shot you dead from half-a-mile away. And you never knew.

Lorie Wilson had, and could. She'd been trained and conditioned for high-speed critical displacement of the president. She would drive, unless he had some sort of male ego problem with that. He didn't, Dwayne Michaels tempted every so often to utter a "holy shit!"

They arrived at the warehouse fifteen minutes later, 10:20 AM, Michaels' eyes scarcely leaving the screen until reaching to the backseat for his camera.

Two cars were parked side by side in the front. He photographed the tag of the one they didn't recognize. Whoever he was, he wasn't from Boston. The car was a rental, though they weren't leaving anything to chance. They would wait. They would trail the man to the airport, his hotel, wherever, another warehouse. Who knew?

Searching the car was unnecessarily risky. Dozens of bay doors were open; too many windows open, too many potentially curious eyes. They would wait, listen and observe.

The men were talking about deliveries and personnel,

some of the names familiar to Wilson and Michaels. The first man spoke about the restaurant, possibly extending the week to increase revenues. The second man, Basil, whoever he was, disagreeing. His boss would not approve.

What boss? The only boss Wilson and Michaels were aware of was the Primary reporting directly to the president. What the hell was going on? The guy was working both sides of the fence.

Their Primary checked his watch, asking for a few minutes alone. He put certain papers into his attaché, placed a call, spoke for five minutes, disconnected and walked into the other office at 11:40.

He was leaving. The men shook hands without exchanging names, accustomed to seeing each other, meeting regularly. The second guy would send an FYI in advance of his next trip. He was pressed for time, wanted to touch base. He had urgent family matters requiring his attention in New York that PM. Such was the extent of the niceties.

Michaels reached for his camera, framing the man from the entrance to the rental sedan at three per second. The white family model would be easy to follow. The guy didn't look reckless in a three-piece brown suit, beige shirt, yellow tie and laced shoes. Michaels remembered the shoes.

He was going to Logan, leaving town. He was on the Ted Williams exit ramp leading to the airport. He would be a while at the rental counter. He wouldn't 'drop and run, bill me later'. He wasn't speeding. He wasn't in much of a hurry.

Wilson drove toward Departures, stopping, placing her shield on the dash. Michaels stepped out, making his way to the trunk for their headsets. Wilson joined him. A whistle blew. They ignored the cop. They would separate and stay out of sight. They would be conspicuous together: A young and good-looking couple in shape, well-dressed and obviously in love. Wilson smiled. She liked the young and in love parts.

The cop was blowing his whistle, coming towards them.

Basil, whoever he was, would recognize them instantly; he had complete dossiers on them, though he wouldn't expect to see them in Boston. Or did she want to wait in the car, he suggested, maybe paint her nails? She loved him and punched him, striding away to the left. The whistle shrieked, Michaels slamming the trunk, somehow exposing his chrome-plated Beretta.

The cop stopped, ready, gripping his weapon.

"You, at the Ford, hands high! Do it, now!"

He didn't think so. "I'm a federal agent. You blow your little whistle at me once more; I'll shove it up your ass. The ID's on the dash. Have a good time with that."

The cop gave him wide berth. The guy looked dangerous, like he wouldn't take shit. He saw the gold and blue badge.

"FBI?" he asked.

Michaels checked his weapon for show, thinking the cop's bowels were still churning to a liquid state. He walked away talking to Wilson.

They were in place, Wilson concealed within sight of Basil, Michaels inside Security.

Basil was done, walking, approaching Security. Michaels melded with the crowd. Basil passed Security easily, no mess, no fuss. Good. No weapon.

At the gate he sat patiently, first reading documents from his attaché, working on his tablet. Apart from that he didn't move. He was a frequent traveller, accustomed to long-durations of immobility.

He was the last to board on the final call, the flight departing at 1:55, American to Dulles. He was flying to DC, not New York. So what was with the subterfuge of urgent family matters? He didn't trust the guy at the warehouse.

Wilson and Michaels came together, waiting until the gate closed to approach the attendant. Michaels showed his

ID. The young woman was impressed. Wilson wasn't. The passenger was Goodman, Vince. Was she certain, Wilson questioned? The woman checked again. Yes, she was, answering to Michaels. Did the passenger manifest show a Hilary Basil? She checked. No. She addressed Wilson, that special interaction between females. And, yes, she was certain.

So who the hell was Hilary Basil?

Michaels thanked her with a smile and walked away. Wilson just walked away: A female thing.

They changed their flight to New York. Departure: 5:10 PM. The flight to Dulles would leave JFK at 7:35 Saturday morning.

The cop was whistling at another car. They returned to the hotel, packed and returned to Logan.

*

Climbing into bed Lorie asked Dwayne if SEALs ever slept eight hours. He couldn't recall that he had, kissing her, waking her gently at 4:00 AM.

The weekend passed slowly despite dinner and the theatre, Lorie making the best of her Saturday hours shopping, Dwayne carrying the bags. Sunday they alternated between working out in the fitness centre and relaxing by the pool. The DMV was closed. Vince Goodman was unlisted and nothing would happen until Monday morning.

*

Vince Goodman did exist. He was forty-eight, lived on the outskirts in upscale Arlington and drove a chocolate brown Bentley. Nice ride, shitty colour. To the best of their knowledge there was no female Goodman, Mrs. or Miss.

There were also ten vehicles registered to TDC, Inc. operating right under Priscilla Vendôme's nose in downtown Washington.

They drove first to the industrial park six miles out in

Mount Rainier where they saw five cars parked by the main entrance. They photographed the five, noting the tag numbers. They saw no Bentley with too many hours to wait. Instead they crossed DC to Arlington.

They had his phone number from the DMV, different from the 1-888 on their speed-dials.

The two-story carriage house was stately, the property manicured. He fit in. The neighbourhood was posh, the snotty 'hey, look at me' kind of posh. The guy had money, possibly cameras and possibly motion detectors, certainly an alarm system.

Michaels needed to reconnoitre the house, study the back of the property. The fence and the gate were the problem, if a neighbour spotted them. He needed the cover of darkness. They had no idea who Goodman was. Not a good situation in Washington. Neither was sitting in a car staring at a house, not knowing who or what might be staring at you. They left. They wanted to record the shift change.

Nothing in Mount Rainer was different from Salem. People started circulating at eight. They photographed the ten drivers, the helpers and their vehicles. At 9:05 the last dark green truck rolled out. Someone, whoever he was, remaining behind to lock-up

She loved him.

This time they knew what to search for and where to search. They were in the building at 9:30, gone by 10:30 with detailed information on Washington area Gourmands transferred to their flash drives. Who ate when didn't matter. Who delivered the food and from where didn't matter. That would come later. They had the faces and licence plates of fifty TDC personnel in two cities and a conspirator in The Agency.

Time to go.

Wilson dropped him off in front of the house moments past midnight. She loved him.

The Fatal Diners' Club

The street was illuminated with an amber glow. The windows of most homes were dark sheets of glass. He disappeared into the shadows of trees and shrubs in seconds. Goodman was either out, in bed, at or in the back of the house. Regardless, guys in brown suits didn't pose a problem.

At the gate he didn't scramble over the pyramided wire top, he leaped over. Inside the fence he pushed his back into the brown brick, inching his way. At the rear corner of the house he scanned the side and rear soffits. No cameras or motion detectors, which were his free pass, his way in.

Garden doors led into the house from the deck, he thought most likely into the kitchen. Good. Cheaper patio doors were a bitch to open without leaving proof of entry. The NID was located at the corner of the deck. Not so good. More time needed to sprint to the doors, break in, locate the screeching siren and sever the wires before all hell broke loose.

The cops he could control, not gossiping neighbours.

He estimated three seconds from the NID to the doors, fifteen more if the lock was hardware store variety and ten to deactivate the siren, assuming the typical front foyer location. Possibly thirty more if Goodman had the foresight to position the siren near the less insulated garage door.

He needed the twenty-eight seconds of noise in a perfect world discounting interior locks, an unreachable siren, a rooftop siren or a Doberman, a dead Doberman. He didn't have a choice. Fifty-eight would be a total fuck-up.

He needed to economize his timing, reduce his daytime visibility. He needed to see the lock, predetermine the quality, the best tool.

The yard was 150 feet deep, 100 wide, best guess. At the far end he was invisible, surprised. He thought more people would be up watching the late news. This was, after all, News Town. The house was dark. Nothing was happening. The backs of all the homes were dark.

Goodman was either a bachelor or his wife didn't drive. The assumption wasn't his to make. Morning would tell him and, in the morning, he would tell his female ninja fiancée who was getting off on her first covert operation. Either way, Goodman didn't have kids. There was no swimming pool, no bicycles, nothing a kid would want. Nor was a car parked in the driveway of a two-car garage. No spoiled teenager.

He snickered, standing in the shadows. He wanted to ask her. He wanted to ask her a lot of things, like about the president's private island. Her face always took on a warm glow when talking about Vendôme. What he really wanted to know was whether, during all those wasted years, she had silently told him that she loved him before each Gourmand…or something less endearing.

His money was on the less endearing. It was her thing, a female thing. But he did have to admit he was curious about her presidential secret.

Gliding along the side fence, he side-stepped to the house. At the NID he snipped the lock in two, taking the pieces. Why the things even had locks was a mystery to him. Homeowners never thought about them and those who did have an interest would come prepared: Case in point.

The concrete deck was large, uncluttered, some privacy provided by mature maples. Better than nothing, though certainly not optimal. The lock was solid, good quality from a specialty store. Nothing he couldn't manage on schedule.

He whispered to Wilson to meet him. At the gate he was over with another single leap, no effort, removing his goggles, continuing along the driveway to the sidewalk, to the slowing vehicle. This time he loved her.

They parked farther up the street a few car lengths beyond an intersection, alone and conspicuous, their shields ready, though he doubted anyone was peering from behind their closed blinds.

Wilson put her holstered gun on the dashboard between

her stocking feet, reclined her seat and closed her eyes.

"Hey, shouldn't we be making plans, dream-girl? You know, for tomorrow?"

Her eyes stayed closed. "You already have. And I am making plans, sweetheart…for my wedding."

*

The hustle and bustle began at 7:20. Most of the cars exiting garages were imports or high-end American products glistening in colours not available to the minions standing at bus stops with sandwiches in otherwise empty briefcases. Though Goodman's street didn't have a single bus stop and no one older than ten was walking.

They drove closer, studying the double doors opening and closing. No one was taking notice of them. Things were looking good. Apparently most of the homes required double incomes to keep up with the Joneses who were keeping up with the Joneses and the kids were days away from year-end.

Goodman left at 8:15 in a tan suit, Wilson wondering aloud if he had a good night's sleep.

They waited until they were alone once again, the morning rush dwindling to an empty street and sidewalks. They circled the block, parking on a cross street where they shouldn't. Wilson left her shield on the dash.

They walked naturally, hand in hand, possibly tourists, a young couple possibly searching for their dream home.

At the house they didn't bother with the front door. The gate was picked in a blink. She loved him. No heads were centred to neighbouring windows. At the deck he placed the requisite pick by the door; Wilson laid out two face masks. At the NID he set his chronograph. He snipped the ring and tip wires and ran. Wilson closed the box, retrieving the tool from the grass. At the door he was through without counting, his face covered. Wilson followed, retrieving the pick, her face concealed. He bolted through the house to the foyer, to a closet. The siren was shrieking. Wilson wasn't worried, shocked by abrupt silence. He pressed the crown of his watch: Twenty-four seconds.

He needed thirty minutes, tops. And quiet, no talking. He'd previously cautioned her that homes were easy to spy on, both ways. As much as Goodman wouldn't detect their equipment, they might not detect his.

They didn't waste time searching through the main floor living room, dining room or kitchen. The office was the first obvious choice. They were time-restricted.

While he worked to make Goodman's life less private, Wilson went through files and drawers. Two loose cables for tablet computers lay on the floor; another for an external hard drive, which she assumed was in the safe with other more compact storage devices and whatever else he didn't want her to see.

They would have to pay him another visit.

The second floor bedroom was next, where they could observe Goodman preparing to leave home and for how long.

While Michaels was working, Wilson first searched through the walk-in. The man was single. He wore quality clothes, though he was certainly no Dwayne. The colours were boring and the styles lacked flair. He either had a girlfriend or the occasional stay-over. One rack was lined with empty hangers, not many, a few drawers were empty, and his en suite had a drawer for products a man wouldn't necessarily need unless women weren't his thing.

The other rooms weren't used as bedrooms. One was set up for home entertainment; another for working out, another was empty and the bathroom was in showroom condition. That was weird. The guy should be living in a one-bedroom condo.

She went to the bedroom, pointing with a forefinger towards the floor. He nodded. The kitchen was spotless with modern appliances, the refrigerator and pantry telling her that he ate most meals in restaurants. All she could see was cereal, coffee and imported beer with a dozen or so frozen pizzas.

Michaels was done. Mission accomplished in twenty-nine minutes. They were strolling along the sidewalk holding hands in thirty.

*

They slept until noon, Lorie threatening severe damage to the epicentre of his male ego if he even thought of touching her poor exhausted body.

At noon they tuned-in to the spy network, alternating their hours at the fitness centre and competing for most laps in the pool.

Goodman walked into his office at six, dropping his briefcase onto his desk, charging one tablet before stepping from sight, reappearing in the bedroom with a beer in his hand, removing his suit jacket, his tie. Dwayne told her to have a good time with that and went to check his equipment.

Goodman disappeared, reappearing ten minutes later in yellow boxers, a towel draped around his neck and a collection of clothes over his arm. No way was he a Dwayne. Beige Dockers with a beige canvas belt, beige socks and a beige polo shirt. She wondered when she would see his beige fedora. The man had no taste, no pizazz. Her man did, especially in his leathers.

So she'd been wrong.

Goodman checked himself in the mirror, his opinion differing greatly from Wilson's. The man was full of himself. Why? Then he was gone, a blur passing the office. The squealing beeps of the keypad, the sound of a door closing.

Dwayne and Lorie went for a cocktail and casual meal served by the pool. They weren't in a hurry. Goodman would be a while. Dining out anywhere near Washington demanded patience.

They were observing Goodman's office two hours later. The house was beginning to darken.

They spent the time looking through the Salem files. Goodman came home at ten, changing the colour on Lorie's screen from infra-red silver grey to pastel shades of green. Dwayne designating her as number one spy for the rest of the evening.

Goodman spent an hour in his office writing notes without the distraction of television or radio, not speaking a word, preparing his briefcase presumably for the next day. He was checking an airline ticket, studying his watch, contemplating.

He made one call. He was confirming a second-quarter meeting. What she waited to hear was with whom and where and where would he stay? Was he travelling for The Agency or for TDC, Inc.? All he told her was when and for what reason.

"Sweetheart, he's departing Dulles at 6:05. He's not saying when. He's got a luncheon thing going-on on Friday at noon. He's not being very helpful."

Goodman closed his attaché and the office light, disappearing until she saw him again in the bedroom disappearing into the walk-in. Not many minutes later she burst into hysterical laughter. He was dressed in pale yellow pyjamas buttoned to the neck and trimmed with white ribbing. His slippers were caramel. No way. No wonder he lived alone. All he was missing was a cap with a pompom.

She hadn't dressed for sleep since leaving her parents' home. What was the point? She turned to Dwayne. He was wearing an Italian straight-back and nothing else. Her man didn't wear jammies. Then she saw the suitcase. Goodman wasn't planning a day trip. Four shirts, four ties, four of everything neatly folded into the dark brown bag, enough for a couple of extra days and nights. She recounted his every move to Dwayne. He was leaving the next day, sweetheart.

She was a good girl, he told her. She threw a glare at him. He chuckled. What did she expect?

Goodman put his luggage by the door. He was good to go. He read for an hour in bed before flipping the bedside light switch, Lorie hoping he wouldn't do anything nasty.

Lorie slid her computer into its case, stretching. She had her own packing to do, again. She didn't have to wonder what Dwayne was thinking.

"What are you doing, dream-girl?"

"We're getting to the airport before him, aren't we?"

"No point. We'll leave for Dulles after the rush-hour. We'll identify the airline; verify the manifest, check for a Hilary Basil onboard, find out where Goodman's going, when he's returning and we'll stop by his house. Guys like that have expenses, and accountants, which means he's got receipts in those files you saw. You don't live where he does and stay in three-stars. If we luck out we find a trend and locate him, discover who he was talking to, who he's meeting. If not, we use the yellow pages of wherever he flies into. We don't need him until then. Either way, he's royally screwed. We've got him. What we don't know is who else we've got."

46
Proof Positive

Goodman woke at 3:30.

Lorie was purring. Dwayne was at the computer making certain Goodman was leaving home per his schedule. He did, in a green suit, green socks and pale green boxers, which was decidedly too much information.

Now Basil, whoever he was, was secondary. He wanted Goodman big time. The guy was a turncoat and that was a major problem. Who then could they trust? The question was rhetorical, the rule of survival dictating that they trust no one. Why would he now believe the guy reporting to Vendôme was any cleaner, or Vendôme herself for that matter? Or was the president reporting to someone, someone tugging her leash? Not good, and for the moment he would keep the potentially hazardous thought to himself.

He eased under the covers, spooning into Lorie's warm curves, surprised when she kissed him awake, their suite infused with early morning light.

They had time. She was impossible to refuse, making up for lost time. And whose fault was that, sweetheart?
*

Dressed like the fashionable young couple they were, Wilson and Michaels drew quite some attention at American's Dulles office. They were not garden variety feds.

Goodman was the one familiar name on the Dulles –

517

O'Hare flight. His scheduled return was 6:10 PM Friday. Michaels booked First-Class seats for late Wednesday afternoon and the flight departing after Goodman's on Friday, the reservations manager smiling. She'd seen a lot of cops, FBI, and federal blowhards in her time, never like these two with the eyes and the Dwayne and the Lorie. That wasn't professional synergy. Not a chance. Agent Lorie Wilson was getting some and Agent Dwayne Michaels was the 'some' in someone.

This time Wilson did thank the airline personnel before sauntering into the concourse beaming, her skirt swaying, Michaels beside her, taking her hand after closing the glass door, feeling the slightest pressure. He could imagine the giggles and the comments behind them, part of his ongoing study of the female condition from which he would never graduate.

They drove to Arlington, parking on a different block, leaving her ID on the dash, walking to the house. The street was deserted. From the sidewalk to the kitchen was a twenty-second delay with a simple twist of the tumbler. This time they were interested strictly in the office. He went to the desk; Wilson went straight to his credenza, hum-humming.

The drawers were locked. Would he mind, if he wasn't too busy?

Didn't they teach her anything in Secret Service School, in the girl's classes?

She punched him, like a girl.

What? She didn't love him this time?

She pushed him away.

Goodman was organized, with good reason. The file drawers were remarkably well categorized, first by year from 2017 to 2024, subcategorized by city, warehouse and personnel, restaurant and personnel, the DMV, the suppliers, the legal firm in each city and his weekly travel expenses. With the exception of one city in which file they saw travel receipts and not much more.

Eleven cities in all, several dozen sub-files, with no mention whatsoever of the other three quadrants. Someone had a serious case of CYA.

Michaels was aware if he dared to speak against Vendôme he would never make love again. Not to Lorie, not to any other woman, and not due to lack of heated passion. All humour aside, he'd met with Vendôme; he believed in her, had voted for her both times. She was good people. That said, he was far from naïve. His head was crammed with top secret Black Ops Intel; he could well imagine what was in Vendôme's head.

He was in a situation he was unaccustomed to. SEALs did not fuck SEALs up the backside. Their Primary did, was. That set the tone. All was fair. What wasn't fair was anything happening to Lorie. That would not happen. Not unless people were willing to die. No exceptions.

He cleared his mind. At the moment their focus was Chicago.

Ninety trips in seven plus years, almost six months of nights at The Excelsior Regency. That was certainly a pattern. The man never stayed home. His favourite Chicago diner was Dan's Platter situated in the hotel, when he ate alone; his favourite dinner venue, or when he was stuck with the tab for lunch, was Finesse.

Clearly he was a man of varied tastes. They toured both locations on the web. Neither was a tactical issue.
*

The flight attendants understood the First-Class couple were armed federal agents, which made the fact they were leaning into each other and holding hands something to whisper about, not the weapons or that they were the only premier passengers not drinking. They were actually nice people, not self-infatuated and demanding.

The Fatal Diners' Club

They disembarked first.

They weren't booked into the Excelsior Regency. They chose a five-star across the street, once again sharing a suite. Screw the pretence. The game rules had changed.

They waited until ten, crossing the street. He was in 1710, checking out Friday. They called his suite. No answer. By 10:30 the suite was wired for audio before they enjoyed a late breakfast at Dan's, a 100-dollar bill ensuring the maître d' would lead Goodman to the proper table at lunch and possibly dinner.

Midafternoon they went to Finesse for a light meal. Goodman was reserved for noon the following day with two separate tables. He was expecting five guests. Waiting for their wine Michaels worked with as little effort as sticking a wad of chewing gum in place, another 100 dollars changing hands to ensure where Goodman would sit.

With lunch finished they drove to the warehouse to photograph cars, faces and dark green trucks.

That evening they sat in the Excelsior lobby listening to Goodman eat by himself at Dan's, watching him leave, the elevator doors closing behind him, listening to him rustle papers in his room and the tap, tap, tap of his keyboard. He didn't speak a single word throughout the entire evening.

The next morning Michaels took his time dressing. His normally dark brown hair was streaked with yellow that wasn't blond, combed differently; his clear eyes were covered with steel-rimmed reading glasses, his grey off-the-rack suit cut for a middle-management type. His shirt was white, the cuffs buttoned, his tie a boring shade of grey. There was nothing remarkable about him. He'd aged ten years and was entirely forgettable, she told him.

Wilson dressed in a two-piece cream-coloured suit, the hem of her skirt below her knees. Her low-heeled shoes were cream-coloured, her pink blouse buttoned to the neck. Her new blonde hair was combed into a ponytail tied with a pink barrette; bangs shielded her forehead, red glasses shielding her new blue eyes. Her lips were painted red, the kind that wasn't bright or inviting. She wore no jewellery, her make-up lighter and thicker than usual. The Beretta she hid in her cream-coloured hobo bag.

She was a businesswoman from Idaho, strait-laced, no one to ruin a marriage over, he told her.

That was cruel. She loved him.

So what? She was from Idaho.

She punched him, leaving him to follow behind. They arrived at Finesse at 11:40 AM. The recorder was in his briefcase. The clear buds in their ears were on the side facing the window. Three couples were seated, a fourth table occupied by two men. He didn't pay them any attention, surprised to see them. Instead he opened his attaché, activated the microcassette, placed a notepad on the table and reached into his suit jacket for a pen.

That's what business people did.

Goodman walked in at 11:55, acknowledging the two men before sitting alone at his table. The restaurant by then was half-full.

Michaels didn't like what he was seeing, even less what he was thinking, thankful his dream-girl was so intent on speaking fluent French for her honeymoon. He jotted notes as she answered. That's what business people did. She shared his concern, pleased she'd taken extra time with her Idaho façade, she told him, the one not to ruin a marriage over.

At twelve noon Michaels' normally steady heart rate skipped a beat. The proverbial sixth sense was kicking in, except that what he was feeling was real. The two limousines arrived moments apart. He didn't have to guess who the passengers had come to meet.

One man exited the first car, waiting for the chauffeur to open the door. One man exited the front passenger side of the second car, opening the door for the man seated behind him. He stepped back, the passengers greeting each other, shaking hands, entering the restaurant, their bodyguard opening the door. A few heads turned, most patrons too engrossed to notice.

Goodman stood. The three men shook hands formally. They weren't friends. This was a business meeting. They sat, Goodman ordering a round of drinks.

Banal niceties weren't exchanged. They didn't care about the wonderful weather, kids or summer vacations. They had a single purpose: The Diners' Club.

The bodyguard joined the two others who'd taken notice of Wilson and Michaels walking in.

Now Michaels wasn't certain at all that Angela Bangles had done them a favour. Stepping on a rattler was never a problem, stepping off was.

They listened until 1:20, enjoying their meal, lingering a while longer with their wine. Michaels was trained to blend in as much as Wilson was trained to identify a problem situation. Conversely she knew how not to be identified. She let Michaels pay the bill. When they stood and walked out, they did so unnoticed despite being observed.

In the fresh air they kept walking, Wilson blowing a stream of air through her lips. That was close. No, Michaels corrected, that was covert. She did good. She was a pro.

An hour later Goodman and his associates stepped out onto the sidewalk, two men preceding them, searching the avenue, one man following, opening the door of the second vehicle.

They didn't notice Lorie Wilson far to the north or Dwayne Michaels who peered into a storefront as both limos drove by.

Michaels and Wilson came together. Further surveillance of Goodman was pointless. They boarded the next flight to Washington, not caring who they bumped on a Friday afternoon. Shit happened. Shit was happening.

Screaming for help when falling or pushed overboard in the middle of the ocean is useless, better to get things done

quickly. Suck it in, as it were. Face reality. Their reality was
Goodman.

47
Hell Hath no Fury, Like a President Scorned

Vince Goodman walked into his home from the garage at 11:04 PM. He went directly into his office, dropping his briefcase, checking his voicemails before walking to the kitchen, flipping the light switch, a guttural gasp erupting from his throat

"Good evening, Vince Goodman. Or should we call you Primary?"

Wilson was sitting on a counter, her legs crossed, one leg swinging, one elbow resting on her knee, her Beretta in her hand.

"Wilson, what the hell are you doing here? How did you even get in?"

"That's it, not curious about the gun I'm holding?"

"Don't threaten me."

"I'm not. Michaels is."

"This is entirely against protocol. This is not how things work. There's procedure to follow. And where is Michaels? I can't tell you the trouble you're in."

"He's behind you."

Goodman jerked to the side.

"Welcome home, Goodman." He passed Goodman, leaning against the counter where Wilson was sitting. "Quite a day you've had, buddy. You must be anxious to get out of those green shorts you're wearing." He paused for affect. "That's right, your bedroom and your office for audio and visual as well as the Salem operation. Have to say, though, the yellow jammies the other night didn't do much for the lady here. Starting to get the picture, asshole?"

Goodman's mind was racing, processing. How the hell did they find him?

He chortled, feigning arrogance or actually believing his world hadn't imploded.

"Michaels, you're the asshole. You and this so-called partner of yours have thrown yourselves into one big shit pile. You're finished, both of you, gone once my Primary hears about this. There's no way the president will tolerate your breach. She'll have your balls for this."

"I'll let you know when I speak with her later tonight."

Goodman coughed a laugh. "You're pretty stupid for an ex-SEAL, Michaels. You have no idea who you're dealing with, what you've walked into. Be my guest. Use my phone. Call her."

Michaels pressed the PLAY button of his microcassette. Goodman took a moment, choking on air.

"Yeah, we do know. And I will use your phone. How was lunch by the way? Ours was a tad rich, though not as rich as yours." He pressed the red button. "We've also gone through your files. We know about the ten cities. We've been to Salem and Mount Rainier. What we had no clue about was the other city or who your buddies were, not until today. Thank you for the up-date. Good timing."

"You're fucking with the goddamn president."

"No, we're not. You are," Wilson added. "Worse, you're fucking with him."

Michaels drew his Beretta from its holster, reaching into his pocket. "Goodman, notice the suppressor. You're familiar with my past. However what you might not know is that SEALs get in and they get out. They're not theatrical, not in it for the glory or the medals. They get the job done, quick and not always easy." He screwed the suppressor onto the barrel of the weapon. "We have a few questions. Please, the tape is on the table. Do your mouth and sit. I won't tie you. What we need is for you not to wake the next door neighbours when you're not inclined to answer. And remove your shoes." Wilson knew he was counting down from ten. "Okay, at least tape your mouth. Meet me halfway."

Goodman obeyed, reaching for the tape. He cut an eight-inch strip, sealing his mouth. A second later Michaels shot him through the toe of his shoe, sending Goodman sprawling into the dining room, crashing into the chairs.

Neither man saw Wilson smothering her intake of air. Michaels had meant what he said. Why hadn't she believed him?

"That was for Baltimore. I hate Baltimore. And, really, keep the shoes on. No big difference. What was I thinking?" He waved the gun. "Sit."

Goodman did as he was told, his breathing rapid, his nostrils flaring.

Wilson slid from the counter. "Who are your counterparts in the three other zones and are they involved?"

She pulled back the tape, waiting.

He wasn't playing nice.

"You are so fucked, Wilson. You have no idea. Or weren't you paying attention at the restaurant?"

She didn't doubt the response in Michaels' eyes. She replaced the tape, stepping away from Goodman, well out of splatter range. She wasn't taking any chances. Her outfit was brand-new and expensive.

Michaels shot through the toe of the other shoe. Goodman lurched from the chair, his eyes screaming, flailing his arms, his dancing frantic, blood spurting, spraying the walls, his fingers tearing at the tape.

"I didn't tell you to stand. Sit, and answer the lady's questions. Also, say fuck to her once more, the next round goes through your zipper. There's no reason to be discourteous."

"Your counterparts, who are they?" she repeated. "And who the hell is Hilary Basil?"

Goodman was losing blood through the gaps in his toes, blood beginning to seep past his ankles.

"There are no others. No other locations exist, just the Gourmands. The agents receive their instructions from me. They have since day one."

She asked, "No warehouses, no restaurants?"

Goodman shook his head. "The ten cities you know about, nothing else."

"And Basil?"

"There is no Basil. Everyone is Basil, anyone who signs a paper or answers the phone is Basil."

Wilson and Michaels exchanged glances.

Michaels asked, "How many members, how many Gourmands?"

"Roughly…500 in each city with a waiting list of a thousand or more here in the Northeast and thousands more across the country."

"In exchange for insurance policies and estates," Wilson prompted.

His surprise was real. "We choose the oldest first, those with the highest BMIs. Think about it. A few thousand have died since Vendôme got in, some of them assisted by you two, many more in the other three zones who died waiting or believing they were waiting. Thousands multiplied by millions. We're talking billions of dollars here. These people, they don't have families. Nobody wants them. We're doing them a service. It's not like we're forcing them. And, believe me, when we put them out of their misery no one cares. Listen, these people are so far gone, so fucked up, even med students can't use them post-mortem. How useless is that? They are the epitome of a useless human being."

Wilson paled. "You said there were no other operations.

So what's the need for other agents?"

"You're not listening, Wilson. Gourmands exist everywhere, signed-up or waiting to sign. And three teams like you with pentobarbital kits and retrieval teams on call to remove No Assists. That's the need."

"How can that be?" She demanded. "And let's keep the bullshit to a minimum."

"We operate in a panhandle. That's what we call the ten cities. They form a panhandle: the biggest cities with the highest concentration of Gourmands. They're real. The thirty others from Miami to LA to Seattle are bogus. Like the Baltimore corpse, meant to keep the teams busy, a distraction."

"You reported the Gourmand in Baltimore as near dead, a possible lead. Now you're saying he was a corpse. How's that?" Wilson questioned, feeling sick.

"How do you think? He was a No Assist. They all are. Some hastened along. Again, keeping you busy, keeping the cash flow flowing. I paid him a visit before I called you." He tried to snicker, coughing. "The face in the bowl he did himself. Quite apropos, don't you think?"

"He had a personalized Diners card thinking he would soon be an active member?"

"That's right. He didn't suffer. But you know that. Like the others he believed he was on a short waiting list. Some sign up immediately, others don't. Those we leave alone. The one in Baltimore signed up a while ago. Guess he was hungry that day. Anyway he died happy, believing he was our newest member."

"That's murder," she accused.

"Prove it. And, after you do, deny it."

Michaels cut in. "How do you know who's a Gourmand?"

"How do you think? Like I said, you're…past your eyes in shit. You have no idea."

Wilson asked, "Is the president involved?"

"Of course she is. Why do you think she implemented her PMC strategy? A perfect scheme for which you're paid for what you do and I'm paid for what I do. The rest isn't my concern." He stared at his feet. "Call her. Ask her, and be ready to run when you don't like the answer." He looked at Michaels. "You of all people should know what she can do."

He fell to the floor.

*

The decision was a no-brainer. Lorie was not involved. Enough said.

Lorie agreed. The man she loved had just proven he had no brain. She waved him away, dialling the White House, mentally crossing her fingers, scrunching her face. His male ego was injured. Get over it.

The call was taken almost instantly.

"Lorie, this is a very happy surprise. You do realize, don't you, that we presidents sleep every so often? Didn't we agree not again until early January? Or am I to assume you have made some progress?"

"Priscilla, we're on hands-free. I'm not alone."

"I understand."

"Priscilla, we have made progress. We're done. We know who they are and where they are. We know absolutely everything about them." She paused, not for affect. "Priscilla, I love you. You know I do and I'm trusting my instincts here, trusting that I really know you, that you are my friend."

"We are friends, Lorie, girlfriends. Not many people know me as well as you do. So where are we going with this?"

"Your involvement, which I don't believe for a moment."

"I've been accused? Really, by whom?"

"Priscilla, I don't trust either side of this line. May I use a code I'm sure you'll understand?"

"By all means, Lorie."

She gulped, moistening her throat. "Dickhead."

Dwayne didn't hear right. He couldn't have.

Priscilla Vendôme was experiencing the same problem.

After several moments, "Lorie, you do realize what you're saying? You're very sure about this, positive." The president wasn't asking.

"It gets worse, much worse."

"And you can't say?"

"Priscilla, we're in Washington. This cannot be said over the phone and I cannot come to you. Not without the possibility of endangering you," she paused, touching Dwayne's arm, "and a very significant other."

Lorie let the silence persist.

"Meet me at Air Force One. I believe you remember the directions. Bring the significant other with you and, Lorie, bring me proof, lots and lots of proof."

"I will. First, though, one of them requires immediate medical attention and detainment. I might not be at the base before you."

Priscilla Vendôme chuckled. "Nobody ever is, Lorie. I'm the president. I get to go first."

The line went dead.

Dwayne took the receiver. He called the Arlington Police, instructing them not wake the neighbourhood and waited. He did not call a retrieval team.

Goodman wasn't doing well.

The cops were stunned by the open-toed shoes, one of them stating the obvious, Michaels asking him if he had an issue. He didn't, the other cop complaining about blood all over their cruiser. Michaels told him to drive fast. They were also instructed to stay with him. He was under arrest for a federal crime and in their care until retrieved.

When they were gone Michaels and Wilson drove from the house in the Bentley. He'd never driven one. He was curious.

"Sweetheart, ever been on Air Force One?"

"No, dream-girl. Ever torpedo from a nuclear submarine in the Mediterranean?"

She scrunched her face. "Now I will definitely never ever tell you."

*

The mammoth VC-25A aircraft sat on the tarmac, the president's Marine One helicopter off to one side.

Eight seriously armed men and women stood at or around the steps. Lorie knew each of them personally, which didn't exempt her. She was relieved of her weapon, scanned and frisked as Dwayne Michaels gave up his weapon before being swept.

Lorie stepped into Air Force One past another ex-colleague. Dwayne followed. Priscilla Vendôme sat waiting, flipping through the pages of a fashion magazine. She was in sneakers, blue jeans and a V-neck sweater. She was alone. She didn't look like a president. She looked cute, Dwayne thought. She stood to greet them, hugging Lorie with a tight squeeze. The women pressed their cheeks together, lightly kissing the very edge of each other's lips before Priscilla extended her hand to Dwayne who believed he was developing a brain tumor.

"Good evening, Madam President."

She glanced at her watch. She was smiling. "Good morning, Mr. Michaels. Please, sit down. May I offer you a coffee? Or does your information require something stronger at this hour?"

Dwayne returned the smile, joking. "I don't think a double scotch would hurt much, Madam President."

Priscilla left them, returning a few moments later with double scotches for her and Dwayne. The joke was on him. She passed Lorie a double Ultimat with a single cube without asking.

Dwayne took his glass, waiting for the president to sit. He couldn't help thinking that up close and personal she was very easy on the eyes even without make-up at 1:00 AM.

"Your engagement ring is lovely, Lorie. Let's get to Mr. Wonderful later. First, tell me about dickhead." She saw the reaction. "Mr. Michaels, Dwayne, we are what we are. Tell me how Frederick Vega figures into this mess. And you do understand I need more than words."

Dwayne opened his tablet, displaying the slideshow.

"Madam President, we took these thirteen hours ago in Chicago. Your husband and Mr. Edward Riley were having lunch with a man whose name is Vince Goodman, our Primary and former employee of Riley Corp.'s Houston legal department. We took the liberty of joining them without a proper invitation. To say the least they were unaware of our presence."

He pressed PLAY on the microcassette, asking for her patience after a few minutes had passed, pausing the recorded voices when the point he intended was made clear.

"Thank you, Dwayne. I've known for a very long time that Vega was inflicted with greed. The marriage isn't real. He's serving a purpose I could not reverse. I hardly ever see him. Edward Riley, however, I must admit, is truly a shock. Lorie, that's what you meant by much worse?"

"Yes, Priscilla. I'm so sorry."

"Don't be. I'm a big girl."

"Madam President, there is no doubt. We've got them. What we did not know about was your possible involvement. Goodman implied you were somehow implicated. What we still don't know about is your Primary."

"You mean Edward Riley. He's my Primary. He's been my connection since The Agency's conception." She sipped her scotch, crossing her legs, seeming 1000 miles away, her eyes brilliant with flashbacks. "Please, tell me everything.

Take as much time as you need. We won't be interrupted."
She patted Lorie's knee. "Smile, Lorie. Three men laughing
at me over lunch isn't the worst thing in the world. Not
when I'll have the last laugh, and I will. Believe me. I may
be the president, but I can still be a supreme and spiteful
bitch. Dwayne..."
*

The president listened without interrupting, stopping once
without asking to serve drinks. As the sun came up she
finished listening to the entire eighty minutes of conspiracy
at the restaurant.

She stood to make coffee, suggesting Lorie give
Dwayne a tour of the 747.

"So it's all about money, as well as ridiculing my
presidency."

Lorie answered. "Billions, Priscilla, divided by three,
though I suppose not equally. In any event Vega's a bit
better off than the thirty million Riley gave him for playing
your perfect husband. I would estimate a few hundred
million. As for Goodman, he passed out before he could tell
us. We should know more once we open his safe. But
Riley's the brains; the other two are go-boys. And what do
you care about ridicule from an old man, a dickhead and a
man with no toes? You are Priscilla Vendôme and you were
a long time before the presidency. So, don't you ever forget
that."

Dwayne was having trouble believing this: Priscilla,
Lorie kissing the president, bitch, dickhead, Lorie chastising
the president, a couple of double scotches, a Danish for
breakfast served by Priscilla Vendôme in killer jeans and a
deadlier sweater, thirty million, dispelling images of them
together on his sixty-inch screen.

The president chuckled. "Dwayne, you shot off his toes.
Really?"

"Yes, ma'am."

"Good. Now you can blow off his head as well." The smiles faded. "Lorie, Dwayne, this situation cannot go public. These three men cannot and will not go to trial. Vega cannot be arrested or sent to prison. Not now, not later. The country would suffer remarkable shame and scandal. Nor can Goodman. They defrauded hundreds of people, thousands, murdered randomly for gain and broke federal laws which I made quite clear are zero tolerance. I want that money. I want his, Vega's and Riley's. No one gets away with this. Am I clear?"

"No, Madam President. You are not. Forgive me, but you know how this works. Did you now order me to kill Vince Goodman?"

"I did. No one can ever know the White House was involved to such an incredible extent with this fatal diners' club. No one would ever believe I wasn't implicated. The presidency would be forever tainted, well beyond my time in office. So, yes, Goodman goes. Live by the sword...Isn't that the expression, Dwayne?"

"Yes, ma'am, that does sound familiar. And what about your husband, ma'am?" he asked.

"We'll get to him in a minute. First, I want those 100 trucks destroyed to the size of a breadbox. Am I clear?"

"Yes, ma'am."

"I want those ten warehouses cleaned out. Put the food to good use. Remove and destroy the liquor and the wine. Remove and destroy every piece of paper, every storage device, every piece of equipment. The buildings I want burned to the ground without injury or collateral damage. The restaurants I want cleaned out completely, everything destroyed. As for the employees, they get a presidential pardon they won't know anything about unless they're completely stupid. I'm pretty sure they'll get the idea once you charge in with the cavalry. They go home or they go to prison. Am I clear?"

"You are."

"I also want Goodman's home cleaned of all files and storage devices. I want Goodman released into your custody and I want the contents of his safe delivered to me personally by you. I want his bank accounts and I want that accomplished today. I also reiterate that Mr. Goodman has designed his own destiny. Am I clear?"

"You are very clear, ma'am."

"I also want to you supervise all activities in all ten cities. I want your old SEAL Team Two to assist. If they think it's too girly. You tell them I disagree. I'll speak with their commander before I leave this plane. You have my full authority. They answer to you. I want you in Virginia tonight. I'll put fighter jets at your disposal. I want those ten cities done in ten days as of tomorrow."

"Ten days, understood."

"Lorie goes with you. She deserves the closure. However not to Goodman's, and you do not let anything happen to my girlfriend. I love this girl very much, Dwayne. Is that understood?"

"That's affirmative, ma'am. And yes, understood."

"That is very affirmative and, Lorie, that's a direct order. You do not assist with Goodman."

"I won't, Priscilla." She clasped Priscilla's hands in hers. "Thank you."

Dwayne Michaels was having a stroke. "Madam President, Mr. Vega…"

"What about him? He's a liar, as well as a deceitful and despicable criminal. He's been doing this for over seven years while living with me at the White House, albeit playacting a role scripted by me, and more than seven years screwing around with bimbos while I'm drier than the frigging Sahara. You name me one other president who's gone through two terms without once getting laid." She waited, staring. No reply, when the question was not rhetorical. "That's right. Now I find out he's a murderer and a thief when all along I thought he was simply an asshole."

He dug his thumb and fingertips into his forehead, massaging away the ache.

"Yes, ma'am. I understand."

"Not unless you're a female president you don't, mister. But thank you for saying so. You're very gallant. I can see why Lorie loves you."

He wanted to skip past that. "Madam President… Mr. Vega, I need you to be very, very clear about this. We're not talking about any Joe Blow here."

"We are, in fact. He's very ordinary in the extreme. I'll see him this morning. He'll spend the next two weeks with his parents in New York. He'll be recovering from exhaustion and he is not to leave New York unless he's in a box and without his family or his security detail being injured. He's caused enough harm. Am I clear?"

"You are, ma'am. No casualties. Understood."

"I also want the parents' home thoroughly searched soon after. They might serve as a convenient hiding place for his bank account numbers. I wouldn't put it past him. The money certainly isn't in this country. And, Dwayne, FYI, all that TDC, Inc. money will be put to good use before I leave office. You are not doing this for me."

"Explanations aren't required, ma'am. Thank you for saying so. My partner, she…"

Lorie cut him off, "Priscilla, what about Houston?"

A pregnant silence permeated the jet.

"You guys can't have all the fun. My final official function will take place at the White House on New Year's Eve to which you're invited. Edward and his wife will also be invited. I can't think of a more appropriate venue to terminate…our relationship. He was the most aware of my cause, of what I wanted to accomplish. He used me, making billions more than he already has. I mean, really, Dwayne, who needs more than a few billion to live comfortably? Despite his few enviable traits, Edward Riley is intrinsically not a good man. He's a disgrace to his family name if either of you have ever read Simple Beginnings, the story of Thatcher and Betty Riley. Talk about a love story. They were good people, honest and loving people, as were Casey and Florence. Edward unfortunately is neither the man Thatcher was, nor does he compare to his father Casey. Decidedly not, and he certainly does not deserve Karina. You leave Riley to me." She snorted. "How the world turns. On the first of January I take over control of Riley Corp., talk about irony, which has also been the intention and legally binding since before my first campaign. You know that, Lorie."

"Dwayne knows that part, Priscilla, nothing else. We both believe in you. It's not an issue."

"Thank you. I might, however, require some technical instruction, Dwayne. May I rely on your expertise to guide me through the experience? I assure you I'm a good student."

What! No! Shit!

"Madam President, whatever you're thinking, it is not a good idea. With complete respect, ma'am, we've had a few drinks here. Please, let me consider our…"

"Yes, drinks with my best friend and her fiancé who must train me well, Dwayne." She beamed, hugging Lorie. "After all I did bring you together, in a way." She curled into Lorie, their arms and hands interlaced. "He's such a good boy, Lorie, and so very handsome. Now tell me, girlfriend, how long have you two been… engaged? What's the current poop and didn't we have some sort of agreement about sleeping with the hired help?"

Dwayne Michaels sat quietly. He didn't exist.

48
Priscilla's Divorce

Later in the morning Lorie wasn't sleeping or relaxing by the pool. She was anxious, afraid for her man.

She had become increasingly daring, almost brash with her poolside bikinis. She had a beautiful body and covering beauty was downright thoughtless according to Dwayne Michaels' Philosophy: 101, which espoused that everyone had an ass, the same way everyone had nipples, admittedly some more perfect and more divine than others.

Irrespective of which that morning Lorie was wearing shorts and a tee-shirt.

Dwayne Michaels left the brown Bentley downtown with the keys in the ignition and the windows down. He'd decided that he preferred Jags.

He escorted Lorie first to the hotel in a taxi, continuing on to a rental agency for a van. He spent the morning emptying Goodman's files and briefcase into the van. Not a single sheet was left.

He searched the house, not a cubic inch ignored, removing the spyware he'd installed. All he found of interest was a gun, which he kept. At noon he drove to a shredding service and waited until the last sheet was confetti. He paid cash and left.

He went to the police station where Goodman was bemoaning his agony in the corner of a grey cell, his feet bandaged in white gauze tipped with red. Michaels had specifically instructed that he not remain in the hospital and that he not be given pain killers or special attention and the local cops saw no reason to fuck with the feds. Not in Washington.

Nor had they processed paperwork on him. He was simply taking up space.

The police thoughtlessly, as local cops are wont to do, put him in the front seat of the van. Michaels didn't think so, pointing to the empty cargo space. Goodman crawled in and fell over.

At the house Michaels watched him crawl out, watching him hobble up the stairs to the bedroom, Goodman's face twisted with pain, his legs trembling, threatening to fail him.

"Goodman, there's no time for glory here, no theatrics. Remember?"

"I can't tell you anything more. You know what I know."

"You don't have to. I'm not here for information. The president wants you dead. That's an FYI. So you've got the choice of the last round in your weapon by your hand or pentobarbital by mine. Here's the deal. Give me the safe combination and you get to do yourself, go out like a man. Click, boom, you're dead. Don't, or fuck me up, and I'll inject you, after I blow out each of your ankles, knees, elbows and shoulders over the next several hours. That bed's going to get pretty soppy, pretty fast if you fuck me up. So don't."

His pain was forgotten. "You can't kill me. That's murder."

"No, that's retribution, payback with presidential authority. You're dead, buddy. So are Vega and Riley. She's really pissed with you guys and, I have to say, you're making things tough on yourself. The fear of one's own death is a total bitch. I get that. Better not to know. But the actual dying part, that's easy. No sweat. So what is it, combination or joint therapy? Either way you're dead. So let's man up. Let's grow a pair and get this over with."

"Please."

He was blubbering, literally spitting out the four digits, Michaels cautioning him to stay put.

The safe opened. Good, Michaels returning to the bedroom. Goodman was convulsing, begging.

"So, Goodman, gun or needle?"

Goodman was losing his mind, trying to kneel, pleading.

Michaels had no time to waste. He'd given the man a choice, reaching into a pocket for his kit. He didn't check for air in the syringe. What was the point? He kicked Goodman onto his side, jabbing the needle into his neck.

"This is for Baltimore," he said distinctly, staring into Goodman's blind eyes.

Pentobarbital was quick and painless. Goodman was dead inside of a minute, somehow placing a post-mortem 9-1-1 call.

An hour later, Michaels was at the White House with the contents of the safe which he handed directly to the president who offered him a scotch.

He respectfully declined. She respectfully insisted. Lorie was en route from the hotel, escorted by the Secret Service. Marine One was waiting to transport them to Andrews Air Force Base where two F-15 fighter aircraft were standing by.

She ordered him onto the sofa. She poured double scotches, kicked off her shoes and sat beside him smiling.

"So, Dwayne, sweetheart, let's you and me talk about my best friend."
*

Vega was in New York, unaware he was saying goodbye to his parents.
*

Saturday morning businessman Vince Goodman's heart

attack was lost in the middle of the obituary pages. He was survived by no one.

*

Lorie Wilson woke late at 4:30 AM. She was a SEAL. Deal with it. No special favours. No special treatment. Get your ass out of that bed and dressed lady or we will do it for you. Do you understand?" He grunted. "I said... do you understand?"

She did. She dressed.

She didn't think she liked him anymore. She was certain she didn't like him anymore. Jerk.

Then the team was running to the plane, jogging. They hadn't eaten breakfast. They were pumped-up. Lorie was walking, yawning. She was hungry. Michaels gave the order. No favours. No special treatment. Then Lorie was jogging, bouncing over some guy's shoulder several feet from the ground and not enjoying the ride. Then she was flailing, flung into the air and caught by another gorilla that dropped her like a sack of potatoes onto a hard bench.

Okay, she'd been wrong all those lonely years. She did not love him, not at all. She hated him. She definitely did not love him.

She had never flown on a plane without seats, squashed up against bare steel siding between incredibly straight-faced macho assholes. Not one of them smiled, unless she was wrong and sneering meant they were happy. No wonder she hadn't liked him when she first saw him at the White House. These men killed for a living on behalf of the president. Shit! Where was she?

Operation Big Meal began on Saturday in Washington moments after sunrise with a unit of heavily armed men in jeans and sweatshirts filling dark green trucks with files and cases of wine, driving them to the airfield where other trucks from the shredder service were waiting to get the job done. The ten green trucks were loaded onto a second military transport that arrived later.

Five cars arrived and were halted, given the choice of arrest or forgetfulness. They chose wisely. Who? What? Don't know.

Food banks were called, grateful for the bountiful windfall. And the Fire Department was called to protect surrounding buildings. Little Lorie struck the symbolic match. Team Two took care of the rest. By midafternoon nothing remained save a melted shell.

Saturday evening they flew by transport to Philadelphia. No way! She was not going to dinner with those disrespectful mongrels, especially not to a grungy pool hall. No way, Dwayne!

Yes, she was, by direct order of the president. Got an issue with that, Wilson?

Okay, good point, but under duress. Got that? And good luck with anything else in your dreams, Michaels.

*

No way! She couldn't believe. The guys were great. They were smiling, laughing, joking, some remembering old times with Dwayne. She loved them. They were nice guys, super guys. They stood when she stood. They didn't touch their meals until she was served. They all wanted to dance with her and each man did, though they did let her win at billiards, which was kind of obvious: A guy thing.

Sunday was a repeat of Saturday; ten more trucks loaded with expensive and very delectable booze being added to the second transport plane. What was different was the lunch break, each member of Team Two sincerely impressed with how Little Lorie could kick serious ass.

Michaels simply shrugged. He hadn't told them that she wasn't quite typical.

They enjoyed her company, respected her, until they discovered whose life she had saved and they began talking behind her back without Michaels hearing.

The Fatal Diners' Club

Things change, though Little Lorie didn't notice the difference. She was too involved.

*

Eight days later Operation Big Meal was accomplished. The Diners' Club was defunct. That Tuesday night the men returned to base. Wednesday Lorie and Dwayne accompanied the 100 green trucks to a demolition foundry. The process took the entire day from dawn until dark, Dwayne visibly saddened by the passing of so many cases of excellent wine.

Wednesday evening Michaels and Wilson flew to New York with three members of the team for a mission that would exclude Little Lorie. She was excluded by Presidential Order. The other men of Team Two understood that as well as their own exclusion. The three SEALs chosen by Michaels had history with him. No sweat. Kick ass.

Frederick Vega had forty-eight hours left to enjoy time away from his wife.

For the team Vega was a holiday, an easy kill. That he was their president's husband didn't matter worth shit. They had presidential authority. So the guy was a fuck-up in bed, or just a fuck-up. Whatever he was didn't matter. He was dead, soon.

Friday, all day, the team was in position. Little Lorie was in a Manhattan hotel, pacing. She felt left out. Worse, she couldn't think of a single reason why they had become so quiet around her.

Friday evening Frederick came out from his parents' high-rise condo. The limousine was waiting. His three-man security detail was waiting. They were professional, good at what they did. Simply put, they weren't SEALs.

The four bullets struck Vega at once in the head, neck and chest. He was dead instantly, his body disfigured and twisted on the sidewalk, his four assassins gone within seconds before wailing sirens screeched to a stop and confusion reigned supreme.

The four men returned to the hotel, three meeting at the bar, waiting for Little Lorie and Michaels to join them.

Walking through the door to their suite, Dwayne didn't have to tell her. Television crews were already on-site, her eyes glued to the screen. The First Gentleman of the United States was dead, assassinated.

History's first.

She wanted to call her friend, knowing she couldn't. The president would be busy; the White House would be on lock-down. She chuckled. Not even Edward Riley would get through.

Saturday morning Dwayne Michaels and his team went to the apartment, instructing the detectives inside to leave, to wait in the corridor. Within ten minutes a large steel-plated combination box was located, irrespective of which they searched another fifteen minutes before leaving, returning the condo to the detectives and Vega's parents who would not be charged with complicity.

Saturday night Team Two had a special mission. They assembled in the hotel bar. Wilson was their target. She knew too much for an outsider, Michaels discovering the plot too late to save her. He had no choice. He would stand against her, face her with his once comrades-in-arms to do what was right. She was done. Men had to stand together or be lost.

Later, Little Lorie Wilson strode to the bar herself from across the lobby, somewhat miffed that her man hadn't waited for her. He was in such a hurry to drink with his buddies.

She was, after all, a woman, his woman. Jerk.

They saw here coming, to a man holding back the oohs and the aahs, each man feeling jealous of Michaels, each man feeling happy for Michaels.

One man pushed open the door, taking her arm, another

man quickly taking her other arm, raising her from the floor, flying her, hoisting her onto the bar. What was happening? Where was Dwayne?

She was confused. She didn't know. They'd been acting so strange around her since…

"Little Lorie Wilson," one man began without preamble, "despite the fact you are a female, a very, very fine female and unfortunately with a man not worth your time, we do here and now, confer upon you the status and title of honorary SEAL in unit Team Two. You are, Little Lorie Wilson, one of us and we salute you." He paused. "We also, as men of distinction and valour, salute your very, very fine legs."

Another SEAL moved his buddy aside, taking over to raucous cheers and applause, no less eager, no less intrigued.

"Little Lorie, with our great respect and to commemorate this special evening for us and for you, we, Team Two, present you this token of our gratitude for having served your country, for having saved the life our Commander-in-Chief, and for having made us proud."

The man who was on one of four rooftops waiting for Vega handed Lorie a cherry wood box. Inside was a gleaming katana they knew she could use with expert ease. Inscribed on each side of the blade were the first names of Team Two, Dwayne's, and the team's insignia.

Subsequent honours included a marching guard to the dance floor, free drinks, too many free drinks, toasts, kisses and hugs. She would absolutely never forget them.

She was really a SEAL. She was one of them. No way!

Michaels, he was just proud and very much in the background.

*

In Houston Edward Riley went to bed for the second night perturbed. What the fuck was going on. Goodman wasn't answering his calls and Vega was dead, murdered.

Priscilla's office had called. He was expected in Washington on the Wednesday for a state funeral. The president was aware of how fond the men had become of one another.

49
The Rose Garden

Wednesday Edward Riley and Karina sat amongst dignitaries and social connections from across the country and the world. Such was Washington's world. No one was conspicuous by their absence. No one would dare.

He expressed his condolences, Karina sincerely sharing Priscilla's grief. Then she was alone. They were gone. Everyone was gone and Vega was forgotten, the sole beneficiaries of his death were the restaurants, hotels and bars of Washington.

Forgotten by all but Riley who chose not to continue his day with those he had no interest in. Instead he was driven to Mount Rainier, telling Karina he would not be long.

He stepped from the limo on his own, not believing his eyes, staring at the twisted metal, the acrid stench of burnt steel lingering in the air. He'd seen enough, ordering the driver to Arlington. The house was deserted, for sale. Goodman was gone. His world was collapsing, the undeniable question being the precise date of his Armageddon.

He placed a call to the police, enquiring after a friend, his mind stunned, his body paralyzed. With all his wealth and resources he had nowhere to run, nowhere to hide. At the hotel Karina showed real concern asking why he was so pale, so uncharacteristically distraught.

He had nothing to say. What could he tell her, that he

would one day in the very near future be killed?

He stayed one sleepless night with her in Washington before flying home, departing early. What he needed was in Houston.

Once at home he locked himself into his office.

Wilson's phone was out of service, Michaels' as well, as were the six others. He dialled each one again, his anxiety mounting. He called The Agency's New York office, Seattle, LA and Miami. The lines were dead. Neither did any of the other nine warehouses respond.

What was happening?

He remained in his office throughout the entire day. The president wasn't taking his calls.

*

Thursday evening Lorie's phone rang at home. She was unemployed, though she wasn't despondent. She was ecstatic. She didn't have to ask who was calling. The voice was Priscilla's.

"Thank you, Lorie, from me, from the country."

"Thank you for the ride in an F-15. How cool is that?"

"That is pretty cool. "Priscilla sighed. "Are we a strange couple, or what? Who would have thought? And now I need a date for your wedding. I'm the frigging president and I can't find a date. That is a total bummer, girlfriend."

"I've been working on that for you and I have the perfect guy now that you're available. I've met him a few times. He's 100 percent you, Priscilla. You'll love this guy."

"There is no perfect guy. You took the last one born in the last fifty years, against my express orders by the way. I should have you arrested."

"You're wrong. He is perfect, if you don't mind a guy with just a few million. So he's not super rich, but he's handsome and charming."

"Does this guy have a name? Please don't tell me he's a

Billy, a Clarence or a Darrell. Please don't tell me that. And more importantly, did he vote for me?"

"He did, twice. And if he's anything like his nephew you'll need to buckle yourself into the saddle. His name is Ned Michaels and I know for a fact he thinks you're hot. And you are. Even my guy thinks you're hot. So can I at least invite him?"

Priscilla's mind leaped into flashback mode. Ned Michaels. Holy crap!

"Don't ask me. It's your wedding. Goodnight, girlfriend. Oh, hey, January is still a date. You do know that, don't you? I want my archery lesson."

"He'll freak, seeing the president in a thong."

She giggled. "Then let's make sure he does, girlfriend. Love you. Bye for now."

The line disconnected.

*

September 06th, 2024 was a Saturday infused with bright and warm sunlight.

A deep-blue sky was the backdrop to the White House rose garden. The lawn was spotted with folding chairs, the intimate crowd including certain well-dressed covert men and their wives and girlfriends anxious to see the bride who had asked for a special favour no one had expected. Not even Gregg Johnson who was the one reporter invited to the wedding and seated by his wife.

Ned Michael stood by his nephew's side. He was honoured. He was also unabashedly studying the Matron of Honour standing alone across from him. He wouldn't get anywhere with a woman like her by being timid. How many times had he watched her speeches, thinking the impossible? Now she was at arm's length staring him down. Damn she was gorgeous, and petite, much smaller in person than her television persona.

She was dressed in a simple satin tube dress with a

bolero jacket to cover her shoulders, the President of the United States studying the best man while waiting to take the bride's flowers. She had invited him to the White House the previous Thursday and Saturday for dinner to break the ice.

On the first occasion he brought the wine, on the second he brought her a dozen long-stemmed roses. She liked him. They liked each other.

The wedding march began, all heads pivoting to see the bride dressed in a full-length strapless gown the colour of a newly minted penny. The tiara was a gift from her girlfriend, given to her the night before at a White House Girls' Night for all the ladies in attendance.

No one heard her father's whispered regrets, how he had thought so little of his daughter's choices in life. How could he have known until Dwayne so rudely opened his eyes? Nor would he ever know more than he did, she whispered, patting his arm. Was he proud? That's all she wanted to hear. He stopped, hugging his daughter for all to see. His daughter risked her life to save the president and God knows what else. What wasn't to be proud? What a silly question.

He beamed at his wife, stepping a few feet forward to give his daughter to an equally proud man.

Minutes later Mrs. Lorie Michaels was embraced and kissed by her husband, the president claiming executive privilege immediately thereafter.

Mr. Wilson could never have imagined that he would one day dance with the president in the White House Ballroom. Nor Mrs. Wilson with Bradley Duncan, the vice-president whom she believed must be the most charming and gracious man she had ever met. All she could think was something she had taught her daughter as a child. No way!

The happy couple reluctantly tore themselves away moments before 10:00 PM. Lorie Michaels would be ordering her Sunday déjeuner without her husband's help at a quaint café-terrasse on the Côte d'Azur.

She hadn't once been tempted to disclose her presidential secret. Nor would she now tell him of Priscilla Vendôme's wedding gift to them, not until New Year's Eve. The girlfriends could play bows and arrows another time soon, Priscilla promised her.

The president stayed late. She hadn't danced in years with anyone whose company she truly enjoyed and she could very clearly imagine herself buckled into his saddle.

50
New Year's Eve, 2024

Minutes remained in Priscilla Vendôme's presidency.

No other president was as popular or as alluring, Gregg Johnson told her as they danced. The nation had slimmed to ninety-seven percent. Graduation rates had sky-rocketed, mortality rates were continuing to decline and families had become families once again.

Yes, and she had him to thank for much of her success. She would miss him. She kissed his cheek: a presidential moment. But now she had one dance remaining. She bid him goodnight and crossed the room to another old and dear friend.

Earlier in the evening Mr. Edward Riley and Mrs. Karina Montoya were announced and Priscilla had gone to greet them personally. The women embraced, pressing warm cheeks together as true friends, though Edward Riley had simply extended his hand as though meeting with a stranger. If no one had discerned the difference in her, he did with his disquiet over the past several months undiminished.

They hadn't spoken more than occasionally since Vega's death. Nor had he ever thought to see Ned Michaels standing by her side as her companion for the evening.

Not once in that time had she mentioned The Agency and now his premier recruiter for The Agency, the man he'd once trusted implicitly, was dancing with her throughout the evening as though neither he nor Vega had ever existed, as though her daughter was not a by-product of their shared aspirations.

However no one would think to refuse the president's personal invitation to the White House, despite his inclination to do so, and no one would think to refuse her invitation to dance.

"We've had so little time together recently, Edward."

"Sadly, I agree. I was beginning to believe our futures were becoming divergent, Priscilla. At times I found myself quite perplexed by the unfamiliar distance between us."

"Divergent? How could that ever be? Not with the girl we share, our lovely daughter. Tell me, do you believe Karina has ever suspected Karina E. is yours?"

"I don't believe so. She adores you unconditionally. Quite frankly I'm more than a little surprised the two of you never attempted a fanciful episode throughout our earlier days."

"Who says she and I didn't? It wasn't all about you, Edward. Our daughter, however, is a bright girl with a bright future. I've become surprisingly fond of her. "

"A bright future indeed, as Karina E. Riley at the head of the corporation with our guidance, I couldn't imagine a more fitting tribute."

"A fitting tribute to what exactly?" she questioned, as though she wasn't aware.

"To the Riley name, the Riley history, naturally," he replied.

"No. That won't happen, Edward. She's Karina E. Vendôme and will remain such."

"We had an agreement, you and I, Priscilla, worth 120 million as I recall."

"We did, until you fucked me, Edward."

They parted several inches, his expression grim.

"Yes, several times as I recall with your eager

permission and your completely unbridled enthusiasm."

"Yes, and each time I saw your face."

"I don't take your meaning. We enjoyed ourselves immensely for a common good."

"Vega was a disappointment."

"He was a means to an end, better off where he now lies."

The president snorted softly, demurely. "He was a means to your end, your lies. You knew he was sterile. That infamous week we shared, you and I, was not in the least spontaneous. You didn't need and didn't want an heir, Edward. You needed a president who trusted you and you needed The Agency as much as you needed The Diners' Club. Tell me, how did you feel seeing Mount Rainier and Goodman's home the night you left here with your good friend Vega dead in the ground? I imagine very much like the way I felt when I discovered the truth about my would-be assassin and Goodman."

"I have no idea where this is going, Priscilla. I have no memory of a Goodman."

"That's curious, considering his previous legal career in Houston. Nor, I suppose, do you remember a luncheon in Chicago with him and Vega when the three of you spent eighty minutes laughing at me, mocking me." She lowered her head imperceptibly, running the tip of her tongue between glossed lips. "I've had both accounts seized, Edward, as are yours as we speak? Or should I say as we dance? As well, their deaths were carried out by Presidential Order as was the annihilation of your ten dinner clubs, your exclusive and fatal Diners' Club. The man who did that for me was Dwayne Michaels. How appropriate, though imagine how I felt when I discovered you were the one who wanted me dead. Too bad for you, Edward, that Alvin Jasper wasn't more nimble."

She felt him stiffen, the fear in his eyes unmistakable.

"We've been friends too long, Priscilla, for you to

misconstrue me this way. What you're saying is reprehensible."

"Laughing at me wasn't very kind, Edward. I never once did anything to hurt you. Not once, not until now. This is what you call the last laugh. However before you leave us, know this. Beginning tomorrow your beloved Riley Corporation will be dismantled piece by piece. Karina will be given one half of the profits, the other half will be used to create a foundation for the betterment of this country's youth. Riley will no longer exist and here's the real irony. The foundation will carry the name of the woman who saved my life by killing your Alvin Jasper. You remember Lorie Wilson. I believe the choice is quite apropos since you once approved her." She glanced past his shoulder. "They're such a delightful couple."

"Priscilla, I must leave. I find this conversation disturbingly unpleasant."

"Oh, you are leaving, Edward, by Presidential Order...my last. You see, my life has taken a wonderful turn. May I introduce my fiancé?"

"Excuse me, Edward, may I have this last dance with my adorable and future wife." Ned Michaels' expression was jovial, his one hand on his Riley's shoulder, the other between their dinner jackets.

"Goodbye, Edward. Give my regards to Vega."

Ned Michaels stepped between them, taking Priscilla's hands.

Edward Riley stood alone for an eternity waiting to die, his face scarred with terror, collapsing to his knees.

Priscilla Vendôme's smirk appeared and disappeared in a flash, suddenly gasping, clasping her mouth.

Ned Michaels lurched toward the dying man, grabbing Edward Riley by the shoulders, easing him to the floor as the president shrieked for help, the Secret Service weaving through the dense crowd in a blur from all directions, rushing to her side.

The Fatal Diners' Club

Riley lay on the floor, clutching his chest, gasping, searching her pitiless and cold green eyes. What he saw last were her arms wrapped tightly around Karina, comforting his grief-stricken wife.

51
January 01ˢᵗ, 2025

Gregg Johnson's special edition headline read:

Houston Billionaire Dies of Sudden Heart Failure during Final Visit to the White House

The byline read:

President Priscilla Vendôme distraught over sudden loss of long-time friend…

*

That Wednesday morning Priscilla Vendôme left politics and the White House en route to Houston. When she left the Riley Ranch Karina Montoya was no longer a grieving widow.

She wasn't surprised by the news which came to her as fact and not a confession. Nor was Edward's treachery a good reason to lose a good friend. She loved Priscilla. She loved Karina E. She always would.

Priscilla made no mention of The Agency, Vega or Goodman, though she did describe in detail what she had always called The Fatal Diners' Club and its single purpose.

She agreed with Priscilla's intention to entirely dismantle Riley Corp., refusing Priscilla's generous offer, suggesting instead that all the money be used to support the

Lorie Wilson Foundation. She would also be moving, she told her friend. She could no longer live in a house once built on love and tainted by treachery. She would, however, do some housecleaning first, starting with certain family treasures stored in her basement.

The women kissed, promising to see each other soon.

On the Thursday Riley Corp. lost its identity and began the process of dissecting Thatcher and Betty Riley's legacy, short-term president and CEO Priscilla Vendôme first writing herself a cheque for 100 million dollars per her contractual agreement with Edward Riley, believing in her heart Thatcher and Betty would agree with her actions and with her foundation.

The same afternoon, two days following his sudden death, Edward Riley was buried without ceremony, taken from the morgue to his gravesite far away from the family plot, buried in a pine box without his family's name on the stone. She didn't attend the interment. He was simply put in the ground as Edward, unknown and forgotten. Nor did she have any idea where.

Karina believed that would have been Casey's and Florence's heartfelt wish, as much as their and her punishment for his lifetime of lies.

*

Priscilla was forging a new life.

She was moving to Florida to marry Ned Michaels and be close to her girlfriend who would work with her at the Lorie Wilson Foundation.

On the Friday she and Ned held hands, waiting in the private lounge at the airport for Lorie and Dwayne to arrive. She was anxious for her archery lessons. That was Priscilla's wedding gift to them, a week on her island that she had decided to keep as part of the foundation as well as the Riley jet which was now repainted and documented as LWF

What she hadn't expected was joining them with a man of her own. How cool was that?

*

Lorie Wilson never thought that from the Secret Service she would become the president of a foundation named for her by a girlfriend she loved very much. Or that Priscilla would be the CEO of that foundation and part of her extended family, moving to Miami to be close to her and work with her.

Owning three bars was Dwayne's dream, not hers, which he understood. Her dream and Priscilla's was carrying on his work he'd told them about with young girls and those unable to help themselves.

What could he say? He was proud, feeling awkward at not calling Priscilla Madam President despite her best effort at trying to assuage his malaise with a romantic embrace and mischievous, raspberry-flavoured kiss much to his uncle's and Lorie's raucous laughter.

Lorie leaned into the porthole. They were landing. She was moments away from hugging and kissing her friend, anxious for walks and talks on the deserted beach.

"I do have to say, dream-girl, I am still a little curious, you know, from a male perspective."

"Pull your head out of the gutter, sweetheart. I told you, we did the bow and arrow thing and we went swimming, tossing around a beach ball...nothing more. We were a couple of girls having fun, having a good time together without men."

He chuckled. "That's it, really, archery on the island of the amazons. Ooh, hot stuff."

Lorie feigned frustration, an exaggerated sigh escaping. She had to muzzle him once and for all.

"Yes, sweetheart, that's right, the island of the amazons, ooh, hot stuff...two beautiful, oily and completely naked amazons. So let your imagination run wild with that. We certainly did."

Dwayne Michaels' eyes flared open. "No way!

The Fatal Diners' Club

Other Mystery – Suspense - Thriller Novels
By Doug Booth:

The Viewing Room
The 4th Man
The Madam
Family Lies
Mother's Pearl Dagger
From Inside Her Bedroom
The Feast of Tombola
Deferred Prejudice
The Hunt for Gilligan Rose
The Fatal Diners' Club
Silent Conviction
A Christmas Killer, Comfort and Joy
Pariah In the Mirror
***
No One to Tell(A Creative Non-Fiction)

www.ingramcontent.com/pod-product-compliance
Lightning Source LLC
Chambersburg PA
CBHW030537020726
47494CB00005B/1398